NORTHERN
OCEAN

GVLF
OF
MVRR

RECLVCE

GVLF
OF
CANDAR

EASTERN
OCEAN

N

VCE

WELLSPRING
OF
CHAOS

TOR BOOKS BY L. E. MODESITT, JR.

THE COREAN CHRONICLES

Legacies
Darknesses
*Scepters**

THE SPELLSONG CYCLE

The Soprano Sorceress
The Spellsong War
Darksong Rising
The Shadow Sorceress
Shadowsinger

THE SAGA OF RECLUCE

The Magic of Recluce
The Towers of the Sunset
The Magic Engineer
The Order War
The Death of Chaos
Fall of Angels
The Chaos Balance
The White Order
Colors of Chaos
Magi'i of Cyador
Scion of Cyador
Wellspring of Chaos

THE ECOLITAN MATTER

The Ecologic Envoy
The Ecolitan Operation
The Ecologic Secession
The Ecolitan Enigma

THE FOREVER HERO

Dawn for a Distant Earth
The Silent Warrior
In Endless Twilight

* Forthcoming

*Forthcoming

L. E. Modesitt, Jr.

WELLSPRING
OF
CHAOS

TOR®

A Tom Doherty Associates Book / New York

WELLSPRING OF CHAOS: A RECLUCE NOVEL

Copyright © 2004 by L. E. Modesitt, Jr.

This book is printed on acid-free paper.

Edited by David G. Hartwell

A Tor Book
Published by Tom Doherty Associates, LLC
175 Fifth Avenue
New York, NY 10010

www.tor.com

Tor® is a registered trademark of Tom Doherty Associates, LLC.

Library of Congress Cataloging-in-Publication Data

Modesitt, L. E.
    Wellspring of chaos: a Recluce novel / L. E. Modesitt, Jr.—1st ed.
        p. cm.
    ISBN 0-765-30907-6 (acid-free paper)
    EAN 978-0765-30907-5
    1. Recluce (Imaginary place)—Fiction. I. Title.

    PS3563.O264W45 2004
    813'.54—dc22   2003065049

First Edition: April 2004

Printed in the United States of America

0 9 8 7 6 5 4 3 2 1

For Jeff:
Brother, friend . . . and woodworker

NORTHERN OCEAN

Cape Devalin

Spidlaria

SPIDLAR

Kleth

East
Horns

Elparta

Quend

Passera

Yrjna

Tellura

Weevett

Meltosia

KYPHROS

Dasir   Telsen

koya   Arastia

thga

Faklaar

STURBAL   HIGH
DESERT

Ruzor

FAKLA RIVER

Tyrhaven

SLIGO

Rytel

Lavah

CERTIS

Jellico

MONTGREN

Vergren

Fyven

Freetown

Hydolar

OHYDE   RIVER

HYDLEN

Asula

Sunta

FREETOWN
(LYDIAR)

Renklaar

Pyrdya

Worrak

Gulf of Candar

NORTH BAY

Gulf of Murr

Black Holding

Alberth

Reflin

Lands
End

Extina

Lydkler

Alaren

FEYN

IRON
WORKS

Mattra   Feyn

Wandernaught

Clarion   Einstronn

Nylan   Sigil

Southpoint

RECLUCE

EASTERN OCEAN

C. Mitchell 1995

Cooper

I

Kharl stood at the front window of his shop, looking westward for a moment at the wedge of twilight sky visible between the slate roofs of the buildings on the far side of the narrow Crafters' Lane. A single lamp was visible through the middle window of Gharan's quarters, above the weaver's shop. Next door, at Hamyl's, both the lower floor and the rooms above were dark. That wasn't surprising, Kharl told himself, since Hamyl's consort had taken the children to her parents' holding to help with the early-midsummer gathering. That had left the potter free to indulge himself at the Tankard, and the lane peaceful, since Kharl's neighbor, the scrivener Tyrbel, was a widower and kept a quiet establishment.

Lowering his eyes, the cooper glanced at the five barrels in his display, all tight cooperage from the best white oak, ranging from the hogshead to the standard barrel and down to the quarter barrel and the fine-finished fifth barrel with the brass spigot, used by anyone who wanted to store and dispense expensive liquids, mostly spirits. Then he barred the front door and closed the shutters behind the lead-glassed panes that his grandsire had installed before Kharl had been born. At that time, glass windows had been considered particularly foolish for a cooper, unlike a goldsmith or an artisan—or even a weaver or a potter—who had to display work to attract buyers. Times had changed, and most shops along the lane had come to display their wares behind windows.

"A barrel's a barrel. So's a hogshead. People buy barrels because they need barrels." Kharl smiled as he recalled the acerbic words of his grandmother, who had never let his grandsire forget what she regarded as the foolishness of the glass.

Foolishness? Kharl didn't think so. He still got orders from passersby who otherwise hadn't thought about barrels. Not many, never more than one an eightday, and sometimes only a few a season. Over time, though, the windows had paid for themselves.

He picked up the lamp and walked toward the rear of the shop, past the high racks that held the billets he would form into staves. Most of the billets were oak, white for the tight cooperage and red for slack. There were also some billets of tight-grained black oak, and a few of chestnut. He passed the workbench and the tool rack, with every tool in place. On the left side of the rear wall was the small forge where he sized and shaped the hoops for tight cooperage. Beside the forge on the brick flooring was the fire pot and, beside it, the steaming ring. The faintest smell of ashes and charcoal drifted toward Kharl from the banked coals of the forge.

Just short of the rear wall, and the door to the loading dock, the cooper stopped and looked at the fifteen white oak barrels waiting there. Each was identical to the next, with the iron bands, set just so, and the smooth finish, with a medium toasting on the inside. Korlan was supposed to pick them up in the morning—pick them up and pay the balance due. The vintner had taken the first fifteen barrels an eightday earlier. Kharl only hoped that the vintner did not come up with some excuse, as he had the summer before, waiting almost two eightdays before showing up, but, then, that was the problem in dealing with someone who lived more than ten kays to the south of Brysta.

Kharl half smiled, then nodded, and turned, the carry-lamp in hand, to head up the stairs.

> ". . . silvers and coppers are not for me,
> but a pretty girl whose charms are free . . ."

He frowned. Had he heard singing in the alley? The Tankard was four doors toward the harbor, but seldom did roisterers come wandering down the alley, even early in the evening. Kharl cocked his head.

> ". . . for when there's no lamps to see,
> any woman's as fair as fair can be . . ."

"No . . . let go of me!"

The woman's voice—no, it was a girl's voice—was familiar, but Kharl could not place it. He moved to the far side of the loading dock and swept up the cudgel in his left hand, then, leaving the lamp behind, eased the door open.

"Let me go!"

". . . mean you no harm, little woman." A raucous laugh followed. "We'll even pay you for what you give others for free . . ."

"Let go! Let . . . mmmpphhh . . ." The girl's words were choked off.

Kharl closed the door behind him so that he would not be silhouetted by the light from the lamp. He glanced toward the Tankard, but saw no one. He looked back to the north. There, less than a rod away, perhaps less than ten cubits, in the fading light and the dimness of the alley, were three figures that Kharl could barely make out. Two men held the girl, a thin figure with dark ringlets over a green summer blouse. The hair and the blouse belonged to Sanyle, the youngest of Tyrbel's daughters.

One of the men had Sanyle's arms cruelly twisted behind her, and the other had his hand on her shoulder, pulling the summer blouse down. Both men were laughing.

Kharl took three quick steps, then two more, bringing the cudgel up.

The nearer man, the one who had started to rip away Sanyle's blouse, turned. A blade hissed from the scabbard at his belt.

Kharl took another step and struck the blade and the man's hand with the cudgel before the man had finished turning toward the cooper. The shortsword dropped on the cobblestones of the alley with a muffled *clank*.

"Ah . . . swine-slime . . . misbegotten . . ." The youth jumped back, cradling his hand. The dark blue velvet of his tunic was almost lost in the dimness.

The second man let go of Sanyle, and his right hand darted toward the hilt of his blade.

"Don't . . ." growled the cooper. " 'Less you want a broken arm. Just let her go, and back away and head back where you came from. Have fun with your own or those you pay."

As soon as the man had released her, Sanyle slipped away into the shadows. There was a glint on the heavy brass key she held, and then the rear door of the structure beside the cooperage opened, and quickly shut.

"You can't do this." The taller young man, who was still half a head shorter than the cooper, kept his hand on the hilt of his blade, but did not draw it. "You don't know who you're talking to . . ."

"Doesn't matter," growled the cooper. "Don't force girls barely old enough to know the difference 'tween boys and men."

"They're all the same."

Kharl raised the cudgel slightly. "Back off, little man, 'less you never want to use that arm again."

The shorter youth scooped up the fallen blade with his left hand and backed away. After a moment, the taller one followed.

Kharl stood watching until the two were out of sight, and until the alley was quiet once more. Then he turned and reentered the cooperage, wondering from what merchants' houses had come the overdressed and spoiled youths. With a snort, he set down the heavy cudgel and barred the door.

After reclaiming the lamp, he started up the steps to the quarters above the cooperage. His boots thumped heavily on the wood, and the fourth step creaked, as it had for years.

Charee stood just inside the door at the top of the stairs. Shoulder-length black hair was bound back from her face, making it seem even narrower than it was. Her green eyes were cool. "Your supper's cold. Thought you were coming up sooner."

"I was. Heard something out back. Wanted to make sure that it wasn't someone trying to break in. Just a pair of youngsters thought they were men, drinking too much for ones so young." Kharl had no intention of saying more about the would-be bravos. For all her virtues, Charee lacked one—that of circumspection. The young men could scarcely have picked out one crafter in gray from another, not unless Charee told the entire lane. Because she well might have, while suggesting that Kharl was being foolish, Kharl saw little point in calling attention to the incident. Sanyle would doubtless tell her widower father, but the scrivener was more than taciturn, as were his children.

"Won't you ever leave well enough alone, Kharl? Leave the roisterers alone. Or if you must, call them to the attention of Lord West's Watch. That's what he draws his tariffs for. You've got a consort and sons that need you . . ."

"My hard-won coins, leastwise." Kharl shut the door to the stairs and the shop below and walked toward the washroom on the right side of the landing.

"Let's not be starting that again."

Kharl forced a smile. "I won't, dearest. I need to wash up." The pitcher on the wash table was full, and the basin empty and clean, with a worn but clean gray towel and a narrow bar of fat soap laid out on the left side. He closed the washroom door and began to wash, enjoying the faint rose scent that came from the petals in the soap. It took time to get the sawdust off his face and hands and arms, and out of his dark beard, short-cropped as it was.

When Kharl stepped into the main room, it was still warm from the day, but the harbor breeze blowing through the open windows offered a welcoming coolness, even if it did bear the scents of salt and fish and caused the two wall lamps to flicker.

The cooper walked toward the round table where Arthal and Warrl waited, their eyes following him, but not exactly looking at him.

"Did you finish your lessons?" Kharl's eyes fixed on Warrl, his younger son, by three years.

"Yes, ser. I did." After a moment, the younger boy asked, "How much longer will I have to go to Master Fonwyl?"

"Until he says you can read and write well enough to pass the craftmaster's tests." Kharl seated himself.

"I don't see why," interrupted Arthal. "It's not as though we'll ever have the golds to post the bond for mastercrafter."

"Maybe so, and maybe not," replied Kharl. "But if you get the chance, I don't want you looking back and complaining that I didn't prepare you. Reading and writing aren't something you can pick up easy-like when you're older."

"But what use is it if you're not a mastercrafter or a merchant or a lord? You scarce have a chance to read a broadsheet—"

"But I can, and once or twice it's saved me good coins. Enough." Kharl managed not to snap. "Let's enjoy supper."

As if she had been waiting for them to stop, Charee lifted the heavy cast-iron stewpot off the stove and carried it to the table. There, she set it on the well-browned trivet in the center of the oval oak table that had been one of the first pieces of actual furniture that Kharl had made after he had taken over the cooperage.

His consort set the large basket of afternoon-baked bread on the table and seated herself at the opposite end of the oval table from Kharl. Kharl began to ladle the stew into the chipped brown crockery bowls that had come from Charee's mother.

"Smells good," offered Kharl.

"It does," added Warrl.

"More summer squash and potatoes than meat," murmured Arthal.

"It's tasty, and it's hot, and you didn't have to spend the day cooking it," Kharl pointed out. "If you'd rather not eat, you can leave the table right now."

"No, Da . . . I'm sorry, Ma." Arthal's voice was barely apologetic.

Kharl didn't feel like calling his older son on his borderline rudeness, not after a long day finishing the last of the barrels for Korlan, especially when he knew that Arthal would just make some other comment.

"What was going on outside, Da?" asked Warrl.

"Just some young fellows who'd had too much at the Tankard. Had more ale than sense, and didn't know it."

"Will the Watch catch them?"

"They settled down," Kharl said, after taking a mouthful of the stew, still warm and peppery, despite Charee's comments about it getting cold. "Good stew." He broke off a chunk of the crusty bread, then dipped it into the stew before chewing off the dipped end. "Good bread."

"They'd better settle down," offered Arthal. "Lord West likes Brysta peaceful."

"The justicers worry more about thieves and killers," Kharl said, taking a swallow of the warm ale, really only about half a mug for each of them, but that had been all that was left in the quarter barrel in the cellar, and he couldn't afford any more—not until Korlan paid him for the wine barrels.

"Cossal said they hung three brigands in the Justicers' Hall on twoday," added Warrl. "He was there."

"They hung three men. That's true. They might even have been guilty." Kharl had his doubts that everyone hanged was as guilty as charged.

"Does it matter, if one brigand is strung up for something he didn't do?" asked Charee. "Anyone they catch has done more than enough anyway. Weren't for Lord West, we'd have thieves overrunning Brysta, like in his sire's time."

"That was a different time," Kharl said. "Fairven had fallen. The more powerful steam engines had exploded. Many trading ventures had failed. People were starving, and white wizards were everywhere."

"Better the whites than those blackstaffers from Recluce," Charee sniffed. "Them and their fine clothes, and their noses in the air. Think they know everything. Father Jorum says that we're all equal in the eyes of the Sovereign."

Kharl wasn't about to get into debating the opinions of the priest of the one-god believers. "I can't see as they harm anyone, but it's better that they stay in Recluce." He took another chunk of bread and wiped out his empty bowl with it. "Good dinner, dearest."

"How would we know? The lords won't touch 'em, not unless they're caught doing something right awful. Merayni, she listened to one of 'em, last winter's end it was, and he was telling terrible tales. Terrible tales."

"What kind of tales?" asked Kharl, in spite of himself. He had his doubts about Charee's older sister Merayni, although Merayni was certainly good-hearted, and she and her consort were more than successful with the pearapple and peach orchard that Dowsyl had inherited from his father. He paused. "Didn't know blackstaffers got so far south as Peachill or Eolya."

"They get everywhere, Merayni was saying, and the tales he told! Terrible, she said. About how a body can't even walk across some hills in Candar without turnin' black and shriveling up and dyin' right there on the spot."

"That may be," Kharl replied. "That's Candar, and not Nordla. Lord West is lucky to have one or two wizards that he can count on. Rather have him with wizards than some of the other Lords of the Quadrant."

"This young blackstaffer, he said that the lord's wizards weren't proper mages. 'A course, Father Jorum says all wizardry is evil."

"I wouldn't know if they're proper wizards." Kharl tilted his mug to get the last drop of ale. "I'm a cooper, not a wizard or a lord. That's their business. Mine's barrels. Solid barrels."

"Terrible stuff, magery." Charee sniffed again. "As bad as thieves and brigands, if you ask me."

"I'm sure there are good mages and bad ones. There are good lords and bad ones, good coopers and bad ones."

"No such thing as a good mage, if you ask me. Lord West can have them all. Be better if he hung 'em."

"That's what lords are for. Deal with raiders, and invaders, and brigands, and mages. Rather be a cooper."

Warrl yawned. So did Arthal.

"You two can take the bowls to the wash table," Charee said.

"Wish we had a sister, like Aubret does," mumbled Warrl. "Do all the dishes."

"You don't have a sister," Charee said. "Two of you are enough."

". . . always say that . . ." murmured Arthal.

"Did you say something?" asked Kharl.

"No, ser."

"I didn't think so." Kharl pushed back his chair and walked to the window, letting the cool evening air flow around him. He hoped that Korlan would pick up the barrels in the morning.

II

Right after his early breakfast, Kharl took the broom and stepped outside the front of the cooperage to sweep the stones of the narrow sidewalk. Warrl was supposed to have done it, but the boy was already laying out the white oak shooks that Kharl would be jointing for the hogshead ordered by Captain Hagen for the *Seastag*. It was less trouble for Kharl to sweep than to rail at Warrl, and at least the boy was already working, unlike his older brother. Since the cooper didn't want to be caught out front if Korlan drove his wagon up to the loading door in the rear, Kharl swept quickly.

Every few moments, Kharl stopped briefly to listen, although he doubted that the vintner would arrive before midmorning, but with Korlan, one could never tell. The air already felt hot and damp. He glanced to the east, at the barrel set on the stone slab between the cooperage and Derdan's woolen shop, the barrel filled with damp sand for use against fires. The water barrel was more toward the harbor, past Tyrbel's scriptorium.

He began to sweep again, trying not to sneeze. As gently as he moved the broom, dust still rose from the stones, dust from a long and dry summer. With the prevailing easterlies, Brysta was hot and damp, but seldom had much rain until late summer. So the air was moist, and the streets were dusty. Finally, he lifted the broom and turned to reenter the cooperage.

"Ahhh . . ."

Kharl looked up.

Tyrbel stood there, with a small smudge of ink on his jaw. "Kharl . . . just wanted to . . . last night . . . Sanyle." The angular scrivener did not met the cooper's eyes. ". . . asked her to deliver some fancy cards up the hill. They must have followed her back."

"Just fortunate to be back by the loading dock. Might not have heard otherwise."

"Some would have heard, and done nothing," Tyrbel replied. "I owe you thanks and more."

"You don't owe me. Neighbors don't look out for neighbors . . . who will?" Kharl smiled. "She's a good girl."

"Best of them all," Tyrbel agreed. "Do you know who they were?"

Kharl shook his head, still listening for Korlan's team and wagon. "No. Wore velvets and blades. Looked like some merchant's spoiled brats. Had too much to drink and didn't care who they hurt."

"Sanyle said they drew against you."

"Had my cudgel. Worked better." Kharl laughed brusquely.

"I hope they were very drunk and didn't know exactly where they were," offered Tyrbel. "Merchants' sons . . . well, some of them don't forget. Sometimes wealth is the wellspring of chaos."

"It was dark," Kharl replied, glancing toward the inside of his shop.

"I won't keep you."

"I'm waiting for Korlan, and I don't want him to load his barrels without leaving what's in his purse."

Tyrbel laughed. "I understand. It took me four eightdays to collect from him for making a copy of *Emyl's Tales*." The scrivener paused. "But I did want to thank you. Neighbors or not, most wouldn't put themselves out."

"Been my daughter, I'd have wanted someone to put themselves out," Kharl said. "She's always been thoughtful to us."

"She is." Tyrbel smiled. "That she is." After a moment, he cleared his throat. "I must be going. I have to go to the Quadrant Hall."

"Copying some records?"

"Exactly. I can't really say who or why, you understand?"

Kharl didn't and never had, but he nodded anyway.

"Thank you, my friend," said Tyrbel as he turned.

Kharl lifted the broom and headed back into the shop.

Warrl looked up. "The shooks are here, Da, and there are two extra, like you said."

Except for the two of them, the cooperage was empty.

"Good." Kharl looked around. "Arthal?"

"I'm coming." The lanky dark-haired youth slumped as he made his way down the stairs from above. "I'm coming." He paused on the fourth step and rocked back and forth, until the step squeaked.

"So is year-end," suggested Kharl, "and it well might get here before you." He waited until his older son reached the workbench before continuing. "Smythal promised he would have the iron blanks for the hogshead last night. I need you to pick them up. Tell him I'll stop by with the coins later today."

"Yes, ser. What if he wants the coins now?"

"He won't. But if he does, then come get me."

Kharl watched for a moment as Arthal left, not quite slouching, but not exactly hastening, either. Then he turned. During Kharl's conversation with Arthal, Warrl had laid out the hollowing knife and the round shave. The younger boy stood at the end of the main workbench.

"Have you sharpened the hollowing knife? And the planer blade?" Kharl looked at Warrl.

"I sharpened the blade the day before yesterday, Da . . ." The redhead looked down, not meeting his father's eyes.

"That was the day before yesterday. Today, we have heavy oak to joint."

"Yes, ser."

Warrl's tone was so resigned that Kharl had trouble not smiling in response before he replied, "The sooner you start, the sooner you'll be done, and then you can head off to Master Fonwyl's."

"Yes, ser." The younger boy's tone was even more resigned.

Kharl was not amused at Warrl's lack of enthusiasm about his tutor and his lessons, not with the coppers they were costing Kharl.

III

First thing on fiveday, Kharl had opened the loading door and left it ajar, waiting as he was for a teamster he'd hired to cart the finished hogshead standing just inside the door down to the *Seastag*. Kharl had tried to complete the cask earlier, but he'd had to wait for Smythal to finish the iron blanks that Kharl forged into hoops, and that had meant sending Arthal twice.

The Austran trader wasn't due to cast off until tomorrow, on sixday, but Kharl found himself glancing at the large cask and loading door again and again as he continued to plane and joint the small black oak staves for the set of fancy fifth-barrels for Yualt. He'd already commissioned the brass spigots, and he'd have to pay a silver to Cupret before eightday.

Arthal was at the other workbench, rough-shaping red oak shooks into proper staves for flour barrels, not that Kharl had any orders, but because he always had some from Wassyt, the miller, come harvest. That was good, because, fast as he made coins, it seemed as though he had to spend them almost as swiftly.

Hot damp air seeped into the shop as always in summer in Brysta. Kharl hoped it wouldn't be too long before the winds changed, and Nordla got some rain, but the easterlies had lasted longer this summer.

The cooper blotted his forehead with the back of his forearm before pausing and readjusting the plane.

"Ge-ha!"

At the teamster's call and the crack of a whip, Kharl set aside the plane. "Arthal! The teamster's here. I'll need you to help load the hogshead."

"Yes, ser." Arthal straightened.

The two walked back to the loading door. Kharl opened the door wide. From there Kharl watched as the teamster brought the wagon and team to a halt. Kharl knew many of the teamsters, but not the burly and bearded young man on the wagon seat. Not that he'd had a choice. A crafter put in a request at the teamsters' hall and took what he got.

He stepped into the alley. "I'm Kharl, the cooper with the hogshead for the ocean pier."

"Morat." The teamster spat out onto the alley, the side of the wagon away from Kharl. "Be two coppers down to the pier—and two back if it comes to that."

Kharl showed four coppers. "But not until we're at the pier."

"And you tie the hogshead in place, and I check it. We don't move till I think it's secure."

"I expected that."

The brawny teamster lowered the rear wagon gate, and Kharl and Arthal lifted the hogshead and eased it into the wagon. While Kharl lashed the cask—equivalent to three barrels—in place in the wagon bed, Morat closed the rear gate.

Arthal watched both men.

Kharl tied the last knot and looked at his eldest. "Close the loading door and watch the shop until I get back. Keep working on those staves."

"Yes, ser," replied Arthal.

With a nod to his son, the cooper looked to the teamster. "Cask's in place." Kharl climbed up into the wagon seat, waiting for Morat to finish checking the lashings.

After a moment, the teamster vaulted into his seat and released the wagon brake. "We'll be going." He flicked the leads to his team. The wagon rolled forward, slowly.

After Morat had the wagon and team clear of the alley behind the cooperage and onto Fifth Cross, he kept the team on the crossing street until they reached Cargo Road. There he turned westward toward the harbor. "First ocean pier, you said."

"The *Seastag*—Austran deepwater."

Once the wagon passed the square at Third Cross, Kharl could see the piers, because Cargo Road sloped downward just enough so that the harbor of Brysta could be seen spread out to the west. All the piers were to the north of the River Westlich, except for the stubby ferry pier. The ferry served those who wanted to cross to the peninsula road that ran south-southeast along the western side of the river. There, the marshes farther north and west, bordered by rock escarpments, had prevented much settlement on the southern part of the harbor. To the north of the piers was the flatland for the lower market and the slateyard.

Kharl checked the fair weather banner on the pole on the outer breakwater—a green oval against a white background. There were no clouds in the western sky, but Lord West's wizards used their glasses to scree well beyond mere sight to determine which banner flew.

There were only eight vessels spread across the three oceangoing piers and the two coastal wharfs, illustrating that late summer was the slowest time in the fair weather months. Closer to harvest and all through the fall, almost every berth on every pier would be taken, and in good times, merchanters would even anchor out beyond the breakwaters.

Lord West had but a handful of warships, iron-hulled steamers with but two single-gun turrets. Brysta's real defenses were the two forts facing each other at the entrance to the harbor—the south fort at the end of one breakwater, and the north fort at the end of the other. Twin chains lay on the stones of the channel between them. Each chain was attached to a modified capstan so that the chains could be raised to deny access to the harbor.

Once every four eightdays, the chains were raised briefly and inspected, and one of Lord West's wizards renewed the order-spell on them. Kharl knew that well. For a year he had served as an assistant to the cooper at the south fort, and had been pressed into the work gang that turned the capstan.

The first ocean pier was empty—except for the *Seastag*, two-masted, like a brig, but with side paddle wheels. The Austran ensign drooped from the jackstaff in the heavy still air that blanketed the harbor. Several wagons were lined up and unloading barrels and crates, and the work gang was using a crane to swing lengths of timbers from a stack on the pier to the midships hold.

The teamster eased the wagon past the timber pallets and brought it to a stop a rod or so past the gangway. "This is the best I can do."

"That's fine." Kharl handed three coppers to the teamster. "It will only be a moment."

Hagen was halfway down the gangway before Kharl finished unlashing the hogshead. The Austran captain had three sailors with him. "Cooper, your timing could not have been better."

"I said today," Kharl replied.

"So you did." The master of the *Seastag* hopped up into the wagon bed and began to inspect the hogshead.

Kharl waited.

Finally, Hagen jumped down and gestured to the three sailors—two men and a hard-faced woman as well muscled as the men. "Take the cask up and set it just aft of the mainmast for now."

"Yes, ser."

Kharl watched as the three eased the cask out of the wagon and carried it across the pier, past the timber being loaded, and up the gangway. Hagen watched as well, until the cask was on board the *Seastag*, before turning to the cooper. "You charge a bit more than the Austrans, but no one makes a better hogshead." Hagen laughed and handed Kharl the three silvers, then added a pair of coppers.

"Thank you, ser." Kharl inclined his head.

Behind them the teamster finished turning the wagon on the wide pier and headed back toward the city proper. He gave the slightest of waves to Kharl.

In return, Kharl nodded to the teamster.

"I'll be thanking you, cooper," said Hagen. "That I will. Next trip, it might be sand barrels."

"Sand barrels?"

"Been reports of raiders out of Lydiar, and the Black Brethren have those rockets. A chaos-wizard's teamed up with pirates out of a place called Renklaar. Water doesn't always stop those chaos-flames. We're fortunate only one pirate's got a wizard."

"How long before you come back this way?" asked Kharl.

"I'm only making a short voyage this time. Maybe half the ports in Candar before we return to Valmurl. Then, after an eightday there, we'll be headed here on the long trip of the winter." He laughed. "We'll end up in Hamor, where it's warm."

The cooper nodded. "You thinking of oak for the sand barrels?"

"The only thing for a vessel. The only thing." The graying Hagen tipped his battered cap to Kharl. "Be seeing you next trip, cooper."

"I look forward to it, ser."

Hagen nodded and turned.

Kharl walked past the timber, careful to avoid the empty sling coming down. Halfway back along the pier from the *Seastag*, he stopped as he noted—and recognized—the low vessel moored at the outboard end of the second pier, a ship entirely of shimmering black, without masts and with but one gun in a single forward turret. Two guards in the black of Recluce marines stood at the foot of the gangway.

The cooper studied the warship for a moment, then shook his head as he continued back along the pier for the kay-long walk back to the cooperage. He just hoped that no one had come by in his absence, but he wouldn't have dared to send Arthal with the hogshead.

"Youth . . ." he muttered under his breath. "Not what they used to be. Paid attention to my da. They'd just as soon spit."

He squared his shoulders and stretched out his stride. He could have paid the teamster for a return ride, but he had better uses for his coppers.

IV

From the angle of the light slanting through the front windows of the cooperage, Kharl could tell it was getting on to late afternoon. He checked the brass spigot he'd set into the first barrel. He'd augured the hole almost perfectly, so that he only needed the slightest bit of cordage between the wood and the brass flange and pipe. The second one was almost as good. He could start sealing the inside of the barrels in the morning. He didn't like doing barrels that required sealing, but Yualt had insisted on only the lightest of toasting and sealant afterward, saying that even the tightest grained oak would absorb some aspect of the contents and thus change them. Since Kharl was neither alchemist nor apothecary, and since the alchemist had refused to tell Kharl what he was putting in the fancy barrel, there wasn't much the cooper could say—especially since Yualt was paying a premium that Kharl needed.

He checked the first barrel before him a last time, running his fingers slowly over the inside of the finely finished staves, nodding in satisfaction, before carrying it over to the finishing bench against the south rear wall. Then he returned to the turning bench and did the same with the second. The heads for both barrels were also laid out—single round sections, rather than sections of quartersawn wood doweled in place.

With a smile, he eased over to the quarter barrel that held sealant.

The smile vanished, and he looked up. "Arthal!"

There was no answer, not that he expected one. After a moment, he walked to the steps and climbed up, and peered into the main room, where Charee was seated at her sewing table, working on the embroidery that she did for Fyona, the seamstress fancied by most of the consorts of the wealthier merchants.

"Where's Arthal?" Kharl asked his consort.

"He said you were finished with him, and he had to meet some friends."

Kharl pursed his lips tightly for a long moment. "I said he was free if he'd done everything. He did today. But he didn't yesterday, and he didn't tell me. I'm out of sealant, and he was supposed to get two buckets from Hyesal. He said he'd taken care of it, and he didn't, and that means . . . oh . . . never mind . . ." The cooper started to close the door, then turned back to Charee. "If anyone should come by, I'll be back shortly. I'm going over to Hyesal's to get the sealant Arthal didn't. I'll leave the door open so you can hear if anyone comes in. Or if Warrl gets back from his lessons."

"Don't be angry, Kharl. Arthal's still young."

"He's near-on double-eight, and I don't like being misled." Kharl snorted, then headed down the steps. "I should have asked him direct . . . have to ask 'em every little thing . . . thinks he's so bright . . ." he muttered to himself as he crossed the shop.

Kharl left by the front door. Outside, on Crafters' Lane, he heard a low rumble and glanced up. Clouds were massing over the Eastern Ocean to the west of the harbor, and the wind had finally shifted from out of the east to the west, bringing with it an actual hint of rain, not just soggy air, and the chance that the long-overdue and welcome late-summer rains would finally arrive.

He glanced at Tyrbel's small display window, which held several books, including a red leather-bound *Book of Godly Prayer*—a work that Tyrbel had done on his own as an offering to his faith. Kharl shook his head, thinking about the one-god believers. How could anyone believe that everything from the Great Western Ocean and beyond the Heavens to the Rational Stars could have been created by one god? Or that the same god knew everything everywhere, down to the smallest beetle? Or more important, from Kharl's viewpoint, that such a god cared equally for all men, women, and children? Given what he saw on the streets of Brysta, Kharl didn't put much faith in such a god.

He laughed to himself at the last thought. He didn't put any faith *at all* in such a god. Tyrbel did. With a rueful smile, he kept walking.

Two blocks down toward the harbor, he came to the upper market square, although most of the peddlers and vendors had already packed up their wares and left. A one-handed beggar was seated on the low stone wall that surrounded the near-empty square. Topped with redstone with rounded edges, the wall was a good place for sitting and resting.

"A copper, ser, just a copper for a poor fellow." The bearded beggar, in a tattered gray tunic and trousers, held his cap upside down, lifting it toward Kharl.

The cooper ignored him and kept walking.

"Just a copper, ser. Just a copper . . ."

Another thirty cubits down Crafters' Lane, also seated on the wall, was a young woman, with short-cropped dark hair and wearing a tan tunic and trousers. Her skin was pale, but unblemished. Her boots were sturdy and brown, and beside her was a canvas pack, against which rested a shimmering black staff. She was small enough that her boots did not touch the cobblestones beneath the wall.

As Kharl neared her, he took in the blackstaffer, then nodded politely.

She looked up. "Good day to you, ser." Her brown eyes smiled with her mouth.

"And you as well," Kharl replied, almost in spite of himself. But her expression had been warm and friendly on a cloudy afternoon, and not asking for anything. He found himself smiling as he left the square behind and made his way the last hundred cubits to Hyesal's apothecary shop, clearly marked with the crossed pestles above the door.

Kharl entered and stepped up to the long counter, time-aged golden oak, on which were arrayed various health tinctures. He looked around the small front room, but didn't see the apothecary. "Hyesal?"

There was no answer.

"Hyesal!"

"Just a moment!" came the querulous reply. "If you're someone I know, just wait. If you're someone I don't, you can take that chance, too."

Kharl grinned and stood there, waiting, his eyes going over the bottles lined up at the back of the counter, taking in the labels—*Morning Tonic, Digestive Tincture, Rheumatism Salve* . . .

The small but angular apothecary appeared behind the counter, as if by magery. "Well, Kharl . . . what is it that won't wait but a moment?"

"Sealant, the one you make for the good barrels. Arthal was supposed to come by—"

"Never did. I would have had it waiting here for you."

"Do you have any ready?"

"I can't say as I do, Kharl, and it's not something I can slop together while you stand there. 'Sides, it's got to stand overnight."

Kharl could feel his anger rising, but Hyesal hadn't created the problem. Arthal had. So he held his tongue.

"Tell you what. After I finish this tincture, I'll get to work on it, and you can pick it up first thing in the morning."

"I'd appreciate that. I would. I've been working on these fancy fifth-barrels for Yualt . . . Arthal . . . he told me he'd come by . . ."

"And you never forgot anything when you were young and starstruck over some lass?"

"He doesn't have enough brains to be starstruck at the moment." Kharl snorted.

Hyesal laughed. "Be ready in the morning." The apothecary turned and left Kharl standing at the counter.

With a shrug, the cooper stepped back and left the shop. In most cities, he would have gotten sealant from an alchemist, but not in Brysta, not that it mattered to Kharl so long as the sealant worked. What worked, that was what mattered, not which craft produced it.

Outside, he could smell the dampness of the rain that had already begun to fall on the ocean beyond the breakwaters, and he lengthened his stride as he hurried back up the gentle incline of Crafters' Lane toward the square and his own shop.

The blackstaffer and the beggar had left the square, but a small figure in gray accosted Kharl as he passed the empty stone sitting wall. "Master Kharl! How be the best cooper in Brysta?"

"Jekat . . . how's the most flattering urchin in Brysta?"

"Not bad, Master Kharl. 'Course a copper or two'd help." A grin crossed the towhead's grimy face.

"Coppers always help." The cooper grinned. "You know anyone who needs barrels?"

"I heard the renderer—Werwal—he's going to be needing some barrels 'fore long. I told Sikal—that's his man—he ought to see you. Werwal won't talk to me, but Sikal will."

Kharl slipped a copper from his purse. "Take this, you worthless urchin." He couldn't help smiling.

"Thank you, ser, and I'll not be telling no one 'bout your kindness." Jekat skipped away across the square.

Kharl was less than half a block from the shop when the rain began to fall—fat drops that splattered against everything. He began to hurry, but the shoulders of his gray tunic were black with water by the time he dashed into the shop.

"Is that you, Kharl?" called Charee from up the stairs.

"Sure as life." Kharl raised his voice to make sure Charee could hear him above the heavy rain pelting down on the roof. "Almost made it back before it started raining. Arthal never ordered the sealant. Won't be ready before tomorrow. Where's Warrl?"

"I sent him to Fyona's with the embroidery. He came in right after you left."

Kharl stopped by the workbench, then turned as Arthal ran inside, his tunic and trousers darkened with rain.

Arthal stopped as he saw his father.

"I'm not too happy with you, young fellow."

"You're never happy with me, Da." Arthal did not meet Kharl's eyes.

"You told me, yesterday, that you'd taken care of all the chores. I just got back from Hyesal's, and you never ordered the sealant. You told me you'd done that."

"I said I'd do it. I was going down there—" Arthal stepped back.

"When? Next end-day? Whenever it met your fancy?"

"It's not like that."

"How is it like?" asked Kharl. "I could have used the sealant today. It would have been ready today. You're almost a double-eight, and I shouldn't have to follow up on everything you do."

"You said you wouldn't finish those today." Arthal's voice was low.

"That isn't the blade's edge, Arthal." Kharl's tone dropped into resignation. "You led me to believe that you'd ordered the sealant. That's deception."

Arthal did not answer.

"Isn't that deception?"

"Yes, ser. I'm sorry, ser."

"You get a reputation for that, and no one will trust you to do anything. Don't you understand that? A man's worth is his reputation. Never forget that."

"I said I was sorry, Da."

Kharl held in a sigh. "Go on upstairs and see if your mother needs any help or any coal for the stove."

Arthal trudged past his father and started up the stairs. ". . . worse than Father Jorum . . ."

The words were not supposed to reach Kharl.

"What did you say?" snapped the cooper.

"Nothing, ser. I was just telling myself that you and Father Jorum feel the same way."

"That's about the only thing we agree on," Kharl snorted.

Once Arthal shut the door to the upstairs, Kharl walked back to the front window, looking out into the still-heavy rain. "Children," he muttered to himself, "so sure of themselves . . . so stupid."

V

Carrying two covered buckets of sealant, Kharl left Hyesal's so early in the morning that few people were out on the lane. He had placed a broom in Arthal's hands before he had departed the shop, and told his older son to sweep the stones before the shop clear of standing water and mud from the rain of the night before. He'd even remembered to make it clear to his son that Arthal was to sweep gently, so that mud and water did not splatter up on the glass of the display window.

Because of the weight of the sealant, Kharl stopped at the uphill side of the square to readjust his grip on the buckets. Early as it was, there were no stalls or carts or peddlers set up. After a moment's respite, he hurried up Crafters' Lane toward his shop. As he passed the short serviceway between Fourth Cross and Fifth, a narrow passage little more than four cubits wide, he slowed.

Had he heard someone? Was there someone lying in the shadows where he could not see? Moaning? In early morning? He shook his head and continued the last hundred cubits to the shop. But his thoughts drifted back—who could be in the serviceway?

Once he reached the shop, he noted that the stones outside the door had indeed been swept clean and were already dry—and that there was no mud on the bricks or glass of the display window. After opening the door, he entered the cooperage and lowered both buckets to the wooden floor.

Abruptly, he turned and walked out, closing the door behind him. On the lane, he headed back down toward the serviceway.

". . . a fool . . . that's what you are . . . stupid . . ." But despite his own words, he stepped into the darkness of the serviceway, checking carefully to make sure that no ruffians or cutpurses might be lingering. For a moment, he saw nothing. Then his eyes made out a bundle against the brick wall, a long bundle.

". . . ooo . . ." An arm twitched.

Kharl glanced around, but the serviceway remained empty except for him and whoever lay near the wall. He bent down, and, as his eyes adjusted to the dimness, he could make out a slender figure—and the end of a smooth black staff. The figure was that of the young woman blackstaffer. Blood and mud splattered the tannish clothes, which had been partly ripped away from her for all too obvious purposes.

Kharl glanced around again, then took a deep breath, and bent down. He pulled her torn cloak back across her exposed body, then eased the nearly limp figure into his arms. Her back felt humped, but he realized that the lumpiness was her pack. He managed to grasp the staff, which, despite the cold damp stones and the mud, felt warm to his touch. Then he lurched to his feet and began to walk out of the serviceway.

Both Arthal and Charee were standing inside the open door to the shop as he carried the young woman through the doorway. Warrl stood farther back, his eyes darting from his father back to his mother.

"Aryl was here. He said he might—" Charee broke off her words. "What have you there?"

"A girl . . . young woman. She was attacked and beaten. I heard her moaning in the serviceway." Kharl looked for somewhere to put her down. His eyes went to the stairs at the rear of the shop.

Charee's eyes went to the section of shimmering black staff that extended beyond the figure Kharl held. She stepped back. "She's one of those. She's one of those blackstaffers from Recluce. I won't have her in my house."

Kharl repressed a sigh and bit back a retort. "Then pull out that apprentice's pallet by the rear bench. You don't have to have her upstairs."

"Why . . . how could you?"

"I was supposed to leave her there, where she could have been attacked again or killed? Or died from the rain and cold?"

Charee sighed. "No. Suppose you couldn't do that." There was only the slightest hint of emphasis on the word *you*.

"Isn't Father Jorum always saying that his god wants us to help strangers and those who cannot help themselves?" asked Kharl.

Arthal and Warrl exchanged quick glances.

"Put her on the pallet," Charee said. "I'll get a blanket to put under her head and some damp cloths to clean away the blood."

Kharl waited as his consort pulled out the apprentice's pallet, which had not been used in years, and wiped it off with a cloth. Then he eased the woman—little more than a girl, he thought, and certainly slender and light as one—onto the pallet. Then he put the staff against the wall.

The cloak slipped slightly.

Charee's hand went to her mouth. "Oh . . ."

"I said she'd been attacked. She might need a dry cover of some sort."

"That'd be best. I'll be back in a moment. Warrl, you come with me!" Charee drew herself up and headed for the stairs, bustling up them in a way that conveyed offended dignity. Warrl followed.

"Ohhhh . . ." The young woman's eyes opened for a moment, then closed.

Arthal looked closely at the uncovered woman's exposed thigh, then away, almost guiltily, Kharl thought.

"What do you know about this?" Kharl partly lifted the woman and eased the pack off her shoulders, lowering her as gently as he could. Then he placed the pack next to the wall beside the black staff.

"Do you know who did it?" He straightened and looked at Arthal.

"No, ser."

Kharl continued to stare at his son.

"Some of the fellows, the ones who work in the carpentry shop on the piers, they were saying that she was really good-looking, and they'd like to get her alone . . . but that was all I heard."

"They said a lot more, but nothing about hurting her?" pressed Kharl. "Or did they—"

"No, ser. They didn't say anything like that. In fact, Derket said that she could be real dangerous. He once saw a woman from Recluce with a staff take down three of Lord North's guards . . ."

Kharl had the feeling Arthal was telling the truth, and some of the tenseness he felt lessened.

Charee reappeared, carrying warm cloths and a thin brown coverlet. "You two . . . Don't you have some fancy barrels to finish, Kharl?"

The cooper nodded and stepped back. "You can bring those buckets over to the finishing bench, Arthal."

"Yes, Da."

After leaving the injured girl to Charee's ministrations, Kharl turned to his workbench. There, he thinned, then stirred the sealant gently before he began to apply it to the black oak fifth-barrels. He could hear Charee murmuring.

". . . don't care much . . . blackstaffers . . . sending women . . . shouldn't come to this . . . Now . . . just take it easy, dear . . ."

"Where . . . ?"

"You're safe now. You're at the cooper's. Kharl found you in the serviceway . . . You'd been hurt . . . just rest." Charee looked across the shop at Kharl. "I'll be getting her some water."

Kharl decided against mentioning ale, not when they were short themselves. "I'm not going anywhere."

As Charee headed up the steps once more, Arthal cleared his throat. "Ah . . . Da?"

"Oh . . . Arthal. You can get out some more shooks—the red oak ones—and you'll have to use the ladder because they're in the upper front section of the racks. I'll need you to sharpen the knives, the shave, and the blade in the planer. After I put one coat on the fine fifth-barrels, then we'll work on those shooks while the barrels are drying."

Charee reappeared with a chipped mug. She went to the prostrate woman and held the water to her lips. "Just a few sips at first. That's it . . ."

Kharl took out the finish brush and dipped it into the sealant, deftly but slowly coating the interior of the barrel, something he would not have done for a vintner's barrel, but how and whether a barrel needed sealing depended on what the final use was, and when an alchemist like Yualt wanted a sealed black oak barrel with spigots, Kharl provided the best he could, even if he had no exact idea what Yualt intended to store in it.

He'd almost finished the first barrel when Charee stepped up to his shoulder, and whispered, "She's asleep. Got a knot on the back of her head. She's still seeing two instead of one. Say you should keep 'em awake, but I couldn't."

"We can only do what we can," Kharl pointed out.

"Beasts . . ." muttered Charee. "She shouldn't be going around like that, but . . . no excuse to knock around anyone that way."

"After I finish the barrels, I'll send Arthal off to tell the Watch."

"You'll do no such thing, Kharl. The Watch can do nothing. There was a scrap of velvet in her hand. Who wears velvet? You think they'll find anyone? And then all of Brysta will know you've been harboring a blackstaffer. You think that will help business?"

Kharl knew she was right. "What color velvet?"

"Doesn't matter." After a moment, Charee added, "Dark blue, almost black."

"I won't tell the Watch."

"See that you don't, and I'll be telling Arthal and Warrl to say nothing. The sooner she's well and out of here, the happier I'll be."

Kharl already knew that. The fact that Charee didn't want to say anything was another indication of how worried his consort was.

After Charee went back upstairs to work on the piecework for Fyona, Kharl motioned to Arthal.

"Yes, Da?" Arthal stepped away from the stacked shooks. "I got down enough for two barrels, and finished sharpening the planer blade and clamped it back in place."

Kharl didn't point out that Arthal had been done for some time. "You need to run some errands. Smythal, first. We need the iron blanks for four flour barrels."

"He'll want something."

Kharl took five coppers from his purse and handed them to Arthal. "Then go out to the mill and see what the timber looks like. Don't talk to Vetrad, just see if his racks, especially the oak racks, are full or empty. And make sure that the billets in our section have been turned. If he asks what you want, say that you were checking the billets, then beg some scrap oak and tell him you need it for detailing practice."

Arthal nodded.

"Before you go, your mother wants a word with you."

The youth frowned.

"She told me she wanted to talk to you. Now, go, and don't dawdle, but your mother first."

"Yes, ser."

After Arthal went upstairs, then came down and left, Kharl finished sealing the first barrel, then the second. As he wiped the brush as clean as he could, then dipped it into the small container of solvent, he became conscious that the blackstaffer had awakened and was looking at him.

He left the brush in the open solvent jar and turned.

"What are you doing?" The words were fluent, but strangely accented.

Kharl glanced over to the pallet where the young woman lay, her head propped up slightly on an old blanket that Charee must have provided. "I'm finishing a fancy fifth-barrel." He paused. "How are you feeling?"

"My head is splitting. It looks like there are two of you sometimes. Most of my body hurts. They weren't gentle."

Kharl looked around the shop, but, for the moment, no one else was there. "Do you know who they were?"

"I don't know anyone here. I just arrived two days ago. I'd left the tavern, and there were two men. I'd never seen them. They wore . . . their clothes were fancier . . ."

"Dark velvet . . . mayhap?"

"Their tunics were well cut, and they both had blades. But . . . I was ready for them. I didn't see the third one, and he hit me in the head with something . . . from behind . . ." She swallowed. "Thirsty . . ." She reached for the old chipped mug Charee had left. Her hands trembled as she lifted it and drank.

Kharl could see thin lines of wetness along her cheeks, but he said nothing.

After several small swallows, she set down the mug, using both hands, and lay back. Her eyes closed.

Kharl watched for a moment, then finished cleaning the brush. He moved to the workbench where he checked the settings on the planer. He watched the blackstaffer as he began to pump the foot pedal, but she did not stir, despite the whirring of the planer when he guided the first red oak shook into position to rough-shape it into a stave. He was halfway through the staves for the third flour barrel when he could see the young woman began to wake again, but she said nothing, and he continued to work.

He had almost finished another set of staves when Charee came down the steps with a chamber pot, looking long at Kharl. The cooper finished shaping the stave he was working on and stopped pumping the foot pedal. He stepped back and walked to the front of the shop, then outside.

Standing before the window, taking in the breeze from the harbor, he still couldn't understand why the young swells had beaten the young woman so badly. Was it just because she had resisted their advances, or

because she was a blackstaffer? He wondered if it had been the same
pair that had tried to force themselves on young Sanyle. If it had been,
they were truly a bad lot, and if it hadn't been, there were all too many
rotten young swells around. Kharl didn't like either possibility, not that
there was much he could do.

VI

When Kharl came down to the shop early the next morning, he
found that Charee had been there earlier, and that the blackstaffer was
propped into a sitting position, sipping hot cider, the coverlet across her
legs and midsection. The bruise on her cheek, one he hadn't noticed
before, had begun to show a yellowish shade along with the purple.

"How are you doing, young woman?"

"My name is Jenevra. You are . . . Kharl?"

"That's right. Kharl."

"I am better, but I am still seeing two of you at times. My head still
aches."

"You'll need to rest for a time, I think."

"I did not need this," Jenevra said. "I should have been more
careful."

With that, Kharl silently agreed, as he readjusted the blade on
the planer. Then he tested the foot pedal, and moved the carry-cart with
the red oak shooks next to the planer where he could easily reach the
shooks. He glanced toward the stairs, but neither Warrl nor Arthal had yet
appeared. He snorted quietly to himself.

Jenevra watched, without saying a word, just occasionally sipping
the cooling cider.

"Why do you blackstaffers come to Brysta?" Kharl asked, moving
back to the planer.

"Many go to Candar and some to Hamor. A few go to Austra," she
replied. "We must go somewhere."

Kharl didn't understand that at all, and his face must have shown it,
even to Jenevra's blurred vision.

"If we do not accept the tenets of order, as set forth in the book of order, and judged by the Council, and by the Institute, then we must undertake a dangergeld—that's a trip away from Recluce to learn who we are and where we should fit in the world."

"Fancy way of throwing you out if you don't agree, sounds like to me," Kharl replied. "Don't go along, and out you go."

"Sometimes it is, and sometimes people return with greater understanding."

"I'd wager not many return."

For a time, Jenevra was silent. Finally, she spoke. "That may be true. There are always those in any town or city who do not fit in. Is it not kinder to allow them a chance, rather than executing or enslaving them?"

"They might not fit anywhere, and they may end up being killed elsewhere. People anywhere don't much care for those who are different."

"You don't think much of people, do you?" she asked gently.

"I know what I see. For every kind act, there's one or more not so kind. People talk kindness. Don't always act that way."

"I suppose kindness and unkindness must balance, like order and chaos."

"You don't sound so certain about that," Kharl said.

"I'm too young to be certain."

Kharl laughed. "Most young-'uns are certain. Only when we get older that we see that naught's as sure as we thought."

Jenevra's eyes moved to the right, looking past Kharl.

He nodded to her and turned to see Arthal almost tiptoeing down the steps. "Arthal! I was wondering when you'd be coming down. You can take the hollowing knife and smooth the inner side of the staves on the ones I've already shaped."

"Ah . . . I'd thought I'd . . . well . . . Derket was saying that they might be looking for a carpenter's apprentice at the shipworks. It pays a half silver an eightday."

"You think you'd find that work more pleasing than being a mere cooper?"

"Da . . . the shop's good for but one of us, and Warrl's better at it already than I am." Arthal did not quite meet his father's gaze.

Kharl waited for a moment, then nodded. "Mayhap you ought to go see, then."

"You'll let me?"

"Arthal, I can't make you be a cooper. Go and see."

The young man looked at Kharl, then said, "They might not want me."

"You won't know that, will you, 'less you ask."

"No, ser."

"Then go and ask. But when you're done, come on back here, unless they offer you a position right then."

"Yes, ser." Arthal nodded and was gone almost before his words died away.

"You don't think they'll take him, do you?" asked Jenevra.

"I don't know. Know it's harder to get a position than he thinks, but he's got more skill than he wants to admit." Kharl picked up the first of the red oak shooks, hoping that someone else would come in before long with an order for more barrels. Senstad had ordered twenty barrels for harvesttime, and that was good, except it would be four to six eightdays before Kharl could collect. Korlan had asked for another thirty, but, again, not until the end of harvest, and that was a good five eightdays away. Kharl would have to start soon, but he didn't have enough of the seasoned oak billets for all of them, and that meant more golds to Vetrad—as Vetrad had told Arthal.

Aryl had been in the shop three times, talking about barrels for his apples, but he'd wanted them for almost less than the cost of the oak and iron.

Warrl had long since gone to his lessons, and Charee had left with her stitchery for Fyona, and Jenevra had drifted into a dozing sleep by the time Kharl had finished turning the shooks into rough staves. He checked the hollowing knife and began to work on smoothing and fine-shaping the staves. He'd finished the staves for one barrel and was working on the second, when he saw Charee coming back into the shop.

His consort slipped up to him, and said in a whisper, "Kharl . . . you've got to get her out of here."

"Her name's Jenevra."

"I don't care what her name is," Charee replied. "Fyona told me that Mallamet was going to put a complaint before the Crafters' Council that you're using the blackstaffer's magic on your barrels."

"That's stupid. The poor girl can't even see straight yet. Mallamet's a poor excuse for a cooper who just wants to cause me trouble."

"That well may be . . . but if the Council decides you're using order-magery in support of a craft . . ."

"How about tomorrow morning?" Kharl said quietly. "You could walk her down to Father Jorum's, and she could rest there for the day." If Jenevra weren't much better in the morning, perhaps he could persuade Charee to let her stay another day. He didn't want to think about what might happen after that day.

"Why not now?"

"She can't even sit up for long without getting dizzy."

"First thing tomorrow," Charee said. "I'll make sure Father Jorum will be around, but I won't let him know why. But it will be first thing in the morning."

"After breakfast," Kharl said.

"After breakfast, but no later." Charee headed for the stairs, carrying another bundle of fabric and thread.

Kharl looked at the dozing blackstaffer, then slowly lifted the hollowing knife once more.

VII

In the early afternoon, somewhat to Kharl's surprise, a lanky man ambled into the cooperage, an unpleasant odor clinging to him, for all of his neat and clean appearance, although his leather trousers bore stains that had clearly resisted all efforts at fullering. His heavy boots thudded on the floor.

Kharl set down the drawing knife and went to meet him.

"You Kharl?"

"That I am. How might I help you?"

"I'm looking for slack cooperage that's close to tight. Heard you were the best at that." The man gestured at the range of barrels on display. "Those look to be tight."

"They are, but I've just finished a few slack barrels out of red oak. They're here in the back."

"Be pleased to see them."

The two men walked to the back of the cooperage, past Arthal, who was slowly, as always, hollowing a red oak stave, and Jenevra, who was almost invisible against the wall and had drifted back into sleep.

"Good slack work . . . you see?" Kharl gestured to the red oak barrel, open-topped, but otherwise completed.

"Might I handle it?"

Kharl nodded.

The other man inspected the barrel carefully, paying particular attention to the joints and the iron hoops. Finally, he straightened. "How much?"

"A silver a barrel."

"Mallamet sells them for eight coppers."

"He does. They're not as tight."

"For ten, nine silvers," offered the man.

"Nine and five coppers," countered Kharl.

"Nine and four," offered the other.

"Done."

"You have three here, I see. When could you have the other seven?"

"I have eight ready now. The others are on the other side."

"Better yet. Five now, and five in two eightdays? I'll pay you six silvers and four now, and the rest when I pick up the others."

"That would be good." Kharl paused. "I must apologize, ser, but since we have not done business before . . ."

The man laughed. "We have not. I had thought you might have guessed. I'm Werwal."

"The renderer? I have heard of you."

"And I you. That is why I am here." Werwal counted out the coins. "My wagon will be here shortly for the five barrels."

"They'll be ready."

With a smile, Werwal bowed slightly and left.

Kharl was smiling as well. The copper he'd given Jekat had been well spent, even if that had not been his intention. He'd have to remember to slip another to the cheerful urchin. Jekat had probably given him more business than his own sons.

The cooper shook his head, sadly, and headed back toward the staves he'd been fine-drawing.

Arthal coughed. "Da . . . he smelled."

"That's not surprising. He's a renderer."

"Shouldn't let him in . . ."

"He bought ten barrels, Arthal. He can't help the smell. That's what he does. Someone has to do it."

"Stinks . . ."

Arthal's mutter was so low that Kharl decided to ignore it as he went back to work. If he corrected Arthal on every word his son said, these days, he reflected, he'd do little enough coopering and Arthal would get even more angry than he always seemed to be.

By late afternoon, Werwal's man Sikal had arrived with a small—and smelly—wagon and collected the barrels, and Arthal had gone with Charee to the market square. Kharl was getting the forge ready to set some hoops when the door to the cooperage opened.

He did not know the man who stepped into the shop, but the cooper stopped pumping the bellows in the small forge and stepped forward past the planer. He skirted Jenevra, who looked up silently, and moved to the sharp-featured figure in the rich brown tunic.

"Might I help you, ser?" asked Kharl, trying to determine what sort of merchant the man might be.

"You might be Kharl, the cooper?" The man's muddy brown eyes flicked up to the racks of billets, then toward the stairs in the rear, before settling on Kharl.

"That I am. And you might be?"

"Let us just say that I have an interest in barrels. Special barrels." A faint smile appeared on the slender but muscular man's lips.

Kharl smelled scent on the man, more than even a wealthy man should use. Lavender, he thought. "Large or small, slack or tight?"

"I was thinking of large slack barrels, for winter transport of seasonal game, and I understand such barrels could hold ice above the game, that would keep the game cold."

"That's possible, but only for an eightday in harvest. In winter, the ice would keep for a season, or longer."

"I would be interested in a . . . large barrel." The man gestured toward the hogshead in the window. "Could you make one a third smaller than the largest there?"

"That is possible."

"Good." The man in brown flashed a smile, then slipped around Kharl and studied the shop, moving toward the tool rack. His eyes took in the tools, implement by implement, then the forge and the open hearth that held the fire pot. His eyes passed over the blackstaffer on the pallet against the wall and returned to Kharl. "You have a well-laid-out cooperage."

"Thank you. When would you like the hogshead?"

"I will have to think about that. When I return, we'll talk about the details. I needed to know whether it was possible." He bowed, then turned.

Kharl watched as the other left. He shook his head. For all his words, the man hadn't felt like someone who bought barrels. The lavender scent suggested a bravo of some sort, but Kharl hadn't the faintest idea why a bravo would find a cooperage of interest. It wasn't as though Kharl had large stocks of coins stashed away.

"That man," said Jenevra, "he was evil."

"Is that something blackstaffers can tell?" Kharl asked.

"Not always," she replied. "I wouldn't be here if we could. But that one, he carries the white of chaos around him like a cloak."

"He's a white mage?"

"No. It's not the same. His is the chaos of murder and destruction."

Why would one such as that, if Jenevra were indeed correct, be visiting a cooper? He hadn't even really looked at the blackstaffer, or at Kharl. "You think he's an assassin? Or a thief?"

Jenevra shrugged, then winced. "He carries chaos. He could be an assassin or an armsman, or he could be an outland merchant who sails close to the wind. Or he could be a thief, or anything else. He is evil, whatever else he may be."

"That's not much help." Kharl paused. "You speak well. You speak too well for a peasant's daughter or for someone who works at hard labor."

"I do? That may be because the Brethren want us prepared when we travel elsewhere."

"The Brethren?"

"The Council of Recluce. They decide how we are prepared. That is, if your family can pay for the training."

"Yours could," Kharl said.

"It was difficult, but they did not wish me ill prepared." She laughed, ironically, a hint of bitterness behind the words. "Much good it has done me—or them."

"You were trained with the staff?"

"I was. Some are trained with blades, or axes, or other weapons for self-protection."

"Are all women trained with the staff?"

"No. It is . . . what weapons are in accord with what we are."

"In accord?" The woman's words were more than a little puzzling. How could a weapon be in accord with a person?

"Every person grows—or comes to be ordered—in a certain fashion. Edged weapons make some uneasy with them. So a staff is better. It is not good to fight your weapon when you are trying to defend yourself."

Although her explanation was strange, the last words made sense to Kharl. He certainly could not fight his tools if he wanted to make good barrels, and he had no trouble seeing that it could apply to weapons as well. While he would have liked to talk longer, talking would not help get the barrels done, and those needed doing so that, if other business arrived, he would still have the slack barrels for harvesttime.

Kharl nodded, then turned back to the forge. He still needed to finish shaping and riveting the hoops for the remaining oak barrels that Werwal had ordered and for the ones that Wassyt the miller would be wanting, sooner or later. If the harvest were really good, Rensan might even buy a few if Mallamet couldn't supply them—which was certainly likely, since Mallamet was neither that good a cooper nor that productive. He was cheap, though, Kharl had to admit.

The cooper also hoped that Jenevra felt much better in the morning.

If she did not . . . Kharl pushed that thought away. He had worries enough.

VIII

When Kharl hurried down to the cooperage after his breakfast, he found that Jenevra had turned so that she was sitting with her back against the wall. She was dressed, and wearing her boots once more, although her face was still pale.

"You're going to have to move today—" Kharl began.

"Charee told me when she brought me breakfast and my clothes. She repaired them. She's very good with a needle." Jenevra smiled wanly for a moment before the expression faded. "I'm much better. Your consort does not like my being here."

Kharl didn't reply.

"It is clear. She thinks I will hurt your business. If I stayed, I probably would. No one likes having blackstaffers around. They told us that, but I did not believe it then."

"In a few moments," Kharl finally said, unable to refute her words, "we're going to take you out to Father Jorum's—"

"One of the one-god priests? He will not be that pleased."

"They preach kindness to all—"

"Except to those from Recluce."

"I have never heard him say anything against Recluce," Kharl protested, although he seldom accompanied Charee to the end-day services.

"What is not said—"

Both Jenevra and Kharl looked up at the sharp *crack*ing sound, followed by the tinkling clank of glass falling on stone. His eyes darted toward the front window of his shop, but all the leaded glass panes were in place.

He frowned.

A muffled low *boom* rumbled past him, shaking the walls. One of the shooks left on the workbench fell to the floor with a flat, slapping sound.

Jenevra started to rise, then put her hand down to steady herself. Her face paled even more, until it was sheet-white.

"Stay put!" commanded Kharl. "You're still weak."

"Fire! Fire at the scrivener's!"

"Fire!" The second voice was that of Tyrbel.

Kharl looked at Jenevra. "You just stay there, unless the fire spreads here, and then you get out as fast as you can."

"Yes, master cooper."

Kharl didn't argue that he wasn't a master cooper, because he'd never had enough golds to pay the Crafters' Guild. He didn't have time to explain as he rushed out of the cooperage. Outside and to the west a line of men had formed up, passing buckets from the fire barrel some forty cubits farther west from the door of Tyrbel's scriptorium. Kharl could see that there weren't enough buckets, not to stop the fierce flames darting from the broken glass of Tyrbel's display window. From the jagged-edged hole in the display window, along with the flames, came lines of thick black smoke, oily-smelling smoke.

A tall man—Gharan—threw the first bucket of water on the flames, and was rewarded with a hissing—and very little diminution of flame.

Kharl looked for the nearest sand barrel, before belatedly realizing that it was at the front of his own cooperage, except on the east side, next to Derdan's. He dashed for it and pulled off the cover, fumbling for the scoop bucket inside. As quickly as he could, he filled the bucket with the damp sand, then ran back toward the display window of the scriptorium.

Gharan was about to throw another bucket of water, and Kharl waited, then followed with the sand. This time, the flames from the bottom of the display area, where the books were burning fiercely, actually subsided. Kharl hurried back to the sand barrel.

Between the flames and the men running to and fro, and the urgency of combating the fire, Kharl didn't know how many trips he had made before the display area was merely scorched and blackened wood, with water and sand oozing everywhere. Most of the leaded-glass panes in Tyrbel's display window had been broken, and shards of glass littered the stones of the narrow sidewalk. The volumes that had been on display were charred scraps.

The odor of charcoal and soot was strong, but Kharl could still smell, if faintly, another acrid scent. He just stood for a moment, breathing hard, his eyes watering as he looked at the ruined front of the scriptorium.

Gharan looked at the cooper. "Good thinking with the sand."

"Had to try something. Water wasn't working very well."

The weaver nodded.

Behind him so did Hamyl the potter.

Tyrbel moved toward Kharl. His face was ashen. "Someone set it. They broke the glass." The scrivener shook his head slowly. "Ten golds' worth of work . . . gone. You know, I was going to give the one—*The Book of Godly Prayer*—I was going to give it to Father Jorum. I'd promised it to him."

"I know," Kharl replied. "You told me." He paused. "It . . . the fire . . . smelled like oils. That's why I went for the sand."

"Why would anyone . . . why?" Tyrbel sounded both puzzled and defeated. "I'm just a scrivener. I don't understand . . ."

"Give way for the Watch! Way for the Watch!" The call came from farther down Crafters' Lane, toward the harbor.

"Trust the Watch to show up after honest men have already put out the fire," groused Gharan from behind the cooper and the scrivener. "Where were they when the fire started? Why bother now?"

"It didn't just start," Tyrbel repeated himself. "Someone set it, but why? Who would do such a terrible thing?"

"Someone who didn't like the documents you were copying for trials before the justicers?" suggested Kharl.

"But . . . why would anyone . . . that's not personal. Lord West likes my work, old as he's getting. Any scrivener would do the same for whoever—"

"Way for the Watch!"

Kharl glanced toward the approaching armsmen, eight of them, with a young-faced captain, scarcely more than a boy, or so he looked to Kharl. They were less than thirty cubits away. The cooper wondered why there were so many for a fire, and how the officer had gathered that number so quickly.

"No!" screamed a woman.

Kharl looked away from the oncoming Watch. He recognized the voice, if belatedly. It was Charee's voice.

Charee came running out of the cooperage, blood smeared across her blouse. "She's dead. She's dead!" Her voice broke with the words.

"Who's dead?" blurted Gharan from behind Kharl and Tyrbel.

"She is . . . the blackstaffer . . . someone cut her throat."

"Jenevra? She'd dead?" Kharl said stupidly. "But she was fine."

"She's dead," Charee said. "Her throat's cut." She looked at Kharl. "I told you she'd be trouble. I told you. I told you."

"She was barely more than a girl. She hadn't done anything," Kharl protested. "Why . . . how . . .?"

"I knew. But no . . . you had to do things the way you always do."

"Silence!"

Kharl turned from Charee to see that the armsmen of the Watch were but a few cubits from the group in front of the cooperage and scriptorium. After several moments, the words and murmurs died away.

"You! In the gray!"

Kharl could feel his stomach tightening as he saw the young captain of the Watch—the same young swell who had been pawing Sanyle—and possibly one of those who had attacked and beaten Jenevra. The captain jabbed his finger at Kharl. "You!"

"Yes, ser?"

"You own this cooperage?"

"Yes, ser."

"Take him away. He killed the girl inside." Behind the captain's voice was a hint of something, something almost like satisfaction, Kharl thought.

Three armsmen moved out from behind the captain and toward Kharl, each with a long truncheon at the ready.

"No! I didn't kill her. I didn't kill anyone." Kharl stepped back.

"That's what they all say." The captain made a motion.

Kharl took another step backward. "You've got the wrong person. I was out here fighting the fire. Everyone here knows that."

"A convenient diversion, no doubt." The young captain smiled. "You and all your friends down here need to learn some respect for the law, and for those who rule Brysta."

"I didn't do it," Kharl protested.

"Take him," snapped the captain, still smiling.

Kharl wondered if he should try to run.

Then a searing blow struck him from behind. He tried to turn, and he was struck again.

"No!" screamed someone.

That was the last word Kharl heard before he toppled into blackness.

IX

There was a low groan, then another. After a time, Kharl realized that he was the one groaning. He closed his mouth, and the sound stopped. Around him was darkness. Underneath him was something hard—very hard, slimy, and damp. His head was pounding. He levered one hand under him, then the other. His hand slipped, and he tried again. It took him more tries than he could count to get into a sitting position.

He put his hand to the back of his head, gently, wincing as his fingers touched the huge lump there. As he lowered his hand, in the dimness that was like night, he could barely make out the dark substance on his fingertips— blood.

His eyes took in the area around him. He was in a small, stone-walled chamber with a heavy door that had but the smallest peephole, through which a faint glow of light seeped, so little that he could not tell whether it was day or night.

"What you in here for?"

Kharl turned his head quickly, and more pain lanced through his skull. The words came from a figure sitting propped against the outside stone wall.

"They say I killed someone. I didn't."

"That's what everyone says." The shadowy figure cackled. "None of us did nothin', we didn't, and some of us didn't."

Kharl started to respond, but then winced as pain stabbed through his skull.

"Don't matter what you did. Justicer's going to say you did, 'less he finds someone else who did. That doesn't happen much."

Kharl eased himself across the damp and slimy stone floor to the other side of the cell, leaning back gingerly, careful not to bang his head against the rough wall stones.

"You don't look like an assassin or a docker," offered the other man.

"I'm a cooper." Kharl took a deeper breath and wished he had not. The air was rank with the odors of unwashed bodies, filth, and worse.

"Cooper, huh. You a good cooper?"

"I thought so."

"Why'd you kill someone, risk losing all that?"

"I didn't," Kharl said tiredly. "My neighbor's shop caught on fire. I was fighting the fire, and someone cut the throat of one of those black-staffers in my shop."

"Ha! They'll hang you quick as they can. Lord West, he don't want to tell the black demons that the murderer got away. Don't want them shelling Brysta. No, ser. That he don't. Hang anyone he can to stop that."

Kharl could see the truth in what the other had said. But what could he do? "They don't let anyone see you here?"

"You jesting? Won't see anyone till you go before the justicer. That'd be Reynol, 'cause he hangs everyone, and that's what they'll want. Four sentences—that's all they got. Flogging, time in the quarries, cut off a hand or foot or both, or hang you. You, they'll hang. Don't matter you did it or not."

"You're cheerful." Kharl swallowed.

"Yep. Cheerful Kaj, that's what they call me."

"What about you? Why are you here?"

"Me? I called that pigswill Egen a bawdson."

"For that, you're in here?"

"Lucky to be alive. Egen's Lord West's youngest, captain in the Watch. Likes girls, young girls. Didn't know he was watchin' . . . said he wasn't man enough to handle a real woman. Whole tavern laughed. Didn't say nothing. When I came out later, his men were waitin' . . . and here I am."

Kharl had the sinking feeling that Egen and the young swell who'd attacked Sanyle and Jenevra were the same man. There were too many coincidences . . . far too many.

He could feel himself beginning to sweat, and with the nausea he was feeling intermittently, he wondered if he could hold his guts in.

"Egen . . . real pissprick . . . and his daddy just looks the other way . . ."

That didn't surprise Kharl.

X

A day passed, and then another. Kharl thought it might have been three days since the fire, and since someone had killed Jenevra. That was if he'd only been knocked out for less than a day. He walked back and forth, if taking three small steps between walls could be called walking. He stopped and coughed, then walked some more.

"That won't do any good," observed Kaj from the corner of the cell—the opposite outside corner from the slop bucket.

"I know," Kharl replied, "but I can't just sit here."

"Might as well. Not goin' anywhere. Except dancin' on air."

"If it's so important to hang me," Kharl said, "why hasn't anyone done anything?"

"You in a hurry to get strung up?" asked Kaj.

"No."

"Then don't ask for it."

"But, I'd think . . ."

"Simple. They brought you in on sixday. Justicers and lords like long end-days. Lord West is gettin' old. Needs the days off to keep his sons at bay. Today's oneday, I figure. Takes a day for the scriveners to write up things formal like. Maybe longer. They don't hurry once you're locked away. They won't come for you till tomorrow, earliest."

"What about you?"

"Leave me here for another eightday. Drag me out and flog me, if I'm lucky . . . Egen's still a pissprick."

"Why doesn't Lord West rein him in?"

" 'Cause he's a smart pissprick. Never gets caught. Always brings you in law-like. Me, drunk too much. Claimed I was soused and disorderly. Was lucky. He'd been really put out, and he'd a planted a lady's brooch or somethin' on me. That's what he did to Fliser. Twice. Second time, they hung him."

"Lord West knows that?"

"Knows some of it. Doesn't care, I'd say. Older son, Osten, he's more like his father. Rotten, but not all the way through like Egen. What they say anyway . . ."

Kharl wanted to shake his head. He'd always suspected those sorts of things happened, but when he'd suggested it to Charee, she'd have nothing to do with his suggestions. For her, all that mattered was that the streets were orderly, no matter how Lord West and his justicers got the job done.

"Not so bad as Gorl, though . . ."

Kharl was certain that he didn't want to hear about Gorl, but there was no way to stop the garrulous Kaj, and he supposed, no reason to. All Kharl could do was to walk a few steps and fret, or sit and stew.

He tried not to breathe deeply as he walked back across the cell.

XI

Despite Kaj's predictions, the gaolers did not come for Kharl until threeday, slightly before midmorning. They took a bucket and splashed water over his hands and face and let him dry both with a small rough towel. Then they bound his hands before him and marched him up the narrow stone staircase. He climbed three flights of steps with centers hollowed by years of wear before they reached a door that led out into the courtyard of the Justicers' Hall. The sky was gray, threatening rain, but the stone pavement was dry. Kharl glanced at the gallows scaffold at the north end of the courtyard, and below it, the flogging frames.

How had it all come to pass? All he'd done was try to help two women and a neighbor, and he was going to be hanged for a killing he hadn't done?

The unseasonably cool wind carried a sour odor to and around Kharl, a smell similar to rotting fish, even as he kept looking at the scaffold.

"You'll be seeing that soon enough, fellow." One of the gaoler's armsmen said, yanking Kharl to start him across the courtyard toward the narrow door at the back of the Hall.

Kharl stumbled, then caught his balance, walking deliberately. The armsmen did not try to hurry him. When they reached the outer door, one stepped ahead and opened it. Inside, they guided Kharl along a narrow corridor that ended at another door, which the same armsman opened, and which led into a foyer. On the left side of the foyer was a single set of double doors, through which the three proceeded.

The chamber in which Kharl found himself was large, but not so large as the outside of the Justicers' Hall would have suggested. The width was about thirty cubits, the length fifty, and the ceiling height was roughly ten. At the end of the chamber were two daises, one behind the other, each holding a podium desk of age-darkened white oak that had turned a deep brownish gold. At the seat behind the lower dais sat a round-faced, blocky, and gray-haired man with a square-cut gray beard who wore a blue velvet gown, trimmed in black.

The single seat on the upper dais, its high, carved back gilded and upholstered in blue velvet, was vacant.

Kharl and the two armsmen stopped beside a heavyset man in a blue-and-gold tunic, who looked to the armsmen. "You should have brought him sooner." Then he lifted the heavy staff and rapped it on the stones of the floor three times, hard enough that the sound echoed through the chamber. All the murmurs died away. "All stand!"

Since Kharl was on his feet, he merely kept standing.

"Is there one who would take the Justicer's Challenge?" intoned the bailiff, barely pausing before continuing. "There being none, the cooper Kharl is here, accused of murder, to be brought before justice!"

Kharl wondered what the Justicer's Challenge was, and who might take it—or why—but no one said anything about it.

The man at the lower dais stood, his eyes fixing on the armsmen and Kharl.

"Bailiff," intoned the justicer after he stood, "bring forth the cooper Kharl."

"That's you," murmured one of the armsmen. "Step firm."

Escorted by the two armsmen, Kharl walked to the armless chair set in the open space forward of the rows of benches. Standing before the benches to the right were several armsman and the Watch captain who had ordered Kharl taken. Before the benches to the left were Charee, Father Jorum, and Mallamet, the cooper whose shop was on Eighth Cross and Cargo Road.

"Keep standing," whispered the armsman.

"You, the cooper Kharl, have been charged with the murder of the blackstaffer Jenevra. What you say or believe is not a question. We are here to do justice, and that justice is to determine whether you killed that blackstaffer." The justicer cleared his throat, then seated himself.

From behind Kharl came a rap of the staff. "All may sit."

"Sit down," hissed the armsman.

Kharl sat, arms still bound before him. He looked at the justicer, but the man never seemed to look back at him.

"Justice calls upon Egen, captain of the Watch," called the justicer.

The captain stood and stepped forward until he was but four paces back from the dais. He bowed. "Lord Justicer Reynol."

"You arrested the cooper. Please tell the Hall what happened."

"Yes, Lord Justicer." Egen bowed again before speaking. "It was last sixday. Someone rang the fire bells, and we proceeded up Crafters' Lane. When we arrived at the fire—it was at the scriptorium—the crafters and the scrivener had quenched the fire, but someone was screaming. She said something like, 'No! She's dead. You cut her throat.' That was what I heard."

"That's not—" Kharl started.

"Silence! You will be heard, cooper," added the justicer. "Continue, if you will, Captain Egen."

"We'd come because of the fire. Sometimes, thieves set them, and sometimes people try to loot shops. So, when I heard that, I went into the cooper's shop and found the blackstaffer. She was on the floor, and her throat had been cut." Egen inclined his head slightly. "There was a bloody knife next to the body. The cooper's apprentice admitted that the knife belonged to the cooper, that it was a drawing knife. His consort had accused him in public. He tried to escape, and it took three armsmen to subdue him."

Reynol nodded. "That will be all for the moment. Please remain here in the Hall."

"Yes, Lord Justicer." Egen bowed again, politely.

"Charee, consort of Kharl, please stand and come forward."

Charee stood. Her steps toward the dais were unsteady. She did not look at Kharl, and her eyes were fixed on the floor stones before her.

"You are Charee, consort of Kharl. Is that correct?"

"Yes . . . Lord."

"You understand that you must tell the truth, and that if you do not, you also will be punished?"

"Yes, Lord." Charee's voice trembled.

"How did the blackstaffer come to the cooperage?"

"Kharl carried her in. She'd been beaten, bad, ser, left in the serviceway to die. We couldn't leave her on the street, but . . ." Charee looked down.

"Go on."

"Um . . . blackstaffers . . . I'd heard tales . . . and I told Kharl she could stay, but only in the shop, not in our quarters up the stairs, and that she had to leave soon as she could."

"What did he say?"

"He said we couldn't throw her out on the street."

"What happened after that?"

"We put her on the old apprentice's pallet in the shop, and I cleaned her up, and got her some blankets. She slept some, then woke up, but she couldn't see proper. Said she was seeing two instead of one—"

"How long was she in the shop?"

"Let's see, ser. It was fourday when Kharl found her, and sixday when . . . when the fire happened."

"Tell us what happened that morning."

"I brought down some bread and cider, and the blackstaffer's clothes. I'd mended them. I helped her dress. See . . . we were going to take her to Father Jorum so she wouldn't be in the shop once she could walk and get around. Then I went upstairs to get the morning meal for Kharl and the boys. Kharl ate and came down to the shop. A while later, I heard a boom, and people yelling, and then there was smoke. I came down and . . . I thought she was lying down . . . except there was blood . . . and she wasn't moving, and I ran out front and told everyone."

"What did you say? Do you recall the exact words?"

"I . . . I said . . . I think I said . . . 'No! She's dead. Someone cut her throat.' "

"You didn't say that your consort cut her throat?"

"No, ser." Charee straightened.

"Are you certain? Why didn't you?"

"It . . . well, ser . . . didn't seem hardly likely. He could have just left her. No reason for him to bring her home, then cut her throat. 'Sides, he was out front fighting the fire."

After a moment, Reynol nodded. "You may return to the bench. I must ask you to remain."

"The cooper Mallamet, step forward."

The stoop-shouldered older cooper stepped toward the dais with a gait that was not quite a shuffle.

"Your name?"

"Mallamet. I'm a cooper, honored justicer."

"You know you must tell the truth or face punishment?"

"Yes, ser."

"What do you know of the prisoner Kharl?"

"He's a cooper, ser." Mallamet looked at the smooth stone floor tiles.

"He's accused of killing a blackstaffer from Recluce. What do you know of this?"

"He had her in his shop. I knew that, ser. And he was making black oak barrels. He was using her to use order to make his barrels better than he could hisself."

"How did you know that?"

"Everyone knew that."

"How did *you* know that?"

"Folks at the Tankard were talking about it, how he was workin' late, no one around, and they heard her chanting stuff."

"Lord West's wizard has inspected those barrels, and there is no additional order infused in them."

"I was just tellin' what I knew."

"Did you tell everyone this so that you could take business from the cooper Kharl?"

"Ser?"

"You heard the question, cooper."

"Ser . . . I was just tellin' what I heard . . ."

"Bailiff!"

"Lord Justicer." The bailiff stepped forward.

"Have the cooper Mallamet taken into custody for false witness. Ten lashes."

"Armsmen! To the fore!"

"Ser . . . no, ser. I was just tellin'."

"Silence!"

Kharl just watched, totally puzzled, as two armsmen escorted Mallamet out of the Hall of Justice. If the justicer and Lord West wanted to hang Kharl, why were they arresting Mallamet? But why had the justicer not asked more questions about what had happened?

"The cooper Kharl."

"Stand," hissed one of the armsmen behind Kharl.

Kharl lurched to his feet, unsteadily. "Lord Justicer." He bowed his head, then looked up, straight at the justicer.

"Earlier, cooper, you had objected to the testimony of Captain Egen. Now, you have a chance to tell what happened."

"Honored justicer," Kharl began carefully, "it all started when I was carrying sealant back from Hyesal the apothecary's shop . . ." He told the entire story as it had happened, ending with, ". . . and when the captain said I'd killed her, I tried to explain that I hadn't done anything. I didn't run. I didn't do anything except I said I didn't do it, and then someone hit me over the head, and I woke up in gaol."

"How do you explain that the blackstaffer was killed with one of your drawing knives?"

"There were lots of people around the front of the shop, ser. Anyone could have walked in. Also, I'm not a killer. I mean, I don't know how to use a knife that way. I wouldn't know where to start."

"Most crafters have a way to defend their shops. What is yours?"

"I keep a cudgel close by, ser. It's close enough to a forge hammer . . ."

"And you are a cooper, and that means using a forge. Had you unbanked your forge that morning?"

"No, ser. Charee and I had to walk Jenevra—she was the blackstaffer—to Father Jorum's. I didn't want to waste the charcoal."

"Have you anything else to say?"

"I didn't do it, ser."

"But you did try to get away from the armsmen, did you not?"

"No, ser. I said I didn't do it. I might have backed up one step, but I didn't try to get away. They were saying I did something I didn't."

"That will be all. Please be seated."

Kharl felt as though the justicer hadn't really paid any attention to his words. But there was no way out of the Hall, not with his hands bound, and armsmen behind him and all around the Hall.

"Lord justicer!" The bailiff in gold and blue rapped his staff on the stone floor of the chamber.

The justicer looked at the functionary. "Yes, bailiff?"

"Your honor . . . there is a witness. He has a pass from the Quadrancy."

The frown of the justicer was so fleeting that Kharl would not have seen it had he even blinked. "Very well. Have him step forward and state his name."

There was a slight sound behind the justicer, and a slender, gray-haired man, clean-shaven and in blue velvet, his tunic trimmed in gold, slipped into the seat at the higher dais behind the justicer, a seat that had been vacant throughout the trial. Even from where he sat, Kharl could see that the newcomer was old, and that there were dark circles ringing his deep-set eyes.

The figure who stepped forward from beside the bailiff as a witness was Tyrbel, wearing the black robe that he had told Kharl was for appearances before the justicers.

"State your name."

"I am Tyrbel, scrivener of Brysta, your honor of justice." The scrivener bowed deeply.

"What have you to say to what has been offered as evidence, master scrivener?"

"What I have to say, your honor of justice, is most plain." Tyrbel looked squarely at the justicer. "Kharl could not have killed the blackstaffer. He is a good man, but there is another reason why he could not have killed her. She was still alive when he left his cooperage to fight the fire, and he was still with me and the others using the buckets when his consort came out to tell him that something terrible had happened."

"How do you know the blackstaffer was still alive?" The justicer's face bore more curiosity than anger.

"I saw her leaning on his workbench through the window when I called for help. She was still standing there when Kharl came out."

"So your scriptorium was burning, and you had time to watch?" The justicer's sarcasm was scarcely veiled.

Kharl looked at Tyrbel. The scrivener was perfectly calm. What Tyrbel said was true. Jenevra had been alive. But Tyrbel had not actually seen that, and Kharl had not talked to Tyrbel since the murder.

"I only watched for a moment. It was long enough to see that Kharl had heard and was coming to help."

"Justicer?" interjected the clean-shaven and elderly man in the high seat, before another word could be said.

"Yes, Lord West?"

Lord West looked squarely at the scrivener. "Are you absolutely certain that the cooper could not have turned back and killed the blackstaffer?"

"Yes, Lord. I had barely reached the fire barrel when Kharl was beside me."

"And he had no blood on him?" asked the lord.

"No, ser."

"Does he wear the same garments now as then?"

Tyrbel turned and studied Kharl. "Yes, ser. They are more soiled, but they are the same."

"I would note, Lord Justicer, that while there is filth on his tunic, there does not seem to be any blood."

"It is so noted," replied Reynol.

Lord West sat back, an amused expression on his face.

Kharl didn't know what to think. One moment, he was convinced he would be hanged, and the next Lord West was suggesting that he could not have killed Jenevra.

"Jorum, priest of the Sovereign, please come forward."

Father Jorum rose from one of the benches to the left and walked forward, past Kharl.

"I will not trouble you with reminders, Jorum. Just answer directly."

"Yes, Lord Justicer."

"What did the woman Charee say to you about the blackstaffer?"

"Very little, ser. She said that someone had been hurt and that she wanted them to finish recovering away from the cooperage."

"Away from the cooperage? Did she say why?"

"She only said that she didn't want the person to stay at the cooperage."

"She gave no reason?"

"No, ser. Except she said that she was having trouble with Kharl over it. She said that she might ask me to talk to the cooper."

"Did you?"

"No, ser. She never did ask me."

"Has she talked to you since?"

"She came to me on sixday, and asked me what to do about her consort. She told me that the Watch had taken the body of the blackstaffer and that they had taken Kharl. She was very upset."

"Did she say anything about the killing?"

"She only said that she wished it had not happened, that she wished the blackstaffer had never come to Brysta, and that she wished that she had not allowed the woman even in the cooperage."

"Was that all?"

"She asked for me to pray for her and her children."

"You may return to the bench, Jorum."

The priest inclined his head, then stepped back.

"Captain Egen," Reynol stated. "Approach the dais."

Egen rose, almost languidly, and stepped forward, stopping and bowing.

"When you arrived with the Watch, Captain, did anyone have blood on their clothing?" asked the justicer.

Egen frowned for a moment, as if recalling, before speaking. "The cooper's consort did. She was the only one. There was blood on her blouse."

"Did you examine the body?"

"Yes, ser."

"How was the blackstaffer killed?"

"The blackstaffer had a large jagged cut across her neck, ser."

"A jagged cut?"

"Yes, ser."

"Did you look at the barrels of the cooper?"

Kharl frowned. What did his barrels have to do with anything?

"Yes, ser."

"Are they well made?"

"Very well made, ser, in my judgment, but I am not a cooper."

"And the cooper was not ill or trembling, or drunk when your men took him into custody?"

"No, ser. He was quite in possession of himself."

"You may stand back, captain." The justicer looked to the bailiff. "Have the woman Charee step forward."

Charee looked from the justicer to the bailiff before stepping toward the dais.

"Did you like the blackstaffer?"

Charee seemed to step back.

"Would you answer the question?"

"No, ser."

"Why not?"

"They're . . ."

"They're what?"

"They're evil . . ."

Reynol nodded. "Do you ever work with the cooper's tools?"

"No, ser. I see 'em, but I don't work with them."

"Could you explain why you had blood on your blouse?"

"Blood . . . on me? 'Cause I saw her lyin' there, and I bent down to see what was the matter. She was dead."

"Are you certain of that?" asked the justicer.

" 'Course she was dead."

"I'll ask you again. Are you certain the blackstaffer was dead?"

Kharl glanced from the justicer to his consort, and back again. He didn't understand the questions, or the reason for them.

"She was dead."

Reynol nodded, then gestured to the bailiff. "Restrain her."

"No! I didn't do nothing!" Charee protested, turning, then stopping as two armsmen appeared and bound her hands behind her back.

"The Hall of Justice has heard enough."

"All stand!" The bailiff rapped the stone floor with the staff.

One of the armsmen had to drag Kharl to his feet. The cooper looked blankly at the justicer.

"There are a number of facts of great import here. First, the cooper was fighting the fire, and noted witnesses saw him doing so, and also saw the blackstaffer alive. Second, dead bodies do not bleed profusely. There may be some blood, but it is limited. Third, the slash on the black-staffer's neck was a jagged cut. Although the cut was made with a cooper's knife, the cooper is a man skilled with the use of a knife, and the cut was made with a less skilled hand. Fourth, the cooper had no signs of blood on his tunic. Only one person did, and that person had to be the killer of the blackstaffer."

"No!" Kharl exclaimed.

"Silence!"

"Keep your trap shut," hissed one of the armsmen holding Kharl.

The justicer looked squarely at Charee. "You would have let your consort die for an act you committed. That is most heinous. You have been found guilty of the murder of the blackstaffer Jenevra."

"No . . . no . . . " The slightest of sobs escaped Charee.

Reynol turned his eyes upon Kharl. "You did not kill, but you allowed the killing to take place. Further, you resisted the lawful author-ity of the Watch. Of both offenses are you guilty." The justicer turned and looked to Lord West. "The woman Charee has been found guilty of murdering the backstaffer, and the cooper Kharl has been found guilty of failing to protect the defenseless under his care and of resisting lawful authority."

"So be it," intoned the lord. He looked to Charee, who looked down at the polished stones of the floor, then to Kharl.

The cooper returned the gaze of the Lord of the Quadrant, fearlessly.

"The sentence for the woman Charee is death by hanging. The cooper is sentenced to twenty lashes for neglect, and another ten for insolence to civil authority. Let the sentences be carried out immediately. Justice delayed is justice denied." West struck the silver chime that rested on the desk of the dais before him. "Justicing is done."

The two armsmen tightened their grip on Kharl.

"You aren't going to make trouble, now, cooper?"

"No . . ." Kharl choked.

How could he? What could he do, with armsmen all around him, and the insufferable swell Egen and another group of armsmen standing by? He watched, silently, as Charee was half carried, half dragged, away.

"Just turn real easy, cooper."

Kharl turned. He still didn't understand. Charee couldn't have killed Jenevra, could she? Why would she have done that? It didn't feel right.

His legs moved, and he saw, but he was not really aware of what he saw or where he walked, not until the armsmen brought him up short outside in the courtyard under the gray sky, just short of the center flogging frame.

"Now, we're going to untie your hands, cooper. You try to get away, and it's another twenty strokes. That makes fifty, and most men don't live with fifty."

Kharl nodded. He understood, not that it mattered in some ways, but he didn't see any point in doing something stupid that could get him killed for nothing.

Once Kharl was secured to the flogging frame, Captain Egen appeared, stepping forward and motioning the armsmen away, including the one with the whip. He stopped less than two cubits from the cooper. When the captain spoke, his voice was soft and very low. "Usually, we do the flogging first, but then you wouldn't be able to see what happened to your consort, and I want you to see that, cooper. I want you to understand that Lord West is the law. I want you to understand that it is not ever a good idea to think that you should judge or question your betters." Egen paused. "Now, do you have anything to say?"

Kharl had plenty to say, but not where he was. "No, ser."

"You should never have intruded on the affairs of your betters, cooper. Perhaps you can learn. If you cannot . . . well, you will see how you'll end up. It's only a matter of time." Egen smiled and stepped back.

Kharl wanted to look away, but thought that would be cowardice of a sort. He watched as Charee half walked, and was half dragged, up the steps to the scaffold platform. Overhead, the gray clouds roiled and darkened, but without thunder, and without rain.

Two of the armsmen tied her wrists together, behind her back.

"I didn't do it—" Charee's words were faint but clear. "I didn't. She was dead—"

"Enough." The burly hangman pulled a heavy black bag over Charee's head, then put the noose in place.

An off-tempo drumroll echoed through the courtyard, although Kharl could not see the drummer.

The hangman stepped back and pulled a lever. The trap dropped.

Kharl winced.

Within moments, Charee's body hung limply.

"Begin the flogging!" snapped Egen.

Kharl didn't feel the lash for the first stroke, and not much for the second.

He lost track after ten, and he didn't feel the last ones, either. That was because he felt nothing at all.

XII

At some point, Kharl recalled being dragged into a cart, facedown. But each time the cart rolled over something, his back turned from a mass of pain into lightning strikes of agony, followed by blackness. About the time when he struggled into wakefulness again, despite the searing pain across his back, several people carried him somewhere, saying things he should have recalled, but didn't.

When he woke, thin knives of pain slashed down his back.

"Ohh . . ."

"I know. It has to hurt. But they flogged your tunic and undertunic into your skin, and if I don't clean it out, it will fester, and you will die."

Kharl knew he should recognize the woman's voice, but the pain washed over him so frequently that he could not concentrate. "Go ahead," he mumbled, his fingers digging into something.

Another strip of pain lanced down his back.

"I'm sorry, but the cloth, some of it, is matted into your flesh, and there's even salt they poured in some places." The voice trembled for a moment.

In a moment of clarity, Kharl recognized the speaker. "Sanyle?"

"Yes. Father asked if I'd help. I've been cooking for the boys and watching over you."

"Thank . . . you . . ."

"Just try to lie still. I'm mostly finished. Then I can clean out the rest of the wounds. Father gave me something that will help numb your back when I'm done."

"Go . . . on . . ."

Agony alternated with blackness until he finally succumbed totally to the darkness. Even then, the darkness was filled with unseen flame.

When Kharl woke again, he was lying facedown on his own bed—the bed he and Charee had shared for so many years. He swallowed, thinking, for there had been good times, if few in recent years. The thoughts of what had happened so suddenly and for so little reason swirled through his mind. At the same time, his back was still a mass of pain, and even the slightest movement intensified the agony.

Between the two kinds of pain, it was a while before he realized someone else was in the small bedchamber. Even so, he had to squint to make out the figure sitting on the stool opposite the side of the bed his head faced.

"Warrl?" Kharl croaked the single name.

"It's me, Da." Warrl stood and went to the door. "He's awake." Then he returned and sat back down.

Kharl said nothing. What could he say?"

"Da . . . Sanyle said . . . she said . . . they hung Ma . . . Why did they do it? Ma didn't do anything."

Kharl tried to speak, but all he could do was cough, and for a moment, or longer, blackness washed over him.

Warrl was still sitting there when Kharl could see once more.

"Da?"

"They . . . discovered . . . no way . . . I could have . . . killed the blackstaffer . . . wanted someone to hang . . . tell the black demons . . ."

"Why didn't you stop them? Why didn't you . . . ?"

"Warrl," came a voice from behind Kharl, Sanyle's soft voice, "your father tried. My father saw it all. Your da struggled against the armsmen, but there were scores of them. That's why they whipped him so badly. He tried to stop them, and they whipped him more."

". . . why? He didn't kill anyone. Ma didn't, neither . . ."

"Let him rest, Warrl. He did the best he could. He did more than most men in Brysta would ever try."

Before the blackness reclaimed him, Kharl could hear Warrl sniffling, and he wanted to reach out, to say more.

XIII

Kharl woke abruptly, at the sound of voices beyond the closed bedchamber door. From the light coming through the windows, and the damp warmth, it seemed to be late afternoon or early evening. Slowly, he managed to stand, even though every movement hurt, even after three days when he'd done little except eat and sleep. He made his way to the door, putting his hand on the latch-lever. Then he stopped as the words in the main room began to make sense.

"... he'd never understand ..."

"... sees more than you think ..." Kharl thought the voice was Sanyle's, but it was hard to tell because she was speaking much less loudly than Arthal.

"... never done except what he wanted ... never listened to any of us. He should have listened to Ma ... he should have ..." Arthal's voice was loud and angry.

"... done more than you've seen, Arthal ..."

"... you're just sweet on him ... Ma not even gone an eightday ..."

"... who would cook and take care of him? You? You can't fire the stove or boil water."

"... can, too ..."

"... not that I've seen ..."

"Why should I ... after what he did ... hasn't even written Aunt Merayni ..."

Kharl winced at that. He should write Merayni, or even take a day to go visit his consort's sister. The thought was painful, because Merayni would blame him. She had a tongue far sharper than Charee's had ever been.

The words died away.

Kharl coughed, then rattled the latch-lever before easing the door open. He stepped through the doorway, then stopped. The two who had been arguing were Arthal and Sanyle. Tyrbel's youngest daughter, more than two years older than Arthal, was slim and dark-haired, but with overlarge eyes and a nose slightly larger and sharper than her face merited.

"Da . . .?" began Arthal, looking toward Kharl.

"It hurts," Kharl admitted. "But lying around isn't going to keep the cooperage going, or bring in coins."

"I suppose not," Arthal replied.

"Doing too much too soon won't help much either," suggested Sanyle. "Why don't you sit down at the table? Supper's almost ready."

"Where's Warrl?"

"He was checking the door bars down below," Sanyle said. "He should be back here any moment." She turned back toward the stove.

Kharl eased his way into the chair where he usually sat, but he had to sit on the edge so that his shoulders wouldn't touch the wooden spokes. He glanced toward the stove, where Sanyle was standing and where Charee had so often stood. For a moment, his eyes clouded, and he could not even see. His lips tightened. Charee had been right about Jenevra bringing trouble. Charee had been right about many things. But what was he supposed to have done? Let the blackstaffer die?

The door from the shop swung open, then closed with a *thud.*

"Everything's barred up, and I closed the shutters, too," Warrl announced even before he stepped into the main room.

"Thank you," Kharl said.

"Da . . . you're up."

"After a fashion," Kharl admitted. "I'm slow. Probably be a few days before I can do much in the shop." Or anywhere else, he suspected.

"You going to keep on with the shop?" asked Warrl.

"I'm a cooper. What else would I do?"

"Without Ma . . .?"

"It will be hard," Kharl admitted.

Sanyle carried the stewpot to the table, setting it on the old wooden trivet.

Kharl just looked at the pot, but his eyes blurred, and he couldn't really see. After a moment, he said, "Sanyle . . . best . . . you serve . . ."

"It's the best I could do . . . and the bread's a little too crisp . . ."

"Be . . . fine . . ." Kharl choked.

"Father sent over some ale. Said it would help you. It's in your mug."

"You . . . thank him . . ." Kharl reached gratefully for the mug and the ale it held. The ale might help. It might.

XIV

Two mornings later, Kharl donned just an undertunic—a soft and old one—above his heavy brown boots and trousers and made his way down to the cooperage. He slowly walked around the shop. The coals in the forge, banked so many days ago, had long since turned to ashes, and the hearth was covered in a fine film of ash powder around the fire pot. There was a film of dust over everything.

He walked toward the wall where the apprentice's pallet had been. It was gone, and someone had scrubbed the floor planks. He leaned over. Set on the bottom of the finishing bench were the black staff and Jenevra's pack. He wondered why the staff had been left. Because no one wanted to touch it? Or had it just been overlooked and forgotten?

His fingers brushed the staff. For all that it had lain under the bench for more than an eightday, the wood still felt warm to his touch. So did the iron bands. He picked up the staff. He'd initially thought that it had merely been stained dark, or that it was black oak. When he studied it and held it, he could see that he'd been wrong. The staff was lorken, fine-grained, and almost as strong as iron, if far lighter. The bands on it, one near each end, and the other two equidistant between those at the ends, were also not plain iron, but mage-fired black iron, the black iron that could only be created in Recluce. Or so it was said.

". . . a warrior's staff . . ." He shook his head and leaned the staff against the wall. Then he stooped and picked up the canvas pack and set it on the finishing bench.

Had Jenevra left anything in it that might have allowed someone to contact family? Did she even have any? Slowly, he untied the thongs and opened the flaps, before looking inside. There were clean under-clothes, and one spare set of trousers, and beneath that a soiled tunic and undertunic, and beneath them a leather-bound book and a pouch. In the pouch were clean rags and a bar of rose soap. That was all.

Kharl replaced everything in the pack, except for the book, which he placed on the corner of the finishing bench before walking toward the front of the shop. There, he deliberately unfastened the shutters and swung them back. After that, he unbarred the front door, opened it, and peered out. The day was cloudy, although the clouds were high and light gray, if thick. Rain would not arrive before afternoon, if at all. He glanced westward. Tyrbel's glass had been repaired, and the window frames replaced and painted, but, without walking over to the window and peering through it, there was no way to tell if the scrivener had placed other books in the display window.

The cooper stepped back into his cooperage, counting the barrel shooks still in the high racks. He moved to the tool rack. Everything was there, except for his best drawing knife. He'd miss that, but he counted himself well off that nothing else seemed to be gone. He turned to the planer, as dusty as everything else.

There was the sound of boots on the steps, and Kharl looked to the stairs.

Arthal stood halfway down, with a canvas duffel slung over his right shoulder. He looked at his father without speaking.

"You might have told me," Kharl said, mildly.

"What is there to say?" Arthal's voice was flat.

"Where you're going," the cooper suggested.

"The *Fleuryl* had an opening for a carpenter's apprentice. I took it. You already said that you wouldn't stop me if there was a position."

Kharl refrained from saying that he had been speaking of a position in Brysta. After what he had heard of the conversation between Sanyle and Arthal two nights before, he saw no point in arguing over his past words. He finally spoke. "I wish you well, son. I hope it turns out as you would like."

"Could it turn out worse than staying here?" asked Arthal coldly, making his way to the bottom of the steps, then shifting the duffel to the other shoulder.

"It could, but, for your sake, I hope it doesn't." Kharl forced a faint smile. "You might remember that I was your age once. We all were."

Arthal was silent, his eyes avoiding Kharl's.

"You think I could have done more. You think that you could have done more had you been in my boots. I hope you never find yourself in them, not that way."

"Da . . . I don't want to say more."

After a moment, Kharl nodded. "Then you'd better go. You're welcome here anytime if you change your thoughts."

Arthal walked silently to the door of the cooperage.

Kharl did not follow him.

Then the younger man stopped. "Good-bye, Da." He turned without waiting for a response.

"Good-bye." Kharl watched as the door closed. His vision blurred for a moment, and he lifted his arm to blot his eyes, ignoring the additional pain the motion caused. Neither boy was happy with him. Not happy? Both were filled with anger and bitterness directed at him, as if he alone had killed their mother.

Arthal was ready to waste his life at sea, and Warrl had bolted out early, saying he had to catch up on his lessons with Master Fonwyl, rather than stay anywhere near his father.

Kharl took a deep breath and walked to the racks where the shooks were stacked, slowly taking down enough for a single red oak slack barrel. Each motion hurt.

He'd have to take his time. That he knew. But what else could he do?

He'd laid out the shooks, set up the planer, and shaped four of the shooks into rough staves when the door to the cooperage opened, and Tyrbel walked in.

Kharl eased the shook he was working away from the planer and took his foot off the drive pedal. He set the shook on the bench and walked forward to meet the scrivener.

"Kharl . . . I am so sorry . . ." began Tyrbel.

The cooper shook his head. "You have nothing to be sorry about. Should have come over to thank you—for my life twice over. Without you and Sanyle, I'd not be here. I'm still not thinking as a man should . . ."

"You've lost your consort, and you've taken a flogging that would have killed a lesser man, my friend." Tyrbel smiled warmly. "Perhaps because I work with words, I know their limits. I've seen your acts, and they are far more eloquent than any words. I did what I could." The scrivener looked down. "I didn't have any idea that . . . Justicer Reynol . . . I didn't know he could do something that base . . ."

"Until I was in the gaol, neither did I." Kharl cleared his throat. "The man with me . . . Kaj . . . he said that I'd hang. He said that Lord West needed to hang someone to keep Recluce from shelling Brysta."

"Recluce is not that vindictive," replied Tyrbel. "That was an excuse because you stood up to Egen."

"Kaj said he was a pissprick."

"I know. They hung Kaj yesterday. I had to be at the Hall for something else when it happened."

"They hung him? For calling Captain Egen a name? For being drunk?"

"The charge was that he was a thief, that he'd stolen some of the coin he'd used at the Tankard, and that the other was counterfeit, and that he'd been found guilty four times before."

"I don't know," Kharl said heavily. "He didn't seem that type."

"I doubt he was," Tyrbel said. "Light! I wish that we had someone of character these days, someone who would take the Justicer's Challenge and remove Reynol. He's but a tool of young Egen." Tyrbel laughed ruefully. "Of course, Lurtedd is a tool of Osten."

"Justicer's Challenge?" He'd heard of it, but would anyone dare? How did it work?

"Oh . . . it's a way that a man learned in law and justice can challenge a justicer. But it's seldom done, because, if he fails, he suffers the punishment of those five people whose cases he takes."

"Oh." After a moment of silence, Kharl added, "Arthal left this morning. He's going to be a carpenter's apprentice on some ship."

"I'm sure that hurts. But, given the way he feels, it would be worse for him to stay here. Worse for him and much worse for you."

"Did Sanyle tell you?"

"That the boys think it's your fault? Yes . . . we won't tell anyone else, but she needed to talk to someone." Tyrbel paused. "It wasn't your fault. A man has to be a man, or he's nothing."

Kharl nodded. "You spoke for me. Will that hurt you?"

"I would hope not." The angular scrivener shrugged, then brushed back a lock of brown-and-silver hair. "But you risked your life for Sanyle. How could I not say the truth?"

"I am grateful. You were the only one."

"Gharan would have. I asked him not to, unless something happened to me. He has small children. I also let it be known that there were many who saw that you could not have murdered the girl."

"That way . . . ?"

Tyrbel nodded. "But . . . that may not have been wise. I did not think that they would turn on Charee when they heard in open justice that you were innocent. They did not let anyone speak for her."

"I tried."

"They added extra lashes for that." Tyrbel paused. "Egen was one of those who tried to force Sanyle, wasn't he?"

"Yes. I didn't know that until the Watch came. Kaj told me who he was. He told me—Captain Egen did—before they whipped me, that I should never question my betters. He said that he'd hang me if I ever did again."

"He's petty, and meaner than a mountain cat in heat, but he's cunning. Never says anything where anyone can hear, and always has some reason in the law for what he does. You know that they gave Mallamet just ten lashes for false witness. The lashes barely broke the skin."

"So they can say they treated everything fair." Kharl snorted.

Tyrbel cleared his throat. "I know some scriveners in Hemmen and Vizyn. I wrote them to see if there might be a need for coopers there."

"You think I should leave Brysta?"

Tyrbel shrugged. "I don't know. But best you keep both eyes open. You end up in gaol again, for whatever reason, and you won't walk out, except to the gallows."

Kharl nodded slowly.

"You've got some time. Egen's cunning. Anything happens to you soon, and people will talk, especially the crafters, and that would upset Lord West." Tyrbel looked to the door. "I have to go."

"Thank you. You have been a friend. A true friend."

"You told me that was what neighbors were for." The scrivener smiled. "Take your time in healing. You'll need your strength."

"I can pay Sanyle some," Kharl said.

"She would like that, but you don't have to."

Kharl felt he did, but he only smiled. "You've both been good to us."

After Tyrbel left, as Kharl walked back to the planer, he saw the leather-bound book on the edge of the finishing bench. Perhaps he should look at it in the evening. He couldn't afford enough ale to take his mind off Charee, and he still needed to write Merayni . . . if he could only find the words.

Maybe puzzling through the book would help, one way or another. He needed something.

XV

Because he knew how Warrl felt, Kharl did not press the boy to speak, except for his work, or request that his son stay too close to the cooperage for the next several days. He did insist on Warrl doing his chores, and his lessons, and on eating with Kharl and Sanyle.

On fiveday evening, as they were finishing supper, Kharl looked at Warrl. "How are your lessons going?"

"I'm going every day. You know that. Master Fonwyl says I'll never pass the craftmaster examination."

"He said that?"

"Yes, ser," Warrl averred.

"Did he say why?"

Warrl did not meet Kharl's eyes. Kharl waited.

"He said . . . all order would turn to chaos before a son of yours was allowed to be a craftmaster in Brysta." Warrl looked up at Kharl. "Why do they all hate you? What did you do to make them hate me?"

"They don't all hate me. Tyrbel doesn't. Gharan doesn't. Hyesal doesn't."

"They don't matter. Lord West and the justicers matter. The craftmasters matter. And they all hate you."

"Everyone matters," Kharl offered, not sure what he could say.

"It's not right. They shouldn't hate me. Not because of what you did. Not because I'm your son."

"They shouldn't. People don't always do what's right. You know that . . . don't you?"

"Why . . ." Warrl looked up. "I'm sorry, Da . . ."

"Your father did the best he could," Sanyle said. "There are evil people in Brysta. Some of them are powerful. Do you think he should not do good because of them?"

"What good does it do?" Warrl asked. "The blackstaffer died, and Ma died, and Da, he almost died."

Kharl looked at Sanyle and gave the slightest of headshakes. He did not want her to mention what he had done for her. That would just give Warrl a chance to direct his anger at her. The young woman waited for a moment before she answered Warrl. "My father always has said that if you do good because you expect to be rewarded, it is not good at all, but greed."

"Then I'll be greedy when I get older," Warrl said. "What good is it if you can't live to enjoy it?"

Kharl cleared his throat. "Did Master Fonwyl say if you had learned enough to pass the mastercrafter examination if you weren't my son?"

Warrl looked up, surprised. After a moment, he replied. "He said I know enough."

"Are you telling me what he said or what you think?"

"No, Da. He said I knew as much as most craftmasters."

"Then, there's no reason for you to keep taking lessons, is there?"

"You mean that, Da?"

"I wouldn't say it if I didn't mean it. Of course, that means you'll be able to help in the shop more."

"That's more interesting than Master Fonwyl." Warrl paused. "Can I go over to Hergan's now?"

"If you're careful and back before full dark."

"Thank you, Da . . ." Warrl looked at Sanyle. "Thank you for dinner."

"You're welcome, Warrl."

Neither Sanyle nor Kharl spoke until Warrl had closed the door and headed down the stairs and through the cooperage. Kharl heard the front door shut.

"You don't want him to know that some of what you did saved others?" asked Sanyle.

"That would make him angry at you. It wouldn't make him less angry at me." The cooper shrugged. "Not much I can do about that." He rose and carried his bowl and Warrl's to the wash table.

After a moment, Sanyle followed his example. "I'll do the dishes." She smiled briefly. "You are paying me."

"Not enough," Kharl said. "I appreciate the cooking. Not something I'd do well. Not well enough to eat what I fixed."

He did let Sanyle do the dishes, although he put them away in the single cupboard, another piece of furniture he had made years before. Thinking of that time, his eyes misted for a moment, and he shook his head. What had happened? Did it happen to others?

He could not answer his own questions. So he put the last bowl away.

After Sanyle had left, and he was alone in the main room, he adjusted the wick in the lamp on the table by the one easy chair and picked up the black leather book he had brought up from the shop. He had to lean back into the chair very gingerly.

Slowly, he studied the slender tome, noting the fineness of the binding. There were no words on the cover or on the spine, just smooth black leather. He opened the front cover to the title page and read the words: *The Basis of Order*. That was all. There was no explanation, and no name for an author. He turned another page. The text began abruptly, under a simple numeral "1." He began to read.

> Order is life; chaos is death. This is fact, not belief. Each living creature consists of ordered parts that must function together . . .

> Order extends down to the smallest fragments of the world. By influencing the smallest ordered segments to create a new and ordered form, an order-master may change where land exists and where it does not, where rain will fall and where it will not . . . In contrast, control of chaos is simply the ability to sever one ordered segment of the world from another . . . without the use of order, focused destruction is the highest level of control to which a chaos-master can aspire . . .

> Simple as these words are, learning about what order and chaos truly are is far from simple. One might say that order is like water, that it can change forms, and that it is vital to life, and that without it nothing lives . . . That is less than the beginning . . .

Kharl skipped to the next page.

> Learning without understanding can but increase the frustration of the impatient, for knowledge is like the hammer of a

smith, useless in the hands of the unskilled and able to do nothing but injure the user who has not both knowledge and understanding . . . All things are not possible, even to the greatest, and even to those with understanding . . .

Kharl lowered the book, frowning, but not closing it, thinking.

XVI

On sixday, Kharl was feeling stronger, but not strong enough to use the forge to finish the hoops for the slack barrels. Instead, he contented himself with working on the red oak shooks, first with the planer, then spending time with the hollowing knife, including some time working with Warrl, showing him some of the finer points of using the knife.

Just before noon, the door opened, and a short wiry figure with a ginger beard and wearing a brown overtunic stepped into the cooperage. He glanced around, then, catching sight of Kharl, squared his shoulders, and moved toward the planer where Kharl stood. From the other workbench, Warrl watched.

"Master Senstad," the cooper said politely.

"Cooper."

Kharl waited, suspecting he knew what was coming, but not wanting to make matters easy for the grower.

"I'd ordered twenty barrels, tight cooperage."

"You did, for harvest."

"I can only use five, Kharl. I'm sorry . . . but the harvest isn't going to be that good. Too dry early in the summer." Senstad's eyes never once met Kharl's.

Kharl could sense the lie, but he only nodded. "Been a bad year for many folk. Least, that's what they say."

"I'll pick up the five next sixday . . . pay you then. That be all right?"

"The barrels'll be ready."

"Good." Senstad paused. "I'm sorry. You know how these things are."

"Yes. I do. It happens."

The grower nodded and turned. At the door, he turned back. "Next sixday."

"They'll be ready," Kharl promised, and that was one he could keep. The door closed.

"He's lying," Warrl said. "Hergan said the growers are having a good year, best in a long time. Why?"

"He probably owes tariffs or money to Lord West. He rents some of his land from the lord, I think."

"Why did he say he wanted five barrels, then?" Warrl's face showed puzzlement.

"If he canceled the order, he'd still owe a quarter—that'd be what he'd pay for five barrels. So . . . this way, he gets five good barrels, and he doesn't lose anything, and he can tell . . . everyone that was all he could do."

"Da . . ." Warrl finally looked down without saying more.

"You can go over to Hergan's for a time, if you'd like."

"I'd like that. You don't mind?"

"You can go," Kharl said. "I'll be all right."

Warrl didn't wait, and within moments Kharl was alone in the cooperage.

He went back to the planer.

In midafternoon there was a solid rap on the loading dock door.

Kharl frowned, but walked back to the door and opened it.

Werwal stood there, in his soiled leathers, his wagon in the alley behind him. "Good afternoon, cooper."

"Good afternoon, Werwal."

"Wasn't sure I'd be seeing you. Not after everything I heard," offered the renderer. "You feeling all right?"

"I've felt better," Kharl confessed. "Good thing I'd finished your barrels last eightday. Still too sore to use the forge."

Werwal laughed, a rueful sound. "Most fellows wouldn't be standing after what you went through." He paused. "I could hold off on the barrels, if you need them for someone else . . ."

"They're ready. If you want them, they're yours. Can't say as I've been overrun with orders the past few days."

"You won't be, I fear. Egen's . . . let's just say that he dislikes losing. Because you're alive, he feels he's lost."

"How do you know so much about him . . . about what goes on?"

Werwal's laugh was more open this time. "No one holds their tongue around renderers and rag-pickers. Who are we, dealing with the dregs of offal?"

Kharl realized something else that he should have noticed sooner. The renderer was far better spoken than most crafters, but that was hardly something that he could mention. "Always felt how a man does his craft reckons his value more than what it is."

"Your barrels show it." Werwal gestured to the slack barrels by the loading door. "Are those mine?"

"That they are—the first five."

"I'll get them. You don't need to be lifting them right now."

"I can help . . ."

"You roll them over, and I'll lift 'em," suggested the renderer.

Rolling the empty barrels was no problem for the cooper, and before long all five were in the renderer's wagon.

Werwal closed the wagon gate and walked back to the loading door where Kharl stood.

"I owe you three silvers and four coppers." The renderer extended the coins. "Long as you're here, I'll be ordering barrels. I don't need too many, but they need to be good."

"I thank you," Kharl replied. "You seem free to say what you think when others will not even hint at it."

The lanky man grinned. "Who else would do what I do? That gives me the freedom to say a bit more, though there are those to whom I would not speak so freely."

"You don't worry about it?"

"I don't worry too much," Werwal replied. "No one else wishes to do what I do." The renderer smiled. "You're always welcome . . . if you don't mind the odor."

"You're always welcome here," Kharl responded.

"For that, cooper, I thank you." Werwal offered a last smile. "I need to get back." He turned and lithely vaulted up onto the wagon seat.

As the wagon rolled down the alley away from the loading dock, Kharl wondered about Werwal's invitation.

Would things change that much, so much that the only place he might be welcome was with Brysta's renderer?

XVII

By the beginning of the next eightday, Kharl was almost back to feeling normal, except that too much bending still sent shivers of pain through his back. He was only slightly slower than usual, but he'd seen few of his normal customers. Some, like Korlan, he didn't expect to see for several more eightdays, although he'd begun work on the vintner's white oak barrels, after finishing the five for Senstad.

About midmorning on threeday, as Kharl was planing white oak shooks into staves for Korlan's barrels, Aryl eased through the door of the cooperage.

Kharl glanced at Warrl, who had been working with the chiv to smooth the rims of a red oak slack barrel. "You can take a break, if you'd like."

"Thank you, Da. Might I go outside?"

"If you don't go too far."

With a nod and a smile, Warrl turned, sliding something thin and white and oblong into his tunic, like a folded sheet of paper, better than the kind Warrl had used for his lessons. Kharl wondered what it was, but didn't want to ask when Aryl was headed toward him.

The boy slipped to the side away from Aryl, waiting until Aryl was farther inside the cooperage before easing behind the brown-bearded and stocky man, then out the door.

"How you doing, Kharl?" asked the square-faced apple grower.

"Been better . . . been worse. You ready to order some barrels?" Kharl set the stave he had just finished aside and took his foot off the drive pedal of the planer.

"Depends . . . you wouldn't talk much when I was offering seven coppers apiece."

"Still wouldn't," Kharl said. "Not much sense in selling something for less than the iron and oak cost. Told you that the price was ten coppers each."

"I don't know, Kharl . . . A silver a barrel . . . that's a lot . . . Mallamet offers slack barrels for eight coppers."

"You get what you pay for, Aryl," Kharl replied.

"Doesn't matter that much for slack barrels when you're shippin' apples, and two coppers a barrel adds up when you need twenty. That's four silvers."

"What about the ones you used for the apples you dry and put on Nenalt's ships?" asked the cooper.

Aryl fingered his beard. "You'd have the right of it there. But I'd be needing just ten of those."

"What about twenty for nine coppers each?" suggested Kharl.

"Hmmm . . . eighteen silvers, that'd be."

"You'd be getting more than two silvers' worth in the better barrels." Kharl didn't like cutting his prices. That led to ruin, but he'd also checked the strongbox, and he needed more coin, or at least the promise of it, in order to claim the seasoned shook billets from Vetrad.

"Well . . . seeing the way things are . . . I'll try twenty at nine each. Be needing them the end of next eightday."

Kharl waited.

"Five silvers now; four on oneday, and the other nine when I pick up the barrels."

Kharl thought. Usually, Aryl paid half with the order, but oneday was less than an eightday away, and he did need the orders. "Seeing as it's you, Aryl, that'd be fine, and your barrels'll be ready an eightday from sixday."

"That'd be good." The grower reached for his belt wallet and laid out four silvers and ten coppers.

"They'll be ready. Good slack barrels."

"That's what I'm payin' for."

"And what you'll get. What you've always gotten."

Aryl nodded, glancing around the cooperage. "Seems a little light on billets."

"Got a full rack of seasoned oaks out at Vetrad's. Wanted 'em seasoned well. Coming in before end-days."

"Glad to hear it." Aryl did not look particularly glad, but merely speculative as he turned and left the cooperage.

After slipping the coins into his belt wallet, Kharl returned to planing the shooks into staves, although he had to stop and rest a bit more often than was his wont.

Before too long, Warrl reappeared, easing his way back to the barrel whose rims he'd been smoothing.

"What was that you took with you?" Kharl asked. "It looked like a good piece of paper."

"Ah . . . I owed Hergan some sheets from when I didn't have any. I begged the paper from Sanyle. You always said I should repay what I owed."

"That you should." Kharl was convinced Warrl wasn't telling the whole truth, and he wasn't so sure begging from Sanyle to pay back Hergan was the best, either. But he didn't want to press it, not when his younger son had been so good about helping and doing his chores, and not so soon after his mother's death.

Before Kharl could say more, Warrl looked at his father, and asked, "Did Aryl order any, Da?"

"We'll be doing twenty for him." Kharl didn't mention that he'd be making ten percent less than normal on the barrels, and he hoped that the cut in price wouldn't prove too costly, when others found out. But he hadn't been getting that many orders, even before the killing.

"You worried, Da?"

"That I am. Orders are slower than I'd like. Mayhap it's the times. Gharan says that he's not doing so well, either, and even Hamyl's been fretting."

"Ma . . . she wasn't getting so much, either . . . Fyona said she wouldn't have had . . ." Warrl looked down.

"Could be that times are getting harder for everyone," Kharl said quickly. But he had to wonder as he turned back to the planer.

XVIII

That evening, after Sanyle had left and Warrl had climbed into his bed in the corner of the main room, Kharl sat at the table, with a pen in hand, looking at the paper before him. Only two words were on the paper—"Dear Merayni."

What could he write? That Charee had been hanged for a murder she didn't commit? That he'd been unable to do anything about it? That because he'd prevented Egen from raping Sanyle and taken pity on a beaten blackstaffer, the lord's son had tried to destroy Kharl, and failing that, had taken his vengeance out on Charee? Merayni would blame Kharl no matter what had happened.

Finally, he folded the paper and tucked it away. He stood and glanced to the corner, but Warrl seemed to be sleeping. With a faint smile, Kharl took the lamp and *The Basis of Order* into his bedchamber. There he stretched out on his stomach—on the left side of the bed, where he had always slept.

He turned his head, and for a moment, with the faintest scent of rose, he thought he could almost feel Charee. And then the sense of her presence was gone. He still had trouble, especially at night, when he lay in the bed alone, accepting that she was gone. And for what? No matter what the justicer had said, Charee had not killed anyone.

He blinked several times, then blotted his eyes.

Finally, he opened the book and forced himself to look at the words on the page. He had to think of something else. He had to. For a moment, he could not make out the print. He blotted his eyes once more, then concentrated on the book.

All physical items—unlike fire or *pure* chaos—must have some structure, or they would not exist . . .

Because all wrought iron has a grain created from the forging of its crystals, the strength of the iron lies in the alignment and length of the grain. Using order to reinforce that grain is the basis of black iron . . . Its strength lies in the ordering of unbruised or unstrained grains along the length of the metal . . .

The cooper nodded. Those words made sense. Even with his limited work in forging the hoops from iron blanks, he could see where what the book said would make sense—except for one thing. *How* could a mage actually infuse iron with order? What he had read so far gave no hint of how such might be done. Yet he had seen the bands on Jenevra's staff and the warship from Recluce in the harbor. Even from a pier away, there was no doubt that it had been constructed of black iron, and that it was a deadly vessel.

Yet he had never seen more than one warship of Recluce at a time, and those most seldom. Why did Lord West fear the demon isle? Or did he? Had he used the isle as an excuse? Kharl frowned. Lord West had used the law—or his youngest son had—to increase his power over Kharl and those in Brysta and the western quadrant of Nordla. He had no need to mention Recluce.

Kharl's eyes dropped to the book once more. What was it about Recluce? Would the book tell him more? He flipped back several pages, more toward the beginning of the first part, and reread a section that had bothered him.

> The purpose of order is to support that life which can order chaos; and without chaos to be ordered, there can be no purpose to life.

> The function of chaos is to destroy order. Without order, no structure can exist—no man nor woman, no plant, not even an earth upon which to walk . . .

He frowned. Was Egen the kind of man who was like chaos, destroying order even as he talked of maintaining it? What did maintain order in Brysta? Justicers? The armsmen under Lord West?

Those questions and thoughts were more than Kharl wanted to contemplate, and he closed the book, setting it aside as he prepared for bed. He still had more barrels to finish in the days ahead, and he needed the sleep. He just hoped he could.

XIX

On fourday, dark gray clouds, wind, and heavy showers buffeted Brysta, and no one came to the cooperage. Fiveday dawned cloudy, but without rain. No one came into the shop through the morning. Finally, in midafternoon, with the sun promising to burn away the clouds, Wassyt lumbered into the cooperage. The miller was a good half head taller than

Kharl, one of few men in Brysta who clearly overtopped the cooper. Wassyt was also considerably broader, his girth cinched in by a tight leather vest. Although he was a good ten years older than Kharl, his hair remained the same light brown that it had been since when Kharl had met him as a youth, and it still fell across the left side of his forehead.

"Good afternoon," Kharl offered.

"Same to you, Kharl." Wassyt glanced toward Warrl, who was rough-hollowing some white oak staves.

"Warrl, you can take some time outside," Kharl suggested.

Warrl nodded, set down the hollowing knife, and left, quietly.

Wassyt stopped short of the fire pot, where Kharl had been checking the coals before toasting one of the white oak barrels for Korlan, and began to speak. "You know I'd never put anyone else's barrels against yours."

"I'd like to believe that they're that good." Kharl managed to keep his expression pleasant, although he knew what would follow would not be something he wanted to hear.

"They're the best," the miller replied. "Not a cooper in Nordla's any better. Maybe a few as good on the eastern shore, but not around here."

Kharl waited for what had to come.

"Wanted you to know that." The miller pushed back the lank brown hair, then blotted his forehead. "I told everyone I'd already ordered my harvest barrels from you, and paid for 'em, the half that goes first. Said I'd ordered thirty."

"I'll have them ready in two eightdays," Kharl said.

"Three's fine. Harvest's a bit late." Wassyt laid out a gold and five silvers, right on the bench. "You got this even before . . . the trouble."

"That's the way it is," Kharl agreed.

"I heard Lord West is short of coin," the miller said. "That's what Sorkan was telling me."

"Hard to believe that a lord would be short of coin."

"You know, the tariff assessments be coming out, right after harvest," Wassyt observed. "Maybe even quicker. Lord West's middle son is reviewing the assessments. That's what Fyngel told me. You know Fyngel—he's the tariff farmer for our section?"

"He's mine, too."

"You'll probably be seein' him afore long, Kharl. Might not want to. I didn't, light knows."

"You think he's close to Lord West's son?"

"Don't know as close. I'd say Fyngel's very respectful, do whatever young Lord Egen suggests. Fyngel, he's not quite a friend, but he's not so bad as some tariff farmers. Well, he was telling me that Lord West's worried about the Austrans. Seems like they're thinking of getting friendly with the Emperor of Hamor, and using that to look across the gulf."

"I've heard talk about that," Kharl said cautiously.

"So the Lords of the Quadrant need to build more ships, and ships take coins." Wassyt spread his beefy hands. "Coins come from us, specially millwrights, crafters, and artisans. Fyngel was given a list. A special-like list. Told that those crafters and artisans had paid too little in tariffs for too long."

"I gather that a certain cooperage might be on that list?"

"Aye. It might." Wassyt cleared his throat. "So might others, and this was what Fyngel told me as he was talking to me about my new tariffs. He was saying that folks who bought casks and barrels from some coopers, well, they just might have their tariffs doubled twice over."

"That's an interesting tale," Kharl said, trying to keep his voice level.

"Then, right after Fyngel left the mill, couldn't say that it was more than a glass, if that, Overcaptain Vielam—that's Lord West's middle son—he came a-riding up to my door . . ."

Kharl had feared that what Wassyt would say wouldn't be good, but Wassyt's words were far worse than he'd expected.

". . . told me that I milled the best of anyone in the western quadrant, and that he'd be pleased to keep having the lord's grains milled, but that his sire had decided that . . . well, that if I put it in certain barrels . . ."

"My barrels?"

"In certain barrels, they'd have to find another miller," Wassyt concluded.

"That would make it hard on you and your family."

"That's when I told the overcaptain that I heard him, but asked him for some care, seeing as I'd already half paid for thirty barrels of that kind, and surely he could understand that, seeing how close it is to harvest. Well . . . he hemmed, and tilted his head, but he said that he could see that, and so long as I'd order no more, he'd overlook it this one time, and he'd make sure that my tariffs didn't rise like those would who hadn't supported his sire." Wassyt shrugged his overlarge shoulders. "And there you have it."

"I thank you for what you did and could do," Kharl said. "There isn't more that you could, and those thirty barrels will be the best you could wish for."

"I'd be wishing I could do more, Master Kharl . . ."

"I've felt and seen what happens to those who cross Lord West and his sons. I'd not wish that on anyone."

"Thought you might understand."

"I do."

"Well . . . best I be going for now. Just wanted to see things square."

"Thank you."

The miller took several steps toward the door, before stopping and looking back at Kharl. "Got a cousin in Jelenn. He's a cooper. Better than Mallamet, not so good as you. He's been thinkin' of coming south. If you ever think of lettin' the place go . . . I'd be staking him."

"Until . . . the trouble . . . I wouldn't have thought about it," Kharl said. "It's still hard."

"Understand." Wassyt shifted his weight. "All right if I send a teamster three eightdays from now?"

"That'd be fine."

After the miller left, Kharl just stared at the bench and the coins lying there. He couldn't blame the miller, not when the tariffs were laid by Lord West. And unlike some, such as Aryl, Wassyt was trying to be fair and do the best he could in a difficult situation.

Kharl eased the coins into his belt wallet, then slowly turned to check the white oak barrel he was about to toast.

The cooperage door opened, and Warrl hurried back to the hearth area. "Da? Did the miller order some barrels?"

"Not exactly, Warrl. He'd already ordered them."

"You didn't—"

"After . . . everything . . . well . . . I wasn't sure, but he's stood by his words, and we'll be making twenty more slack barrels—that's in addition to the ones we've already got ready."

"Thirty barrels . . . you don't look so happy for all that."

"I'm still worried, son," Kharl confessed. "Outside of Aryl and Wassyt, it's been a slow harvest season, and people don't need near as many barrels in the late fall and in winter."

"Sometimes they break them."

"They don't break many of mine," Kharl pointed out.

"Then why don't they buy more from you?"

"Mine cost a few coppers more, and people don't think about how long a barrel will last. And some of them don't need really good barrels."

"Why don't you make two kinds of barrels, then?"

"Because most people would buy the cheap ones, and then they'd complain that they weren't as good as the others, and I'd have to make the good barrels for less to keep them buying from me." And, because, he had to admit to himself, he hated the idea of making barrels that weren't as well crafted as they should be.

"Oh . . ." Warrl didn't sound convinced.

"You can get back to working on those staves."

"Yes, Da." Warrl stepped back toward the front of the cooperage. He picked up the hollowing knife, then stopped. He looked out the window for a long time.

Kharl watched his son, wondering what the youth was dreaming about . . . and whether there was really anything he could do about it.

XX

Another three days passed, and the end-days arrived with no one buying or ordering any barrels or casks. No one else even peered into the cooperage. It had not been that hot for harvest, and except for fourday it had not rained, although the sky had been overcast for most of the past two eightdays. Eightday had been quiet, the shop shuttered, and finally, oneday morning, the sun had finally come out in full brilliance. As on the previous few days, no one had even walked into the cooperage. Kharl was not surprised, but he still had to finish the barrels for Wassyt and Aryl, although he fretted that he'd gotten no new orders since those two.

Around late morning, Kharl stepped back from the planer.

He glanced toward the steps upstairs, as he had so many times over the years, thinking about dinner. He swallowed, once more realizing that Charee was not there to fix it . . . or there for anything else.

He looked down at the empty flask on the side of the bench.

"Da?" asked Warrl, whose eyes had been as much on the front window as on the shakes he was hollowing.

"We're almost out of sharpening oil," Kharl said. "I need to get some, and it will help to stretch my legs. You can watch the shop, and then you can take some time to eat when I get back."

"I can do that."

"Good. I don't plan to be long."

Kharl brushed off his garments, then, with a nod at his son, picked up the leather flask and hurried out of the cooperage into a bright sunny day, one more like midsummer than early harvest. He dodged around a well-dressed man who was studying the books in Tyrbel's window and continued down Crafters' Lane.

Less than a block farther west, Kharl saw Dhulat—the cabinetmaker whose shop was on the corner of Fourth Cross and Cargo. The cooper started to lift his hand in greeting to the older man, but as he did Dhulat abruptly looked down and crossed the lane, clearly not wanting to meet Kharl.

For a moment, Kharl almost stopped walking. People in Brysta were usually friendly, and he'd even bought a chest from Dhulat several years back, a modest piece to be sure, but the cabinetmaker had seemed pleased enough to sell it. So why was the cabinetmaker avoiding Kharl? Were Egen and his brothers telling everyone about Kharl, warning them not to buy from him?

As he kept walking Kharl glanced around, but he saw none of the Watch nearby, just a few crafters, some women shopping, and a laundress with her wash in a tall basket on her head. The day was hot, hotter than it had been in more than an eightday, and he blotted his forehead as he continued along the lane.

He reached Hyesal's shop without any other incidents, passing a few crafters or assistants that he knew, and trading nods, but no words. He stepped into the apothecary shop, with its faintly acrid odor.

The angular Hyesal was behind the counter, watching as Kharl approached. He said nothing until Kharl set the empty flask on the counter. "Can't say I'm surprised to see you, Kharl. You always did have more backbone than sense."

"I just need a bit of that sharpening oil." Kharl gestured to the flask.

"You need to have your head sharpened, and that doesn't take oil. Stupidity is the wellspring of chaos." Hyesal picked up the flask. "I'll get your oil." Without another word, he slipped into the back room.

His head sharpened? Kharl grimaced. Hyesal had never been known for his unwillingness to call a clipped coin, no matter who had tendered it.

The apothecary returned shortly and set the flask back on the counter. "One copper. Same as always."

Kharl handed over the coin. "You're sharper than I am, Hyesal. That's why you're the apothecary. What good would sharpening my head do?"

"Might point you out of Brysta while you still have it. Your head, that is."

"You think—"

"Does a bull have horns? Does a winter sea storm? You wager against either, and you lose. Always. You make good barrels. Make them someplace else." He shook his head. "I've said my piece. More than my piece. Do as you please." The apothecary turned and left Kharl standing there.

Slowly, the cooper picked up the flask and headed for the door. As he stepped out of the apothecary shop and turned eastward, away from the harbor and back toward the cooperage, Kharl could feel eyes on his back—or so he thought. The feeling didn't go away. So, just opposite the square, Kharl stopped to look at the torque on display in the goldsmith's window. He wasn't that interested in it, even as artistry, but he wanted to see if someone happened to be following him—or if he were imagining it. After a moment, he turned slowly, letting his eyes travel back along the lane.

A single figure in the dark blue and black of the Watch stood waiting a half a block back toward the harbor. The squarish Watchman made no secret of his interest in Kharl, and his eyes met Kharl's as the cooper continued to scan the square, looking past the Watchman.

Kharl nodded, as if to himself, then crossed the lane to the square, his eyes falling on the section of wall where he'd first seen Jenevra. He shook his head.

"Ser! A copper for a poor lad? A copper!" A small figure in gray appeared and went to his knees in front of the cooper, totally abject. The bright eyes belied the position.

Kharl fumbled for a copper. He owed Jekat for Werwal's business.

"Pisser Egen's after you," whispered Jekat. "Tellin' everyone to order from you isn't a good thing." He raised his voice. "A copper, ser? Just a copper."

Kharl fumbled out two coppers. "Why?"

"You made him look stupid . . . you and the scrivener . . . Scrivener's got friends in high places . . . you don't . . ."

"Here's your copper." Kharl extended two.

"Thank you, ser!" exclaimed the urchin loudly, adding in a lower voice, "More 'n one of his bullies watching you. You're supposed to see one, not the other . . ."

"Thank you," murmured Kharl.

"Do what we can . . ." murmured Jekat, before scampering away.

Kharl resumed his progress back to the shop, wondering what he could do. He knew no one outside of Brysta and the surrounding area—and there was Warrl to consider. For the moment, he could pay Sanyle to cook and help, but what would he do elsewhere? How would he get there?

The flask in his hand felt like a weight.

XXI

Kharl's hope that he could somehow avoid the unpleasantness predicted by Wassyt was shattered when the cooperage door opened late on threeday. A hearty-faced blond man taller than Kharl walked inside. While he came into the cooperage alone, before the door shut Kharl could see the pair of burly personal guards in green and gray station themselves outside, one on each side of the cooperage door.

Warrl looked to his father.

"You can go upstairs and see how Sanyle's coming with supper," Kharl said. His words were far closer to a command than a mere suggestion. The cooper set the drawing knife down on the bench.

"Yes, Da." Warrl slipped away.

"Now . . . cooper, you'll be having the boy think that I'm a demon of some sort," called the man who'd entered.

"Not a demon, Fyngel, just a tariff farmer to be treated with respect."

Fyngel laughed. "You put it better than most, cooper. You don't think different. You just speak nicer."

As Kharl watched, Fyngel surveyed the cooperage, walking to one side and counting the billets of oak set in the racks, then surveying those barrels on display in the window. "Good-looking barrels you got there, cooper. First-rate, I'd say."

"I do the best I can."

Fyngel checked the workbenches, and the forge and the hearth, as well as the fire pots, then the loading door and the barrels stacked beside the door. He came back and studied the planer. "Doin' well, it looks like."

"It's the slowest harvest in many years," Kharl pointed out.

"That's what everyone says when the tariff farmer shows. Every harvesttime is the slowest." Fyngel laughed once more, producing a ledger-like book that he set down and opened on the finishing bench.

Kharl waited.

"Best you come here and take a look, cooper. Book hasn't been updated in some years," the tariff farmer said. "Lord West told us we had to go out and check all the crafters, make sure that everything was down right."

Kharl walked to the finishing bench. Fyngel reeked of grease and a sweet rose scent.

"Now, you got a forge here. Book doesn't show that."

"It's only a half forge. A farrier could use it, but a smith wouldn't be able to do all that he needed on it, and the hearth space isn't big enough."

"Forge is a forge, so far as tariffs go. That's another five golds." The tariff farmer made a note with his grease markstick.

Kharl held his tongue. His total tariffs due the previous winter had only been three golds, and he'd had trouble raising the coin. Three golds didn't sound that large, not until you had to count out three hundred coppers—and that was roughly Kharl's margin on 150 barrels—or twice that many barrels on arrangements like the one he'd been forced into with Aryl.

"Then you got racks for your lumber. Those aren't in the book. Say another gold for that." Fyngel smiled as he wrote a few more numbers, but the expression was anything but friendly.

"The racks were there when the cooperage was first built," Kharl said. "That was in my grandsire's time."

"That may be, cooper, but they're not in the book. Looks like your sire got a good deal. The rear loading door isn't in the book, either. So that'll add another three to your tariff."

Kharl waited.

After making a last notation, Fyngel looked up. "Twelve golds. Be due the first eightday of winter, same as always." With another less-than-friendly smile, he closed the book. "Lord West also says that any tariffs paid after the second eightday of winter, I have to charge another gold for each eightday they're late."

Kharl just nodded.

"We'll be seeing you and your golds in a season, cooper." Fyngel smiled a last time before turning and walking out.

Kharl walked toward the door, watching as the tariff farmer rejoined his guards, men bigger than Fyngel himself, and the three walked eastward along the lane. Kharl stood just inside the door, trying to unclench his fists.

Tyrbel appeared outside his scriptorium and walked slowly to the cooperage, stepping inside. He looked at Kharl. "You look less than pleased."

"Did he visit you?"

"Before you," Tyrbel announced. "I pleaded with him about my expenses in repairing the display window. He was not moved."

"So he upped your tariffs, too?"

"Twice what they were last year," admitted the scrivener. "And you?"

"Mine are four times last year's."

"If you pay it, next year, it will be double that. If you survive that long."

"You're cheerful," Kharl said dourly.

"I see what I see. Do you think otherwise?"

"No."

"I wrote to some I know in Hemmen and Vizyn. I told you that."

"Vizyn . . ." mused Kharl. "Would the Austrans let in a Nordlan?"

"A cooper who was mistreated by one of the Lords of the Quadrant? I would think so." Tyrbel nodded. "I have not heard back, but the scrivener I know there is called Taleas."

"Taleas in Vizyn." Then Kharl laughed, ruefully. "As if I could even get there. Golds for passage, and then what? Throw myself upon the town, begging that I'm a good cooper?"

"You could sell the cooperage here."

"For what? A handful of coppers? Everyone would know, and Mallamet might bid a gold, if that, and I'd still owe the tariff."

Tyrbel shook his head. "They cannot collect from a man who does not live in Nordla."

"I don't run."

"My friend . . . if you do not run, you had best find twelve golds in a season." Tyrbel paused. "I will write others I know as well. It cannot hurt."

"Thank you." Kharl doubted it would help, but he wasn't about to say that to one of the few men who had stood up for him against Egen and Lord West.

"Good evening." Tyrbel nodded, then turned and slipped out the door.

After Tyrbel left, it was late enough that Kharl did not feel like working longer. Slowly, deliberately, he barred the doors, including the loading door, and closed and locked the shutters. Then he started up the steps to the upper level. He stopped at the door, slightly ajar, when he heard Warrl's voice.

". . . tariff farmers?"

". . . collect tariffs for Lord West . . . best not to cross them," replied Sanyle.

"Da . . . he didn't do anything . . . he just stood there . . ."

"Were you watching? Did he not tell you to come up here?"

". . . just watched from the door . . . no one could see . . . but he just stood there."

"What would you have him do? Fyngel has his own armsmen, and he has the warrant to send anyone who opposes him to prison."

"But Da . . . he can't pay . . . all those golds . . ."

"You want him to fight the tariff farmer, get thrown into prison, flogged again, and still owe the tariffs while he's too hurt to work?" asked Sanyle.

". . . you're just like Da . . . always telling me why I can't do things . . . miss Ma . . . she wasn't like that . . ."

That had been one of Charee's faults, Kharl knew, one he'd indulged. She'd never wanted to point out limits. He banged on the door. "Supper ready, yet?"

"Almost," called back Sanyle.

"I'll wash up."

When Kharl made his way into the main room, Warrl looked up from where he sat on a stool beside the serving table, but the boy did not speak.

"Just sit down, and I'll have the dumplings out in a moment," Sanyle said.

As Kharl passed the single easy chair, his eyes dropped to the book lying there—*The Basis of Order*. He had not read much of it, just skipped through it. He was a cooper, not a youth, and not an order-master. What good would learning more about order do him? It certainly wouldn't pay his tariffs. But then, it didn't look like coopering would, either.

XXII

The remainder of the eightday passed without another buyer even entering the cooperage, and eightday itself dawned bright. Because so few shopped or purchased anything on the second end-day, Kharl did not open the cooperage doors, although he often worked. The present eightday was no exception, since he did not have all the barrels he needed for Korlan, or for Wassyt and Aryl. With the increased tariff he would owe to Fyngel at the first of winter, every copper counted more than ever.

While Kharl ran the shooks through the planer, Warrl was laying out more of the white oak billets, now that Kharl had scraped together enough to pay Vetrad the balance owed for the seasoned oak, which had finally been delivered the day before.

A *thumping* came from somewhere, barely audible above the noise of the planer.

"There's someone at the door," Warrl called.

"We're not open," Kharl pointed out.

Warrl peered through the shutters. "It's Aunt Merayni and Uncle Dowsyl."

With a feeling of dread about what was to come, Kharl stepped back from the planer and set the half-finished stave on the bench, then walked to the doorway and unbarred the door. He held it open until the man and the woman standing on the sidewalk stones stepped inside. He closed the door, but did not replace the bar.

"How long before you were going to tell us, Kharl?" snapped Merayni, a tall and broad woman only a fraction of a head shorter than the cooper, wearing a brown tunic and trousers. She stepped past Kharl and into the cooperage.

Dowsyl was only slightly taller than Merayni, but broader. His sleeveless tunic and half-sleeved undertunic showed arms that were heavily muscled. He said nothing as he followed his consort.

"Shortly," Kharl replied. "I've tried . . ." He closed the door.

"Tried? I never got a word from you. How about never? It takes a message from my nephew for me to find out that my sister is dead, that one nephew has fled Nordla, and that you have angered every important person in the Quadrant."

"You seem to know more than I do," Kharl replied.

Dowsyl cleared his throat, then spoke into the silence that followed. "Charee is dead. Arthal is gone. You will lose the cooperage before winter. This is what Warrl wrote. Is that all true?"

"Charee . . . Arthal . . . those are true," Kharl admitted.

"How do you plan to care for Warrl?" asked Merayni.

"We've managed. We will manage."

"Managed? For the sake of a woman you didn't even know, you got my sister killed. Is that how you'll manage?" asked Merayni.

Kharl looked to Warrl. The youth had edged toward Merayni. Kharl just looked. Finally, he spoke. "We have managed. Warrl is my son. He is fed and taught and cared for."

"For how long?" questioned Merayni.

The cooper didn't have an answer, not one that would have been truthful.

"Warrl's coming to the holding with us, Kharl." Merayni's voice softened. "It's better that way. You must know it is."

"What about the cooperage?" asked Kharl, knowing his words were futile, but feeling that he had to say something. "Someday, it will be his, but not if he doesn't learn to be a cooper."

"You promise that? How many orders for barrels did you get in the last eightdays?"

"I'm to deliver thirty barrels to Korlan, thirty to Wassyt, and twenty to Aryl, all in the next two eightdays." Kharl gestured to the stacks of unfinished shooks and semifinished staves.

"Did any of them order any more?" demanded Merayni.

"They only need barrels just before and during harvest."

"Kharl . . ." Merayni paused, then spoke slowly. "We may live a day away from Brysta, but we know people, and we've asked around. No one will order more from you. They're too afraid of Lord West and his tariff farmers. You won't be able to pay your tariffs, and you'll lose the cooperage. In a few eightdays . . ."

"Enough . . . enough . . ." Kharl looked at Warrl. "So you wrote your aunt?"

"I had to, Da . . . I had to. You didn't." Warrl met his father's gaze without flinching. "I know you tried . . . I saw . . . but you didn't."

Kharl turned to Merayni, but did not speak.

Neither did she.

"I tried to save a woman . . . she was little more than a girl. She wasn't much older than your Dowlan, Merayni. She'd been beaten and abused. She would have died. I was supposed to let her die?"

"She was a blackstaffer from Recluce. You *know* how people feel about them. Nothing good could possibly come from trying to save her. What good did it do? She died anyway."

"I was supposed to know that?"

"Sometimes, Kharl . . . you have to think of your own. That's always been your problem. You have too big a heart, and people take advantage of you. Charee knew that. We all know that. But this time, when you didn't think of your own, everyone suffered. Charee's dead. Arthal's on a ship somewhere—"

"The *Fleuryl*," Kharl interjected.

"You're going to lose everything you ever worked for," Merayni continued implacably, "and Warrl has to choose between leaving his father and becoming a beggar or an orphan. That's all because you wouldn't think first of your consort and your family." She looked to Warrl. "You can do whatever you will, but I am *not* letting my sister's son suffer any more because of your stubbornness."

Warrl looked helplessly at his father, even as he moved up beside his aunt. "I . . . didn't want to write . . . but . . . you . . . someone had to tell Auntie . . ."

"Someone had to," Kharl said heavily. "I was wrong not to write. I should have written. Do you . . ." He stopped. Whatever he said would make no difference. No difference at all. He could fight . . . but for what? Keeping his son for another season before he lost everything? And if he didn't . . . well, then, he could always make his way out to their holding and orchards and prove them wrong.

His eyes went to Warrl. "You'd better get your things. Take anything you want." He turned and walked to the back of the shop, opposite the forge.

"Da . . ."

Kharl did not turn.

Behind him, there were whispers, then footsteps on the stairs.

Dowsyl walked back to the forge. "Kharl?"

"What?"

"You get through this, and Warrl would come back. He's lost his mother. He's worried, and he's scared. He needs to be someplace safe."

"I can see that."

"Can you?"

"He and Merayni have made it clear." Kharl paused, then looked squarely at Dowsyl. "I'll get through it."

"If you do, you're welcome. Even if you don't, you're welcome. Place could hold you and Warrl."

"Thank you."

"Glad it wasn't me found that blackstaffer," Dowsyl said. "Can't make a right choice in a spot like that."

"Dowsyl!" called Merayni. "I need some help here."

The grower nodded to Kharl. "I meant it."

"Thank you," Kharl said again.

Dowsyl turned and made his way up the steps.

Some time passed. Kharl didn't know how much. He heard footsteps coming down the steps. He didn't look.

"Da . . . please don't be angry at me . . ."

Kharl turned. He looked at the thin, tear-streaked face of his son. "We all have to do what we think is right. I did what I thought was right. You did what you thought was right. I'm angry, but I'm not angry at you for that. I hope you understand someday."

"Da . . ."

Kharl stepped forward and put his arms around Warrl. "It's all right. It is."

"Come . . . see me . . . please . . ."

"As I can, son . . . as I can . . ." Kharl stepped back.

"Are you ready, Warrl?" asked Merayni.

"Yes, Auntie." Warrl stepped back.

"You can come to see Warrl anytime you want, Kharl," Merayni said. "Anytime . . ."

Kharl just nodded.

"Until then," she added.

Kharl just watched as the trio left the cooperage, carrying three large bundles.

The shop door shut. For a time Kharl just looked at the closed door.

Then, he stepped away from the cold forge, back toward the planer.

His eyes fell to the black staff, still where he had left it under the bench. He bent down and pulled it out. Once more, the wood felt warm, comfortable, in his hands. After studying the staff for a long moment, he leaned it against the wall. He still had barrels to do . . . if he ever wanted to pay the tariffs.

XXIII

Oneday came, and went, and no one walked in the door, and Kharl finished the red oak slack barrels for Aryl. Twoday came . . . and went, and so did threeday and fourday. Kharl continued to work, planing, drawing, fitting, firing, toasting . . . And not a single buyer, or even anyone who might buy, came into the cooperage.

On fiveday morning, Kharl just looked blankly at the planer and the white oak shooks stacked on the carry-cart. Almost five days, and he'd talked to no one except Sanyle, when she had brought him his midday dinner. At night, he'd tried to read *The Basis of Order*, but the words drifted by and around him, their meaning not reaching him, as though he were a desert isle in the middle of the ocean, unable to drink the water surrounding him.

In less than half a season, he'd gone from being a successful cooper with a good consort and two sons to a man who'd lost both his consort and his sons, and who would soon lose his cooperage, if not more, unless matters changed much for the better. And he saw no way to make that change.

He stepped away from the planer and absently brushed the thin strips of wood off his tunic and out of his beard, a beard that needed trimming.

He walked slowly to the display window, looking out and watching Crafters' Lane for a time, noting the man in a grayish blue tunic standing on the corner. Over the past few days, he'd seen the same man, more than a few times. Was he one of the Watchmen who were keeping an eye on Kharl?

Why did anyone care? Was Egen that vindictive? Because he'd been thwarted of his pleasure with Sanyle? And because a mere cooper had dared to stand up to the son of a lord? Kharl hadn't even known who Egen was when all that had happened.

After a time, Kharl walked back to the planer. He still had more than a few staves to shape for the barrels already ordered. His eyes dropped to the cudgel that he'd taken to keeping close by him. Then he began to pump the foot pedal.

XXIV

Those who do not understand order or chaos say that the two belong only to those with the gift for one or the other, and that those who have such gifts are few. This is a truth, and it is also a falsehood. Many men and women have gifts. Some are more intelligent than others; some are stronger; some are more patient; some have great courage; some have greater understanding. So to say that one has a gift for order or chaos can be a truth. Yet, to suggest that there is something improper about understanding order or chaos because it requires a gift is a falsehood. Each and every great talent, whatever it may be, requires a gift of greater ability. A man may have a gift for letters, and for distilling truth. A woman may have a gift for numbers, and for trading of goods.

A youth may have the gift of song, and another the gift of hands that can shape iron or wood. So it is with order and chaos.

Yet many would claim that the gift to understand order and chaos is different from the gift of understanding other aspects of the world, that anyone can be a crafter or an engineer, but that only a special few can become order-mages or chaos-masters. This is a falsehood, for the great ones in any area of endeavor are few, whether that area be engineering, cabinetry, fishing, or order-magery . . .

In the beginning, as a child, a boy or girl can have a gift, not for one or the other, but for either, or, if the gift is great enough, for both . . . So can a man or woman, once grown, if he or she approaches order as might a child. For order is a wonder, and those who can yet wonder as children can have their eyes opened at any age . . .

—The Basis of Order

XXV

After shaping the slope of the barrel chime of yet another red oak slack barrel, Kharl set the adze down and blotted his forehead with the back of his forearm. After almost an eightday of clear and sunny weather, it had rained earlier in the day, and then the sun had come out full force. By midafternoon all of Brysta was enveloped in hot wet air. Even the interior of the cooperage was hot and sticky. Kharl had left both the loading door and the front door open, because there was a slight breeze that seemed to make the cooperage fractionally cooler.

The back section of the shop was filled with barrels—both slack and tight, and Kharl had all of those ordered by Korlan ready, as well as most of those for Wassyt and Aryl. Who would order or purchase more barrels, Kharl didn't know, but that was a stream he'd ford later. With so few customers, he couldn't afford not to have barrels at the ready.

He laughed once, a harsh bark, then blotted his forehead again. He didn't have any choice but to wait and see.

He picked up the adze, turned the next barrel, and began shaping.

He stopped. Had he heard something? He frowned, and lifted the adze once more. Then he lowered it, listening.

"Help! Thieves! . . ." The yell died out.

As he recognized Tyrbel's voice, Kharl grabbed the cudgel that he had kept handy and, still holding the adze in the other hand, dashed to the front of the cooperage and out through the door, elbowing it full open, onto Crafters' Lane and into the full sunlight. In a handful of long steps, he was just outside the scrivener's door, still blinking as his eyes struggled to adjust to the afternoon glare.

A wiry figure in brown darted from the scriptorium, dodging away from Kharl.

The cooper recognized the man, and, without thinking, threw the adze full force and straight into the man's shoulder and chest. The man lurched back, one hand grasping, then pulling at the adze wedged in his shoulder. Annoyance and pain flashed across the man's face.

Kharl stepped forward and brought the cudgel around in a short arc, with all the force he'd developed over the years at the bench and forge. The heavy cudgel head crashed into the smaller man's temple, and his eyes widened, as if he could not believe he had been struck. He pitched forward, hand still on the haft of the adze. He shuddered once and was still.

Kharl stood there, cudgel still in his hand, looking blankly down, realizing that he had killed the man who had visited the cooperage the afternoon before Jenevra had been killed. While the cooper could not have proved anything, he *knew* the dead man at his feet had been her killer.

From inside the scriptorium came a long piercing scream that seemed to go on and on.

Kharl turned. Sanyle was screaming. Tyrbel was dead.

A squat laundress coming up the lane staggered as she saw the body on the stones and Kharl and his cudgel, then put up her hand to straighten the basket balanced on her head before crossing the lane away from the dead man and Kharl. The Watchman in blue—the one who had been watching the cooperage—sprinted down Crafters' Lane.

Gharan appeared and ran across the lane. So did Hamyl.

"Kharl! Get a pack and leave!" Gharan ordered. "You've got to run. Now."

"What?" Kharl couldn't believe the weaver's words.

"You think you'll walk out of the Hall of Justicers' this time?"

"Lord West'll have you hanging from the scaffold by tomorrow night," added Hamyl. "Unless the Watch get you first."

"We'll tell everyone what happened," Gharan promised. "We will, but it'll be too late if the Watch gets you."

The words finally broke through to the cooper.

He could not speak, but nodded. Then he hurried back into and through the cooperage, dropping the cudgel as he took the steps upstairs two at a time. Once into the bedchamber, he threw his best trousers, a good tunic, and underclothes into the pack, then another pair of boots and a winter jacket. He took the bag of silvers from the strongbox, hung it around his neck under his undertunic on the leather thongs. He scooped all of the coppers into the pack. As he straightened up, he saw the book on the table and stuffed it inside his still unfastened pack. Then he tied the pack shut.

He'd taken the book because, if the Watch found that, there was no telling what lies they might spread. He hurried down the steps, swinging the pack onto his back. Once on the shop floor, he started for the loading door that was still open to the alley.

He stopped as he saw the staff still leaning against the wall, then dashed to the far side of the shop and grabbed it. No one questioned staffs, and it was something else he didn't want to leave, although he couldn't have said why.

"Hurry!" hissed a voice from the loading door. "The Watch is almost out front."

Kharl whirled.

Jekat gestured through the partly open loading door. "This way, ser! You got to run! Watch'll get you otherwise."

Should he follow the urchin?

Who else could he trust—who knew the alleys and the back streets?

Kharl ran, straight through the loading door. Abruptly, he stopped but for an instant to close the loading door behind him, before sprinting to catch up to the urchin who had begun to run, if slowly, toward the northeastern end of the alley.

"Can't catch me!" Jekat yelled as he ran out of the alley and turned on Fifth Cross.

"I'll get you!" Kharl yelled back. "You miserable urchin!"

Some of those on the cross street looked scandalized, others amused, and only one man tried to grab the elusive Jekat as Kharl raced after the urchin, trying to counterfeit the rage of a man robbed by a light-fingered boy.

Jekat darted into a serviceway, and Kharl followed, panting heavily. He might work hard in the cooperage, but he had not run so fast nor so far in years. The urchin slowed some and turned westward into the alley, again downhill. Kharl lumbered after him, down another road and up Fourth Cross, finally catching up with the beggar youth near the intersection of the alley off Fourth Cross and Old Mill Road, some five blocks southwest of where the chase had started behind his cooperage.

Jekat ducked into another serviceway, moving into the shadows.

". . . give it to you, ser . . . can run . . ." panted Jekat.

". . . give it to you . . . good idea . . . counterfeiting . . . theft . . ."

"No one . . . heeds . . . man . . . chasing a beggar lad . . ."

Kharl took some more deep breaths, half–bent over. He was still panting and soaked in sweat. "How . . . did you know?"

". . . was watchin'. I saw the Watch run off. Coward."

"So . . . now what do I do to keep out of Lord West's hands?" asked Kharl. "Or Egen's."

"Same as I do," replied Jekat. "You'll learn."

XXVI

In the twilight of early evening, Kharl leaned against the stones, trying to get comfortable in the narrow space between the two walls, one ancient brick and the other even more ancient stone, while attempting to ignore the greater stench from beyond the stone wall and the lesser from beyond the brick. Overhead was a roof of sorts, composed of odd pieces of timber and wood and covered with layers of discarded fabric and molded leather, but there was open space on each end of the makeshift roof. To the east the space ended in a wall of yellow brick. At the west end was a jury-rigged partition of woven branches and cloth. The ground had been scraped smooth and clean, but it was still hard.

"No one's going to come here," Jekat said.

"With the rendering yard on one side and the tanner on the other . . . and with no one knowing this space is here . . . I can see why," observed Kharl.

"Even Werwal doesn't know." The towhead brushed back ragged-cut hair.

"You sure about that?" asked the cooper.

"Maybe . . . he does. But he wouldn't say. Him and Sikal, they understand. Drenzel, he doesn't know, never even comes back behind the dumping vats." After a moment, the urchin looked at Kharl. "Suppose you don't have many coppers?"

"I have a few," Kharl replied. "I could only grab a handful or so before I got out of the cooperage. Didn't have long." For some reason, the deception bothered him, necessary as he felt it was.

"You give me a pair . . . I can get us a good chunk of fowl. Clean and hot. Tasty, too."

"How will you manage that?"

"Enelya—she's at the White Pony. Long as I got coin, they'll get grub for me." Jekat grinned. "Won't do ale. She says Durol watches the barrels too close. See . . . what she does is put the fowl or whatever on the tab for someone. Slips it off to me then. Durol doesn't care, so long as the coins match." Jekat frowned in the dimness. "Mayhap, need three to get enough for us both."

"You're still a thief," Kharl said, ruefully.

"Watch what you say. Without me and yer friends . . ."

"I know. I'd be dead or laid out in a gaol chamber, waiting to be hung."

"If you were lucky. They took Quelyn and flogged him, then poured salt and tanning acid across his back—that was before—"

"Don't think I need to know that, young fellow."

"You should . . . Egen don't like you. Never seen him put so many men after a fellow."

"It's enough to know he'll do his worst if he catches me."

"Real pissprick . . . girls at the Bardo say he doesn't get excited 'less he thinks he's hurtin' 'em. Likes 'em young, too. Some of 'em cry real quick . . . real tears . . . They have to . . ."

Kharl winced. How could a lord accept that kind of man as his son? The more he learned about Captain Egen, the more despicable the image of him became in Kharl's mind.

"You got those coppers?" questioned Jekat.

Kharl fumbled with his belt wallet and handed three to the boy.

"Good. There's not a clipped one there."

"You don't think it'd be better for me to come with you?"

"Nah. Egen's still got the Watch lookin' for you, and you don't know the alleys and the serviceways. Maybe we can find you some rags tonight." Jekat eased along the uneven stone wall until he came to what seemed the dead end of yellow brick. There, after putting his foot up on a projection of stone, he climbed over the wall and vanished.

Kharl wondered if Jekat would ever return, but looking toward the cavelike area in the stone wall, where there were items like candle stubs, a rough pallet, and even a battered chamber pot, he had the feeling that the youth had nowhere else to go.

Like Kharl himself, the cooper reflected.

As the oblong of sky that Kharl could see to the west dimmed, he wondered how long before Jekat would return.

He looked from one wall to another, a space narrower than the gaol cell he'd been thrown into, if longer, and then back up at the patch of evening sky. He still had to ask how so many people accepted the evil around them. He shook his head. Most were like Charee. So long as things seemed orderly and life went on, they didn't care about what didn't affect them. After a moment, he laughed. He'd been no better.

The sky darkened into full night, and still Jekat had not returned.

Kharl frowned, more worried about the boy's safety than about whether he would return.

Then there was the faintest of scraping sounds, a scuffing, and a muted thump, and the small figure in shapeless gray reappeared out of the darkness.

"It took Enelya a while tonight. White Pony was busy, but the bird's good." Jekat handed a bundle to Kharl, a goodly chunk of fowl wrapped in two huge slabs of bread.

"I take it back, Jekat," Kharl mumbled after a large mouthful. "Couldn't manage this . . . 'less you're very good."

"Wasn't my doin', not all the way, leastwise. Some sort of party. Had extras. Durol was probably happy to get the coppers. Or Enelya was."

Even through the darkness, Kharl could make out a grin as the urchin raised a crockery mug without handles. "Have a swallow."

"Ale?" asked Kharl as he carefully took the chipped and handleless mug.

"First time in a season, but a fellow won't turn that down."

Kharl took a sip to make sure it was ale, then a swallow. "Good stuff." Was it good because he was so hungry? Probably.

"Durol told Enelya he'd look the other way if the serving girls wanted some. Some fellow paid for the whole keg."

"I thank you and Enelya. Greatly. How did you work out this . . . arrangement with her?"

"She's from Sagana. That's where I come from. She was a friend of my sis. When Sis and Ma died, I came here, heard she'd found work at a tavern. Found her. She helps as she can. Sometimes I can help her. Got to find folks who will. That's . . . the only way . . ." Jekat yawned.

Kharl handed back the mug.

"Mosta that's for you. Drank half a mug there." Jekat took a small swallow and handed the mug back, then chewed on something. "You know . . . won't be this good most nights. You need to get outa Brysta."

"I need to get out of Nordla," Kharl said tiredly. "To Austra, if I can."

"How you goin' to do that?"

"Know a ship-master. Calls here every season, sometimes more often. Think he might take me."

"How long afore he calls again?"

Kharl shrugged. "Don't know. He was here, maybe half a season ago, maybe a bit longer. Said he'd be back late fall, early winter."

"It'll take some doing to stay away from the Watch for that long."

"You have."

"No one cares about a beggar boy. You pissed off Egen good. He still has people looking for you. What you going to do?"

"Wait . . . listen to you. Then . . . if the ship-master from Austra comes back, I'll try and get aboard. Could be a while, though."

"Better lie low till then. Egen's mean."

"Why are you helping me?" asked Kharl.

"Why not? You always treated me good as you could. Most don't. Also, you stood up to Egen. Most don't." Jekat yawned. "'Sides, you're strong. Might need that."

Might need that? Kharl wondered as he took another swallow of the ale. With it and the fowl, he could almost ignore the stenches from the renderer and the tanner.

After they finished eating and drinking the last of the ale, Jekat took back the mug and crawled into his cubbyhole and curled up under a tattered and soiled cover that looked to have been a drapery or hanging many long years before, doubtless before the boy had even been born.

Kharl made himself as comfortable as he could under the makeshift roof between the two walls, using his pack for a pillow. He looked upward into the darkness. Eventually, he did drift into sleep, a sort of restless dozing.

XXVII

Kharl woke with the gray light of dawn, and the crowing of a rooster that he could have done without. Every muscle ached, even muscles he hadn't known he had.

The moment he moved, Jekat's blond head peered out of the tattered hanging masking the cubbyhole. "We need to get some grub."

"You have a plan for that?"

"You got coins, we can try the lower market, except everyone's looking for you. Even be some Watch down there."

"Got some smelly rags?"

"Most 'round here smell . . ." Jekat grinned. "I grabbed stuff last night. Got a really old cloak. You leave behind the undertunic and tunic. See if it'll do."

Kharl didn't want to leave the clothes and the pack and staff, but neither would have matched the beggarly image. But he'd need to tie the pouch with the silvers around his leg, fasten it somehow to the inside of his thigh. While Jekat rummaged through the corner of the cubbyhole, he made the switch, but left the undertunic on, at least until he had something to wear. It was getting later in harvest, and mornings were chill. He probably should have pulled out the winter jacket for a cover to sleep under, but he'd been so tired he hadn't even thought of it.

Then, after he took care of other necessities well down the wall in the place suggested by Jekat, he returned and donned the ragged hooded cloak that half concealed his face.

The urchin—in patched and shapeless gray—looked up from under a ragged thatch of curly hair, more sandy than true blond. "Let me go over the wall and look around first . . ."

That bothered Kharl, but he couldn't say why. "Be careful."

"I'm always careful."

Jekat scrambled up the wall nimbly, vanishing silently over the top. Kharl listened.

Then he heard a scuffling, and a single sharp cry, followed by low words.

"Been layin' for you, beggar boy . . . seen you comin' and goin'. You got coin hidden in there, and you're gonna share it all with us . . ."

"Mmmmhph . . ."

"Hold him . . . goin' over. Oh . . . now, what do we have here." A laugh followed. "This is going to be fun . . . real fun . . . Geehm . . . you take a look-see what's there."

On the far side of the wall that was only a cubit more than head high, Kharl slowly took hold of the staff, far too long to be really useful in the narrow space between the walls, and probably beyond, but the staff was all he had, and he certainly owed Jekat. He stepped back, waiting.

A lean man in a grimy brown tunic and dark gray trousers, with boots bound together with strips of leather, scrambled down over the wall, a stubby knife shimmering in his right hand. Even before the man could register Kharl's presence, the cooper drove the end of the staff into the other's gut with all the force he could manage.

"Uuufff . . ."

"You all right, Geehm?" came from the other side of the wall.

Before the intruder could reply, Kharl brought the staff back and jabbed at the man's knife hand because there was no room to do anything but jab, even with his grip halfway down the smooth black wood.

"Aeeii . . ." The knife dropped from the attacker's hand, although Kharl hadn't struck that hard.

Kharl shifted his grip on the warm wood.

"Not going to be easy . . . not now, you bastard . . ." The intruder bent down.

Kharl could sense . . . something, and almost without thinking he slammed the staff into the other's shoulder. A second knife went flying against the wall. Kharl brought the staff up, then down, in an awkward sideways blow, but one hard enough to drop the man, because he pitched forward, clearly unconscious the way he sprawled.

Kharl half vaulted over the fallen figure and leaned the staff against the end and corner of the walls as he scrambled up to the top of the wall, then reached down and grabbed the staff. As he turned he could see a smaller man holding Jekat and a third man, somewhat larger, moving to meet him even as Kharl dropped down into the end of the ancient serviceway.

"Oh . . . so you had someone guarding your loot," hissed the man holding Jekat. "Get him, Brot."

Brot lumbered forward, a long knife in each hand.

The serviceway was wider than the space of Jekat's hideaway, and that allowed Kharl to shift his hands inside the middle iron bands, so that he could use the staff properly. He hadn't used one in years, although his father had taught him the basics years before, when he'd still been a boy, since staffs or cudgels were the only weapons permitted to artisans and crafters.

Still, it seemed like the staff had a mind of its own, because Kharl could almost sense what the bigger man was about to do, and within moments one of the knives was on the dirt-covered stones, and one of Brot's wrists hung almost limply. Yet the man charged Kharl again.

Kharl struck once more, then again, and there was a sickening *crack*, and Brot clutched his arm and shoulder, then sank to the stones.

"Demon . . ." the smaller man started to thrust Jekat away, but his eyes went wide, then he crumpled, blood welling across the gray cloth that covered his guts. He started to moan.

Jekat bent, then straightened.

Kharl could see the redness across the fallen man's neck. The moans had stopped.

"Go away!" Jekat snapped at Brot. "Far away!"

The big man Kharl had wounded staggered to his feet, arms dangling limply, and lumbered out of the serviceway, not even looking back, not saying a word despite what had to be great pain.

"What . . .?" Kharl blurted.

"Brot's a no-mind. He lost it to a wizard years back. Did whatever his brother asked." Jekat gestured to the dead man on the stones, then looked up. "The other one?"

"Knocked him out."

"Let me look." Jekat scrambled to the top of the lower section of wall between the tanner's wall and the renderer's wall. He peered over, then looked back down at Kharl. "Think you killed him. He's not moving at all."

"I didn't hit him that hard," Kharl said.

Jekat dropped back down to the pavement, eyes on the staff Kharl still held. "That's a black staff. Must be something about it."

Kharl had wondered, but he'd scarcely had time to think about it. He looked at the staff once more. It had certainly been well made, and of lorken and black iron . . . but that shouldn't have given it any special powers.

"Anyway . . . we need to get rid of these two."

Kharl looked at Jekat, taking in the shapeless gray clothes, the raggedly cut hair, the smooth skin, carefully smudged with grime. He'd never bothered to look closely before. Who studied urchins? A lot of things made much more sense.

"Maybe you'd better go . . ."

"What is your name?" he asked. "Jekai, Jekati?"

"Jeka. Easy enough to add a 't.' "

"Where do you want me to go?" Kharl asked. "You know I don't know the alleys and serviceways."

"You stay, nothing changes." Her voice was wary.

"Do you really think I'd force anything?" he asked. "Besides, that was why you helped me, wasn't it? You must have seen something."

Jeka nodded. "Saw you save the scrivener's girl. Heard about the blackstaffer. Some men'd save one. I don't know any who'd risk for two. Leastwise, I never saw any." A brief smile crossed her face. "Three, I guess, now." The smile vanished. "Nothin' changes."

"Nothing," Kharl promised.

"We still got to get rid of him and the other," Jeka pointed out.

"After dark," Kharl suggested. "Lift this one over the wall for now. When it's dark, I'll drag them out and over a street or two. Leave 'em in the shadows. Try that now, and someone would see. Watch won't come here, will they?"

"Haven't ever."

"Do you think they told anyone else?"

"No. That kind'd want to keep the loot to themselves."

As he lifted the dead man's body and pushed it up over the wall, Kharl hoped so.

He turned to Jeka. "Might as well go."

She nodded. "Leave the staff . . . and bend over. Shuffle. Uncomb your beard."

Kharl couldn't exactly uncomb his beard, but he tried to make it look less groomed. In a few days, the way it grew, it would look disreputable enough. He didn't like leaving the staff, but she was right. It was too good for a beggar, far too good. He eased it back over the wall, then shuffled after Jeka out onto Copper Road.

"Should I beg?" muttered Kharl.

"You don't, and some'll be looking at you funny, 'less you want to twitch and mumble, something like that."

"A copper, just a copper . . . copper, please . . ." Kharl mumbled.

"Whine more," suggested Jeka under her breath.

"A copper . . . just one . . . hungry . . . please . . ."

"Better," she said. "Now . . . you got a few more coppers?"

Kharl handed over three, trying to keep stooped over and shuffling. He was finding that holding that position was hard work.

The lower market was in the open space on the north side of the harbor, below First Cross, a flat area that had once held warehouses before they'd been swept away by the great flood and storm in Kharl's grandsire's time. The odors of ripe—and rotten—fruit mixed with the smell of fish and freshly lighted charcoal on small braziers, and with other less obvious odors.

As they drew nearer, Jeka motioned. "You squat over there . . . by that post. Beggars not supposed to be in the market."

The post was half of a rotting bollard that lay on its side twenty cubits from the first cart, and Kharl sat down cross-legged, the rags covering his trousers and boots.

Jeka slipped away.

The cooper began to beg. ". . . copper . . . just a copper . . ." He tensed as he saw two men in Watch uniforms strolling down Copper Road toward the market, but for him to move would call more attention than remaining huddled by the decayed bollard. Instead, he dropped his voice into a mumble, careful to keep his face down and partly shielded by the ragged hood.

Surprisingly, the two Watchmen ignored him, as if he did not exist, and stood less than fifteen cubits away, their eyes on the mélange of carts, goods spread on ground cloths, and even on the counters of portable stalls.

"... what about that business with the silversmith ..."

"... sort of thing that reeks of Egen and his lavender ..."

"... who could say ... no traces ..."

"... never any traces ... deadly little sneak ..."

The taller man laughed. "... fine ... when he's with you ... needs you ... but better wear plate on your back ... dealing with him ... rather be down here ..."

"... safer than in the Justicers' Halls. That's certain ..."

After a silence, one of two Watchmen asked, "... you seen the new one at Bardo's?"

"From Hamor, they say ..."

"Frigging amazing ..."

"Uh-oh ..."

The two hurried toward a stall where the counter had been knocked down and a wizened woman held a thin youth in blue.

"Tried to steal my silks, he did!"

The youth saw the two in Watch blue, and tried to bolt. He almost broke free before one of the Watch coshed him with his truncheon.

"Hsst ..."

Kharl turned his head.

Jeka beckoned. "Need to get you clear 'fore those two head this way."

Kharl didn't argue, but mock-struggled to his feet and hobble-shuffled after Jeka.

"I got some bread and dried figs, and a wedge of hard cheese. Watch'll come up Cargo Road. Be a good thing to be gone. We can fill the flask at the fountain on Second Cross."

Kharl hadn't seen the flask, but Jeka could have concealed that and more in the shapeless garments. She had, in fact.

They kept to the side of the road, making their way back along the alleyway off Copper Road up to Second Cross. The fountain there was for horses, but there was only one spavined cart mare drinking from the stone trough under the fountain. Without direction from Jeka, Kharl eased into the morning shadows and settled down into a heap against the brick wall across the street.

A tradesman walking swiftly by glanced toward Kharl.

"A copper . . . just a copper . . ."

"Go work for it, fellow. No time for lazy beggars."

". . . worked hard, ser . . . can't now . . ."

". . . all say that . . ." With a snort, the tradesman walked on by.

From somewhere else a copper clattered on the stones. Kharl swept it in, almost feeling guilty.

Jeka waited until the ashman led the limping mare away, then rinsed the flask and filled it.

Kharl made his hobbling and stooped way northward along Second Cross, then downhill, following the alley to First Cross, keeping Jeka at a distance until they passed the last wall of the slateyard, where she made her way to a pile of stones above the ancient breakwater and settled onto a wide and flat stone.

Kharl took the stone across from her. His eyes surveyed the harbor and the piers to the south. There were but five oceangoing vessels tied up, and none bore the twin square-rigged masts of the *Seastag,* not that he'd expected the vessel to return to Brysta so soon.

"Looking for that ship?" asked Jeka, extending a chunk of bread and a section of the hard cheese.

"It's not there. Won't be for two or three eightdays, at least. Maybe longer. Good view of the harbor from here."

"We can see anyone coming from here. Can't really see us, not with the slateyard wall."

"Why did you come here from Sagana?" he asked after a mouthful of bread and cheese.

"What else could I do? My da died when his mule bolted and the harness broke, metal buckle slashed his neck. Ma found him in the field. Strong woman, she was. She farmed the plot and sheared the flock from the time I could recall. Me and Sis, we spun and wove. Got to be pretty good. Fever got Ma and Sis, three years back. Tariff farmer, he claimed the place owed tariffs, loom and all. He said he was goin' to indenture me to Gelhal—ran the same sort of place as Bardo's, 'cept worse. I took the coins and ran. I'm small . . . been passing for a beggar boy. Figured I'd have to leave soon. People notice when you don't grow." Jeka stopped to eat, then passed the water flask to Kharl.

"Thank you."

"What happened to your boys?" Jeka asked. "Saw 'em, and then they were gone."

"Arthal . . . he signed on a ship as a carpenter's apprentice, and Charee's sister took Warrl. Couldn't fight that. Knew, I guess, I was going to lose the cooperage."

" 'Fore that business with Vexon?"

"Vexon?"

"Fellow you killed with the cudgel. He's an assassin. He was till you killed him, anyway. Lotsa folk be pleased you did him in. They say he worked for Egen."

"Thought so," Kharl mumbled.

"Why'd you say you'd lose the place?"

"Tariff farmer—Fyngel. Twice-doubled my tariff. Said he'd been ordered to by Lord West. Egen, I figure. No way I'd be able to raise twelve golds by the turn of winter."

"Twelve . . . golds?"

Kharl nodded.

"Like a fortune. Egen musta wanted to hurt you bad," said Jeka. "Don't know which is worse, lord or tariff farmer."

"Lord," suggested Kharl. "Tariff farmers do as they're told. May be greedy, but that's what the lords want."

"Justicers aren't much better."

"Not from what I've seen," Kharl agreed. "My father, he said they were better in the old times, when Lord West's grandsire was lord."

"Can't go back. Past doesn't come again."

"No." Kharl swallowed, a lump in his throat at the words, sitting on stone rubble on the ruined northern side of the harbor, realizing again all that he'd lost. "It doesn't."

XXVIII

For the next eightday, every morning Kharl woke up listening, wondering whether that day would be the one that the Watch would find him, or whether another set of beggar-brigands would track and attack them. Neither happened—not in the space between the walls nor on their journeys down the shadowed sides of streets, alleys, and serviceways, but he was all too aware that either could—and still might.

After two days, he'd found a length of cast-off timber, and, over the next several, managed to use his belt knife to carve a grip on it, so that it could function as half staff or cudgel, while looking like a walking stick for a creaky old man. Since Kharl felt it was unwise to take the black staff with him, the makeshift stick and weapon offered some reassurance.

On sixday—at least, he thought it was sixday—Kharl woke early, almost shivering in a morning that verged on frosty. Jeka was still asleep behind her canvases. He wondered how long it might be before Hagan returned, but he knew that was eightdays away, maybe a half season at best, even with the so-called short voyage the Austran captain was making. If matters got too bad, perhaps Kharl could find another ship. Too bad? He nearly laughed out loud, but that would have wakened Jeka. He wasn't certain how things could get much worse, not unless Egen caught him and tortured and hanged him. Had he been wrong just to leave the cooperage? He frowned, thinking. He couldn't have sold the building and the business for enough golds even to pay the tariffs due. That was clear. But he still wondered.

The canvas shivered, and before long, Jeka appeared.

"You look as if someone was goin' to hang you."

Kharl almost burst into laughter at the cheerful tone of her voice expressing such dour thoughts. "Sad to think I don't dare show my face to buy food."

"You do, and the Watch'll be lookin' for you, quick-like. They keep asking for you."

"You haven't—"

"Haven't told no one. Vaskal—one of 'em sorta nice to me—get a copper from him now 'n then, he told me if I ever ran across you—said the cooper Kharl—be a gold in it for me . . ."

Kharl shook his head.

"I wouldn't take no gold. Wouldn't turn anyone over to Egen." Jeka's voice turned dark.

After a moment, Kharl spoke. "I was thinking about the cooperage. Was my da's and my grandsire's. Thought I'd be able to pass it on to my boys."

"Not with pisser Egen after you. They say . . ." Jeka broke off her words.

"What?"

". . . just things. He's mean, a lot meaner 'n he should be."

Kharl could agree with that. "I thought I'd go out for a bit."

"If you want . . . best be careful . . . still don't know the alleys well as you should . . ."

Kharl stood. "I'll be careful. Can't always ask you to do everything." After taking his makeshift stick and weapon, and gathering the ragged cloak that was far from warm enough around him, he eased his way up the wall. Once he was certain no one was in the serviceway, he clambered over and scuttled out of the serviceway and onto the street.

It was early enough that there were few about, just servants headed down to the fish market, and dockers and laborers. No one looked at the ragged beggar moving uphill toward the crafters' section of Brysta, and when he began to ask for coppers, most moved well away from him.

As he neared his cooperage, Kharl moved from the main street into the alley that ran behind the Tankard, an alley likely to be empty in the morning. He kept his eyes open, and listened carefully, as he neared the rear of the cooperage. Both the rear door and the loading dock doorway had been carelessly boarded up. He watched for a time, but neither saw nor heard anyone.

He edged past the cooperage to Fifth Cross, where he turned back toward Crafters' Lane. There he turned and limped slowly past the tinsmith's, then Derdan's woolen shop, and finally past the cooperage, as slowly as he could. The display window of the cooperage was covered with boards, and what he could see of the glass was streaked with dirt and a few pigeon droppings.

On the door, also boarded shut, was an oblong of parchment with a blue wax seal and a blue ribbon. Both parchment and ribbon showed signs of water spots and dust. Kharl peered and squinted at the parchment.

> . . . know all by these present that the premises and contents will be presented at public auction on sevenday, the tenth week of fall . . . all may bid, save any related by blood to the former owner, the cooper Kharl . . .

Kharl caught sight of someone walking up the far side of the lane and looked away, slowly limping toward the square. From what he'd glimpsed, the rest of the notice had declared that no bid under fifteen golds would be accepted and had then merely spelled out the need for the winning bidder to be prepared to pay in gold at the conclusion of the auction.

The signature had been that of Reynol, Lord Justicer.

That didn't surprise Kharl in the slightest, nor did the minimum price. Lord West wanted his tariffs, one way or another.

Kharl kept limping past Tyrbel's scriptorium. The door was closed, but not boarded up. He wondered if Sanyle still lived there, or if she had gone to live with one of her older sisters—or if, horribly, Egen had taken her for his own purposes. The cooper's lips tightened as he limped downhill toward the upper market square, the one now too good for him, where a beggar would be run off.

XXIX

Sevenday came and went, as did eightday and oneday. Kharl's stomach growled most of the time. The end-days had been lean, with fewer places for Jeka or Kharl to cadge or buy food cheaply. Thin clouds promised a brisk and cool day, but one without rain, and one suited for what Kharl needed to do. He opened his pack and took out a tunic.

Jeka looked at Kharl, quizzically, but not speaking.

"I'm going to leave for a few days," he said. "You want to come?"

"Where?"

"Out to the southeast, a hamlet called Peachill."

Jeka cocked her head. "No. Better that you go alone."

"You be all right?"

She laughed. "I was fine 'fore you came . . . be all right if you go."

"I'll be back in a day or so."

"That's what—"

"I will," Kharl said.

"I'll see you then." Jeka turned her head away.

"I'm going out to see my boy." Kharl didn't know why he had to explain to Jeka, but he did. "I want to know if he's all right." He knew that, in some ways, going to Peachill was dangerous. Dangerous or not, he *had* to know that Warrl was all right.

"Why'd you leave him?"

"I didn't. I told you. He left me. He was afraid I'd lose everything, and that somehow it was all my fault, and he wrote his aunt, and she came, and he left with her."

Jeka looked up at him.

Kharl wasn't sure how to read the darkness in her eyes. "I knew they were right, but how . . . how could I have just given up the cooperage?"

She didn't say anything, but she might as well have stated that he'd lost it anyway, and lost his sons as well.

"I have to make sure he's all right." Kharl knew he was repeating himself, but she had to understand.

Jeka nodded. "I'll be here." She turned away.

Kharl pulled on his tunic and winter jacket. He'd wear the ragged cloak over the jacket until he was clear of Brysta, but he wasn't going to see Warrl as a beggar. Especially not when his son was staying with Merayni.

Once he left the space between the walls, it took him more than a glass to reach the southeast road at the foot of the harbor on the outskirts of Brysta. No one seemed to be following him, but he kept walking until he was a good kay beyond the pillars that marked the limits of Brysta and until the road was empty. Only then did he shed the ragged cloak, roll it into a cylinder, and hide it in the hedgerow behind the stone wall. He paused a moment, trying to mark the location in his memory.

He kept the short walking stick, and it was almost a pleasure to be able to straighten up and stretch his legs along the gently curving road.

Midmorning came . . . and went, and he was still on the road.

Early in the afternoon, he saw a woman cleaning out her garden, and for several coppers, persuaded her to provide him with a half a loaf of bread, some hard cheese, a leek, and permission to use her well for water. The water and the food added some spring to his step, at least for another three or four kays, when his feet began to ache, and his steps slowed.

Still, by late afternoon, he reached the kaystone that announced Peachill. He knew that Dowsyl's orchards were off a lane on the west side of the road, somewhere short of the hamlet, but it had been more than five years since he and Charee had visited Merayni, and Kharl could not remember the lane exactly. He walked another five rods, and stopped.

With a sigh, he walked another fifty cubits to a hutlike dwelling set amid gardens needing preparation for the winter. There, he knocked.

After several moments, the oblong peep-door opened. "Don't need nothing sharpened," came a woman's voice.

"I'm not a tinker. I'm a traveler. Could you tell me which lane leads to Dowsyl's place?"

"Why you want to know?"

"Because they're family," Kharl replied.

While the small part of the woman's face Kharl could see expressed doubt, she cleared her throat. "If you were coming south, you already passed it. Last lane back. Go in about two kays, and the house is just past the peach trees."

"He still have the little barn between the pearapples and peaches?"

"Yes." Even with the single word, some of the suspicion lifted from the woman's face. Then, the peep-door closed with a *click*.

"Thank you." Even with the door closed, Kharl bowed. Then he headed back northward to the first lane.

It could have been that he was tired, but the distance to Dowsyl's orchards seemed far longer than two kays. The sun hung low in the western sky above the rolling hills covered with a mixture of graying broadleaf trees and pines before Kharl stopped at the low stone wall that bordered the lane.

Beyond the peach trees, their leaves now almost entirely winter-gray, Kharl could see the square dwelling with the heavy thatched roof, and beyond the house, the rows of pearapple trees, with some leaves still showing patches of green. After standing in the lane for a time, he walked through the gateless opening in the stone wall. He had almost reached the clear area around the house when he heard footsteps to his right and turned.

"Da! You came!" Warrl ran from the small barn toward his father. He looked as though he might throw his arms around his father, then stopped. "You came. I wasn't sure you would."

"Your aunt said I was welcome, and I wanted to see how you were doing."

"I've learned a lot, and . . ." Warrl stopped and looked past Kharl.

Kharl turned. The broad-shouldered Merayni, wearing a ragged apron covered with flour, appeared on the narrow porch of the orchard cottage.

The cooper nodded toward Charee's sister, then began to walk toward her.

Warrl walked beside his father. "Aunt Merayni . . . Da came."

"I see that." Merayni's voice was level.

"Merayni . . ." Dowsyl appeared behind Warrl. "Kharl's walked a long way. I'm sure he could use something for his thirst."

Merayni looked at her consort, then at Kharl. "I'll find something." She paused. "Everything is wonderful, and you're going to take Warrl?" Her voice was cold and edged.

"No. Things are not wonderful. You were right." Kharl met Merayni's eyes directly. "I lost the cooperage, and I'm getting by best I can. I may have to go to sea. But I wanted to see Warrl."

Abruptly, Merayni looked down, if but slightly.

"Hard thing, to lose something like that," said Dowsyl slowly. "Wouldn't want to lose the orchards and land. Know I wouldn't take to that."

"Da . . . I'm sorry." Warrl's voice was low.

"You didn't do that, son. I made some mistakes. Sometimes . . . you make mistakes, and bad things happen."

"How did you lose it, Da?" asked Warrl.

"I couldn't make the golds for the tariffs. The justicer put it up for public auction. Said no one related to me by blood could bid on it." Kharl was troubled by his own words. Although what he said was truthful, what he implied was not exactly so.

"Comes from upsetting lords . . ." murmured Merayni.

"It does," Kharl agreed. "But there's little I can do now."

Merayni slipped into the squarish dwelling.

Dowsyl stepped closer. "Long walk, Kharl."

"It was, but I wanted to see Warrl. I wasn't sure when I might be able to get back here."

"Said you were welcome to stay here. I meant it."

"I know," Kharl replied. "I thank you for that, but I'm a cooper. I'm not a grower. I don't know trees or the land."

Merayni came back out onto the porch, bearing a large mug. "Just drew this."

Kharl accepted the worn clay mug and took a long swallow of the cool water. "Thank you." He took another, draining the mug and handing it back.

"Well . . . your Da's here, Warrl," Dowsyl said. "He's had a long journey. Least we can do is have a solid supper and offer him a bed for the night."

Before Merayni could say anything, Kharl replied. "Both would be welcome, but just a mat and a blanket in the little barn would be good. I'll have to leave in the morning."

"There's a comfortable pallet there," Merayni said, "and we've blankets to spare."

"Thank you."

"Be a bit before supper, though."

"Anything would be welcome . . . anytime." Kharl bowed his head slightly.

"Da? Can I show you the orchard and the trees Uncle Dowsyl let me prune?" asked Warrl.

"You surely can," replied Kharl.

"Over this way . . . he had me start on the pearapples . . ."

As Kharl followed his son, he could not but overhear the words behind them.

". . . was such a proud man . . . almost feel sorry for him . . . Almost . . ."

". . . not right, what happened . . ."

". . . doesn't matter . . . should have known better. Charee warned him . . . she did . . ."

They were right, Kharl reflected. Charee had warned him. She'd warned him that helping people could hurt her and the children, and Kharl had tried to help Sanyle and Jenevra . . . and one was an orphan and the other was dead—and Kharl had lost his consort and cooperage, and at least one son. For all that Merayni said, a sadness fell across the cooper as he considered that trying to do good had created such awful results. He forced a smile onto his face as he followed and listened to his son.

"This one . . . I had to do twice. There was a graft . . . you see, here . . ."

Kharl just watched Warrl, listening.

XXX

On threeday morning, Kharl was up at dawn and used the well behind the cottage to wash up, chill as the air was, cold as the water was.

Warrl joined him just as the sun flooded a clear fall sky. "You have to go today, Da?"

"I do."

"Uncle Dowsyl said you could stay. I heard him."

Kharl decided against pointing out Merayni's views on that. "Your uncle is a good and kindly man, Warrl. But . . . I'm not a grower. I'm a cooper. I might be able to be a carpenter somewhere, or do other things, but a grower I'm not."

"Aunt Merayni doesn't think you'll ever be a cooper again. She said so. Is it true?"

"I can't be a cooper in Brysta. I'd have to go somewhere else, maybe even another land."

"You could come here."

Kharl shook his head. "Peachill is too small for a cooper. People only need a few barrels a year here."

"You don't want to come?"

"I can't, son."

"You don't want to . . ."

"It's not that . . ." Kharl tried to think of an answer that would express what he felt. "It's . . . I'd rather be with you . . . but if I came here . . . it wouldn't be fair to Merayni or Dowsyl . . . or to you. It's too close to Brysta. It's still part of Lord West's lands."

"How could that be? You work hard. You'd do that, here. I know you would. You always work hard."

"Warrl . . . do you remember what happened in Brysta? Every time I cross the street there, now, I have to look to make sure there aren't any of Lord Egen's bravos around. I'm staying with people, poor people, but I have to sneak in and out. If I came here, and Lord Egen found out . . ." Kharl shook his head slowly.

"No! It can't be . . ." Warrl's headshake was violent. "You're just saying that . . ." He turned and found himself held by Dowsyl. He looked up. "Uncle Dowsyl . . . that . . . it can't be . . ."

"Lad . . . I fear so," said Dowsyl slowly. "Your da's got the right of it, sad as it is."

"I had to make sure you were all right," Kharl said, his eyes fixed on Warrl's narrow face, in some ways so much like his mother's. "But I dare not come back too soon. And if I go to sea, I'll not be able to. Not for a time."

"But . . . why? What did you do?"

"Your da did what was right," answered Dowsyl. "Times . . . when a man does, and a lord's done wrong, all those around the man suffer. It's not fair, lad, but that's the way of the world. But don't be blaming your da for doing right. There's too few that will in these days."

Warrl slowly turned. "Da . . ."

Kharl stepped forward and put his arms around his son. He also mouthed the words, "Thank you," to Dowsyl.

The grower nodded, with a sad smile, before saying, "Merayni's got breakfast for us. Come on in when you're ready." After a moment, he added, "Your da will need a good fill, Warrl. Long walk back to Brysta." He turned and left them.

"I'm sorry, Da," offered Warrl, stepping back from Kharl's embrace.

"So am I. Never thought . . ." Kharl shook his head again.

Warrl looked down.

After another silence, the cooper said, "We'd better go eat."

Breakfast was hearty, with fried apples and pearapples, ham slices, and hot bread from the oven. There was little conversation, because he and Warrl had said what they could, as had Dowsyl, and because Merayni had long since voiced her views. Young Dowlan was interested in having more pearapples, and his sisters chattered about the new goat kid.

Before all that long, the food was gone, and Kharl had given Warrl a last hug, thanked Merayni and Dowsyl. In turn, Merayni had given Kharl some travel bread, cheese, and some dried pearapples. Then Kharl was walking down the long lane toward the main road. The light wind rustled the dry winter-gray leaves still clinging to the grove trees.

The cooper reflected as he walked eastward on the lane toward the road back to Brysta. Dowsyl had seemed concerned, and Kharl had sensed sadness in Warrl. Merayni had been polite. She'd not even said anything nasty and had been hospitable to him, if cool, although he could tell that she had been more than glad to see Kharl leave—without Warrl.

When Kharl reached the main road to Brysta, where he turned north, he could feel eyes on his back—probably those of the woman with the less-than-orderly gardens, watching to see where the stranger might be headed. He kept walking.

By midmorning, he was hungry, and he stopped beside a stream and sampled some of the bread and dried pearapples. He saved the rest of what Merayni had given him for later. He knew he'd be even hungrier then, and who knew when or what he'd eat once he reached Brysta.

He'd walked another glass or so, when, at the sound of hoofs on the road, Kharl glanced behind him. He saw no riders coming from the south, and that suggested that they were on the far side of the curve in the road ahead. He looked around, then spied an opening in the hedgerow behind the stone wall bordering the road. He scrambled into the hedgerow just as the first rider of a column of lancers cantered around the curve and into sight.

While the lancers in blue tunics trimmed in burgundy rode past, Kharl counted more than twoscore riders. None said a word, and none had weapons at the ready, though all bore scabbards holding sabres.

Where were the lancers headed in such a rush—and why?

Kharl wondered if he'd ever know.

Once they had passed, and the sound of hoofs had died away, he eased himself out of his hiding place in the hedgerow and continued walking northward, doubting that he would reach the tannery walls until well after dark. Longer, if he encountered more lancers.

He hoped nothing had happened to Jeka in his absence.

XXXI

Early on fourday morning, Kharl woke to find a cloudy sky, with cold mist half-drifting, half-drizzling through the open ends of the makeshift roof between the walls, a harbinger of late fall and of the winter to come. Intermittently, water dripped down off each end of the roof, and, every so often, from somewhere in the middle.

Kharl drew the winter sheepskin jacket around him, taking comfort in its warmth, but knowing it was too fine to wear on the streets, at least not in his guise as a beggar. He reached out and ran his fingers over the black staff. It wasn't exactly warm, but it didn't feel cold, and somehow, touching it had a calming effect on Kharl. He almost felt as though life had somehow become more clear. He knew that was not true, not at all, but it felt that way.

Jeka had come back late the night before—long after he had trudged through the alleys and serviceways—and she had scuttled into her hidey-hole without speaking.

Kharl pressed his lips together tightly, swallowing. Charee was dead. Her sister despised him. Arthal had stormed out. The cooperage would be sold, and Kharl was hiding like a rat between walls. He'd lost everything and everyone he had loved. While he'd learned long before that fairness was absent in much of life, he hadn't expected such unfairness to descend on him.

His lips quirked into a sardonic smile. He doubted that his life would ever be clear again. If he didn't get out of Brysta before too long, the length of that life was likely to be short indeed. Yet, he couldn't walk far enough because all Nordla was under the laws of the Quadrant. That meant that, if he were discovered elsewhere in Nordla, Lord West—or Egen—could request his return from any other lord. At best, that meant living like Jeka, or living a lie, waiting to be discovered. Neither alternative appealed to Kharl.

"Gettin' cold," observed Jeka as she eased from her cubbyhole. "How was your boy?"

"Doing fine. He's learning how to be a grower."

"So . . . he didn't want to be a cooper?"

"He lost his mother. He'd rather stay with his aunt and uncle than lose more."

"I'da stayed with Ma anywhere," Jeka said in a low voice.

"Your mother was lucky you felt that way."

"Didn't help her none."

From the bleakness of her tone, Kharl decided not to pry. "How do you make it through the winter?"

"Well as I can . . . I keep the cubby sealed, much as I can. It's higher, so water doesn't come in." Jeka shrugged. "Got pretty thin by spring this year."

"You can't keep doing this."

"What else is there? I won't go to a pleasure house. No one else'll have me . . ."

Kharl glanced at the section of sky visible between the wall and the crude roof, dark gray and getting lower. "Won't find much at the lower market today. Anyplace else we can get something to eat?"

"We could go to the White Pony. See if there's stuff left. Sometimes, there is. Durol'll let the girls sell it cheap, copper or two."

"Might as well try." Kharl's stomach was growling, as it often did of late. The slight paunch he had developed over the past few years had already begun to shrink, but the process wasn't pleasant—or noiseless.

"It's all right . . . you know," Jeka said.

"What's all right?" Kharl had no idea what she meant.

"That you got some coppers. Everyone hides their coin. You have to. You been real generous."

"So have you. Sharing your space. You helped me with shelter. I help with food."

"Maybe . . . maybe . . ." Jeka's eyes dropped.

"What?"

"Maybe you're too honest to be . . . a cooper." Her words trailed away.

Too honest to be a cooper? Was Brysta that bad?

". . . shouldn'ta said anything," Jeka mumbled.

"Never thought of that," Kharl replied. Still mulling over her observation, he packed away the winter jacket, regretfully.

Before long, they were over the wall and out of the serviceway, making their way uphill and eastward, toward the slightly better section of the harbor area where the White Pony was located off Third Cross, but farther to the south.

The wind picked up, and the misty rain struck Kharl's face like icy needles, despite the hood of the ragged cloak. The icy needles also penetrated the ragged fabric in too many other places.

"Shoulda holed up for the day," suggested Jeka.

"You want to go back?"

"Not that far now." After a moment, she added, " 'Sides, then I'd have to give back your coppers." A gaminelike grin appeared and quickly vanished.

They walked another long cross block before Jeka turned up a narrow alley. "We take this to the stable."

"Stable?"

"Pony's got a few rooms upstairs. Some folk stay there, those that don't know better." Jeka eased close to a red brick wall irregularly darkened by the misty rain. "Best you wait here just around the corner, by the old gatepost."

Kharl followed her instructions and huddled in the corner formed by a short gate-wall and the corner of the stable nearest the alley. As Jeka scurried urchin-like toward the inn, from under his thin and ragged and increasingly damp cloak, Kharl watched her.

Jeka slipped along the stable wall toward the rear kitchen door of the inn. She had barely passed the open stable door when a squarish man, with an oiled-leather cape to protect him against the damp, stepped out of the stable. A burly man in a dark burgundy wool jacket followed him, and the second carried a knife in his belt, long enough almost to be a shortsword, and a truncheon in his right hand.

A sense of . . . something . . . surrounded the squarish man, something that Kharl couldn't exactly see.

"You, beggar boy!" ordered the man in the cape. "You owe me something."

Jeka froze for a moment, then shook her head and started to dart away, but the bodyguard was quicker and grabbed her arm. A flash of something—white—flared from the fingers of the well-dressed man, and Jeka once more froze.

"Now, young woman dressed as a boy . . . you will wait here with Farn . . . until I return. I will not be gone but a few moments to collect . . .

your companion." The squarish man laughed softly. "Since you owe me . . ." He laughed again.

Jeka said nothing.

A broad and not terribly pleasant smile appeared on Farn's face.

"You will not disturb her, Farn. My uses come first. Two will be far better than one. What a wonderful coincidence, especially in this weather." The broad man walked along the side wall of the White Pony, ignoring the rear kitchen door and heading for the front door. He did so without so much as a look backward.

Kharl eased his way out from the alley, shuffling toward the tavern and leaning on his stick. He tried not to look anywhere near the bodyguard or Jeka, but toward the kitchen door.

"You!" snapped Farn. "Go somewhere else."

"Hungry," whined Kharl. "Copper for a hungry man? Copper, kind ser? Copper . . .?"

Farn let go of Jeka. She did not move. The bodyguard lifted his truncheon.

Kharl moved, bringing his shaped timber up in a single swift motion and driving the sharper end into the other's gut with all the force that a cooper could bring to bear. The bodyguard staggered. His breath puffed out with an explosive grunt, but he held on to the truncheon.

Kharl grabbed the middle of his weapon and, holding it in two hands, slammed it straight up into the other's jaw. There was a dull *crack* as the guard's jawbone snapped. This time the truncheon fell, but the man slowly, so slowly, it seemed to Kharl, reached for Kharl's neck.

Two-handed, again, Kharl drove his crude staff into the other's nose.

Blood welled over the guard's face, and his entire body went slack, slumping, then crumpling onto the muddy ground. For just an instant, Kharl thought he saw a netlike veil of white and black, a spiderweb of sorts within the body of the guard, appear, then disintegrate.

He shook his head, then lowered the makeshift staff.

Jeka still stood immobile, and the stillness and the total lack of expression on her face shocked Kharl. What had the other man done to her? Used some sort of wizardry? He glanced toward the White Pony, but no one seemed to have seen what had happened.

He grabbed Jeka's arm. She didn't move.

"Come on. Follow me."

This time, when he tugged at her arm, she followed, but her

movements were stiff and jerky. Kharl hurried them into the alley and out of sight from the tavern. They had gone almost another block before the mist began to change into a light rain. Still, it took far longer to return to the serviceway leading to Jeka's hidey-hole than it had to travel from it.

Once there, Kharl looked at the wall. He could easily boost Jeka over the wall, but he worried that she'd fall on the other side. He couldn't carry her and climb the wall himself.

"Climb over the wall and down the other side. Wait there," he finally said.

Jeka followed his commands, again awkwardly. After a look back, Kharl scrambled after her. She stood waiting on the other side, her face blank. Drops of rain from the edge of the roof fell on her. Some dribbled down her face. She had not moved.

"Move under the roof." Kharl guided her into the drier section of the makeshift dwelling, then set down his crude short staff.

He just looked at her for a time. What could he do? The wizard had done something with the white flash. White? He frowned, thinking, then nodded. It certainly couldn't hurt. He stepped to one side and slid the long black staff from under the rags.

Then he turned toward Jeka.

Her eyes widened, and she began to tremble. Kharl took her hand.

"No!" she screamed, struggling to get away from the staff.

Kharl pressed the staff to the hand he held.

Hsssttt! The hissing sound was almost like water on a red-hot iron blank.

Jeka collapsed like a street-show marionette whose strings had been cut, and Kharl had to struggle to hold her one-handed, while he set aside the black staff. Then he propped her form into a half-sitting position against the stone wall. The hand that had touched the staff was reddened, as if it had been slightly burned. Yet the staff had not been that hot to Kharl's touch.

Did white and black magic always react that way?

"Ohhh . . ." Jeka looked up, eyes darting around. "What . . ."

"How much do you remember?"

"There was a white flash, then . . ." She shook her head. Tears seeped from the corners of her eyes. "I would have done anything anyone told me."

"That was what he wanted."

"But . . . won't they come after us?"

"The bodyguard won't."

"You killed him."

"I didn't mean to." Kharl thought about his words, then added. "No. He felt so evil that I *had* to. Except I really wasn't thinking that then." His actions still confused him.

"Won't the wizard come after us for that?" Jeka shivered.

"He might," Kharl conceded. "But it's raining, and it's hard to track people in the rain, even with dogs. He didn't see me, I don't think." He paused. "You have any other hiding places?"

"They're not very good. This is the only really good one."

"Then, we'd better stay here. We'll have to be very careful when we go out. And I'm coming with you."

"Guess . . . guess you'd better." The faint tears still oozed from the corners of Jeka's eyes.

Kharl didn't have any idea what he could say to make her feel better.

All that because he'd been hungry.

XXXII

Kharl's stomach had gone well beyond empty and painful by dawn five mornings later, after four days of weather ranging from mist to rain so heavy that it had fallen in walls of icy water. He was sore and stiff because only a small area of the poorly roofed hiding space had remained usable—and that had been damp. When the sun finally rose on a cold and clear oneday, the cloudless sky and bright morning sunlight did little to cheer him. Nor did it ease his aching muscles and empty belly.

Jeka finally crawled out of her cubby, yawning. "Need to sleep when you can. Sleep more, and you don't need to eat so much."

"Could be."

"Least it's oneday," she offered. "Lower market's good on oneday. 'Specially by afternoon."

Before too long, she left, and after a few moments, Kharl followed, carrying his small wooden begging bowl. He had to be careful climbing the wall, because he felt a bit light-headed, but the walking, even at his affected hobble, cleared away some of the faintness.

The rain had washed away much of the stench from the rendering yard and from the tannery, and the cold breeze from the west brought a cleaner smell to Brysta. It wouldn't last that long, Kharl knew, but it helped as he hobbled down Copper Road, trailing Jeka by a good half block, when he could even see her elusive form.

He continued to plead, "A copper, just a copper for a poor man . . ."

As usual, most of those on the street ignored Kharl the beggar either by walking past quickly or by avoiding him. He did get one copper in the battered wooden bowl.

The sun was a good quarter of the way up the eastern sky when Kharl paused on the rubble-strewn corner on the northeast side of the harbor, short of the slateyard. From there, he looked at the lower market with its tents, carts, and portable stalls. He didn't see Jeka. He could see, except it was a feeling, more than a seeing, a patchy area of whiteness on the southern side of the open space that held the market.

Abruptly, and from nowhere, Jeka dashed from a cart and crossed the soggy ground between them. She stopped and extended a half loaf of bread. "Mamata gave it to me. She said she'd eaten some, and couldn't eat any more and couldn't sell it."

Kharl took a bite of the heavy rye, and his mouth watered. He forced himself to hand the bread back to Jeka after another bite.

"I had more than that," she said, refusing the bread.

Kharl didn't argue. He took several more large mouthfuls, and within moments, he started to feel less light-headed. He handed the remaining bread to Jeka.

This time, she took the quarter loaf remaining and finished half of it, then gave the remainder back. He ate it, even licking the crumbs off his fingers.

"I need to see what else I can scrounge or get cheap," she said.

"Stay away from the southern end," he said.

Jeka looked at him.

"Just a feeling," he said, not wanting to explain.

"I'll be careful. Always am."

"Be more careful," he suggested. "Don't know where that wizard might show up."

"Here? Not likely." Jeka laughed, then made her way back toward the carts and stalls.

Kharl followed. Even after the bread, his mouth watered as the scent of roasting fowl wafted around him. How long had it been since he'd sat at his own table and eaten fowl? And ale? And as much bread as he wanted?

He kept moving. Instead of staking out a space and sitting down, he hobbled around the harborside end of the market, occasionally pleading, extending the bowl. "A copper . . . just a copper for a poor man . . ."

Over the eightdays he'd been in hiding, he doubted that he'd collected more than nine or ten coppers, but his efforts made it easier to conceal the source of the coins he'd given to Jeka, not so much for her—she knew better—but from those with whom she dealt. He stopped and slumped, as if tired, but the slump was not all pose, not with the little he had eaten over the end-days.

Then he returned to walking and whining, ". . . copper . . . just a copper . . ."

As he neared the southwestern corner of the market, Kharl could see the patchy whitish fog more clearly, centered around a maroon-painted stall. He blinked, and the fog vanished. Was he seeing things because he was hungry? But the fog had become clearer *after* he'd eaten.

He limped and hobbled farther south, easing himself closer to the maroon stall, finally squatting near the rotten bollard section where he'd often placed himself.

"Copper . . . just a copper . . ." he mumbled, watching the stall where several youths, three girls, two women, and a tall man were gathered.

"Ooos" and "aahhs" came from the group.

"A few coins here, any coin," came a voice, "and you'll see what you've never seen."

After a moment, a flare of bluish flame erupted from somewhere in front of the group, then vanished. It wasn't flame, Kharl could tell, although he didn't really know how he knew, but it looked like it, and everyone stepped back.

For a moment, Kharl caught a glimpse of the wizard, wearing a red cape. Behind and to the left of the wizard stood another man, almost identical to the bodyguard Kharl had killed—or *had* he killed the man outside the White Pony? Kharl swallowed. The wizard was the same man who had ensorceled Jeka. But what was he doing in the lower market? Looking for her? Kharl's fingers tightened around his stick, a poor weapon against a wizard, but the only one he had. He kept watching, more aware of the whiteness that was not fog.

The small crowd once more drew nearer to the wizard.

"You see?" The wizard laughed. "All of you draw near, and you will see something truly special. Closer now . . . and who might have a coin? For miracles do not come without a price." He laughed again, heartily.

Kharl shivered at the laughter, feeling something more behind it.

"A copper? Cannot someone add to it?" asked the wizard. "If not, you must step closer, for what marvels you will see will be smaller."

The cooper frowned. The wizard seemed more to want the crowd closer than to get another copper. Kharl glanced past the stall. Jeka was moving past a cart with scarfs tied around a polished wooden rod, slowly toward the wizard and his booth. Kharl hobbled in toward the crowd, then left, toward Jeka. She slipped right, as if to avoid Kharl.

"Got a copper, brat?" he asked in a louder voice that was half growl, half whine.

Jeka stiffened at the tone.

"Get back," Kharl whispered. "Same wizard. Looking for you . . ."

Jeka darted off to the north.

Kharl hobbled quickly, as if Jeka had taken something. "Stop! Brat!"

Behind him, there was a flash of light, bright enough that he had to blink, even though his back was to the wizard. Screams filled the air, and Kharl looked back.

A column of smoke filled the space around where the wizard's booth had been. More had happened than just a flash of light. Those around the smoke had their hands to their eyes. Some staggered. Two women had collapsed, as had a man.

As Kharl watched, the wizard's guard emerged from the smoke, carrying a bundle of some sort—a very long bundle. To the right of the guard was the wizard, but his figure was blurred, and Kharl had trouble looking at the mage, as the wizard and his guard slipped away from the smoke and the booth it had shrouded.

For a moment, Kharl stood frozen, his eyes flicking from the guard to the almost invisible figure of the wizard, then back to the guard in the burgundy jacket.

The wizard stopped, turned, and looked directly at Kharl. His eyes seemed to burn. "You will not thwart me again, half creature. Next time, the weather will not favor you, and she will repay me."

Although the words were spoken from more than thirty cubits away—a good two rods—Kharl heard them clearly, and wondered how he had.

The wizard turned and strode swiftly away from the market, moving more quickly than the guard burdened with the large and long bundle.

Sellers and would-be buyers alike were turning toward the column of dissipating smoke and the booth emerging from the smoke, a squarish stall that looked only vaguely like the burgundy-walled stall before which the wizard had performed. More illusion? Kharl wondered how the stall could have changed so much, then looked back toward the wizard and the guard. They had reached a coach waiting east of the market.

"She's gone! Gone!"

Kharl turned back toward the stall where one of the women had staggered upright. "She's gone!"

Belatedly, Kharl realized that the bundle must have held a body—a small live body, and probably that of a girl. He glanced back to find the two men, but both the coach holding the guard and the wizard had already vanished.

The cooper began to hobble back uphill, even as the wizard's words echoed through his thoughts. . . . *not thwart me again* . . .

Kharl kept moving. He would have liked to tell someone, even the Watch, about the girl, but there wasn't much he could do, not now, and who would believe him if he told anyone there?

Slowly, he made his way back to the wall shelter adjoining the rendering yard. He did not enter the serviceway until the nearby street was empty. He quickly scaled the wall, then settled down to wait.

As time passed, Kharl began to worry, but he had no idea where he might find Jeka, none at all. She did not return to the space between the walls until close to sunset, but Kharl could smell the fowl she carried as she dropped over the wall.

"I got some-at for you," Jeka announced.

"What about you?" asked Kharl.

"Had some already. That dustup at the market . . . found some coppers. Bought fowl for us both. You always buy." Jeka did not quite look at Kharl as she handed him the fowl in stale bread.

Kharl kept from frowning. Jeka was telling the truth. That he knew, although he could not have said why. She had eaten, and she had found coppers, but he was missing something.

"What's the matter?" he asked.

"Nothing."

"Something's bothering you," he observed, before taking a bite of the fowl.

Jeka did not reply, instead settling down with her back against the ancient brick wall.

Kharl did not press her as he ate several more bites, before holding out the fowl. "Sure you wouldn't like some?"

"Had more 'n enough."

After finishing the bread and fowl, Kharl licked his fingers as clean as he could. For the first time in days, his stomach felt comfortably full. Yet he couldn't enjoy it. Something was bothering Jeka. Still. "You're worried. You can't hide it."

Jeka just sat in the early twilight, not looking at Kharl.

He waited.

Finally, Jeka began to speak, slowly at first. "Enelya had a sister. She was younger'n me, lots younger. She was doing the morning dishes . . . when we went to the White Pony . . ."

Kharl knew what Jeka was going to say, but he said nothing.

"She was at the tub . . . and like as disappeared . . ."

"Did anyone find her?"

"Enelya looked . . . much as she could." Jeka took another bite of the fowl. "Found her this morning. In the harbor . . . say she drowned, 'cause there wasn't a mark on her."

"You don't think she did?"

"Enelya says she was scared of water. She almost drowned in the creek where they grew up backhills . . . always stayed away from the harbor."

"The wizard. He took someone else this morning at the market," Kharl said. "He wanted to take you at the White Pony. He talked about two being better than one. And he said you owed him."

"Heard that." Jeka shivered, although it was not that cold. "Today, I woulda gone there. Felt like I was bein' called. Didn't know you for a moment . . ."

"I wondered about that," Kharl said. "That's why I was harsh."

"Saved me . . . maybe . . ." She shivered again. "He's gonna keep lookin' . . ."

"He wants young ones, girls almost . . ." Kharl murmured, more to himself, thinking that the wizard was worse even than Egen. But owing?

"Must need 'em for his wizardry . . ."

"The Watch doesn't say anything?" asked Kharl abruptly.

"They don't care. Not about street girls. Don't even care about poor ones. Safer as a boy than a girl."

"How do you owe him?"

"Don't. Not him."

Although Jeka was lying, Kharl just nodded. What good would it do to press her? Except get him in more trouble. There wasn't much he could say. But he worried about the wizard's words. Had the wet weather helped him in dealing with the wizard before? Why?

His lips curled into a wry smile. Until he'd thought over the wizard's words, he hadn't been aware of anything that seemed to favor him these days.

His eyes dropped to the rag-wrapped black staff. Would it, too, help against the wizard? Would anything help enough?

XXXIII

Kharl kept worrying on twoday, but he had a feeling that threeday or fourday would be when the wizard resumed looking for him—or for Jeka. He still had no idea why the wizard was seeking out one young woman disguised as a beggar boy, but it was clear that he was.

On twoday, Kharl checked the harbor, as he had most days, but there was no sign of the *Seastag,* or either of the other two ships whose masters he knew, if less well than he did Hagen. He tried to push aside the worry that he might not be able to avoid Egen until a captain he knew ported in Brysta.

Jeka woke Kharl early on threeday, even before dawn. "Feel that . . . like a cord I can't see, tuggin' at me."

The cooper looked at the shivering young woman posing as a ragged boy. As he saw the light frost on the stones, he couldn't help feeling guilty for his warm jacket, even if he only dared sleep in it. For a moment, her words didn't mean anything. Then he stiffened and lurched up. "We need to leave here. Now." He tried not to wince. His back and limbs were sore and stiff, as they had been every morning he had awakened between the walls.

"Leave? So's he can catch us in the open?" Jeka pulled her ragged brown cloak around her more tightly.

"If we stay here, he'll follow whatever that cord is until he knows where you are. You want to stay and be cornered?"

"Got a little bread left," Jeka offered. "Let's eat first."

Two chunks of bread took little enough time to eat.

Then Kharl took the rag-covered black staff and his pack and carried them farther along the space between the walls, hiding them—and his jacket—as well as he could beyond the stone-circled hole that served as a necessary, before using the crude latrine.

"Why'd you move that stuff?" asked Jeka.

"So if the wizard or his guard looks, they won't know someone else is here." Kharl's head throbbed faintly at the misstatement. He donned the ragged beggar's cloak.

"Better get on." Jeka turned and scrambled over the wall.

By the time the sun was rising over Brysta on what promised to be a bright fall day, one warmer than the light morning frost indicated, the two stood in the serviceway, flanked by long shadows on one side and the flat light of sunrise on the other.

Kharl looked at Jeka. "Can you feel where the tugging's coming from?"

"No."

Kharl held in the harsh words he felt at Jeka's rebellious tone. "We'll go up the street, say fifty cubits."

The two walked south on the cross street, and Kharl tried not to look back.

"Stop." Kharl waited, then looked at Jeka. "Does it feel stronger?"

"No . . . feels weaker . . . maybe closer . . ." She looked puzzled.

"We go the other way."

"Other way?"

"No pull when a fish on a line swims to the fisherman," Kharl said.

Jeka paled.

Kharl wished he'd used different words. "Come on." He turned back north.

Jeka scrambled to catch up to him. As they walked in the shadows on the east side of the cross street, Kharl wished he'd brought the staff rather than his crude stick. At the end of the block, the cross street ended in a stone wall, and they turned westward, taking the walk on the south side, downhill toward the harbor. Jeka darted ahead, then froze for a moment.

Kharl peered toward the harbor. At the end of the next block, there were three Watchmen and an officer—one whom Kharl recognized even from that distance as Egen. He was certain, although he didn't quite know why. Jeka slipped back toward Kharl.

"Watch ahead," mumbled Jeka.

"And the wizard's somewhere behind." Kharl looked to the service-way to his left, which connected to an east–west alleyway. "Into the serviceway."

"Be Watch at the harborside end of the alley."

"Can't be any worse." Kharl hoped it couldn't be worse, but he wasn't counting on that, not the way the last few seasons had been going.

In a few moments, they reached the point where the serviceway joined the alley. Kharl peered around the corner formed by two brick walls. As Jeka had predicted, there were Watchmen at the end nearer the harbor.

Kharl studied the alley, noting the thin line of shadows on the southern side. He looked at Jeka. "We turn and start uphill on the sunny side, but we move toward the shadows. Once we're in the shadows we crouch down, then come back to the serviceway right across from us."

"It might work." Jeka sounded less than convinced.

"Might not. Got a better idea?"

"No."

"Then we'll try it." Kharl stepped out of the serviceway and began to walk up the alley at a slight angle.

So far as he could tell, the Watchmen below did not move. At least, he heard no steps on the stones, those that were high enough to stand out above the lower muddy stones. They covered close to a hundred cubits before they entered the shadows. Kharl took several more steps before he began to crouch as he slipped to the southern side of the alley.

He ducked into a recess formed by a loading dock, then peered around the corner and down the alley. The Watchmen had not moved.

"The cord thing's stronger," Jeka muttered from behind him.

"We need to slip along the shadow here. Keep low."

"*You* keep low."

Kharl tried to keep low, crouching as he made his way back down the side of the alley.

After fifty cubits, they had to duck behind a refuse bin as a loading door opened.

Rats skittered and rustled in the bin as they waited. It seemed like a glass passed before the heavyset man in brown went back into the shop and closed the door. Finally, they slipped into the serviceway and walked quickly to where it ended short of the next street. Kharl halted.

"Now what?" asked Jeka.

"We run across the street and into that serviceway, and we keep moving south until we get to the fountain. Then we head back uphill."

They sprint-scurried across Wellman Street, and down another serviceway . . . then another, and a third. In time, they turned down the alley south of Cargo Road and made their way to the fountain. There they waited for a teamster to water his pair of mules, then slipped in ahead of a laundress to drink.

After they had drunk, Kharl turned to Jeka. "Can you feel the cord thing?"

Jeka paused. "No. I don't think so."

"Good. We'll keep moving along Second Cross toward the river."

"The river? Can't swim."

"We aren't going to. White wizards have trouble with streams and running water. Leastwise, that's what they say. We'll circle back later today." At least, Kharl hoped that they could, but he didn't know what else to suggest. He also didn't like the idea that the Watch seemed to be helping the wizard.

He had to wonder what Egen had to do with the white wizard. Was the wizard working for Egen? Or did Egen owe something to the wizard?

XXXIV

On threeday night, they did not go back to Jeka's hidey-hole between the tannery and the renderer's yard. Neither did they reach the river or the river road. Instead, they curled up inside a hedgerow beside the road headed southeast from Brysta—the same road that led to the orchards held by Merayni and Dowsyl. Where Kharl hoped Warrl was safe.

Huddled inside the thick wall of brush, shivering at times, Kharl swallowed at that thought, but there was nothing he could do. Trying to see Warrl again would only make matters worse, and, if the wizard was working with Egen, the lord might well now have spared a guard or two to watch the place. More important, with each passing day, Kharl could offer Warrl even less.

"I'm cold," mumbled Jeka.

"So am I." Those were the last words Kharl said before he drifted into a troubled sleep.

He woke in the gray before dawn. The way his body ached when he tried to uncurl, he decided there were worse places to sleep than between renderer's and tanner's walls. Much worse.

"You snore," Jeka said. "Loud."

"So do you. Soft."

"Soft's better 'n loud."

"Probably." Kharl crawled out through the brushy tunnel onto the field side of the hedgerow. The wheat had already been harvested, and the brown stubble jutted skyward from the dark ground. The air was chill enough that Kharl's breath was like fog, and the ground crunched underfoot. The shutters of the hut beyond the small woodlot appeared to be closed. Kharl shifted his weight from one foot to the other, trying to loosen tight muscles.

Shortly, Jeka followed him, glancing toward the cottage, then at Kharl.

After a moment, he asked, "You feel the cord thing tugging at you?"

"A little."

"Frigging wizard," Kharl muttered. "Moved south. We need to circle around Brysta and get back to your place."

"So why'd we leave?"

"So that he didn't catch us there, so he didn't find out that was the only place you sleep."

"It is."

"Not any longer."

"We can't keep moving. We can't get food."

"You want to end up like Enelya's sister?"

"No. We can't keep doing this, either."

Kharl nodded. She was right about that. "Need to get back and pick up your stuff . . . if we can. Somehow." He looked back toward the cottage. At one side of the woodlot, there was a tree, one that looked to be an apple, and despite the thinning leaves, Kharl thought he saw a few fruits hanging. Probably rotten, but they might have good spots.

"Where you goin'?"

"Apple tree."

"Too many'll run your guts," Jeka warned.

"Could be." Kharl kept moving, as quietly as he could. He reached the tree without any noise from the cottage, less than four rods away, although he could smell the smoke of a cooking fire. All of the fruit was beyond his reach from the ground, but the tree looked sturdy, and he levered himself up. From the lowest sturdy branch, he managed to pluck something, but his hand came away gooey. The entire fruit was spoiled. He had better luck with the next several, tucking them inside his under-tunic as he inched out on the branch and stretched upward.

Ruuufff! Rufff! The sharp but deep bark of a dog filled the dawn air, so sudden that it startled Kharl. He had to grab the trunk of the apple tree to keep from falling.

Ruufff . . .

The barking continued. Kharl scrambled down to the ground, scooped up an apple he'd dropped, and began to run. As he scrambled through the stubble of the field, hurrying back toward the hedgerow, the dog barking behind him, he just hoped that the holder didn't have a bow.

"Thief! Coward!" came the call from the cottage, but Kharl did not look back before squeezing through a narrow space in the hedgerow, an overgrown gate path.

Jeka waited on the roadside for Kharl. "Real quiet, you were."

"I was quiet. The dog wasn't."

"That's why they got dogs."

Kharl shook his head. She was right. He wasn't a very good thief. He didn't like being a thief, even of half-rotten apples.

"What did you get?"

He extended two of the apples. "They're half-good. Better than nothing."

"You get any for you?"

Kharl forced two on her, then produced two more. "We'd better start walking."

Jeka nodded, and took several steps. "Need to eat slow."

Kharl caught up to her. "You feel the wizard?"

"We're moving away, I think."

"Let me know if it changes." Kharl took a small bite from the good part of the apple.

Given the growling of his stomach, Kharl had to force himself to take small bites, and make each last as they walked.

"Need to head east and north," Kharl said. "Know there's a ring road ahead."

"Where? How far?"

Kharl shrugged.

They walked south almost a glass before they reached the ring road that looked to circle east and north. Then, for the next glass or so, they walked back northward along the road, ducking behind the low stone wall, since there was no hedgerow, when wagons or riders neared. The road turned almost due north at another crossroads, and after that, for a time, they saw no one, and there were few tracks in the dust of the narrow road.

"How about the wizard?" Kharl finally asked.

"He's got to be back there." Jeka gestured behind them.

"Good."

After a time, well after the apples were gone, and the sun had cleared the low hills to the east of Brysta, Kharl stopped, looking ahead.

"What is it?" asked Jeka.

"Just thinking. Someplace ahead we'll reach the pike. We can come into Brysta from the northeast, down the pike, off Angle Road."

"Lots of road guards, too."

"Not many, and they're not under Egen. His older brother, I think."

"What's his name?"

"Osgard, Osten . . . something like that. There's someone coming." Kharl eased toward the two thorn-olives before the stone wall, then hurried behind them. Jeka reached cover first, again.

To the north, a narrow wagon drawn by a single horse moved away from them. Farther southward, there was a peddler. Kharl couldn't tell which way he was pushing his handcart.

After a time, he said, "We can get back on the road now."

Jeka joined him, glancing back over her shoulder, but the ring road remained mostly empty except for the peddler who was going northward, as they were, but certainly not any faster, and the wagon, which was soon out of sight.

They had covered perhaps two kays, and a hedgerow began on the west side of the road, weedy and sparse at first, but thickening more toward the north.

Another wagon, headed south and drawn by two dark chestnuts, appeared from around a gentle curve to the north and moved quickly toward them. Kharl eased to the side of the road, Jeka moving behind him. Behind the wagon were two mounted guards. A third sat beside the driver, with a cocked crossbow propped beside him. None of the four looked more than once at Kharl and Jeka. As the wagon rolled past, Kharl read the inscription on the side: Tekat & Sons, Merchants in Spirits.

"Fancy wagon," Jeka said. "Wonder what they carry."

"Spirits," Kharl said. "That's what the sign on the side said, anyway."

"Do all coopers know their letters?" Jeka's voice held a trace of wistfulness.

"I don't know. Some do. Some don't. It helps some."

"You have any books . . . I mean, back . . ." Jeka broke off the sentence.

"When I had the shop?" Kharl laughed, softly, not quite bitterly. "I had a few. Got 'em from my da. Books are dear. Some cost a gold or more." The thought of Tyrbel's beautiful books, and the scrivener's death, washed over him. He swallowed. So many deaths—Charee's, Tyrbel's, the assassin's, the wizard's guard . . . and while he could say he knew why, he wasn't sure he truly understood why Egen, why anyone, could be so vindictive.

Kharl thought he heard something, and he glanced back over his shoulder. A man was riding northward, at either a trot or a fast walk. The late-morning sun showed his burgundy jacket clearly. The cooper looked to Jeka. "You feel . . . ?"

"No. Not any more 'n before."

"That looks like one of his guards." Kharl glanced around. "Hide in that patch of weeds. Behind them, anyway."

"What about you?"

"He's far enough away that he might not have seen you. He's probably seen me. I hide, and he looks for us both."

Jeka scuttled into the weedy patch on the far side of the dried-up ditch. Kharl adopted a more laborious hobble. He covered another five rods before he could hear the hoofbeats on the hard and damp road clay clearly. As they drew nearer, he finally looked back, then, as if in fear, he scuttled well back from the road, watching the rider carefully.

The burgundy-jacketed man reined up but did not leave the road. One hand rested on the hilt of the sabre at his side, but he did not draw it. He looked at Kharl. "Old fellow . . . did you see a boy running along here. A boy in gray rags?"

"Eh . . . ?" Kharl whined. "A boy, you say . . . ?"

"That's what I said. If it's the right boy, there's a copper or two in it for you."

"A copper for an old man? A copper?"

"The boy?"

Kharl let his shoulders sag. "Seen no boy. Saw a peddler. Saw a wagon. Saw two." He peered at the rider. "Copper for a poor old man?"

The rider snorted. "Go and starve somewhere else. Get off the road."

Kharl looked around, as if bewildered.

"Get off the road!"

Kharl scuttled backward, seeming almost to trip, before scrambling over the dry ditch and looking around as if wondering where he could go.

The rider laughed, then turned his mount northward.

As he rode away, Kharl realized that the guard had not been the one he had seen at the market, but that the man, like the wizard, had shreds of the unseen white fog clinging to him. Did it have to do with wizardry? What? He just stood and waited until the man was out of sight beyond the next low rise in the road. Before long, Jeka rejoined him.

He looked at her. "What did you do to him?"

"Who?" Jeka did not look at Kharl.

"The wizard. Did you lift his purse, or something? He couldn't be searching so hard for you just to do . . . whatever he does to girls." Kharl glanced to the road and at the heavy wagon rolling southward. "Better duck, just in case."

Jeka dropped flat in the weeds behind Kharl, and the cooper watched as the four-horse team rumbled past, shivering the ground. On the outer side of the road, Kharl could also see three men scything late wheat. Maybe Jeka was right, that they needed to get off the road and follow it from behind the hedgerows. They might run into holders and their families, but it was clear that the wizard had some men patrolling the roads.

Kharl looked down. "You didn't answer me."

"Was only a silver . . . had it in his belt. Goral gave me nine coppers for it."

"When?"

"Two eightdays back."

"So he wants you for two reasons. Because you made a fool of him, and also for his wizardry." Kharl paused. "Why did you steal from a wizard?"

"Didn't know he was. Just a dandy like all the others. How did you know?"

Kharl paused. How had he known? He'd known from the white flash, but . . . He shook his head. "I don't know. I just knew."

"Takes one to know one, maybe?"

"I'm a cooper. You know that."

Jeka just shrugged.

"We need to get moving. Away from the road."

"I told you so."

"Yes, you did."

Walking northward along the edge of the fields beside the hedgerow was slower, but since most of the fields had been harvested, they saw few holders there, save for the areas of meadow where youths and children watched small flocks of sheep. People watched them, closely, until they passed, but said nothing.

Once, Kharl would have watched people who looked the way he did. His beard was untrimmed and scraggly, his clothes ragged, and he was certain he smelled rank, if not worse, although he had mostly gotten used to that. He hadn't gotten used to the itchy skin.

While they avoided any surveillance by not walking the road, going by the hedgerow paths meant it took even longer than Kharl had thought. They also had little to eat, just a few bitter quinces he had retrieved from deep in the thorny branches of an unkempt bush near the hedgerow, and there had been only one small stream that looked clear enough to drink. Both were walking slowly by late afternoon, when they neared the pike and the low ridges through which flowed Souangle Creek. Rather, Kharl corrected himself, the creek flowed into the pond that Vetrad's grandsire had built and through the millrace that powered the sawmill.

Kharl thought they might be able to sneak into Vetrad's lumber barn after dusk. It was dry, and a lot warmer than the hedgerow. There was also an orchard beyond it, and there might be a few apples left, discards, partly rotten, and the like. He hoped so. The mill and lumberyard were off the ring road, less than a kay out Angle Road from it on the creek. Kharl had never known why the same road was called the pike inside the ring road, and Angle Road outside, but it was.

He glanced back at the clouds, darkening and gathering out over the ocean, just beyond the harbor, then to Jeka. Her face was pale.

"The wizard?" he asked.

"Thing's stronger. Stronger 'n it's been."

"Where?"

Jeka half shrugged. "I can't tell."

Kharl could feel that she was exhausted. He was tired, but he doubted that Jeka could have walked another ten rods without falling over. He wished he had the staff, rather than the stick.

"We'll rest for a while." Kharl pointed to a tumbled rock wall bordering the hedgerow.

Jeka slumped onto the rock. "Not much to eat here. There's more in Brysta."

"We're headed back that way. I think I know a safer place to sleep tonight. It's not too far, a little more than a kay."

A low rumble rolled out of the west. Kharl looked over the empty fields and the trees beyond. While he could not see the dwellings and structures of Brysta, he knew they were there, and the harbor was beyond—and the growing thunderheads were rising over the harbor, blocking out the late-afternoon sun.

"I don't think the wizard's that far away," Jeka said tiredly.

"Can you walk some more?" Kharl asked.

"I can try." She stood slowly.

They walked along the narrow path. Kharl let her lead the way, afraid that he might set too fast a pace for her.

"We're moving away from him," Jeka said after they had walked another twenty rods toward the spot where Angle Road met the ring road. "Think so, anyway."

"He's probably stopped south of us, then." Kharl could feel the dampness in the air, and the wind began to gust around them.

"Wind feels good," Jeka said. "Long's it doesn't rain."

A ways farther along, perhaps a quarter kay, Kharl found a break in the hedgerow and squeezed through, watching the road carefully as he did. From beside the hedgerow, he could see Angle Road just ahead, and the old stone bridge where the road crossed Souangle Creek. Two wagons had passed the crossroads, heading out away from Brysta, in the direction of Sagana and Alturan. The road looked clear, and he didn't see any other easy way to cross the creek, except by the Angle Road bridge.

He turned and beckoned. "We need to hurry."

"Wizard's getting closer." Jeka shivered.

Kharl looked to the south on the ring road. He *thought* he saw mounted figures. He grabbed Jeka's arm and stepped up his pace, quickly crossing the ring road and hurrying along the right side of Angle Road, even though every step hurt his already sore feet. He could imagine that every step felt worse to Jeka.

By the time they reached the bridge over the creek, Kharl was almost dragging Jeka, and except for a wedge of blue-green to the east, the sky was filled with gray clouds that seemed to darken more with each moment.

He glanced ahead. There was almost a half a kay to go before they reached the low stone wall that encircled Vetrad's mill and lumber barns. "We'll cross and wait under the bridge."

"Good . . . need to rest," Jeka gasped.

Kharl had to half carry her down the weed-tangled slope and under the bridge. They huddled together on a pile of stones amid the mud and debris gathered against the stone buttress on the north side, the only really solid footing. There they waited.

A gust of wind whipped under the span of the bridge, so strong that Kharl had to gather the tattered beggar's cloak around him to keep it from being blown off him—or so he felt. Then the wind died away. He looked upstream, in the direction of the millrace, but he could not see it. He could see that no rain was yet falling. In the comparative silence after another gust of wind from the oncoming storms, Kharl heard voices.

". . . doesn't know which way she went from the crossroads . . ."

". . . doesn't know? He always knows . . ."

"You want to tell him?"

The riders did not stop and look under the bridge, as Kharl would have done. He wondered why. Did they not think of it? Or did they want to cover as much ground as they could before the storm struck?

Kharl and Jeka continued to wait, amid more gusts of wind, and a pattering of rain that came, then went. In time, the pair of riders returned, the hoofs of their mounts echoing on the paving stones of the span above.

". . . didn't go this way . . . miller was out, and he would have seen them . . ."

". . . tomorrow . . . maybe . . ."

So Vetrad was out? Kharl took a deep breath. That meant they'd have to take the way along the creek.

He waited for a time, then crawled up the steep slope and, crouching beside the stone restraining wall of the bridge, studied Angle Road. It was empty. "Come on," he called down to Jeka.

He waited until she reached him.

"We'll cross the road. Looks like a path along the creek there on the other side. Just about a half kay . . ."

"You said that a kay ago . . ." Jeka attempted a smile.

"Suppose I did."

The path was overgrown and narrow, but it was also mostly shaded by weedy trees, interspersed with an occasional oak and, surprisingly, at one spot, an ancient black lorken. Another pattering of rain on the leaves overhead came and went, and a series of deeper thunderclaps rumbled overhead.

Finally, Kharl could see the stones of the lower spillway of Vetrad's millrace. "We're almost here. Through the berry bushes, and across the narrow meadow to the tall barn."

"I . . . hope . . . so . . ." panted Jeka.

They stopped at the edge of the berry bushes, stripped of every last berry. The meadow looked empty. An even deeper thunder roll rumbled over them, and the rain began to fall. The first raindrops were fat—and far apart. They hit the ground or the meadow grass slowly, then splattered.

Kharl had not taken four steps when Jeka's legs gave way, and she sprawled out full length on tannish meadow grass. He turned, then scooped her up. He was amazed at how light she was, even as tired as he felt.

"Can't carry me . . ."

"It's not far."

From his times of scouting out Vetrad's stocks, Kharl knew that all the barn doors would be locked, but that the rear door facing the small orchard at the edge of the meadow was low enough, with a gap above it, that they could scramble through. Vetrad wasn't worried about people. He just didn't want them taking his timbers and billets, and the doors and locks were more than enough for that. Even so, by the time they huddled under the overhang by the small door, the rumble of thunder was all around them. A bolt of lightning struck somewhere on the ridge to the east of the millpond, so close and so loud that Kharl's ears rang.

"You just wait here," he told Jeka.

"Where are you going?"

"Saw some pearapples on the trees. Looked near ripe, and no one's going to be looking now. Won't be long." Kharl hurried back into the storm.

There was more wind than rain, although his ragged cloak was still damp when he returned with almost a half score of pearapples.

"Door's locked," Jeka said dully.

"Look up." Kharl picked Jeka up and lifted her so that she could scramble through the opening above the doorframe. Then he tucked the fruits into his trousers as best he could and jumped, catching the edge and slowly levering himself up. Going down was easier.

Jeka stood waiting in the dimness.

"This way," he said, leading her along the wide space between the stacks of rough timbers, until they reached the ladder to the oak lofts. "Up there."

Once he reached the top of the ladder, Kharl led them along the catwalk to the left and to the space just under the eaves behind the last row of red oak billets. Kharl hadn't remembered it as that large, but compared to where they had been sleeping, it was spacious, a good five cubits by five, although it was only three in height. "No one comes here. Too dry to cure the oak properly. Dries too fast, uneven."

Jeka sank onto one of the planks, covered in shavings, sitting there.

"They should clean out the billet shavings, but they never have. It's not as hard as it looks." Kharl extended a pearapple. "Eat. There's a place where we can get water, if the rain keeps up."

"Don't feel the wizard at all," Jeka said after several bites of the fruit.

"Not at all?" questioned the cooper as he finished his own pearapple, far better than the poor apples that had begun the day.

"Nah . . ." She cocked her head to the side, gaminelike. "Not since it really started raining."

Kharl frowned. Rain? Could rain do that? Running water was supposed to slow wizards. He wasn't sure that it did, but what was rain but water running down from the skies?

"Feels good." Jeka yawned. "Can we go back tomorrow?"

"We'll see." Kharl found himself yawning.

Later, as the rain streamed down, coming off the roof of the lumber barn in thin sheets, for the first time in days, Kharl fell asleep immediately.

XXXV

The journey back into Brysta proper was far easier than their flight—except that Jeka had been right about the effect of so much fruit on Kharl, and that had slowed their travel. By late afternoon, they had reached the upper cross streets of Brysta. Kharl insisted on observing his cooperage from a distance. While there was no guard, and the proclamation had been taken down, it was boarded shut.

Somewhat later, they had reached the White Pony, where Jeka used some of Kharl's coppers to buy them some fowl and bread. After eating, and visiting the fountain, they had made their way back to Jeka's place. Along the way, Kharl had checked the harbor, but none of the vessels he knew had ported. There had also been no trace or sign of the white wizard, and that bothered Kharl almost as much as if the wizard and his men had been chasing Jeka.

Still . . . she could use the respite, and Kharl had no doubts that sooner or later the wizard would show up once more, although he had to admit to himself that he didn't understand why he felt that way.

While Jeka dozed in her hidey-hole, in the space between the walls, under the inadequate roof, in the last light of day, Kharl leafed through the blackstaffer's book, trying to find something that would give him some insight into what had happened with the wizard.

. . . the greater the effort to concentrate order within material objects, the greater the amount of free chaos within the world . . .

What in light was free chaos? He turned another few pages.

. . . all that is, everything that exists, is little more than the twisting of chaos in a shell of order, and the greater the complexity of those twistings, the more solid the object appears. A thumb of lead or gold may appear more solid than a feather or a flower, and may indeed overbalance the scales, yet there is no difference in the fashion in which they are constructed . . .

He kept turning the pages, reading a phrase here, a sentence there.

. . . the form of everything under the sun is determined by the amount of order and chaos and the way in which they are combined and intertwined . . .

After more than a glass of turning pages, he had found all too many incomprehensible phrases. He turned yet another page, stopping and rereading it.

Water is of both chaos and order, yet it is order, and represents order, for its structure overweighs its parts . . .

Kharl rubbed his forehead. How could water have parts? Water was. You could boil it or freeze it, and it changed to steam or ice, but it was still water. He took a deep breath and kept reading.

Because water is both order and of order, yet comprised of parts that are totally chaotic, it challenges chaos with the depth of its order. Truly a river people or a sea people must hold to order or they will be lost. Chaos fares best upon the dry land, and least in a steady rain or snowfall . . .

Rain or snow affected chaos? A faint smile crossed Kharl's lips.

Even a fog will affect a chaos-wielder, but only those who are of the weaker sort. A steady rain is a patterned fall of ordered chaos. A raindrop is ordered, and the fall of each is unpatterned, chaotic, yet all raindrops falling together results in a pattern ordered by chaos, and that order can weaken or destroy many of the links of power created by those who wield chaos, as the fires of sun itself can weaken those who wield order, if they do not understand that the sun is a furnace of chaos . . .

The cooper blinked. What did the sun have to do with order and chaos? Like water, it was. It gave warmth and light, and how could those be of chaos? And the sun weakened order? The book implied that a chaos-wielder could affect the sun. How could that be? A wizard could no more affect the sun than . . . Kharl couldn't think of a comparison.

After a time, the cooper closed the book and nodded to himself. He did have one answer, but more questions than ever.

XXXVI

On sixday, Kharl was awake with the sun, bright and clear as on the day before, and cool, but without frost. He could see clouds forming out to the west over the open ocean, and there was a brisk wind off the water, promising rain sometime in the afternoon. He thought about reading more from *The Basis of Order*. He'd had to stop the day before when his mind had finally quit grasping the words, as if there had just been too many new ideas banging around inside his skull—ideas he couldn't yet connect to each other. There was so much he didn't know.

What could he do about the wizard? Should he even try? How could he not, when Jeka had been the only one to offer him help and a place to hide? He glanced at his pack, debating whether to take out the book and start once more.

With a sound between a grunt and a groan, Jeka rolled out of her hidey-hole and looked at Kharl. "Need to get us something to eat."

"You don't feel the wizard?"

"No." She shook her head. "I'll go to the lower market."

"I can go."

Jeka shook her head. "No one'd sell cheap or fair to you. No one looks at me. Some folk still watch you. They might tell Egen. You never know."

She was probably right about that, Kharl thought. "But . . . if you see or feel the wizard, you stop and come back here. Quick as you can."

"I can do that. Got some coppers?" The gaminelike urchin grinned.

"Just a few." Kharl grinned back as he handed her three.

He watched her scramble over the wall, gracefully, wondering if he should have insisted on going himself, but he wanted to try to read more in the book, because he still didn't know what he could or should do about the white wizard.

After a moment, Kharl took *The Basis of Order* out from his pack and opened it once more, hoping that the words would make more sense. The first words he read seemed so obvious that he wondered why they were there.

> . . . there is more that lies beneath the surface of anything, whether it be the ocean or the mountains . . . Do not assume that what lies beneath is the same as what lies above, nor that it is different . . .

The next words were far from obvious, and meant nothing to him, nothing at all.

> In substance, there is no difference between chaos and order, for neither has substance in and of itself . . .

Nor did many of the pages that followed help much, either. His head began to ache, but he kept reading, doggedly.

Sometime in early afternoon, Jeka climbed back over the wall and dropped down before Kharl. Her face was contorted.

"Hurts . . . he's after me . . ."

"Who? The wizard?"

Jeka nodded. Then she pulled out half a loaf of bread and a small wedge of hard cheese. "I got you this."

"Have you eaten?" Kharl took the bread and cheese.

"Yes."

"As much as this?"

"About the same."

The words rang true, and Kharl began to eat. The headache he had not thought had come from reading began to subside, if slowly. When he had finished, he made his way along the walls and past the crude latrine to retrieve the black staff.

Jeka looked at him as he brought it back. "You want me to touch it?" She shivered.

"It might help."

Jeka edged forward, then grabbed the staff, suddenly, before Kharl could reach out. Without even a cry or a murmur, her eyes closed; her knees buckled, and she dropped in a heap.

Alarmed, Kharl bent forward, but he could see that she was breathing. He half dragged, half carried her into her sleeping space. When he was certain she was still breathing, and seemed to be sleeping, he eased back away and sat down against the wall.

The staff had some power. That was certain. It could break whatever spell the white wizard laid on Jeka, but the effect didn't last.

Kharl tried to read more of *The Basis of Order,* but the words flowed by him without making much sense. Then he stood and stretched, and tried to figure out how he could deal with the wizard—or if he should even try. Then he just sat against the wall.

A good glass passed before Jeka moaned.

Kharl lifted the canvas and peered into the hidey-hole. "You all right?"

"No . . . my head still hurts."

He waited for a time, and finally Jeka eased out into the indirect light of a cloudy afternoon, although the only place where rain looked to be falling was offshore.

"Wizard . . . he's . . . bastard like Egen," she muttered.

Kharl agreed silently. "Do you feel any better?"

"The cord thing is gone. My head hurts."

Kharl looked at her. "Do you know someone who could tell you where the wizard lives?"

Jeka dropped her eyes.

Kharl waited, but she did not reply.

"You already know? Because that's where you stole the silver from him?"

"He was kicking a peddler woman . . . pushing her . . . she said he hadn't paid . . . He was awful mad . . . served him right."

"But stealing from a wizard?"

"Told you . . . didn't know he was a wizard then. Just thought he was a dandy. Never miss a silver. He was stealin' from her . . . didn't think it was so bad to steal from him . . ."

"I need to know where he lives."

"Not all that far from the White Pony, 'cept it's up the hill and north."

Kharl glanced to the west. The afternoon rain that was so common in mid- and late fall looked to be moving inshore. He hoped that the coming storm would help conceal Jeka from the wizard. "You'll have to take me there."

Jeka looked down. "I'm tired again . . . don't know why."

Kharl gestured in the direction of the wall and the serviceway beyond. "Let's go. You climb over first."

Jeka dragged herself to the wall and over it, with a noticeable lack of enthusiasm. She just stood and watched as Kharl climbed, then descended into the shadowed serviceway.

"You bringing that staff?"

"It might help."

"Long as no one looks too close," she replied.

Kharl stayed almost abreast of Jeka as she wound her way through alleys, serviceways, and, occasionally, streets, but they did not stay on the streets long, and only on those streets that seemed crowded. The general direction was eastward. They did stop by a fountain, one that Kharl had not visited before, and drank. The water helped Kharl some, but Jeka looked pale and drawn, more so than earlier.

As they paused in an alley entrance, Kharl glanced at the cross street. Jeka was turning onto one of the older streets in upper Brysta, where large houses had been set within twenty cubits of the street itself, with ancient brick sidewalks, The yellow bricks were worn and, in some places, had been replaced with more reddish bricks. In other spots, there were just muddy gaps. The dwellings remained imposing two- and three-story edifices, but Kharl could sense the feeling of time and wear.

"Not far . . ." she said in a low voice. "Past the next street, on the right side."

The next block had slightly larger dwellings, but they seemed less well kept—and older—and several had iron fences, and a few had iron-banded doors and shutters.

Jeka suddenly stiffened, then sprinted away from Kharl, moving faster than he'd ever seen her move. She dashed down the street, then turned in at a high wooden gate in the middle of a short stone wall. The gate opened as she neared. A guard in burgundy stepped outside and closed the gate, stationing himself directly in front of the closed gate.

Stunned into momentary stiffness and silence, Kharl drew back into the shaded part of the alley. Trying to grasp what had happened, he stood close to the brick wall that enclosed either a courtyard or a garden. Where he was would have been in the shadow cast by the wall and the dwelling to the left of where he stood, except that the western sky was now completely cloud-covered. After a moment, Kharl shook his head, trying to clear his mind. Then, he bent forward and peered around the corner.

The guard did not even look in Kharl's direction.

The cooper straightened. Now what? What could he do?

He had to do something. For eightday after eightday, he'd just tried to survive, and one of the few who had helped was Jeka. Knowing what he knew about the wizard, he just couldn't walk away. And he couldn't wait. Not with what had happened to the other girls.

Taking a firmer grip on the staff, he edged out of the alley and began to hobble down the irregular stone walk flanking the narrow street. The wind had picked up, out of the west, and the clouds had thickened, but no rain was falling.

As he made his way in the direction of the guard, Kharl was glad he had brought the staff.

The guard watched, bored, but cautious, as Kharl hobbled toward him.

Kharl halted, a good four cubits back from the man. "A copper, ser . . . a copper for a poor man . . . just a copper." He leaned on the staff and took a step sideways, a step that brought him nearer to the brawny guard.

"Be on your way, fellow." The guard turned, catlike.

"A copper . . .? Surely, you can spare a copper?" Kharl asked, as he took a step forward and paused. He could sense some of the white fog around the guard.

"Out of here!" The guard reached for his blade.

Kharl brought the staff up from below, a lesson he'd learned years before, and never forgotten.

The blade went flying. The guard gaped, but only for an instant before the iron-banded end of the staff slammed into his gut. As the man doubled over, Kharl used his two-handed grip to bring the other end into the man's temple. The unseen whiteness around the guard vanished.

A rasping sound followed the collapse of the first guard. Then the gate burst open, and a second guard came charging out, his blade out, glistening in the flat light. Kharl brought the staff into his ready position, noting that the guard's blade was more of a bronzed white than the silver gray he'd expected and seen on occasion when bravos had flashed theirs on the streets of Brysta.

As he struck with the longer staff, Kharl also wondered how the wizard's guards could carry blades, since the wizard wasn't a lord or a merchant. He supposed Lord West would either make an exception for a wizard or just look the other way.

The second guard parried Kharl's first thrust, but had to back up from the force of the blow, dealt by a staff that felt more solid than mere wood. There was little enough space between the open gate and the wall, and Kharl slammed the staff into the guard's knee. The man staggered, but tried to bring his blade around.

The move was too late, and Kharl hit hard enough that he could feel something snap in the man's shoulder area. He didn't wait, but struck again . . . and again.

Then he stood there, dumbly, for a moment, trying to catch his breath, as he looked at the two immobile forms on the stones.

After another series of gasping breaths, he lurched through the open gate and up the three steps onto a small porch just large enough to shelter three or four people from the rain while waiting for entry. He turned the antique brass lever handle, and the door opened.

Kharl was only halfway through the doorway when he heard hurried steps and saw a tall figure stop at the back of the wide, deep, and dim foyer. The ragged cooper could sense the cloud of that same unseen whiteness, and threw the staff up in front of him, even before the wizard flung a burst of whitish red fire at him.

The fire cascaded away from the staff—mostly. Some flame flared against Kharl's left leg, but he kept the staff up as he took two steps forward, ignoring the searing pain.

Another firebolt flashed toward Kharl, running up his left arm, hotter than the coals of the forge, hot enough to bring up patches of flame on the ragged cloak.

Charging forward through the pain and the heat, and the smell of burned hair, Kharl thrust the ironbound staff right into the wizard's midsection. For an instant, flame flew in all directions, but not at Kharl. The wizard's mouth dropped open.

Before the wizard could recover, Kharl reversed the staff and tried to bring the other end against the other's jaw and neck. While the blow was not terribly strong, it was enough to jar the wizard and allow Kharl to advance with another blow.

In moments, the wizard collapsed.

Kharl drove one end of the staff straight down into the center of his chest. Ribs and bones cracked, and the wizard went limp, lifeless.

Kharl stood there, stupidly, looking at the figure on the floor. The dark hair turned white. The smooth skin wrinkled, then turned whitish yellow, tightening around the skull. The hair became more wispy, then vanished, as a skull replaced the face that had been there moments before. Before Kharl could even swallow more than once, all that remained of the wizard were his garments and a pile of whitish dust that, in turn, began to vanish.

Kharl stepped past the clothes and to the first door on the left, polished oak that had aged into a deep gold, with dark grain lines. He opened the door gingerly. The chamber beyond, some sort of sitting room, was empty. Kharl closed the door and stepped past the archway to the dining area, also empty.

He hurried through the entire first level, but it was uninhabited, and he struggled up the stairs all too conscious of the growing pain in his arm and leg. Outside, thunder rumbled, and he could hear the patter of raindrops. He just wished that it had started to rain earlier.

In the first small bedchamber at the top of the wide and ancient oak stairs, Jeka lay on the bed, her eyes wide. One wrist was tied to the bedpost on the left side, and a coil of rope lay on a coverlet that was a dull green and so old that Kharl could not make out the pattern on the fabric. He moved around the bed, toward the side where Jeka's hand was tied. Her eyes did not follow him, nor did she offer any sound or movement, still staring sightlessly at the ceiling.

He fumbled with the rope, trying to hurry, but finding the knot difficult with only one hand. Jeka did not move when he untied the one bound wrist.

Kharl doubted that he could carry Jeka and the staff, and he feared that if he touched her with it, she would collapse again.

"Stand up," he ordered her quietly.

Jeka stood.

"Follow me."

He hobbled down the stairs. Jeka followed, woodenly. Kharl didn't even try to find a rear door. He just wanted them out of the dwelling as quickly as possible.

Outside, the wind was gusting, and scattered sheets of rain swept around them as they stepped out of the gate. Unlike the wizard's, the bodies of the guards remained right where they had fallen.

"Murder! Someone's murdered!" came a call from somewhere.

Kharl ignored that, too, and half trotted, half hobbled, not a counterfeited hobble, but one from the pain in his leg, toward the alley. Each step also stabbed through his left arm. There was no one in the alley, and another gust of wind blasted over them, rustling the graying leaves of the trees surrounding the ancient dwellings on both sides of the alley.

Kharl and Jeka managed three blocks before Kharl slowed to a true hobble, finally turning out of the last alley and onto Gemstone Road. Just after they turned the corner, they found themselves less than a rod from a Watchman on patrol.

"You!" snapped the Watchman. "What are you doing here?"

"Just a poor man, ser . . . a poor man . . . my boy, ser, he's not right . . . ran off he did, and I've just gotten him . . ."

Truncheon in hand, the Watchman looked at Kharl, then at Jeka.

Jeka did not look at the Watchman, but remained standing beside Kharl.

"Does he speak, fellow?"

"Sometimes, ser . . ." Kharl looked at Jekat. "Can you tell the man your name, Jekat?"

"Jekat." The two syllables were uninflected, dull, and she continued to look straight ahead.

The Watchman studied Jeka and then Kharl. He shook his head. "On your way! Away from decent folk. And make it quick!"

"Yes, ser . . . yes, ser . . . thank you, ser . . ." Kharl whined.

He just hoped that they didn't run into more Watchmen or, worse, Egen, although he suspected the lord's son might not even recognize him any longer. Not unless they held him and stripped him and found the scars on his back.

The rain began to fall more heavily, and by the time they were back in the serviceway beside the rendering wall, both Kharl and Jeka were soaked through. The rain had come too late to help Kharl with the wizard, but it might have helped them escape.

Kharl took a deep breath. Despite the chill of the rain, the staff continued to feel warm to Kharl's hands. He looked at Jeka.

"Climb over the wall and wait."

She did, and he followed, laboriously, and with inadvertent tears streaming down his face. Every movement sent stabs of pain through his injured arm and leg.

Only when they were under the roof, such as it was, did he touch the staff to Jeka.

She collapsed.

Then he eased her into her hidey-hole, pulling off her wet cloak, but not more, and wrapping her in drier woolen rags. Then, in turn, he collapsed against the stone wall, just sitting there, breathing deeply, and wondering what he had done.

He knew why—but not how.

XXXVII

Sevenday was cool and cloudy, even at dawn, but the clouds were high. Kharl thought it was unlikely there would be rain. For that he was grateful as he sat against the stone wall and checked his wounds. Three sets of half-scabbed and oozing lines ran from the knee to just above Kharl's boot tops on his left leg. A shorter trio of lines ran between Kharl's elbow and shoulder, also on his left arm. The pain from the night before had faded into a dull aching in both his injured leg and arm, unless he moved suddenly, then it sharpened.

Kharl still did not understand exactly what had happened. He knew that he had fought well enough to disable the guards, but he doubted that he had struck hard enough to kill them; and he certainly had not struck the wizard hard enough to stun him—yet he had. Or was Kharl deceiving himself? Had he really used that much force? He wasn't sure he'd ever know. What he did know was that, if he couldn't find a friendly ship soon, he needed another way to get out of Brysta. All around him bodies continued to mount, and if Egen ever suspected that Kharl was alive in Brysta and had killed his wizard, there would be more Watchmen looking everywhere.

He glanced up to find Jeka sitting on the edge of the hidey-hole ledge, studying him. While there were dark circles under her eyes, her face was not so drawn as the day before.

"How are you feeling?" he asked.

"You came after me."

Kharl nodded, not knowing exactly what to say.

"You killed the wizard."

He nodded again. "I was lucky."

"You were brave."

"I'm not brave." How could he explain that he wasn't, that he'd just had to try, because it might have been the only chance left in his life to try to help someone who had helped him? He looked at Jeka carefully.

Her face was still pale. "I've got a few coppers. I'm going with you to the lower market. You need to eat."

"You shoulda taken coins from the wizard."

"I was more interested in getting us out of there before anyone found us. Coins don't do much good if they hang you."

"Coulda grabbed 'em without stopping."

"*You* could have," Kharl said. "I'm not that good. Besides . . ." He paused and offered a grin. "Wasn't that what got you in trouble with the wizard in the first place?"

"Yeah . . ." Jeka looked away slightly, then back. "But if he was dead . . ."

"If there were coins missing, the Watch might be looking for us a lot more. This way . . . the wizard's dead. So are his guards, and there's a rope tied to a bedpost. No wizard's going to kidnap a ragged urchin everyone thinks is a boy. Clearly . . ." Kharl paused. He hoped it was clear. "The wizard kidnapped the wrong person and paid for it."

"That's what you hope."

"You think Egen is going to believe that a beggar and an urchin killed two guards and a wizard—and didn't take a thing?" countered Kharl.

"Probably not," Jeka agreed.

"Now . . . let's go get something to eat."

"I could do it myself."

"You aren't going alone."

"You got hurt. Maybe you shouldn't walk that far."

"We both got hurt. Besides, I can limp for real."

Jeka smiled.

Kharl stood. He would take the staff.

XXXVIII

Fog finally rolled in early on eightday, sometime well before Kharl woke. The air was cold and clammy. Even his hair was damp. He glanced toward the canvas that covered Jeka's hidey-hole, hoping she was warm enough. He stood quietly, trying to stretch out sore muscles without pulling the scabs on his injured leg and arm. The burns weren't deep, but at times they were painful, and doubtless would remain so for days.

The *Seastag* hadn't tied up in the harbor by sunset the night before, and with the fog, wasn't likely to in the next day. It could be eightdays before Hagen's ship showed up, and there wasn't even any certainty that Kharl could buy or beg his way aboard. Even if he did, what about Jeka? Sooner or later, she'd run into something she couldn't handle. What could he do for her?

He laughed silently, ruefully. He couldn't even solve his own problems, and he thought he could do something for Jeka, an urchin whose only skills were cadging food? But were they? She'd mentioned once that she'd been a weaver.

Kharl frowned, thinking.

He was still thinking about it a glass later, when he slipped out of the serviceway, the dark staff in his hand. Jeka was still dozing. He'd listened to Jeka enough to know that the market was dangerous, even for her at times, and there were few he could trust in buying or cadging food. But he wanted to do his share, and with the wizard gone, he could try the White Pony.

With the fog covering Brysta, the Watch wasn't likely to be able to follow him, although he doubted that they were all that interested in a ragged beggar. He walked slowly, trying not to stretch his left leg too much. The fog was so thin at times that Kharl could see almost a hundred cubits, and then so thick moments later that he could scarcely glimpse the tip of the staff he carried. He made his way southward until he reached Copper Road, where he paused.

He heard heavy steps, close by, and he ducked into the alley and flattened himself against the wall as the two members of the Watch walked down Copper Road toward the harbor.

"... cold day ..."

"... just the fog ... always have hot and cold days in midfall ..."

Kharl waited for the two to go on, but they stopped opposite the alley.

"... say that fog makes it harder for the white wizards ..."

"... you really think someone killed Hanryl? All they found was his garments."

"... two dead guards."

"... had their blades out. Clubbed ... couldn't have happened without wizardry. Lord Egen's worried ... thinks there's another wizard loose, stronger ..."

"Long as they fight each other ... don't much care."

"Better get on over to Cargo Road ..."

Kharl waited until the footsteps had long died away before heading toward the White Pony, where he hoped that Enelya would accord him the same courtesy as she did Jeka.

XXXIX

In the late afternoon, from the point of rock north of the slateyard, Kharl watched as the *Seastag* maneuvered toward the outermost pier. More than an eightday had passed since he had managed to rescue Jeka from the wizard, and, every day, he had checked the harbor, but few vessels had entered, although he had seen Lord West's gunboats more than a few times.

He took a last look at the Austran vessel, sails furled and using her steam engine and paddle wheels to move toward the pier, before he began to walk southward toward the piers, his eyes open for the Watch. It would probably take him several glasses to circle the harbor to the piers from where he was, but Hagen spent at least three days in Brysta.

By the time Kharl had made his way past the warehouses, avoiding two harbor posts of the Watch, and reached the pier holding the Austran ship, several wagons had already appeared and were being readied to take cargo about to be off-loaded.

Kharl eased out along the pier, moving from unused bollard to bollard until he was almost at the stern of the *Seastag*. Then he watched for a time as palleted bundles were winched up from the center hold. Hagen stood on the poop deck watching.

After several loads filled the first wagon, the winching stopped.

Kharl slipped forward until he was on the pier, just below the captain. "Hagen!" Kharl hissed.

The master of the *Seastag* glanced down, frowning as he took in Kharl.

"It's Kharl, the cooper."

For a moment, Hagen studied Kharl. "What happened to you?"

"Could I work a passage to Austra?"

"Work a passage? What happened to you?" repeated Hagen, as his eyes continued to study the ragged figure.

"Lord's son doesn't exactly like me. Doubled my tariffs twice over. No way I could pay that. Lost the cooperage. Lost most everything." All of what Kharl said was true, but he dared not be more truthful.

"You look that way."

"I can still work. Carpenter's assistant until you make landfall in Austra?"

"I just came from there. I won't be making landfall there for half a season.

"Could you use a carpenter's assistant for half a season?"

Hagen glanced down the pier, then back toward Kharl. "What about your boys?"

"One left to be an apprentice ship's carpenter on the *Fleuryl*. The other's with Charee's sister. She said I had no business raising Warrl. He agreed. He'd even written her . . ."

Hagen fingered his chin. "I don't know . . ."

"I know how to work. You know that."

"You look . . ."

"Disguise," Kharl admitted. "I don't want anyone to see me. You can understand that. I'll come aboard in a good tunic and trousers."

"I don't know. Been a hard trip already."

"You can't get a good worker for less."

"Passage is about all I can afford, Kharl."

"That's all I'm asking."

Hagen frowned. "Suppose . . . I suppose."

"I'll be back later tonight with my gear. Would that be all right?"

"How much gear?"

"Very little. Some clothes, a pack. No tools."

Hagen shook his head. "Hate to see a man so down on his luck."

"I'll be fine once I'm away from Brysta."

"We'll be here in port almost an eightday."

"I'll stay on board. Give you an extra body to help load and unload."

The captain laughed. "For that, I could even pay you bottom level."

"I won't object." Kharl smiled. "Later tonight?"

"I'll tell the deck watch to get me."

"Thank you." Kharl nodded, then hurried down the pier. He had more than a few loose ends he wanted to tie up, and he wanted to get back before Hagen had a chance to change his mind, although he didn't think Hagen was that kind of man. Still, he had a lot to do, including trying to do something for Jeka. What he had in mind might not work . . . but it was all he had been able to come up with, and he had to try.

On his way back to the walled hideout, Kharl stopped by the fountain and, when no one was too close, washed up as he could, removing the worst of the dirt and grime.

Still, for all his concerns about Jeka, she was not between the walls when Kharl returned. He hoped she would not be too long in returning. In the meantime, he rummaged through his pack until he found the old scissors. By feel, he slowly trimmed his beard and mustache, making sure that it was shorter and more rounded than it had been before.

Then he dressed in his spare tunic and trousers. He hoped that he could get the dirt and soil out of the clothes he had been wearing, which he folded and put into his pack.

"Well . . . you're looking good." Jeka stood at the foot of the wall. "Are you going somewhere?"

"The ship I was waiting for is here."

"Goin' to miss you," Jeka said warily, her eyes avoiding Kharl's.

Despite the stench of the hidey-hole, and the dirt, Kharl realized he was going to miss Jeka as well. "I'll miss you, but . . ." He shook his head. "Can't stay here. You know that. Sooner . . . later, Egen'd find me."

"You can go, be a cooper anywhere. Me . . . ?" She spread her hands.

"You were a weaver once, you said?" Kharl asked.

"It was a long time ago."

"Were you good at it?"

"Light-fired good, Ma said. So did Hunat, but he had three sons and a daughter there."

Kharl nodded to himself, then eased his fingers into the pouch he'd replaced around his neck and slipped out a silver. He handed it to her. "This might help."

"You had silvers?" Jeka looked at the coin. "Had this, and you stayed here?"

"Know anyplace I'd have been any safer?" he asked. "With Egen wanting my head?"

The trace of a smile crossed her lips. "You got more alley-smarts than you let on."

"Come on . . ." He pulled his pack into place and arranged the ragged cloak over both tunic and pack. Then he picked up the staff.

"Where we goin'?"

"To see a man. He's a good man. The only one who helped me and stood by me." Who was still alive—but Kharl wasn't about to say that.

"Why . . . ?"

Kharl took her arm. "We don't have that much time."

Jeka followed Kharl over the wall and out into the serviceway, clearly reluctant, and then along the alleys and cross streets until they were in the alley paralleling Crafters' Lane—the alley on the south side, not the one on the north that ran behind the cooperage. In time, they came to the rear door of Gharan's shop.

Kharl glanced around, then drew back the ragged hooded cloak enough to reveal his face and the better tunic underneath. He rapped on the door.

Amyla opened it. Her eyes widened.

"Get Gharan. I won't be a moment."

After a long look at the cooper, Amyla stepped back, leaving the door slightly ajar.

Gharan appeared instantly. "Kharl . . ." He looked down the alley, then back at the cooper.

"There's no one out here. Not now. You've stood up for me, and you've been honest," Kharl said. "I'm leaving Brysta, but I have a favor to ask—not for me."

Gharan looked from Kharl to Jeka, quizzically.

"Jekat isn't Jekat, exactly. She's Jeka, and an orphan. She's also a good weaver." Kharl fumbled at the pouch around his neck and under his undertunic, then handed three silvers to Gharan. "I'll pay you to try her as a helper or an apprentice for two eightdays. You like what she does, then you keep her on. You don't, at least try to find her a place."

Gharan looked to Jeka again. "Where are you from?"

"Sagana."

"Why didn't you stay there?"

"I couldn't. Hunat had three sons and a daughter, and the tariff farmer took everything when Ma died, wanted to indenture me to a pleasure house."

Gharan winced, then looked at Kharl. "Two eightdays' trial. There is a chance."

"Say she's a distant cousin." Kharl turned to Jeka. "You stay here now. You don't need anything back there." He handed her two silvers. "These are for decent clothes for you." He straightened. "I'd better go."

He stepped back, leaving Jeka standing there with Gharan, then ducked back along the alley, almost at a run, before anyone could say anything. He did not slow down until he was several blocks away. He forced himself not to look back.

He reached the pier where the *Seastag* was docked just after sunset. He stopped to study the area around the ship, but saw no Watchmen. He slipped off the ragged cloak and rolled it up, slipping it next to an unused bollard, then straightened up and walked toward the Austran vessel.

The crewman at the top of the gangway watched as Kharl approached.

The cooper stopped at the foot of gangway. "I'm Kharl. Captain Hagen is expecting me . . ." He wasn't sure what else to say.

"He told me. You're to come aboard and wait here on the quarter-deck."

Kharl walked up the gangway and stepped down onto the deck planks, although he saw nothing that resembled a quarterdeck.

The sailor on watch looked strangely at the ironbound staff.

Kharl did not offer to explain.

The sailor took a tin whistle and piped something. Shortly, Hagen appeared with a muscular and blocky man who looked to be about Kharl's age.

Hagen smiled as he saw Kharl. "You look somewhat better than this afternoon." He turned to the other man. "Furwyl . . . we're payin' a debt and getting some help. Kharl here's a cooper. Lost his consort and his family, then his cooperage to the tariff farmer. Done a lot of good work for us in the past. Working his way to Austra, as assistant to the carpenter. Doesn't do rigging, but anything else you need him for."

Furwyl smiled. "He's a mite big to put up there."

"Furwyl is first mate, number two," Hagen said to Kharl. "You answer him and any of the other mates, like they were me. Mates are the ones with the vests, or the jackets with the stripes on the sleeves."

"Yes, ser."

"I'll need a moment more with Kharl, Furwyl. Then you can get him squared away in the fo'c's'le and take him down to the carpenter. I already told Tarkyn."

"Yes, ser."

"Oh, Furwyl . . . I think we'd better change the shore leave while we're here. It's too late for tonight, but from now on, I want the crew to go in pairs. Anyone who leaves alone, or returns alone, loses a silver. There's something going on. There's a renegade wizard loose—killed a white mage, one serving Lord West's youngest son. We don't want anyone tied up with that."

"The crew won't like that."

"Better that than no leave. We don't want to lose crew, and they don't want to end up dead or left here, either."

"Yes, ser." Furwyl stepped away, moving toward the bow along the pierside railing.

Hagen turned his attention on Kharl. "I made a quick trip to your cooperage. Someone else is there. He said he bought it at a tariff auction because you abandoned it. Why?"

"To stay alive," Kharl replied. "I stopped Lord West's son from forcing himself on my neighbor's daughter, and he had my Charee killed. He had the tariff farmer raise my levy to twelve golds, and had an assassin kill my neighbor because he testified for me before the justicers . . ."

Hagen winced. "I thought it might be something like that. You stay on board and out of sight when the port inspectors are around."

"I can do that."

"And you do whatever you're told by the mates, by Tarkyn—he's the carpenter—or by me."

"Yes, ser."

Hagen beckoned. "Furwyl . . . you can take him now."

As Kharl followed the first mate, Furwyl looked at the cooper. "You've made some of our hogsheads and barrels?"

"Yes, ser. Some of them."

"Wouldn't hurt Tarkyn to have some help. It's been a rough fall. In here." Furwyl gestured to the open hatchway on the starboard side, leading into the forecastle.

Kharl had to duck as he entered the passageway, dimly lit by a single lamp in a bulkhead bracket. A closed hatch was on the right, an open hatch straight ahead.

Furwyl gestured to the closed hatch. "Women's crew quarters. Off-limits at all times. You'll be in the main section forward. Even have an extra bunk or so."

Most of the bunk spaces were empty, except for three. In two, the sailors were sleeping. The third sailor looked at the mate and Kharl.

"Kharl's the assistant to the carpenter," Furwyl explained.

The sailor nodded and rolled over.

The bunk spaces were about four cubits long, two high, and two deep, set against the hull. Each was painted white, and there was a thin mattress with a single blanket on each. Between each set of bunks were two open spaces with nets.

The mate pointed to the last bunk on the port side. "That one'll be yours. Your gear goes in the bin at the foot of your bunk. Have to lash that staff away down in the carpenter shop."

The bin was certainly large enough to hold Kharl's pack, but as he looked around the triangular space, he could see why the staff would not fit anywhere. He stepped forward and put his pack in the bin, then tied the net in place.

Furwyl turned, expecting Kharl to follow. The cooper did, back outside, then into the passageway on the starboard side, and down a ladder one level, and forward into a narrow space where a sailor in gray sat on a stool carving something out of what looked to be a white bone. He looked up, but did not rise.

"Tarkyn," the first mate said, "this is Kharl. The captain said he'd told you."

"Didn't ask me, ser. Told me." The carpenter was a good decade older than Kharl, grizzled, and white-haired, and he wore a gray shirt, not either tunic or undertunic, and matching gray trousers. He surveyed Kharl. "Least he's no youngster."

Furwyl nodded to Kharl. "I'll leave you two." He looked to Tarkyn. "Captain said you could store his staff here. It won't fit in the fo'c's'le. Hope he doesn't need it, but we will be sailing offshore of Renklaar."

"We'll find a place."

Furwyl left.

Tarkyn looked at the staff. "You from Recluce?"

"No. The staff came from a blackstaffer. It's useful in strange places."

"You can rack it there." Tarkyn pointed at the overhead wood bin that stretched aft.

Kharl eased the staff into the long wood bin on one side, carefully rearranging two timbers so that it fit snugly.

Tarkyn looked hard at Kharl. "You after my spot?"

Kharl laughed. "No. I offered my services to help pay my passage. I'm a cooper—"

"Captain told me that. You a good cooper?"

"One of the better ones."

"Why you here?"

"The Lord's tariff farmer took a dislike to me. I couldn't come up with twelve golds in four eightdays. Not when the tariff had only been three golds the year before."

"One thing about being a ship's carpenter . . . don't have to worry about such. Worry about pirates, storms, spoiled food, broken spars— but not tariff farmers." Tarkyn laughed. "Be here after morning muster, and I'll show you around. See what you can do."

"Thank you."

"Don't thank me yet." Tarkyn looked down at the carving he held, barely illuminated by the bronze lamp, and lifted the knife. "See you first thing in the morning."

"I'll be here," Kharl promised, stepping back out of the carpenter shop. For all of Tarkyn's taciturn welcome, Kharl had sensed the basic soundness of the man, and the organization of the shop, from the wood set just so in the bins and bays to the tool chests that were care- fully stowed and restrained.

He climbed up the ladder, then back onto the main deck. After a moment, he climbed the forward ladder and walked to the base of the bowsprit. There he stood, at the railing on the seaward side, looking into the darkness ... wondering how he had ended up on the *Seastag* ... and where it would all lead.

After a time, he turned to view the lights of Brysta. He'd never thought of leaving the city where he'd been born. But then, he'd never thought that the city—or its rulers—would have cost him his consort, his family, his livelihood, then driven him out.

Looking at the scattered lights spread across the harbor front, and the low hills overlooking the harbor, he swallowed, feeling the lump in his throat, and his eyes began to burn.

XL

Kharl spent the first five days, when not sleeping or eating, either with the winch crew or in the carpenter shop. Adjusting to the in-port morning muster was easy enough; he'd always gotten up early anyway. Having regular meals turned out harder on his guts and system, much as he knew he needed them.

After testing Kharl on a few minor projects, such as replacing a smashed panel on an inside door-hatch and rebuilding a storm-damaged section of the poop deck rail, Tarkyn just asked if Kharl could do something. Most things he was asked to do, he could, and some, like turning a spar, were easy enough to pick up.

He had no idea about others, as when the carpenter had asked him how he'd reset the rudder posts.

"I suppose I could take it apart and learn," the cooper had offered, "but I don't know as you and the captain would wish that."

Tarkyn had laughed. "Wise man who knows what he can do. Wiser man who knows what he can't."

Kharl wasn't certain about that. He'd done a few things in the past eightdays he'd never believed he could have done, and, before that, he certainly would have told anyone that he couldn't have done them.

He'd not seen either Watch or harbor inspectors, but the Watch usually didn't patrol the piers, and the harbor inspectors were only interested in tariffs and quiet on the vessels tied to the piers—and the *Seastag* was a very quiet ship.

By late afternoon on threeday, all the outbound cargo had been loaded, and the hatches secured, with everything battened down. Then the steam engine had been fired up, and with a slapping *thwup, thwup*, the midships paddle wheels had begun to turn.

Kharl stood at the railing as the *Seastag* eased away from the pier, out into the harbor, then westward past the outer breakwater. He looked back at Brysta, the afternoon light illuminating the city in a golden glow, giving it a beauty he had not seen—or experienced—in recent seasons.

"You! Second carpenter!" called a voice.

Kharl turned at the voice, recognizing the third, a hard-faced wiry woman with short-cropped hair and broad shoulders. "Ser?"

"We'll be setting canvas once we clear. You're lead on the mainmast winch."

"Yes, ser." Kharl moved toward the winch. There he stood, waiting for orders, and looking back, wondering if he would ever see Nordla again, if he would ever want to, yet knowing that he would.

Carpenter

XLI

Thirteen days had passed since the *Seastag* had steamed out of Brysta and hoisted sail. Once well clear of Nordla, Hagen had shut down the steam engine to conserve coal. All thirteen days had seen very rough seas, except for the last few glasses, when the seas had begun to calm. Kharl hadn't realized how much continual work was required of a ship's carpenter, much of it while standing on a moving deck. Most of it was simple, in terms of craft, but necessary. He'd replaced railing spokes. He'd turned pulley brackets. He'd fashioned a replacement bar for the capstan, when the iron one had broken loose and rolled over the side during one of the heavier blows. He could have reinforced it with iron bands, but there was no forge available on the ship.

The cooper grinned at his recollection of Hagen's anger over that. The fourth mate—the bosun—had practically backed himself over the railing stepping away from the captain as Hagen berated the man for not making sure that the capstan locker had been secured for heavy weather.

It was near midday, and Kharl stood near the bow, just forward of the foremast, since the *Seastag* was only twin-masted, but full-rigged, a brig's rigging on a full ship's hull, spread to allow engine and paddle wheels midships. He was taking a break from the pedal-powered lathe in the carpenter's shop and enjoying the fresh air. Unlike some of the newer sailors, the weather hadn't bothered Kharl, and he found that merely working, eating, and sleeping on a regular schedule had improved both his attitude and his health. The thin mattress felt almost luxurious after nearly a season on rags and hard ground, and even the ship's food wasn't that bad, although the fruit was dried and limited, and the biscuits that went with every meal tended to get rock-hard the moment they cooled.

"Land ahead!" came down the call from the lookout.

"Land where?" called back Furwyl, who had the con, on the platform before the steersman.

"Ten off the starboard bow!"

Within moments, Kharl could feel the *Seastag* turning to starboard. He couldn't see what the lookout had, not yet, and he headed back down to the carpenter shop.

Tarkyn stepped back from the lathe. "You're younger. You can finish."

Kharl took the turning chisel from the older man. "The lookout sighted land."

"Thought as much," replied Tarkyn. "Shifted course."

"We came starboard. It looked like we were headed too far south."

"Not too far if the captain could see land. Means he was right within fifty kays after fifteen hundred on the open sea. Not many captains that good."

"Do you mind if I watch as we come into port?" Kharl adjusted the foot pedal and began pumping, so that the spruce in the lathe began to spin.

"No. Not after you finish that gaff. Bemyr'll want you up on the winch crew anyway."

Kharl didn't rush the turning. There was no point in spoiling the wood, and it would be a good glass, if not two or three, before the *Seastag* came anywhere near the shore. When he did finish, he handed the smoothed gaff to Tarkyn.

"Not bad."

Kharl took out one of the rags and cleaned off the lathe, then got out the small broom and the handled flat scoop. He swept up the shavings and put them in the burn box, where the cook would collect them later. By the time he had finished, Tarkyn was back working on his scrimshaw, what would be a full-rigged ship carved into a red deer antler.

"How long have you been working on that?" the cooper asked.

"This voyage and the last." Tarkyn looked toward the open hatch.

Kharl took the hint and slipped out of the carpenter shop and up to the bow. At times, the carpenter didn't want to talk at all—not to Kharl.

The ship was headed due north, and Kharl could smell the smoke from the engine being fired up. The third mate was barking commands at the riggers, terms Kharl didn't understand, except in general terms, naming sails to be furled, and those to be left in place. He had picked up some of the names, but he had no idea which sail the mizzen skysail was, nor the fore topgallant. So he just stayed out of the way near the bow and watched as the *Seastag* drew nearer to the coast. Before long, he could make out a long black line above the water—a breakwater. Hagen, on the poop, brought the ship more to the west.

The third, her voice hard and sharp, issued another series of commands, and the rest of the sails were furled as the paddle wheels began to move. The *Seastag* moved slowly northward, then hove to off the southern breakwater, waiting, the paddle wheels turning just enough to keep the ship with bare steerageway.

In less than a fraction of a glass, a pilot boat steamed up. The boat kept perfect station on the *Seastag* while the ladder went over the side. Shortly, a man in blue trousers and jacket climbed aboard. Furwyl met him on the deck and escorted him back to the poop, where he stood beside the captain and began to give orders to the helm.

The *Seastag* crept forward, wallowing slightly before gaining true headway, then picked up speed to perhaps three kays, Kharl judged, moving toward a channel marked with red and black buoys. The channel ran almost due east between the two long breakwaters of black stone. The breakwaters rose a good ten cubits above the water and seemed to be at least three times that wide, with the flat surface of a lord's causeway.

"Never seen breakwaters like that . . ." murmured Hodal, one of the few deckhands who was actually taller and broader than Kharl—and a good fifteen years younger.

"Lots of things you'll see here you never saw before," someone else replied. "Nothing like Nylan. Nothing nowhere."

"Winch crew! Stand by!" ordered Bemyr, the bosun.

Kharl moved aft to join the others, but continued to watch as the *Seastag* entered the harbor, not all that much larger than the one at Brysta. The difference was that there were piers and more piers, all of them stone, with clean lines and no signs of missing mortar, seemingly in perfect repair, with timbered rails and hempen buffers.

"Is this part of Recluce called Nylan, or is it just the harbor?" Kharl asked Reisl, who was the closest of the winch crew to him.

"Who knows?" Reisl shrugged.

The bosun looked at Kharl. "The southern tip of Recluce is called Southpoint. The port here is Nylan, named after some old hero. He was a smith, I think. Anyway, we've been coming north past the point 'fore coming inshore. That's 'cause the harbor's on the west side, north of the southern tip. Pretty big port, more than a half score piers for deep-ocean traders, a few more for coasters from Candar and fishing vessels. Most of the time, it's crowded."

"They got girls there?" asked the fresh-faced Wylat.

"The tavern maids are prettier here than anyplace you'll ever be. And all you can do is look." Bemyr laughed.

"Don't believe that," came a voice from the other side of the winch crew.

"You better believe it. This is the place that flattened Fairven some fifty–sixty years back. They got more mages here in Nylan than in the whole rest of the world. You see all that black stone out there? They got ships that move faster than the fastest war-steamers out of Hamor, and half the time you can't see 'em. They got patrollers on every street. You won't lose any coin to brigands there, and you'll get fair measure for your coin. But you can't buy a woman for all the golds the captain's got."

"You can't?"

As the *Seastag* eased past the inner end of the breakwaters, Kharl's attention drifted from the comments about women to the harbor and the city to the north of it. Outside of a few blocks immediately north of the harbor, the city was built on a long sloping hill, an almost symmetrical ridge that was more than two kays from the harbor to the crest and nearly twice that wide. The dwellings and the buildings he could see were constructed of a blackish stone, with dark roofs, and the streets were wide and straight.

"Anywhere you can buy a good woman . . . a woman, anyway," another crew member said.

"Except on board," cracked the third mate from across the deck.

"Can't buy women in Nylan," stated Bemyr. "Better not try, either. Now . . . once in a while, one'll take a liking to a sailor . . . and that's something. Only knew of two fellows that happened to . . ." Bemyr broke off. "Enough of that. They've already got the wagons moving down the pier. They move cargo fast here."

"Lines out!" ordered Furwyl. "Tighten up forward! Bring her in!"

The *Seastag*'s paddle wheel slowed to a stop.

"Double up!" ordered Furwyl. "Bosun!"

Bemyr put his whistle to his mouth and blew two shrill blasts. "Before long, cargo hatch'll be off. Winch crew in place! Step lively, now!"

Kharl took his place and waited.

XLII

For the next two days, Kharl labored as a deckhand, shifting cargo, moving pallets. Not until midafternoon of the third day was he granted shore leave, along with Tarkyn and half the rigging crew. He had managed, with some difficulty, to wash his once-better outfit clean, but a close look would have revealed muted stains in the tunic. He also had the staff, which he felt he needed to return, although he wasn't quite sure where to take it, only that it had come from Recluce, and he thought Jenevra had mentioned Nylan.

He stood on the section of the deck behind the gangway, in that ill-defined area that was called the quarterdeck, along with the others going on shore leave, sunlight and shadows from the masts and rigging falling across them.

"Don't be too long, or too late," Bemyr told those going on shore leave. "You don't need a friend with you, not here, but be careful. Captain says we sail just after dawn. That's when the winds turn and blow out of the northeast."

Kharl stepped back and let the younger men surge down the gangway.

As the cooper waited, the captain appeared, looking at the staff. "I'd forgotten that. Where did you get it?"

"It belongs here. I need to return it."

"That's probably a very good idea. Enjoy yourself."

"Yes, ser," Kharl said politely, but Hagen had already stepped away.

Kharl looked around as he walked down the gangway onto the pier. All the piers were of dressed stone, and the stonework was simple but flawless, the joins between stones as tight as those of his best barrels, and with only the thinnest lines of mortar.

The pier itself was almost clear of wagons, except for one last one holding barrels, probably of provisions. Kharl walked past it, then stopped at the end of the pier and looked up the long, inclined hillside that held most of the city. Even though it was well past harvest, everything seemed either black or green. The streets and even the one alley he could see to his left were all paved in a dark gray stone that was almost black. The late-afternoon light glinting off it made it look gray, but as he looked closer, he could see that it was indeed black. In fact, he hadn't realized just how black, and how pervasive the black stone truly was. All of the buildings, all of the dwellings, were of the same black stone, and the roofs of the buildings and dwellings were of a stone that looked like split black slate.

There were trees, tall and green, and open areas of grass, also green at a time of year when most grass in Nordla was brown. The buildings and dwellings were set in their own greenery, and placed much farther apart than in Brysta, spreading the city out and giving a feeling of spaciousness.

Kharl looked at the open area, a rectangular paved square, separating the piers from the warehouses and buildings, then picked the widest-looking boulevard and walked toward it, his staff in hand. He stopped at the corner where it intersected the square and walked toward a man in a black-and-tan uniform, a patroller, from what Bemyr had said. "Could you help me? I'm looking for the Brethren."

"All of Nylan's got Brethren. Any ones special?" The man's accent was so clipped it took Kharl several moments to piece together what the fellow had actually said.

"The ones . . . the place that sends people to other lands . . ."

"Where they train the dangergelders, you mean? Up the hill, almost three kays, and there's a building on the left, with a green triangle on a stone marker outside. That's the place. Only one with the green triangle."

"Thank you."

The patroller nodded in response.

As he continued uphill, Kharl noted something else. Almost all the buildings were but one story, and most of those near the harbor looked newish, certainly not more than a generation old, and some more recently constructed than that. Yet the port had a feeling of being much older.

He had walked no more than a block when he realized that several passersby and others in the street had taken a quick glance at him and the staff, and looked away. No one said anything, but they definitely looked at him strangely. Because of his clothing, not that of a typical sailor? Or the staff? Or both?

He was breathing harder by the time he reached his destination, nearly a glass later. The structure was more than just a building. From what he could tell, looking over the low stone wall at the green grass and neatly trimmed hedges and well-kept flowers, he was looking at an estate.

Finally, he stepped through the two black stone pillars that served as gateposts, although there was no actual gate, and made his way to the covered porch and the doorway beyond. After a momentary hesitation, he rapped on the door.

Shortly, the door opened, and a young woman stood there. She wore gray all over, except for a shimmering black scarf and a silver pin on the collar of her tunic. The pin was a lightning bolt crossed with a staff. "Might I help you?" Again, the accent was strange, but understandable.

"I hope so," Kharl said. "This staff . . . it's not mine . . . I didn't know what to do with it."

For the first time, the woman, who had been studying the cooper intently enough to make Kharl uneasy, actually looked at the staff. She frowned, briefly. "If you would come in, I think you should see Magister Trelyn." She held the black oak door open wider.

Kharl took the invitation and stepped inside, finding himself in an upper foyer, separated from the lower one by three black stone steps that ran the width of the foyer.

"There are benches below . . . if you would like to rest . . .?"

Kharl stepped down to the lower level and the benches set almost against each wall. His eyes were caught by a painting hanging over one of the benches. The woman portrayed wore black, and her hair was brown. Her eyes were black, and somehow very alive. She didn't look like anyone Kharl knew, yet she reminded him of Jenevra, the black-staffer.

He studied the walls, black oak panels set between heavy black oak timbers, and the floor, also of the black slate. Only the ceiling was light, a white plaster tinged bluish gray. There were three doors that led into other parts of the building. Two were closed, and the third was just ajar.

Kharl could hear voices.

". . . doesn't look like a dangergelder . . . accent . . . but the staff . . . it's not corrupted . . . more ordered than it should be . . ."

". . . just have to see . . ."

Kharl turned and watched as the woman and a man dressed in dark,

dark gray appeared. His hair was silvered, but his face was that of a younger man. Kharl had the feeling that he was older than he looked. He wore black boots, well polished. Like the woman, he wore a silver collar pin, but his looked like a sprig of a plant crossed with a staff. The cooper also realized something else. Just as the wizard in Brysta had been surrounded by a whitish fog that Kharl had sensed more than felt, this man was surrounded by a blackness, a darkness, but the darkness didn't feel cold or evil. Instead, it felt almost warm . . . solid, like well-made tight cooperage.

"I'm Magister Trelyn." The magister smiled. "How could I help you?"

"The staff," Kharl said. "It's not mine. It belonged to a blackstaffer named Jenevra. I thought I should return it."

Trelyn frowned. "Could you tell me what happened to this black-staffer, and where it happened?"

"Her name was Jenevra, and she was from Recluce. She came to Brysta, she said, because she had to take a trip to learn something. She was attacked and beaten badly, and I took her into my shop." Kharl shrugged helplessly. "She was getting better, and was almost well. Then someone set a fire next door, and while I was helping fight it . . . she was killed. The justicers said my consort did it, and they hung her, but she was innocent."

"You left Brysta just to return this?"

Kharl laughed, almost harshly. "No. I left Brysta because, after they flogged me, and increased my tariffs so much that I could not pay them, someone murdered my neighbor, who was the only one who stood up for me against Lord West and his son. I went into hiding until I could get on a ship away from Nordla. The ship ported here, and I thought I should return the staff."

"Has it been the cause of your ill fortune?"

"No. I can't say it has. It wasn't mine. I had barely touched it when everything began to go wrong. I had to use it to save myself and someone else."

The magister nodded more. "Might I see it?"

Kharl might have balked at others touching it, although he could not have said why, but he readily handed it to the older magister. "Here."

Trelyn ran his fingers over the wood and the black iron, his eyes almost closed. After several moments, his eyes opened wide, and he studied Kharl intently. Then he handed the staff back to Kharl.

"It's not mine," Kharl said.

"It may have belonged to Jenevra, and we are sad to hear what happened to her, but it is now yours. It would be useless to anyone else, and it would have to be destroyed. That would not be good for you, either."

"Not good for me?" Kharl didn't want it destroyed, but it had not been his. "But . . . I'm just a cooper . . ."

Trelyn smiled, an expression almost sad. "One of the hardest tasks in life is to discover that we are more than we think we are. Whether you can discover truly what you are . . . that I cannot say, but you are more than a cooper."

Kharl smiled ruefully. "Always be a cooper, I think. Headed to Austra . . . in time."

"I did not say you were not a cooper," Trelyn said quietly, "but that you are, or could be . . . should be . . . more than that. If you have the courage to look into yourself. You have a great affinity for order, and for instilling order."

The words made Kharl uncomfortable, and he shifted his weight from one foot to the other. "I can't stay too long. My ship will be sailing."

"Not that soon," Trelyn observed.

"No," Kharl admitted.

"Were you younger and raised on Recluce, you might have been an engineer or an order-master. Even so . . . are people pleased with your barrels?"

"Always have been, those that buy 'em. Some don't, though."

"Those that did not and will not are likely not to be trusted. They avoid your work because it embodies order."

Kharl frowned, considering what the magister had said. It was true that those who bought his work and kept buying it over the years were those he knew were honest and trustworthy. He'd never looked at it that way, though. Was that why he had been having more and more trouble selling his barrels? Because there were fewer and fewer trustworthy souls in Brysta?

"It's a most disconcerting thought, is it not?" asked the magister. "That those who cannot be trusted do not trust those who produce truly ordered work."

"I hadn't thought of it that way before."

"If you wish to survive and prosper, you will need to think more along those lines," suggested Trelyn. "You will become more aligned with order, and unless your thoughts become equally attuned, your troubles will continue."

"My thoughts . . ."

"Thoughts always precede action, yours or the thoughts of another. If you attune yourself to order, you will find that life will be more rewarding."

"Not easier, though?"

"No," admitted the magister. "Life is seldom easy for those who embody order, although it would seem it should be. But then, what seems is not always what is."

"Why me?"

The magister smiled, warmly, then shrugged. "That I do not know. I do know that those who work with wood often understand order better, as do smiths. You do some of each, and that may be part of the answer. It may be that you are a cooper because that feels right to you."

Kharl's lips quirked. "What do you suggest?"

"Look beyond what you think you see. Learn new things. Reconsider old knowledge. Trust what you feel." Trelyn paused, then drew a book from his tunic. "This might also help."

Kharl took the book, opened the cover, then smiled and handed it back. "I did keep her book. I hope you don't mind."

"I thought you might have, but I wanted to make sure you had a copy. You may have to read it several times—or more. It sometimes helps to skip through it and read those passages that make the most sense at the moment. Dorrin wrote it most logically, but most of us are not that logical."

Somehow, those words relaxed Kharl. "Thank you." He glanced toward the door.

"Also," added Trelyn, "you can find those who understand order everywhere, not just on Recluce. In time, you might be one that others turn to."

"I've been having trouble just surviving." Kharl paused, and added, "Until an eightday ago, anyway."

"That was when you left your old life, I would guess, although sometimes the effects last for a long time. We often create part of our trouble by not wanting to accept who and what we are. You should try to understand yourself, as well as the world." Trelyn smiled again. "Those are really all I can offer in terms of words of wisdom, and I'm not certain that they work for everyone. I do hope they help you." Trelyn moved toward the door.

"Thank you." Kharl followed the magister.

"When you discover yourself, truly, you can return here, if you so wish," Trelyn added, as Kharl stepped through the door and out into the fall sunlight.

"Don't know as I'd want to, then," Kharl replied.

"That is often the way. For it, the world is a better place. Our hopes go with you."

As Kharl walked back down the wide and straight stone street, through a city far cleaner and better-smelling than Brysta, he pondered the magister's words, especially those about people not wanting to accept who they were. Hadn't he always accepted he would be a cooper? The magister had told him bluntly that he was more than that—but had not said what he was, only that Kharl had to discover it, and that it would be hard. Hard? Kharl laughed to himself. He'd already discovered that.

Kharl looked up, sensing something. On the other side of the street were two figures in black, one man and one woman. Both wore silver insignia on their collars, one that looked like a cog crossed with a staff. Like the magister, they held the unseen blackness, if not so deeply or warmly.

The man glanced sharply at Kharl, but the woman leaned toward him and whispered something. Then she looked to Kharl and smiled, saying, "Order always be with you."

What could he say back? After a moment, he replied with the only thing that came to mind, "And with you."

The two both nodded and continued onward, past Kharl and up the hill.

Kharl wondered why the woman had gone out of her way to offer the strange greeting, and what she had said to her companion.

Rather than going straight back to the *Seastag*, Kharl looked for somewhere to eat. He still had silvers left, and a handful of coppers, and after the ship's food, he wanted a good meal, perhaps the first one in a season.

The first inn—the Copper Kettle—he approached, while looking neat enough, and smelling clean enough, did not appeal to him, for reasons he could not have explained. He walked westward along a slightly narrower street, although one still broad by the standards of Brysta, and stopped abruptly at a smaller place, more like a tavern really. He went inside. The public room was not large, holding fewer than ten tables, with only two occupied, but that wasn't exactly unexpected in late afternoon.

A tall woman, broad, but not fat, wearing a dark green shirt and trousers with a spotless white apron, smiled at him. "Any table that's free."

Kharl moved toward a table in a corner, one that was bright from the late-afternoon light slanting through the unshuttered windows, but not painfully so. He leaned the staff into the corner, trying to keep it out of the way, and settled into the armless chair that allowed him to survey the room. In one way, there was nothing at all remarkable—nine round tables and chairs, wooden floors, white-plastered walls, bronze lamps in brackets on the walls. In another, it was all astounding. The tables were well crafted of red oak, covered in a hard finish, and they were clean. The same was true of the chairs. The floors were of wide golden oak planks, also finished with a smooth sort of varnish, Kharl judged, and without a speck of dirt or dust on them. The windows had glass, and the glass had been kept spotless. He'd never seen what might have been called a common eatery so clean.

"Do you know what you want?" asked the white-haired woman who had greeted him. Her eyes flickered to the staff, then back to Kharl.

"I don't even know what you have," he admitted.

"Not everything we usually do. Let's see. White fish or red fish, battered and fried. Always have a fish chowder. Also, we've got a quarter fowl, and chops. Chops might be a bit tough. All comes with mashed potatoes and fried pearapples, except the chowder, of course. Just bread. Fish is two coppers, fowl and chops three. Ale or wine is two, redberry one."

"What's the best?"

"Today . . . the white fish."

"I'll try it, with an ale." Kharl fumbled in his belt wallet.

"Pay when I bring the ale." She smiled and slipped away.

Kharl just watched her go, admiring her grace, even though he knew she was years older than he was.

She returned with the ale almost immediately, and Kharl placed the silver on the table. "Need some change."

"Where are you headed?" she asked as she deftly swept up the silver, then looked strangely at the Brystan coin, then at Kharl, before shrugging. "Silver's silver."

"It is," Kharl agreed. "Some things don't change. Lydiar, I think."

"Better there than Hamor." She smiled politely. "Do you know when you leave?"

"Tomorrow."

"You'll have good weather." With another smile she was gone.

Kharl sipped the ale, far better than any he could recall. Then, that might have been because it had been so long since he'd had good ale. As he took a second swallow, he thought over the servingwoman's questions. There was some sort of honest misunderstanding, he knew, and it centered on the staff. Did she think he was a blackstaffer, being sent out?

Jenevra had been young, but the woman hadn't seemed surprised at all. Did that mean that the Brethren or whoever ruled Recluce could send people out as blackstaffers at any age? He frowned. He should have asked more questions of Trelyn, but he just hadn't thought of them. He'd always been like that, not fully understanding things until much later, if then. That didn't seem to have changed. He took another sip of the ale, enjoying it.

When the server returned with his meal, set on a new-looking crockery platter, accompanied by a small basket of bread as well, she slipped six coppers onto the table.

"Thank you." Kharl left two coppers on the table. He hadn't even thought about coinage. He'd just discovered that silvers converted one for one, but coppers? Who knew? He supposed Tarkyn or the captain did, but he thought he ought to find out, before he ordered anything in Lydiar or anyplace else. He wasn't so sure the Lydians would be as accommodating as people in Recluce.

As the woman had promised, the fish was good—light and flaky under the crisp golden batter, and the potatoes were rich and filling, the pearapples a pleasing combination of tart and sweet. He left nothing—except the coppers.

When he stood to leave, the server smiled from across the room. "Best of fortune."

"Thank you."

Kharl didn't want to return to the ship, not immediately. So he kept walking. In time, he came to a square, except it wasn't a square, but a park, with trimmed hedges, and yellow and orange flowers, and stone walks amid the green grass, grass that was trimmed short. The trees were all evergreens, some of types Kharl had never seen. He stood on the street side of the black stone wall and watched as two boys and a girl played some sort of tag, with two adults looking on from a nearby stone bench.

After a time, he walked farther downhill toward the piers on the western side of the harbor. He was curious, because even with the sun about to set, and the light falling across the westernmost set of piers, a sort of shadow lay across them. Kharl could not make out any of the vessels, although he could see the ships at the other piers clearly, and there were no clouds in the sky.

When he neared the piers, he discovered several things. First, the street ended at a black stone wall, with a guard post in front of the open iron gate manned by two soldiers or marines in black uniforms. Second, the guards had weapons in racks that had to be rifles. He looked again. No, they weren't rifles, exactly, and their barrels were far too large. Third, he could see through the gate the late-day sunlight falling on the piers, yet there was a darkness that blocked any view of the ships.

Kharl knew that there was at least one vessel there; he could almost sense its solidity, but no masts extended above the ten-cubit-high wall. He immediately turned east, because the cross street in front of the piers also ended just to the west, with another black stone wall. He could sense the guards watching him, and he did not look back until the black wall ended—or rather made a right-angle turn harborward. He walked on another fifty cubits before turning.

The way the walls were set, there was no way to see what might be tied at the pier behind the walls, but whatever was tied there did not have masts that extended very high.

The guards and the walls suggested that this section of the harbor held the dreaded warships of Recluce, but if such warships were so fearsome, why were they being hidden? Was there something about them that the rulers of Recluce did not wish known? After a moment, he shrugged and continued walking along the edge of the harbor.

When he finally returned to the ship, after looking at shops, vessels from Hamor and Candar, as well as from Nordla and Austra, it was well into evening.

He took the staff back down to the carpenter shop. For the first time in days, Tarkyn wasn't there. Kharl replaced the staff in the bin and headed back toward the forecastle. He slowed as he passed the women's crew quarters, hearing voices ahead, then stopped just outside the hatch.

". . . tell you . . . something strange about him . . ."

". . . imagining things . . ."

". . . wasn't imagining . . . he's walking down the street, and two of those creepy types in black . . . they greet him . . . like he's one of 'em . . ."

"So? He works hard . . . doesn't slack, and keeps his mouth shut . . ."

". . . tell you . . . strange . . ."

". . . worry too much, Asolf . . . you drank too much, too. Get some shut-eye . . .

". . . tell you . . ."

"Sleep it off."

Kharl waited quietly for a time before entering the forecastle. When he did step in and begin to ready himself for sleep, both Asolf and whomever he had been talking to were asleep, as were about half the crew—those that were aboard.

Kharl lay back on the thin mattress, thinking. How could he discover how he might be more than just a cooper? By further reading of *The Basis of Order*? By looking more deeply into things?

After a time, he drifted into sleep.

XLIII

Is there a source—a wellspring—of order or of chaos? Can something exist without a source? And if there be such, what is indeed the wellspring of chaos? Or that of order? There is but one, for chaos can be said to be the wellspring of order, and order the wellspring of chaos. These are so because, for so long as there is life, neither chaos nor order can exist by itself for long without the other.

Yet for so long as there have been peoples upon the face of the world, there have been those who championed order over chaos, or chaos over order. There have been those who denied the power of one, or of both. All creatures that live are born, and birth is the triumph of life. All creatures, from the largest to the smallest, are brought low by death, and death is the triumph of chaos.

If all things that have been born were never to die, within generations the very earth would be filled until none could move, and there would not be enough sustenance for all. If nothing were to be born, there would be no towns or roads, no grasses upon the ground, no fishes in the sea, and all would be desolation . . .

How can one say, then, that chaos is greater, or that order is?

—*The Basis of Order*

XLIV

After breakfast, before he headed down to the carpenter shop once more, Kharl glanced forward as he stood on the main deck, pitching but slightly. In all directions, he could only see the gray-blue waters of the Northern Ocean. Or they might be sailing the Gulf of Candar by now. He'd asked Furwyl, but the first said he wouldn't know if they were actually in the Gulf until he took his noon sightings. The unseen border between the two varied with every map, in any case, Furwyl had pointed out.

Just another thing that he'd thought was more certain than it was, Kharl reflected as he headed down to the carpenter shop. He stepped inside to find Tarkyn working on his scrimshaw.

"I see that staff is still in the bin," offered the older man.

"I tried to give it back." Kharl shrugged. "The magister wouldn't take it."

"He say why?"

"He said it was mine now, and that I should take care of it."

"Might see a little use, if we're unlucky. Not like it once was. Not like twenty years ago, when there were pirates everywhere," mused Tarkyn. "Nowdays, only have to worry when you're close to shore near Renklaar or Jera . . . maybe Biehl and Quend."

"There were that many pirates? I thought Recluce had always taken care of them."

"Not just Recluce. The white wizards of Fairven hated pirates as well. That one thing they agreed upon, and before the cataclysm, there were few pirates indeed, and most of them did not last long. After the cataclysm . . . then there were many."

"After the fall of Fairven?" asked Kharl. "I didn't realize that was a cataclysm."

"Aye, that it was." Tarkyn set down the scrimshaw on the narrow bench built into the bulkhead. "Great waves swept out of the ocean and smashed into the harbors. Wasn't a war fleet anywhere that survived, not even the ships of Recluce. I heard tell that even the black iron of their mages is not so strong now as then. Many of the steam engines that once worked did no longer, and those that did had not the power they once had . . ." The carpenter coughed and cleared his throat. "My grandsire once said that the ships of Recluce were of black iron and more than two hundred cubits in length, and moved twice as fast as a horse at full gallop. Now . . . they are swift, but not that swift, and little more than half that in length."

"They don't let people see them in Nylan."

"Don't let folk close anywhere. Still mighty ships. Saw one take down a Delapran pirate once. Like a shark half out of water she moved. Shells, something that looked like a cannon but wasn't. Couldn't have been half a glass before the pirate was sinking in flames from stem to stern. No . . . one thing a skipper doesn't want to do is offend Recluce. Even worse than offending the Hamorians, for all their ships and guns. Upset the blacks, and you won't have a ship for long, that's certain. That's why the pirates are few, and why they stay close to shore. At times, makes you wish for the old times, when there were almost none."

"Does anyone know what caused the cataclysm? Fairven is . . . it was . . . somewhere in the middle of Candar. How could its fall cause great waves?"

Tarkyn laughed. "Folks have wondered that for years. Pride . . . that's what it was. Ever since Cerryl the Great, the white mages got more and more sure of themselves. Cocky. First, they took over Certis, and

Hydlen, and then Gallos. Before anyone knew it, they held all of Candar east of the Westhorns." He snorted. "Was that enough? No . . . they started building a great road through the Westhorns, so as they could march their white lancers right into Sarronnyn."

Kharl hadn't heard that part of the story. "What happened?"

"Recluce sent some black mages. They were proud, too. Thought a few troopers and mages 'd be more than enough to stop Fairven. They weren't. The whites smashed 'em and the Tyrant of Sarronnyn. Whites had all of Candar under their thumbs, except the Great Forest, Delapra, and Southwind. Might have gotten them, too, except that something happened." Tarkyn smiled, as if inviting Kharl to ask.

"What?"

"Fairven fell in a single afternoon. No one knows how. Some say mages from Recluce. The one-god believers claim their god leveled it with thunderbolts. Others say the very earth revolted. One thing's sure. Something melted most of the buildings—and they were stone—like they were wax in a furnace. Nothing grows there, and anyone who goes there these days doesn't come back. Some of the hilltops are like black glass. Heard of a fellow who climbed one. Days later, his hair fell out, got sores all over. Two eightdays later he was dead."

"I still don't see how that caused great waves in the oceans."

"Who knows? One thing certain though. The land moved. Some of the roads—the old stone roads . . . in places, they're just split. Other places, the mountains fell on them, buried 'em and anyone who was traveling 'em them."

Kharl shook his head. "It's still hard to believe. They ruled forever, and then, in one day, they were gone."

"Like a mighty ship on the ocean," said Tarkyn. "Proud, with sails billowing, engine pourin' out smoke. No one checks the hull. Shipworms . . . can't see 'em until it's too late. A storm, and the hull gives in, and the ship sinks, just like that. Lands are like ships. Don't see the worms till it's too late." The carpenter glanced at the lathe. "We could use another top gaff."

Kharl nodded. "Spruce?"

"You don't want oak that high . . ."

Kharl stepped toward the overhead wood bin, but he was still thinking about lands being like ships with shipworms. Was Nordla like that? Or Recluce? How would you ever know . . . until it was too late?

XLV

Another day passed before the *Seastag* sailed into the Great North Bay of Lydiar, barely past dawn. The bay was far larger than the harbor at Nylan or at Brysta. That was clear from the moment the *Seastag* passed through the straits formed by the two peninsulas of dark rock separated by more than thirty kays of water. Kharl had to take the second's word that the second peninsula was there, some twenty kays north. Once past the straits, there was no other sign of land, just gray water sparkling in the sunlight.

It took most of the day before the *Seastag* neared the city of Lydiar, on the southwestern end of the bay. Only then, in late afternoon and perhaps five kays offshore, did Hagen order the sails furled and the engine fired up. A pilot boat appeared as the ship neared the outermost pier, off-loading a pilot who climbed aboard and up to the poop without a word to anyone.

As the pilot directed the *Seastag* toward one of the longer and sturdier piers near the northern edge of the hodgepodge of wharfs and piers, Kharl stood with the deck crew on the main deck. He watched, because the only thing Bemyr ever used him for was on the capstan or the winch. That was doubtless wise, because Kharl didn't know that much about other deck duties.

"Ten to port!" ordered the pilot, his voice carrying with the wind to the main deck.

The *thwupping* of the paddle wheels slowed as the ship neared the northernmost pier.

Most of the city was set on a low plateau above the bay, but there were buildings and dwellings on the slope that led down to the water. Lydiar had clearly grown haphazardly over the years, because Kharl couldn't make out a single straight street of any length, and the roofs and walls were of all of different colors, but worn and muted, and all beginning to gray.

"See that pile of grayish white rock on the middle of the hillside there, straight back? Right overlooking the harbor?" asked Bemyr.

"It looks like it was once something," Kharl replied.

"Aye. It was. Used to be the stronghold of the Duke of Lydiar, more 'n eight hundred years back. Maybe longer. Say that the mage Creslin— supposedly founded Recluce—he destroyed it in an afternoon with lightnings from the sky."

Did the mages from Recluce like afternoons? Or was that just the way the stories came down? "They never rebuilt it?"

"Nope. Wondered that myself. Maybe 'cause it was built by wizards and destroyed by other wizards. Wizards, they're the wellspring of chaos."

"There hasn't been anything like that lately, has there?"

"Not since the fall of Fairven, leastwise." The bosun stepped away, moving toward the first mate, who had beckoned to Bemyr.

Kharl looked back at the harbor. There appeared to be more piers at Lydiar than at Nylan, but that might have been because, compared to the spareness and order of the harbor at Nylan, Lydiar was haphazard and disorganized, with piers of all sizes and shapes jutting out from land in no recognizable order, neither by length, nor width, nor depth of water. All the piers were of grayed timber, but some were of heavy construction, with massive circular posts and bollards, and others looked so spindly that they could well fall to the next storm. Next to the spindly piers were smaller vessels, skiffs, fishing craft, and some that Kharl could not identify. The larger piers held oceangoing vessels and coasters, several of them sloop-rigged and without stacks.

The *Seastag* slowed to little more than headway as it turned starboard into the second large pier, one for oceangoing vessels that held but one other vessel, on the far side.

Shortly, lines went out.

"Crew one! Take the forward line," ordered Bemyr. "Crew two . . . you got the stern line."

Once the lines were around the bollards, the paddle wheels slowed to a halt. Kharl was the last man in the first crew as they reeled in the line, walking the ship into the pier and snug against the fenders.

"Double up, and make those lines tight!" ordered Furwyl from the front of the poop deck.

The shrillness of the bosun's whistle cut through the low voices of the deckhands.

"Deck crew to the foremast!" called Bemyr.

Kharl followed the others, standing at the rear of the group.

"No unloading tonight. We got in too late, and their crews are already off," Bemyr added. "No shore leave until tomorrow. Not until we've off-loaded. We'll start early."

A series of groans swept across the deck crew.

"No duties tonight, except sentries on the lines and gangway," Bemyr added.

Kharl waited as most of the others in the deck gang slipped away.

"Didn't bother you, did it?" asked Reisl. "Why not?"

"I don't have anyone to see, and little coin to spend." That was true enough, although Kharl also had little desire, not after Charee's death.

"And you're not interested in women?"

"Not in those likely to be interested in me right now," Kharl replied wryly.

Reisl laughed. "Tell you've been around."

Not as much as he should have been, Kharl reflected.

XLVI

The second day in Lydiar, Bemyr put Kharl in the first shore leave section. The cooper stepped off the gangway in late afternoon, under a clear sky, although a chill fall wind blew out of the northeast off the Great North Bay. Bemyr had admonished the entire leave section to be back by midnight—when the curfew bell rang.

Once more, Kharl waited and let the others pour off the ship and along the pier toward lower Lydiar, past the Sligan merchanter tied on the opposite side of the pier and inshore of the *Seastag*. Then, wearing his heavier tunic, he stepped off, with a nod to the quarterdeck watch. He took deliberate steps along the pier. He had decided against taking the staff into Lydiar. There was little sense in being identified as a blackstaffer from Recluce, and he hoped to avoid areas of the town where he might need the staff—or any weapon.

The timbers of the pier were thick enough, but the wood was grayish, with barely a trace of brown remaining, showing that it had been years since the pier had been built or substantially repaired. Even from looking at Lydiar from the ship, Kharl had gained the impression that most of Lydiar could have used some repair. As he walked off the end of the pier and onto the first waterfront street, Kharl studied the warehouses facing the harbor. One was clearly vacant, with the doors and windows removed. Another had the windows on the upper level boarded up. None looked to have been recently stained or painted.

Kharl turned uphill, passing a chandlery less than fifty rods up the street from the piers. The narrow porch was bowed, and the roof above the porch sagged. The shutters were peeling, and the small windows were splattered with salt and grime. Kharl kept walking, past a tavern— the Red Keg—where he'd seen several of the deck crew enter. Just beyond the tavern was a fuller's, but so dingy that Kharl wouldn't have wanted anything cleaned there.

Two youths glanced from the alley across the street at Kharl, taking in his size, then disappearing into the shadows. Kharl snorted and kept walking, his eyes and senses alert, but he neither sensed nor saw the youths returning.

The street was paved with a combination of older granite blocks and newer red sandstone replacements. At the end of the block on which the tavern sat, the main street crossed a narrow lane before curving to the right and ascending more steeply past narrow two-story dwellings with sharply pitched roofs. Kharl kept walking, until he reached the top of the hill—and found that he hadn't climbed a hill at all, but more of a gentle bluff, because to the west the land neither rose nor fell that much. Perhaps half a kay west was an ancient stone wall that looked to mark the western edge of the city.

On Kharl's right, the area that comprised the edge of the hill or bluff was open ground, rocky, and intermittently grassy, a strip perhaps ten rods in width that ran from the edge of the avenue to where the bluff steepened, then dropped downhill to the meaner dwellings on the hillside below. To his left, were modest dwellings, although several with more pretension had low hedges to separate their grounds from the street.

Kharl turned southeast, following the wide avenue at the edge of the bluff. Within twenty rods, the houses had become noticeably larger and grander, and constructed of solid gray granite, with grayish tile roofs. Each had a gray stone wall before it, slightly more than shoulder high, with iron grille fencing above the stonework. Behind each wall was an enclosed space, some with lawns, and others with formal gardens. The shutters on the grander dwellings were more freshly painted, and in such shades as blue, dark green, or maroon.

A carriage passed Kharl, followed by another, and a man on horseback, wearing a deep blue jacket. A small wagon rumbled down the granite-paved avenue, coming toward the cooper, but the driver scarcely glanced in Kharl's direction. The housemaid on the side porch of one of the houses looked in Kharl's direction, then quickly away.

After half a kay, the houses ended, suddenly, as did the avenue, although a side street led back westward, away from the bluff edge. Directly before Kharl was an unkempt mass of undergrowth extending a good fifty cubits. Beyond that was a mass of tumbled white stone. Kharl realized that he stood at the edge of the former hold of the Dukes of Lydiar.

Following a narrow path, Kharl made his way through the undergrowth. The bushes and twisted high grass ended, abruptly. Nothing grew past a point five cubits from Kharl's boots until somewhere on the farther southern side of the ruins. He could sense why nothing grew there, for the rocky soil looked and felt dead. It did not look evil or menacing, but it was . . . empty. He could sense neither order nor chaos, just a feeling of great age. One of the white stones was a good five cubits long and half that in height and width. It had been cut, as if by a mighty knife, into two pieces, one twice the size of the other. Another stone still bore the imprint of a lightning bolt, black-etched into the white stone. Amid the larger stones were fragments of columns, and roof tiles, as if the entire structure had been smashed and the remnants tossed and stirred.

After a time, Kharl retraced his steps back to the avenue and followed the side street, then another avenue, making his way around the ruins, until he came to another street that led downward toward lower Lydiar.

Less than a hundred cubits down from the edge of the bluff, on the right-hand side of the street, behind a narrow garden surrounded by a knee-high wall, twin lamps beckoned from each side of the doorway of an establishment that billed itself as a café. Kharl paused and looked over the building, then stepped forward. It felt more orderly than any he had seen in Lydiar, and the mixed aromas of food smelled inviting, tinged with seasonings he did not recognize.

A menu was chalked on slate beside the door. It took him several moments to decipher the meanings, and the prices, before he opened the door and stepped inside. He could certainly use a meal other than shipboard cooking, even if the prices were higher than in more modest places.

A slender older woman greeted him. "We only serve ale and wine with meals." Her voice was polite, level, and carried a tone of slight amusement.

"I was looking for a good meal, not for drinks." He paused. "Brystan silver good here?"

"We take anyone's coins, so long as they're not clipped." She turned, gesturing for him to follow her to a square table set beside a brick wall. There were two chairs, unpadded, but with arms. Kharl took the one that let him survey the rest of the café, a space no more than ten cubits wide and twenty long, with but eleven tables of various sizes. Only three of them were occupied, one with a couple, a second large circular table with a family of five around it, and a third with two men in the corner.

"You're not local."

"No. I'm a ship's carpenter."

"How'd you get up here?"

"I walked, past the large houses and the ruins . . ."

"Most sailors don't get out of lower Lydiar."

"I'm not most sailors," he replied with a smile.

"Did you see the bill of fare outside? I can tell you what's on it, if you'd like."

"I think I got most of it," Kharl replied, "except for the langostinos. What are they?"

"You're definitely not most sailors." The woman smiled. "They're a Lydian lobster, with only one large claw. Very tasty."

"Which is better—the langostinos or the burhka with the black mushrooms?"

The server cocked her head to the side. "That's a hard one to answer. The burhka's very spicy, very hot to the taste, but rich, and the mushrooms are at their peak. The langostinos are more delicate in taste, but very filling."

"I'll try the langostinos, and whatever ale or lager you think will go best with them."

"The lager's better; the red ale would overpower them."

Kharl smiled. "Thank you."

She left the table and slipped through a narrow archway, returning almost immediately with a large glass mug, filled to the top with a pale liquid, which she set on the table.

"I hope you like it."

"I'm sure I will." Kharl took a sip, wondering, but after swallowing that small amount, found himself nodding. The lager was excellent, with a smooth bite that wasn't in the slightest bitter. He had the feeling that he might regret the evening, if only because he clearly couldn't afford to eat and drink such fare often—if ever again.

He put that thought behind him as he took another sip of the lager and looked toward the doorway, where a tall man had appeared. The hostess greeted him, and the two exchanged words that Kharl strained to hear.

". . . we'll be full in a bit . . ."

". . . don't look that crowded . . ."

". . . have a number of people coming in within the glass . . ."

". . . couldn't fit us in?"

". . . sorry, but it just isn't possible. The chef had promised . . ."

The tall man scowled, then turned and left. There was . . . something . . . about the man, but he departed so suddenly that Kharl couldn't exactly figure out what it might have been.

Kharl took a slightly larger swallow of the lager, enjoying the taste, and the warmth of the café, feeling more relaxed than he had in days.

Before long, or so it seemed, the server returned with a large platter, on which were the langostinos, steamed in their shells, with a dark brown rice, and a butter cream sauce, and a small, crusty, freshly baked loaf of white bread.

"There you are."

"It looks and smells good. Should I pay now?" Kharl asked apologetically.

"You can pay when you leave. That's our way. If you honestly don't like the food, you don't pay."

"You're very trusting."

She laughed. "We're not trusting at all."

Kharl understood, abruptly. "The man at the door?"

"He wouldn't have been happy here, and it wouldn't have been good for him or us. Can I get you anything else?"

"No. This looks like more than enough."

"Let me know if you need anything." She slipped away from Kharl and moved to the table with the family.

For a moment, Kharl just reflected. Somehow, the woman *knew* who could be trusted and who would enjoy the place, and just didn't let others in. Her remark about not being trusting at all suggested that there were other defenses, but he didn't see any. With a shrug, he began to eat.

He ate every morsel, and finished the lager down to the last drop.

"You liked it, I see." The server smiled broadly as she appeared at his table.

"The best meal I've eaten in years," Kharl confessed.

"Thank you. I'll tell Hasif. He likes it when people appreciate his cooking." The woman smiled. "You're welcome here anytime."

"Thank you." Kharl put a silver and a copper on the table. "I enjoyed it. Greatly."

"That's good to hear."

Kharl rose and made his way from the café, still smiling. The meal and the lager had cost eight coppers and, with the three coppers he left for the server, had been almost twice what he'd paid in Recluce, and he'd thought that high. Then, he had to admit, what he'd just eaten was without a doubt the best food he'd ever put in his mouth.

He walked from the café and out into the darkness, although it seemed more like twilight to him, for some reason. He turned and noted the sign on the far side for the first time—Travelers' Rest Inn and Café. A peaceful place, he decided, and very ordered and restful. As he walked downhill through the dark streets of lower Lydiar, he kept his eyes and ears open, but he'd either picked a good street, or brigands and thieves had decided the night was not for them.

About half the shore leave section had returned when Kharl finally made his way back aboard the *Seastag*. He was undressing and folding his tunic when Argan walked slowly through the hatch, clearly trying to control each step. An overpowering floral scent clung to him, almost sickening to Kharl.

"Where'd you go?" asked Argan.

"Walked around, got something to eat, walked back."

"No girls? No ale?"

"Lager and no girls," Kharl replied with a smile.

"Half's better than none," mumbled Argan, turning toward his own bunk.

Kharl smiled faintly. Those kinds of girls he didn't need. For some reason, the images of Sanyle—and then of Jekat, or Jeka—crossed his mind. He shook his head. He was too old for them, but he hoped they were doing well.

He slipped into his bunk and into sleep.

XLVII

The next day Kharl was hard at work on deck duties, replacing weakened posts in the starboard quarter railing of the *Seastag*, before smoothing, then varnishing it. He had finished the job and been released for the day a glass before supper.

He'd thought about the ruins he'd seen the day before, with the massive stone blocks clearly split in two and left to weather for ages. It did not appear the site had ever been quarried for stones, but perhaps the abundance of timber to the north along the low hills lining the Great North Bay had made using wood more attractive. Certainly, except for the larger dwellings at the top of the bluff, almost all the dwellings and buildings in Lydiar were of wood, and most looked to be decades old, if not older. While he had not felt any of the whiteness he had with the wizard in Brysta, the dead feeling of the soil told him that some great wizardry had to have been involved. Nothing grew around the ruins still. That might have been the reason why no one had tried to quarry them. Perhaps in ages past people had tried and suffered, even died, but that was something about which Kharl could only guess.

Since he still had close to a glass before supper, he slipped *The Basis of Order* from his pack in his bin and carried it with him up onto the deck. He found a space beside the railing where the late and fading light from the setting sun illuminated the pages and began to read, not really trying to puzzle out each phrase, but just letting the words flow over and through him.

"What are you reading?"

Kharl glanced up to find the third mate—Rhylla—looking down at him. "It's a book on order and chaos, ser. Someone left it to me, back in Brysta."

"Not many sailors—or coopers—read," observed Rhylla.

"I suppose not."

"Furwyl said you lost everything to the tariff farmer. Why did he do that?" Rhylla's voice expressed mild concern.

"Because I stopped Lord West's son from having his way with a neighbor girl."

"Aye. That would do it." Rhylla snorted. "What happened to the girl?"

"He had her father murdered. Her mother died years ago."

"So they killed the father and ran you off?"

Kharl nodded.

"You look like it wasn't that simple."

Kharl laughed, half-bitterly. "They hung my consort because she couldn't prove she didn't do something. My eldest son left Brysta as a carpenter's assistant on a ship; my youngest left to live with my consort's sister. The tax farmer demanded twelve golds . . ."

"Twelve . . . golds?"

"Twelve. I got off with a mere thirty lashes, and the deaths of my consort and neighbor."

"Thirty—and you still can walk?"

"I didn't for a while."

"I can see why you wanted to leave Brysta. You think things'll be better elsewhere?"

"Things? No. I figure that people are the same everywhere. But I won't have a lord's son looking to do me in elsewhere."

Rhylla nodded. "Good folk and bastards everywhere. Trick is to keep to the good ones and avoid the others."

"Sometimes that's hard," Kharl pointed out.

"These days . . . harder. One reason why I'm staying here as a third."

"You could be a second on another ship?"

"Been offered twice. Pay'd be better, but the crew share'd be smaller, and I'd end up drinking all the extra coins to forget. Hagen's a good captain. Too few like him. You know that he owns other ships, but still sails as captain?"

"No." It didn't surprise Kharl. Hagen was good, and he couldn't imagine the captain sitting in a countinghouse or a mansion and being happy. He didn't know why he thought that, but he did.

"You hid out waitin' for him, didn't you?"

Kharl smiled ruefully.

"Smartest thing you coulda done." Rhylla nodded. "Need to check on the duty sentries." She stepped away.

Kharl looked down at the page open before him.

> . . . each thing under the sun, be it a man or a machine, a creature or an object created, is unique, no matter how closely it resembles another, and yet all these unique things are created from the sameness of order and chaos, and all that is unique is the manner in which order and chaos are twisted into the unique forms that we are and that surround us . . .

He thought about the words for a time . . . for a long time . . . until the bell rang for supper, and he slipped the book inside his tunic and went below to the long narrow mess.

After eating, he went back on deck to think, and to watch the stars appear in the night sky, brightening as the sky darkened. In time, he returned to the crew quarters.

As he undressed and slipped into his bunk, he hoped he could sleep soundly. He did—except for the time when Reisl staggered back into the forecastle, clearly drunk, and mumbled incoherently before collapsing into his own bunk.

Kharl sighed and went back to sleep.

XLVIII

Kharl had already washed up and trimmed his beard, and was getting ready to head to the mess for what passed for breakfast, when Bemyr's whistle shrilled through the forecastle, announcing that breakfast was ready. Another whistle would call the in-port morning muster, where additional duties might be assigned.

"Frig . . ." mumbled Reisl, turning and sitting on the edge of his bunk, legs dangling as he held his head in his hands.

"Too much ale," called Argan.

Behind them, Wylat just grinned.

Reisl slumped to his feet and began to pull out clothes from his bin, where he had tossed them the night before. He straightened abruptly. "Know I was ale-decked," he mumbled, "but not enough to lose every copper in my wallet."

"You had some when you came back aboard?" asked Kharl.

Reisl nodded, then turned to Hodal. "You know what happened to my coin?"

Hodal looked up at the taller man. "No. You think I'm that stupid?"

Kharl could sense that Hodal was telling the truth. The cooper glanced around the forecastle, taking in the sailors still in their bunks. Some were asleep, others pretending to be so.

"What about you, Kawelt?" asked Reisl, stepping forward toward the next bunk.

"Like to take anything you have, Reisl. Didn't."

Kharl could see/sense just a touch of the strange whiteness that no one else seemed to notice around the third upper bunk—the one holding Asolf. Kharl eased toward it, nodding to Reisl.

Reisl stepped toward Asolf. "Why did you empty my wallet, Asolf?"

The broad-faced sailor cocked his head. "You're one to be making charges. You couldn't have seen the sun if it had risen right in front of you." He eased out of his bunk without looking at Reisl. He already wore trousers, but not deck shoes.

"I just asked if you emptied my wallet."

"Why would I do that?"

Kharl looked at the younger man. "You don't want to answer the question, and usually people who don't want to answer have a reason they don't want to."

"Carpenter . . . it's not your business."

"Theft in the fo'c's'le is everyone's business," snapped Bemyr from the hatchway. "Yes or no?"

"No," replied Asolf.

"That's a lie," Kharl said without thinking.

Asolf drove right toward the cooper. Kharl stepped aside and, as he did, one-handedly flung Asolf to the deck. The deckhand lay there for a moment, then started to gather his feet under him. Kharl wondered if the sailor had a knife or a marlinespike. His own fingers tightened about the carpenter's hammer in his belt.

"You move, and you're off the ship in the clothes on your back," Bemyr stated coldly.

Asolf froze.

"I think I'll take a look in Asolf's bin," Bemyr said, moving forward.

"Yeah . . . I took all three coppers in his wallet," Asolf said tiredly.

"I'm sure you did, and I'm sure you took more than that," Bemyr said. "You and I are going to talk to the captain. Get up."

Asolf slowly rose, glaring at Kharl. "Friggin' half mage."

"Didn't take no mage to figure out you were hiding something," Reisl said.

"Even I could figure it out," added Bemyr. "Let's go."

After the two left the forecastle Reisl looked at Kharl. "Thanks. Always thought he was snitching coppers here and there. Never could get him."

"You seemed to know who it was," Kharl said.

"Knew for a while, but he's mean." Reisl shook his head. "You took him down so quick."

"Just luck," Kharl lied. He'd sensed that Asolf would attack, and he'd been ready. Since he was half a head taller, broader, stronger, and ready, the thieving sailor hadn't had a chance.

"Take that kind of luck any day."

"So will I," replied Kharl with a laugh. As he left and headed for the mess, Kharl wondered why Asolf had called him a half mage. Because the sailor was touched with chaos and had realized Kharl could sense it? Or just to get Kharl distrusted by the other sailors?

Breakfast in port wasn't bad—there was hot bread and an egg mush with scraps of meat. Kharl took his bowl and sat at one end of the narrow table, scooping up the mush with a crust of the rye bread, listening as others entered the mess.

". . . the bosun and the captain threw Asolf off . . . caught him stealing coppers, bosun did . . ."

". . . few morns woke up thinking I shoulda had more in my wallet . . . now I know . . ."

". . . smart . . . only took a few . . ."

"Not smart enough."

Kharl finished and left the mess.

Immediately after muster, and before reporting to the carpenter shop, Kharl made his way to the bow, on the port side, the side where he could look out northward over the Great North Bay. He leaned on the railing, thinking. He'd been lucky that most of the crew had already suspected Asolf, but he'd come close to giving himself away. He frowned. What exactly was he afraid of? That somehow he was able to sense chaos and when people told lies? Or that people would think he was a mage, when he scarcely knew anything about it?

He'd always had a feel for wood, and often Vetrad had complained when Kharl had refused certain lengths of wood, but the ones he'd refused hadn't felt right, and he'd seldom ever found himself with bad billets in the cooperage. Idly, thinking about the wood, he looked down at the solid oak hull, angling toward the gray water of the bay.

He frowned. About ten cubits aft of where he stood, just above the waterline, on the port side, he could sense an overtone of white.

"What are you looking at?"

Kharl straightened at Hagen's question. "Ser, I mean, captain. I think there's something wrong with the hull, the wood, that is, down there, right at the waterline."

"Well . . . you think so, and you go down on a bosun's chair and look real close." Hagen gestured.

Furwyl appeared.

"Bosun's chair," Hagen said. "Kharl's worried about the hull down there. Like to have him take a look. Can't leave until tomorrow anyway."

"Those are new planks and timbers . . ."

"Can't hurt to have him look."

Kharl almost wished he'd said nothing, but he remained silent until Hodal appeared with the rope-slung chair. The two of them attached the ropes and pulleys, then swung the chair over the railing. There Kharl climbed into the chair and was lowered.

The chair stopped two or three cubits too high.

"A little lower," Kharl called.

The chair lurched down.

"That's good."

Up close, Kharl could feel that the damage was worse than he'd thought, although the hull looked normal. An entire patch of hull going at least three cubits below the waterline was rotten—or something like it. He touched the wood and could feel some give.

"Well?" Furwyl called down.

"You got a whole section of hull here. I could drive a maul through it."

Furwyl laughed. "That section's only a year old. Come on up."

"It's rotten."

"Can't be. It's new oak."

Kharl took the hammer from his belt. "Watch."

"Be glad to."

The carpenter who'd been a cooper took one swing, and buried the hammer in the wood just above the waterline. Splinters and chunks of rotten wood flew. Kharl pulled away a fist-sized chunk, holding it in his left hand. "Pull me up. You can see for yourself."

Furwyl's mouth hung open.

Then the first mate and Hodal pulled up the chair, and Kharl scrambled out, handing the chunk of oak to Furwyl.

Furwyl looked at the wood, taking in the strawlike parallel tubes in the fragment. "Shipworms . . . frigging shipworms. That Jeran swine . . . paid for coppered wood . . ." He looked up. "Captain!"

Hagen reappeared.

"Carpenter's right. Shipworms. Bet all those timbers we replaced in Biehl are no good."

Hagen's jaw tightened.

"I'm sorry, ser," Kharl said. "I don't claim to know ships . . . but I know something about wood . . ."

"Not your fault, man." Hagen shook his head. "We hit a bad blow . . . might lose the ship."

"Leave the chair there," Furwyl said.

Kharl stepped aside, sliding down the railing as the two officers talked in low voices.

". . . not the best place to refit and retimber . . ."

". . . put that hammer through that like rotten cheese . . ."

". . . any kind of storm . . . go down by the head . . . quicker 'n a lead barrel . . ."

Kharl looked out across the harbor, not really seeing anything. What had happened to him? He'd known wood, and once he'd touched the hull, he'd known it was weak, but he'd never before been able to see or sense something like that from ten cubits away before.

XLIX

The single dry dock at Lydiar was old, and the steam engine that powered the pump groaned and wheezed as the water gushed in surges over the stone walls of the dock and out into the harbor until the *Seastag* rested on the wide keel blocks. The crew had already moved the cargo in the forward hold, and much of it was under tarpaulins on the aft section of the main deck.

Kharl—still sweating from that effort—stood on the stone rim of the only dry dock in Lydiar, with Tarkyn beside him, looking down at the exposed hull.

"Hamorian merchants soak their planks in copper solution," Tarkyn said. "Then they sheathe the hull in thin copper plates. Costs more to begin with, but they claim that it's cheaper over the life of the vessel. 'Course their warships are iron-hulled steamers. Don't worry about worms with those, but cost of coal will kill a trader . . ."

"Lot of things are like that," replied Kharl. "Most folks want things cheap as they can get them. Cooperage was like that. Good tight white oak cooperage costs two coppers more a barrel, four if it's something as big as a hogshead, but a good barrel'll outlast a poor one by half again as long." He shrugged. "For some folks . . . makes no difference, but for most . . . after five years they'll spend silvers, sometimes even golds, more for what they thought they'd saved . . ." He cleared his throat. "Is there any way the captain can get recompense from the Jeran?"

"Not so as I'd know." Tarkyn laughed. "Revenge, though. That he can get. Just tell every master he meets. In a few years, none'd be dealing with the Jeran. Folks forget that there's a balance to life. Things come back. Not so as the black ones in Recluce say, always prating on about the Balance, but in life. Do a man good, and most will return good. Do a man ill, and few will forget."

"Too bad that doesn't apply to rulers," mused Kharl.

"It does, cooper. We just don't see it. The white wizards of Fairven . . . they got too mighty and proud. Where are they now? Whole city's a ruin. Nothing'll ever live there again. The Prefect of Gallos—he's got more problems than a lathe has shavings. Most 'cause he treats all but a few like serfs." Tarkyn gestured back toward Lydiar. "Lydiar goes through rulers like . . ." Tarkyn stopped to grope for a comparison, then looked at Kharl.

"I suppose so. It just hasn't happened where I've seen it."

"It happens. Trust me." Tarkyn cleared his throat again. "Friggin' frog. Get older, and you spend more time clearing your throat than talkin'. Then, could be, gettin' paid back for talkin' too much when you're young. Anyway . . . you see the captain? He does right well. Know why? 'Cause he treats his crews right. Makes sure his captains on the other ships do, too. Word gets around."

Kharl recalled the third mate talking about staying as a third rather than becoming a second on another ship. "I had that feeling, even when I was a cooper."

" 'Course, sometimes a fellow's got to help matters along. Got to stand up and do the right thing, not wait for others to do it. Captain's like that. When he found out that fellow been lifting coppers, he booted him off just like that, and he took his crew share, divided it among the hands who lost coins." Tarkyn laughed. "Some probably said they lost a copper or two more 'n they did, and some probably lost some they didn't recall, but a lot of skippers, they'd just pocket that share. Not the captain."

Kharl glanced down into the dry dock, where water still swirled around the lower sections of the keel, although the water level continued to drop, revealing greenish moss on the lower stones of the dry dock walls. "He always dealt with me fairly when he bought cooperage."

"You gave him the best, I'd wager, because he did."

Kharl had given everyone the best, but he merely answered, "I did."

"Sooner or later, what you do comes back," Tarkyn declared.

Kharl still had to wonder whether that was truly so. No one had avenged Charee's death, nor had any good come from it that he could see. While he had managed to help Jeka a little, no one had done anything about Lord West's corrupt tariff farmers in either Sagana or Brysta. Tyrbel's death and that of Jenevra had both occurred, and nothing had happened to Egen. Then, Kharl reflected, he had killed Tyrbel's assassin, who had probably been the one who had killed Jenevra. Still . . . nothing had happened to redress the balance with Lord West and his sons, and Kharl had seen nothing to make him believe that it would.

L

Even with the Lydian shipwright's workforce, the crew of the *Seastag*, and the wood-handling skills of Kharl and Tarkyn, it took almost an eightday to replace the worm-damaged hull sections. The actual woodwork had only taken about a third of that time, but the caulking and the finish work, and then the trials in the Great North Bay, and the second round of caulking and ensuring that the hull was both sound and watertight, accounted for the majority of the repair time.

Hagen had not wasted that time, but had the crew work on other repairs that would not have been enough to warrant a dry docking. The rudder was cleaned and repaired, as were several paddle wheel spokes, and all the fittings and piping in the steam engine were checked and cleaned—as well as other small repairs that Kharl could not have explained. More coal was brought on board, and the bunkers refilled.

Kharl was kept busy with the hull work, and, at the end, with refitting the interior timbers and braces against the new hull. Hagen personally inspected every bit of work that affected the seaworthiness of the ship. The *Seastag* finally left Lydiar on a threeday.

Early afternoon on sixday found Kharl on the foredeck, just aft of the bowsprit, taking a break from the lathe. The wind was light, barely enough to puff out the sails, under a bright and cloudless sky that made the day seem warmer than it was. The swells were little more than a cubit and a half from trough to crest, and so long and flat that there was almost no foam at all, making the water look even darker.

Kharl stretched, then glanced to starboard, quickly taking in the headlands to the west and a pair of small islands, possibly as close as three kays away. He turned and looked off to port, out toward the seemingly endless Eastern Ocean. He frowned, seeing in the distance a speck of darkness. At first, he thought it might be the kind of darkness that he'd first seen in Nylan, but it resolved itself into a low black shape a good four kays east. The black ship cut through the choppy waters, moving swiftly northward, first passing abreast of the southward-bound *Seastag*, and then swiftly vanishing.

Kharl shook his head, still not certain he'd seen the ship.

"You saw it all right," said Rhylla, from his right. "Move fast, don't they?"

"That was one of the black warships?"

The third nodded. "Wish it had been headed south, instead of back to Nylan. Do us more good, specially with the wind so light." She turned and crossed the main deck.

Musing on her words, Kharl started back down to the carpenter's shop.

"Long for a short break," Tarkyn said, stepping away from the lathe.

"I'm sorry. I saw one of the black ships. I couldn't believe how fast it was."

"You mark its heading?"

"It was headed north, maybe northeast. Third said it was going back to Nylan." Kharl stepped up to the lathe and readjusted the foot pedal for his longer legs, then took the shaping chisel, studying the section of oak that would become a rough-shaped spare railing support.

"Captain better think about powering up the engine," Tarkyn said.

Kharl looked up from the lathe, lifting the chisel.

"We've barely got headway. We're heavy-laden, 'bout as heavy as we'll be, 'cause we've got copper for the druids. That's what the first said."

Kharl didn't understand.

"We're south of Renklaar, short of Pyrdya, and we're close to shore 'cause the trades blow north farther offshore."

The carpenter's explanation still didn't make any more sense to Kharl.

"Pirates," the carpenter finally said. "Got to worry about 'em till we're well south of here, past Worrak, for sure."

"But Recluce . . . I mean, we're about as close as we can be to Recluce."

"That's the problem. All sorts of ships port at Nylan, with rich cargoes. They come through these waters. All sorts of islets and marshes off the mouth of the Ohyde. Hide a fleet there, if you wanted. Recluce doesn't have too many of those black ships. Can't be everywhere."

"You think pirates would come after us?"

"They'll come after anything they think they can capture. We had wind, with the engine, be a hard chase for them."

Kharl sniffed the air. "Something's burning."

"Good. Captain's lighting off the engine. Doesn't like to. Coal's not cheap, but losing a ship to pirates makes coal cheap at twice the price."

Kharl continued to work the lathe, and neither man spoke until Kharl finished the turning.

"Best you rack that and clean the lathe, stow the brackets and clamps."

Kharl nodded. After putting the railing support in the overhead rack used for partly finished work, he swept up the shavings and sawdust into the flat scoop and emptied them into the burn box. Then came the rags, and finally the oil to coat all the exposed metal.

"Good," grunted Tarkyn.

Somewhere, Kharl could hear the hissing of steam as pressure built up in the boiler aft of the carpenter shop. A slow rumbling echoed through the ship, followed by a regular thumping, and then the deliberate *thwup . . . thwup* of the paddle wheels.

Bemyr's whistle shrilled throughout the ship. "All hands topside to repel boarders! All hands topside to repel boarders!"

"Worried about that," muttered Tarkyn.

Kharl glanced toward the overhead bin, looking for the dark staff.

"The far side," Tarkyn said.

Kharl eased the staff out of the longer of the two overhead bins. He glanced over at the older man, and saw that Tarkyn had opened a locker and was taking out a crossbow, a rewinding assembly, and a quiver of dark bolts, but the bolts didn't look like iron.

"Lorken," the carpenter said. "Can make 'em here on the lathe. Almost as good as iron, and they work real well against pirates, specially those touched with chaos. You better get topside. I'll be up in a moment."

When Kharl left the carpenter shop, the paddle wheels had begun to pick up speed, but only fractionally, and a long groaning told Kharl that the engine was straining, probably because the steam pressure wasn't high enough yet. As he came up the ladder, staff in hand, he was met by the third, who stood by an open locker, filled with weapons of all sorts, ranging from long and short blades to cudgels and spears.

Rhylla looked at Kharl and his staff. "Better put you on the poop." She gestured.

"Yes, ser." Kharl glanced aft, across the main deck where sailors were forming up behind each railing. Most carried cutlasses, but Kharl saw spears and a cudgel as well, and even one woman with a quiver and longbow. He took a quick look to starboard, inshore. There were two pirate vessels, each long and slim, with a bastard rig and a huge balloon sail, each less than a kay away. Both were filled with armed men.

"Cooper!"

"Sorry, ser." Kharl hurried across the deck, waited for a sailor with a broadsword to climb the ladder, then followed him up to the poop.

He had no sooner reached the top when Furwyl motioned for him to take a position abeam the helm, but on the port side. "You can cover more deck, and that means we can use someone else on the main deck."

Kharl nodded. He thought he understood.

"Don't leave your space unless you're ordered to." Furwyl paused. "Or unless they've already overrun the main deck, and no one's climbing the poop."

"Yes, ser." Kharl took the assigned space, but once there, looked back shoreward. With the speed of the paddle wheels increasing, the gap between the two pirate vessels and the *Seastag* was no longer obviously narrowing. In fact, Kharl could begin to see the *Seastag* start to pull away from the leading pirate vessel.

"Port five," ordered Hagen, standing almost directly beside the helm.

"Coming port, ser."

Kharl could barely feel the gentle turn.

"Steady on heading, ser."

"Steady as she goes."

"Steady as she goes, ser."

Slowly, ever so slowly, the gap between the larger ocean trader and the pirate vessels widened, until it was more like a kay and a half.

Kharl kept checking, but the gap was still increasing, and the *Seastag* was edging farther and farther away from land. Hagen was trying not to lose what air he had, but to find a heading that played more to the strengths of the *Seastag*.

A muffled *crummpt* echoed through the *Seastag*. The entire vessel shuddered. Almost immediately flame flared from the stack, hot enough to scorch the limp lower sheets closest to the stack before fading into blackish gray smoke that settled down across the decks. The paddle wheels' *thwup-thwup-thwup* slowed, finally coming to a stop.

Kharl gaped for a moment. The smoke had held, for just an instant, the barest hint of chaos about it. What had happened? Why had the engine exploded?

The gap between the pirate vessels and the *Seastag* began to narrow once more.

An engineman, blackened from crown to boots, pulled himself up the ladder and made his way toward the captain. Kharl tried to listen.

"Firebox . . . exploded, ser . . . awful . . . steam . . . metal . . ."

"Is there a fire below?" Hagen's question was clipped.

"No fire, ser. Not now. Sand and water . . . got that. But . . . no . . . engine, much, neither, ser . . . two stokers . . . didn't make it . . ."

The cooper looked shoreward. The pirates were closer, little more than a kay away, and the sternmost of the two had shifted course slightly, to take a heading that would come up alongside the *Seastag* on the port side. That made sense, unhappily, because the pirates could board from both sides, and divide the defenders' efforts.

"Shut everything down, best you can, and bring the engine crew topside," Hagen told the engineer.

"Yes, ser, those that can." The engineer turned and made his way down.

". . . some sort of wizardry . . ." muttered the captain to Furwyl.

". . . put out the word about Lydiar," returned the first mate.

". . . get through this first . . ."

As he waited for the pirates, Kharl tried to relax, tried to recall the warm-up exercises he had not used or needed in years and replicate them, to ready himself. The wind remained light, and with their smaller craft and larger sails, the pirates steadily closed on the *Seastag,* until they were only rods away, then within fifty cubits, one on each side of the trader.

"Stand by to repel boarders!" ordered Furwyl, and the command was echoed by the three other mates. "Stand back from the railings until they close!"

Kharl moved back, realizing the reason for the command as an arrow whispered past his head. He immediately dropped into a kneeling position, waiting.

Clunk!

At the heavy sound, Kharl turned his head to see a pronged iron that had been catapulted over the railing and onto the deck. Several arrows skidded along the deck as well and one buried itself in the steering platform.

A seaman ran forward, crouching, with an ax and, keeping his head down, began to hack at the line attached to the grappling iron. Another iron arched over the railing, and dragged across the deck until it, too, was wedged behind the poop railing. The seaman with the ax had barely cut through the first line before there were two others wedged in place.

The young man attacked the second, but seemed to make no progress. "Friggin' thing . . . wound with wire . . ."

Kharl's eyes darted across the upper deck, taking in the four grapples still wedged in place. While he couldn't see more, he had no doubts that the same tactics were being employed against the main and forward decks. The seaman managed to part the line on two more grapples, but, by that time, another three had been wedged in place.

Kharl edged forward, because he could hear voices, scuffling, and muttered curses . . .

". . . get your friggin' ass up . . ."

". . . sows carry less lard 'n you . . ."

The cooper saw a brawny arm reach over the railing. He lunged forward and slammed the staff down on the arm, feeling the bones break, and seeing the pirate tumble backward off the rope and into the water just aft of where the two hulls rubbed against each other.

He brought the staff around in a sweep. One pirate ducked, but the lorken staff caught a second in the neck, and he sagged, then slid out of sight, while Kharl reversed the staff. His return was weak, and the one pirate was over the railing, cutlass slashing toward the cooper, and parrying the staff.

Kharl two-handed the staff, using both ends. The wood, almost as hard as iron, and springier, fended off the cuts from the pirate, who tried to circle away from Kharl, and found himself between a sailor with a spear and the cooper. In the pirate's moment of indecision, Kharl struck with an underthrust, and the cutlass spun out of the pirate's hand. The other sailor plunged the spear into the pirate's belly.

Kharl turned back to the port railing, where two more pirates had appeared, one with the ubiquitous cutlass, and a taller man with a hand-and-a-half blade. Kharl took on the taller man, and found himself backing up against a man with far better blade skills than Kharl had staff capabilities.

Thwunk! The huge pirate looked stunned at the quarrel in his left shoulder.

Kharl took the moment and knocked the big blade from his hand and attacked with all his strength. Even badly wounded, the pirate weathered two blows that would have felled a lesser man and ducked away from several that could have stopped him.

Kharl managed another strike, then a solid thrust into the man's guts. The pirate tumbled forward, and Kharl saw the blood from a deep cut across his back.

Two more pirates appeared from somewhere, and Kharl and another sailor found themselves slowly pushing the pair forward, toward the edge of the poop deck. One looked back, and took a spear. The other grabbed the railing and vaulted down.

Kharl stood for a moment, gasping, glancing around the poop deck, but it was empty, except for Kharl, the captain, the helmsman, and two other sailors from the *Seastag*. Below, the main deck swirled with fighters. The defenders were being pressed from both sides, although they did not seem that greatly outnumbered, and some pirates had fallen, but the attackers fought without much thought of caution, it seemed to Kharl, and kept pressing the *Seastag*'s defenders inward.

The cooper glanced down at the pirate vessel to port. Only two men stood on the low rear deck, beside the steersman. All three were watching the main deck of the *Seastag*.

Abruptly, staff in one hand, Kharl swung himself over the railing and clambered down one of the ropes left hanging by the pirates. When he was just slightly higher than the aft deck of the pirate vessel, he twisted his body and jumped. Even as close as the two vessels were, he barely cleared the railing and landed heavily on the deck.

The two pirates remaining were surprised enough that Kharl had a chance to get the staff into position before the first charged.

Kharl parried the slash by the pirate, and the cutlass clanked against the black iron band. The blade shattered, and Kharl reversed the staff into a wicked riposte into the man's guts, then, as the pirate staggered, finished him off with a blow to the side of his head.

The cooper barely managed to get the staff back and balanced in time to ward off the attack of the second helm guard, who was using two shortswords, one in each hand.

Kharl let the other attack, using a balanced two-handed grip on the longer staff to block or deflect the other's slashing attacks, giving a little space, and watching.

Then, after the pirate made a particularly vicious cut that left him slightly unbalanced, Kharl slammed the staff into the other's knee with enough force that something crunched, and the pirate sprawled sideways on the deck. Kharl brained him, then turned to the helmsman.

The helmsman released the helm and grabbed for the cutlass at his belt. His hand closed on the hilt just as one of the iron bands of Kharl's staff crashed into his temple.

As Kharl surveyed the deck, he could see that there was no one near him, and forward on the pirate ship, no one had even looked aft. With a cold smile Kharl strode forward, toward the handful of pirates, along the railing, clearly wanting to board the *Seastag*.

The first two went down, one right after the other, without anyone noticing.

The third turned. "They're behind us!" He got his blade, more of a rapier than a cutlass, up and into a rough guard position. Kharl slammed the blade aside and brought the staff up from below, doubling the man over, and finishing him off with a reverse.

Then . . . there were pirates all around Kharl, and the most he could do was try to weave a defense.

He stepped back, still creating a blur of blackness, when a taller man, taller even than Kharl, lunged forward with a huge broadsword. Because of the force of the cut—that missed—the big man was off-balance for a moment, and Kharl struck.

A shocked expression froze on the pirate's face, and he brought the broadsword around in a last desperate swinging lunge.

Kharl managed to get the strength from somewhere to parry, but he slipped on a deck wet with blood and salt, and the flat side of the blade crashed into his chest, then slammed down into his foot. With a last effort, Kharl brought up the end of the staff straight into the pirate's throat. Kharl could feel something give, and some of the pressure on his leg abate. He tried to lever the staff upward, but it was caught under the body of the fallen pirate.

Then something struck him from behind, and wave of red blackness crashed over him.

LI

A reddish dark haze swam around Kharl, and much as he attempted to grope his way through it, it merely thickened. When he tried to rest, it seemed to constrict around him, like an iron band across his chest and ribs, with an agonizing pain so sharp that he felt he could hardly breathe. He wanted to move, but neither his arms nor his legs would budge, and his head was a mass of flame.

In time—how long it had been, he had no idea—the haze thinned, and an image swam into his view, except that it was a pair of images. Kharl squinted, and the two images resolved into one, that of a single face, one he thought he should recognize, but did not.

"You'll be all right, cooper. You're acting like you're still fighting. You don't have to keep fighting. Try to loosen those muscles."

"Pirates . . . ?" Kharl mumbled, his mouth so dry that the single word was a croak.

"You need to drink. Open your mouth."

Kharl did. The coolness was welcome. His tongue was swollen, and swallowing was difficult.

"Pirates?" he asked again.

"Most of 'em are dead. We brought in their ships. Not bad prizes. Worrak isn't prime, but the captain figures that, even after replacing the engine, be a goodly prize share for everyone. That's for you, too."

Kharl didn't care about that. He just knew his leg hurt, especially his foot—and his chest.

"Hurts . . . a bit . . ."

"Your ribs are cracked . . . bruised, and there's that right foot. It's going to hurt for a while, but you'll walk fine. Your boots won't be so cramped on that side. That last pirate blade took the two smallest toes, but . . . wound came up clean. Healing good. Worried about you. Been a couple of days now."

"Hit my head."

"Big lump, but nothing's broken and no soft spots there. Local healer says you'll be fine. He's looked at all of you."

Kharl finally grasped that Rhylla, the third mate, was talking. He hoped his memory would improve. "Thank you."

"You need to drink some more."

So Kharl did, then drifted back into sleep, back into the reddish haze, except at times there were periods of black coolness.

He woke in dim light, either dawn or twilight, he thought, before realizing that all light was dim in sick bay or anywhere belowdecks. He only saw two other bunks, besides the one above him, and the two—those across from him—were occupied. He lay back on the narrow bunk, closing his eyes and trying to ignore the dull aching in the toes he no longer had, and wondering what would happen next. He could hear voices from the two men in the opposite bunks, whispering as they were.

". . . thought he woke . . ."

". . . back asleep . . ."

". . . you'd be sleeping, too . . . what hit him. Tough old guy . . ."

Kharl didn't think of himself as old, but he must have seemed so to young seamen.

". . . never saw anything like it . . . cleared off everyone on the one . . . looked like . . ."

". . . Reisl said he used that staff and batted down arrows . . ."

Kharl wanted to snort, but it would have taken too much effort. No one could do that.

". . . saw him take out three pirates with that big staff . . . one hit it with a blade, and the blade shattered . . ."

". . . blackstaffer . . ."

". . . he's not . . . used to be a cooper in Brysta . . . what the third said . . . did something to piss off the Lord . . ."

There was a laugh. "Got to like that . . . anyone with enough guts to piss off a lord . . . good man . . ."

Kharl drifted back into sleep.

When he woke for the third time, the space was brighter, and the aching in his skull was only the faintest throbbing, although his foot didn't feel that much better. He was alone in sick bay, and the other bunks had been stripped.

Still, he thought he ought to try to sit up, and he gingerly eased into a sitting position on the edge of the bunk. Knives jabbed through his ribs, and he could barely hold himself erect. Still . . . he wasn't going to get better lying flat.

He slowly levered himself into a standing position, although he was as much leaning against the bulkhead as standing. He coughed, two or three times, and the sharp knives that went through his chest made him wonder if he would collapse right there. He just stood, hanging on until the coughing passed and he could breathe easier. Then he took one step, and another. He finally made it to the hatch, and looked out onto the main deck. It was midafternoon, and the ship was tied to a pier.

He stepped slowly out onto the deck, barefoot he realized, but he had no idea where his boots were, or if he could even bend over to put them on, or if they would fit. A wave of dizziness washed over him and he eased sideways until he reached the ladder to the forecastle deck, where he sat down.

"Cooper?"

Kharl looked up to see Furwyl standing there. "Yes, ser?"

"Third and the healer said it'd be a few more days . . ."

". . . if I got up at all?"

Furwyl laughed. "They didn't say that."

"Not exactly. Figured . . . I'd better walk some. Rest some. Not worth spit . . . right now."

"You know how you feel," the first mate said carefully. "We're leaving Worrak tomorrow."

"Won't be doing much carpentering . . . for a while," Kharl replied.

"If you want to stay, you've got a berth, long as you want it."

"I'd . . . like that." Kharl forced a smile, one that he meant, even if he still hurt so much that he didn't feel like smiling.

"Good. That's settled." Furwyl smiled. "Maybe you'd better lie down for a while . . . get up in a bit for supper."

"Supper . . . sounds good." Kharl realized he had no idea if he'd eaten, or what, or how often. He didn't like the idea that he had no idea what had happened to him. He did appreciate the loyalty of the captain and the first. Slowly, he rose, and putting one foot in front of the other, gingerly, headed back to sick bay.

LII

The *Seastag* waited two days more to leave Worrak, because the captain had been promised a cargo of brimstone for delivery to Dellash. Brimstone was a good cargo, provided it didn't burn or get spilled, and Hagen had planned to port at Dellash anyway, according to Rhylla. Kharl didn't complain about the delay because he appreciated being able to begin to walk on a steady deck. His damaged boot had been patched, but he felt unbalanced, even though he had lost just his littlest toes, rather than his largest.

By the evening before the *Seastag*'s departure, Kharl was walking with a slight limp, and the stabbing in his ribs had receded to a dull ache. He'd tried a little work with the lathe, but he could only manage it for a quarter of a glass before the pain in his ribs began to worsen. He stopped, but that was better than he had been doing.

After sitting on Tarkyn's stool for a time, he made his way back onto the main deck. The sun was hanging above the low hills, just to the south of where the Fakla River entered the harbor. There was enough of a sea breeze to carry the harbor odors inshore and leave the deck with the clean scent of the Eastern Ocean, although the breeze was brisk enough that the deck would be chill once the sun set.

"Cooper?" called a voice.

Kharl turned. Ghart, the second mate, stood several cubits aft.

"Yes, ser?"

"Captain and the first are on the poop. They'd like to see you."

"I'll be right there." Kharl headed aft and went up the ladder, carefully and slowly. So long as he moved smoothly, the pain in his ribs wasn't too bad.

Hagen and Furwyl stood waiting under the aft mast.

Kharl stopped several cubits short of the two officers. "Captain, ser, you asked for me?"

"That I did," replied Hagen. "I've been thinking, Kharl. We've got a long voyage ahead. Tarkyn says you're good, better than most ship's carpenters. You saved us from losing everything. So, we're going to pay you as the carpenter's second." Hagen smiled. "And you start wearing carpenters' grays onboard. You won't be doing deck work, but you'll have to take in-port gangway watches once we get to Ruzor."

"You use any sort of weapon besides that staff?" asked Furwyl.

"I'm not bad with a cudgel," Kharl said.

"That might be a little handier on watch," replied the first, with a laugh.

Hagen handed Kharl a small pouch. "That's your pay for the last eightday."

"Thank you, ser." Kharl wasn't quite sure what else to say.

The captain nodded, as if he did not wish to be thanked. "Ghart is in charge of in-port watches. He'll be letting you know which sections you'll stand."

"Yes, ser."

"Tarkyn's rustled up two sets of grays for you," added Furwyl. "Says they'll fit you just fine. We can use another subofficer."

"I'll do my best, captain, ser."

"You already have," Hagen replied. "More than most. That's why you're crew, now, for so long as you want."

"Yes, ser."

Hagen nodded, as if to dismiss Kharl, and the cooper—carpenter's second—stepped back and climbed down the ladder. He doubted that he really wanted to remain a ship's carpenter, but if he couldn't find a place where he could be a cooper, at least he'd have shelter and coin and something useful to do—and with woods, which he knew.

He stopped as pain shot through his ribs.

Most healers were black mages. He wondered if *The Basis of Order* had sections on healing, and if they might teach him something about how to speed his own healing. He might as well read through it and see. He certainly couldn't work full-time as a carpenter. Not yet.

And, based on what he'd already experienced, the information—if he could understand it—might prove useful.

LIII

Against strong blustering gusts that were nearly direct headwinds, it took the *Seastag* five days—with frequent tacking and the use of the engine—after leaving Worrak to make port in Ruzor. Kharl was glad for the respite, because every time the ship had rolled or pitched heavily, and he had been caught off guard, his ribs had reminded him that they had not yet healed. He thought that the efforts he had made to cultivate a sense of balance within himself had helped speed the healing, but that could have been wishful thinking.

Whatever the reason, there were times—brief moments—when they did not ache, and those seemed more frequent with each day. Even so, he was glad that the *Seastag* had ported, even if Hagen had said that they would be in Ruzor but two days.

Kharl had two in-port watches, but one was that afternoon, and the second the following morning. Ghart had given him an easy watch schedule, clearly in deference to his injuries, but Kharl had no doubts that his duties in other ports would include night and midwatches. He had been down in the carpenter shop since after breakfast, using the tools to tighten the grip on the cudgel he'd taken from the weapons locker, and was headed back up to replace it.

He stopped halfway up the ladder from the carpenter shop as he heard voices from the main deck, as if two people were standing right outside the hatch.

"... most fortunate to have captured the pirates ... understand you have a cargo of two hundred stone of brimstone ..."

"... already have a binding contract for the brimstone ... sell it here ... and Synadar wouldn't give me a copper were I broke and legless ..."

"... understand that, but the Prefect is willing to pay a third more than your contract price ... would free cargo space ..."

"Why is the Prefect of Gallos so interested in my cargo of brimstone?" asked Hagen.

"The Prefect is having trouble with the province of Kyphros . . . the Prince of Analeria is always claiming another part of Gallos . . . The prince has no mages, and gunpowder is useful."

"His troubles don't matter to me," replied Hagen. "All a trader's got is his reputation. I sell out a cargo and a buyer, I lose that buyer, and anyone he tells . . ."

"It's not wise to anger . . ."

"It's not wise for you to anger him." Hagen laughed. "The Prefect doesn't have more than twoscore lancers here in Ruzor. The pier's stone and long. You send 'em down that pier, and I'll cut the lines and be off. Then I'll tell every trader to steer clear. Ruzor's the Prefect's only port, and he's got no fleet."

". . . you're a hard man, captain. Someday, you'll regret that."

"Regret what? Being honest? Being fair?"

There was a long silence.

". . . tariffs are twenty golds on the cotton, the Brystan apples, and the tin ingots."

"That's twice what they were last year," Hagen pointed out, his voice indifferent.

"That's what they are."

"They are what they are, and I'll report them to the buyers."

". . . seeing as you didn't know . . ."

"Whatever they are . . . we report them. And you'll give me a receipt for that amount."

"Eleven golds." The words were nearly spit out.

"We're always happy to pay what is levied by the lord of the land," Hagen said cheerfully. "We want everyone to know what we paid and to whom."

The voices faded as steps on the deck above indicated that the two men had moved away from the forecastle hatch above. Kharl waited several moments before climbing up, then going out on the main deck. He stopped for a moment and looked to the east and north. Ruzor sat on the east side of the Phroan River, underneath the cliffs serving as the western ramparts against the high desert that extended westward from the Little Easthorns. It was an old port town, and despite being located on the northeast edge of a large natural bay, had but a single long stone pier for oceangoing vessels. Farther seaward was a long stone breakwater, with a squarish gray stone tower fortress at its terminus. Under a clear sky and a sun that shed little heat, the *Seastag* was tied between the set of bollards farthest out into the harbor.

Kharl headed for the watch locker, where he replaced the cudgel and secured the locker. Turning slowly, he watched as Hagen handed a leather bag to a bearded and bulky man wearing a dark blue winter jacket, its collar trimmed with golden fur. The bearded man took the pouch, bowed slightly, and walked down the gangway with stiff and jerky steps. His steps lengthened once he was on the pier, but they were still abrupt and forced.

Kharl eased toward Ghart, who had the in-port deck watch until noon.

". . . not a happy man, ser," the second said to Hagen.

"That kind never is. There won't be any shore leave, but tell the crew we'll make that up in Southport. I'm going below. Have to tell the engineer to keep some coals hot in the firebox."

"Yes, ser."

As Hagen neared the carpenter second, he nodded.

"Ser." Kharl returned the nod.

"How are those ribs?"

"Better every day."

"Good to hear that." Hagen stepped past Kharl and across the deck, before heading through the hatch to his cabin.

"Ser." Kharl addressed Ghart, who remained beside the end of the gangway. "I fixed the grip on the cudgel and replaced it in the weapons locker." He handed over the heavy bronze key.

"That's good. No shore leave, and that'll mean your watches will be quiet. 'Less that customs' weasel gets the local lancers riled up."

"Was that who the captain was talking to when I came topside? He didn't look pleased."

"He wasn't. Tried to inflate the tariff, pocket the difference. Weasel. Surprised you couldn't smell him from across the deck." Ghart shook his head. "The Prefect rules Kyphros with folk like that, and he won't be keeping it long."

"I don't know," mused Kharl. "You'd think so, but . . ."

"Could be," replied Ghart. "Folks are always fearing change." He glanced back along the pier, but the customs enumerator had disappeared.

"They're always afraid change will make things worse." Kharl chuckled ruefully. "For most folks, it does."

"You're saying that things never change," Ghart said. " 'Cause the worse they get, the more folk fear they'll get even worse."

"Until they *know* they can't get worse . . ."

"You're a cheerful sort today, carpenter."

Kharl offered a rueful smile. "Experience."

"Don't think I want to know. Seen enough I'd rather not see again." Ghart turned to look at the long wagon being driven down the pier toward the *Seastag*. "Need to get the off-loading crew. Looks like the cotton factor."

Kharl slipped away to the railing near the bow. From there, he looked over the old town once more, taking in the ancient gray stone buildings and those newer dwellings, few as they were, with white plaster walls farther westward on the narrow bluff.

Ghart's words echoed through his thoughts, and Kharl wondered just what it might take to get people to want to change a poor ruler, or if they feared change so much that no ruler would ever be changed except by death or conquest.

LIV

Kharl looked down at the pier, and then out at Ruzor. A glass had passed since he had taken the deck watch, and the cotton factor's wagons had come, been loaded, and departed. Two long and heavy wagons remained on the pier, and the deck crew was finishing the off-loading of tin ingots. Kharl walked slowly in a circle, around the quarterdeck—that ill-defined area on the main deck immediately inboard of the head of the gangway down to the pier.

The late-afternoon wind had picked up, and the sun had dropped behind the bluffs to the west of Ruzor so that the *Seastag* and the pier sat in shadow, chilled further by the wind out of the northeast. Glad that he had kept his winter jacket and was wearing it over the carpenters' grays, Kharl stopped pacing and stood by the railing, looking down and across at the metal factor's men placing the tin ingots in the second wagon. The only movements on the pier were those of the loaders, and the only ones

Kharl could see on the *Seastag* were the winch crew, although he knew some of the deckhands were down in the hold loading the heavy canvas slings.

"Last ingots!" came the call from the hold.

"Last load," Furwyl relayed from where he stood on the forward section of the poop.

The metal factor, a solid figure in a heavy brown work jacket, raised his arm in acknowledgment. The heavy sling rose out of the hold and then swung out to the pier and down onto the stone beside the wagon. The cotton had been loaded directly into the wagons, but the ingots were not. Was that because they were so much heavier that the wrong placement on the wagon could bend or snap an axle? By the time the dock loaders had placed the last ingots on the wagon, the boom was secured in its stowed position and the deck crew was folding up the sling and replacing the hatch cover.

"Winch and deck crew, you can knock off." Bemyr's voice cut through the afternoon.

"For what?" mumbled someone. "Nowhere to go."

"You heard the captain. No shore leave here. More shore leave in Southport. It's warmer there, anyway."

"Yeah . . ."

". . . except the women . . ."

"You couldn't get a woman here, either, Sonlat."

". . . and the ale's flat . . . flat as the women . . ."

"Men aren't any better," cracked one of the women riggers.

A series of laughs followed as the men and the two muscular women drifted into smaller groups.

Kharl turned his attention back to the now-empty pier, a long stretch of gray stone, tinged with pink in some places and the green of algae in others. The only other vessel at the pier was an old fishing schooner. The sunlight falling on the harbor waters to the south and east of the *Seastag* suggested that sunset was still a glass or so away.

"Quiet so far, carpenter?" asked Furwyl, easing up to the quarter-deck.

"Yes, ser."

"I'll be checking the manifests with the captain. Let us know if you see anything strange."

"Yes, ser."

As the first crossed the deck, Kharl glanced at the cudgel set against the railing forward of the gangway, then back to the pier. He looked farther west, toward the town. Was that someone on the harbor road? He scanned the pier and harbor, but his eyes kept going back to the road, and before too long he could see a rider moving at a quick trot toward the squarish heavy-timbered building that held the portmaster and the customs enumerator. The traveler neared the port building and tied his mount outside.

Kharl kept looking back toward the port building, but it was about a quarter of a glass later before the rider emerged and vaulted into his saddle. The rider was in uniform, probably a lancer of some sort, and he was continuing along the road bordering the harbor, his mount carrying him past the pier and toward the breakwater—and the fort that squatted on the seaward end.

Kharl did not want to ring the alarm bell, but he did think that either Furwyl or Hagen should know. He glanced around. No one was nearby. He crossed the deck quickly and stepped into the passageway way leading to the mates' cabins, and that of the captain. The hatch door to the captain's cabin was ajar, and he knocked.

"Yes?"

"Captain, ser, there's a lancer riding from the port building to the fort on the end of the breakwater. I didn't know if you wanted to know, but the second told me that the customs enumerator was not to be trusted . . ."

"He's still riding? How do you know—" began Furwyl, turning.

The captain lurched up from behind the table. "On deck, first. Back to your post, carpenter."

Kharl hurried back to the quarterdeck. From there he watched as Hagen climbed to the poop, a spyglass in hand. The captain only watched for a moment before calling to Furwyl, "Have the engineer go to emergency fire-up!"

"Yes, ser." Furwyl dropped down the ladder to the engine spaces.

Kharl kept watching both the pier and the breakwater. The lancer had not yet reached the breakwater fort. The carpenter second had not realized just how far out the breakwater was and how much the harbor road wound between the base of the pier and the breakwater. Still, it wasn't that long before the lancer was on the breakwater road heading to the fort.

As Kharl watched, he could smell coal smoke, and after a few more moments, a thin line of black began to flow from the stack.

Bemyr's whistle shrilled through the late afternoon. "All hands! All hands! Deck crew, make ready to cast off. Make ready to cast off! Harbor rig! Harbor rig!"

Furwyl appeared beside Kharl. "We'll leave the midships line in place and the gangway down. You know of anyone who's left the ship?"

"No, ser."

"Good." The first turned, and two of the crew—one burly man and an equally burly woman—dashed down the gangway onto the pier, the woman going forward, the man aft.

"Single up!" Furwyl ordered. "Single up!"

"Singling up!"

"Clear the aft line!"

The seaman by the aft line loosened it, then hurried back up the pier to the gangway, but waited. "Aft line clear."

"Clear the forward line."

"Forward line clear." After undoing the forward line, the woman retreated to the single cleat beside the gangway, where the other sailor joined her. Both forward and aft lines were pulled in.

"Clear the midships line."

The two unwound the line from the cleat, down to a single loop, then sprinted up the gangway. Kharl watched as the line flowed away and off the cleat as the deck crew reeled it in.

"Up the gangway."

After the gangway was winched up and back, Kharl locked the quarterdeck railing back in place flush with the fixed railing.

With the cold wind out of the northeast filling the sails, the *Seastag* swung away smartly from the stone pier. The smoke from the stack thickened, and Kharl could hear a low groaning as the engine began to turn over, slowly, then stop because there wasn't enough pressure in the boilers yet. Even without the engine, the ship was headed seaward under sail with fair headway.

Kharl glanced from the pier to the fort at the end of the breakwater. From what he could tell, Hagen was piloting the *Seastag* into the section of the channel closest to the fort. While Kharl knew the captain must have had a reason, he had no idea what that might have been.

The ship was nearing the fort, but was still a good kay away from the closest approach, which Kharl judged to be a kay and a half.

Cruump! Something flew through the forward yards and landed another fifty rods south of the ship. A gout of water gushed skyward.

Kharl realized that the something had been a shell from a cannon in the fort.

Thwup . . . thwup . . . Slowly . . . too slowly, it seemed, the paddle wheels began to turn.

Another shell whistled overhead and landed in the water less than five rods to starboard.

"Hard port!" Hagen ordered.

The *Seastag* turned port, headed almost directly at the breakwater, losing speed with each rod. Yet another shell slammed into the blue-gray harbor waters, barely off the starboard quarter, and another gout of water erupted skyward. Although the paddle wheels were beginning to pick up a slow and even rhythm, even Kharl could tell that the ship was losing headway, and might soon even lose steerageway. He could also see the water ahead lightening as they neared the shallows that sloped up to the breakwater, and the fort.

"Hard starboard!" came the command. "Full power!"

As the *Seastag* turned back to starboard, and the sails caught the wind nearly full once more, the ship seemed to leap forward—and not a moment too soon. There was the faintest scraping on the port side, as if the hull had run against the edge of a sandbar or a rock, and then another cannon shell exploded into the water less than five rods directly aft of the sternpost.

"Steady on zero nine zero!" ordered Hagen.

Another shell slammed through the rigging, and this time, a rain of debris pattered and clattered down onto the poop deck. Kharl looked up. One of the sails on the starboard side had been ripped loose of the bottom rigging and flapped in the wind. The footlines dangled, and the end gaff was missing.

The paddle wheels turned over a shade faster with each moment, and the ship continued to gain speed. The *Seastag* had passed the end of the breakwater and was now moving away from the fort at a goodly clip, the open water between the Gallosian fort and the ship increasing.

"Twenty starboard!" ordered Hagen.

Just as the ship settled onto the new heading, another shell struck just off the port quarter, close enough and with sufficient force to throw a spray of water across the forecastle. Kharl could even feel some of the spray from where he stood midships on the starboard side.

Glancing aft, he could see that once the *Seastag* had cleared the shallower waters seaward from the breakwater, Hagen had turned the ship onto a heading that presented only the stern to the cannon of the fort, keeping the ship's exposure to cannon fire as narrow as possible.

Another shell exploded in the waters aft of the *Seastag*.

Kharl waited for another shell, perhaps to strike the ship itself, but no other shells were fired, not that he could see or hear.

Furwyl took the ladder down from the poop and crossed the deck to Kharl. "Captain thinks we're out of range now." He looked at the chunks of wood and line, and several pulleys, that lay across the main deck. "You and Tarkyn are going to be busy replacing gaffs and booms," Hagen said. "Lucky they didn't hit either of the masts square."

"I don't know as it was luck, ser, was it?"

"Captain did his best, and he's good, carpenter, but there's always luck." Furwyl nodded and headed toward the bosun. "Bemyr! Get a crew here to clean up the mess."

Kharl looked back into the twilight that was beginning to descend on Ruzor and the squat Gallosian fort on the breakwater. Why were people so vindictive? Hagen had done what was right, and the customs enumerator and the Prefect's armsmen had tried to punish him and sink the *Seastag* because they hadn't gotten their way. Yet they would have been outraged had they been the buyers of the brimstone, and Hagen had sold it to someone else.

He shook his head. The Prefect's enumerator and Egen were the same sort, wanting things their own way and vindictive when they were thwarted. Did having power turn people that way?

Kharl laughed. It wasn't as though he'd ever be tempted in that fashion. Coopers and carpenters never got that kind of power.

LV

Another five days passed before the *Seastag* made her way into the port at Diehl, the most sheltered harbor that Kharl had seen. A forested peninsula guarded the seaward approach, looming over the deep channel that was less than two kays wide at the harbor entrance. Once past the entry, the *Seastag* steamed almost due west through a bay more than thirty kays wide, and from the half day that it took to reach the actual port, more than fifty kays in length. Only the Great North Bay at Lydiar had been larger, almost an inland sea, as Kharl recalled.

Kharl had been assigned the morning deck watch the day after the ship had arrived, and Hagen had appeared almost as soon as the carpenter had taken his station on the quarterdeck, opposite the still-empty pier.

"We've got the copper to off-load and some of the woolens we picked up in Nylan. Expect their port-mistress anytime, or one of the assistants. Just give me a call or ring the bell twice. I don't need to tell you, but be exceedingly polite." With a nod, Hagen had turned and returned to his cabin, leaving Kharl on the deck under high clouds, on the warmest morning Kharl had experienced in eightdays.

As Bemyr supervised the deck crew's removal of both hatch covers, Kharl studied the port and the land beyond. Diehl itself was the smallest port town Kharl had seen, not that he had seen many, with only two warehouses behind the port-mistress's structure at the foot of the single pier—a structure of old and heavy timber supported by equally old and massive stone columns. The *Seastag* was the only vessel tied at a pier large enough for two ocean traders.

The water in the bay was a warm blue, unlike the late-autumn dark blue of the Eastern Ocean or the harbor waters at the Candarian towns and cities where the *Seastag* had previously ported, and the air was warmer—and moister. Beyond the port area, everything was green—differing shades of green in a canopy of trees that stretched to the horizon in every direction where there was land.

A glass passed before a silver-haired woman walked down the pier toward the *Seastag*. Kharl had not seen her appear, but he almost nodded to himself, thinking that the port-mistress would probably be older. But as the woman neared, he could see from the unlined face and slender figure that the woman was anything but old. He'd heard that druids were silver-haired, but the druid approaching the ship was the first he had ever seen. He continued to watch, even as he stepped forward to greet her. The silver-haired figure walked up the gangway with a grace that looked youthful and had to be mature. That Kharl knew. Women were almost always the graceful ones, while girls betrayed their age through a myriad of little traits, including a touch of uneasiness and awkwardness with their movements.

"Greetings," Kharl offered, inclining his head. "Are you here about the cargo?"

The druid studied Kharl before finally speaking. "You are not from Recluce."

"No. I'm from Brysta." Kharl almost stepped back from her, so strong was the feeling of her presence . . . and a swirling linkage of both the whiteness—except it was unlike any whiteness he had sensed before—and a deeper blackness, although that seemed more like what he had felt from the mage in Nylan.

She paused. "Will you be here long?"

"The ship? The captain decides that. We have to off-load cargo, for you. Let me summon him. He wanted to know as soon as you arrived."

"No . . . not yet. I will be back with those for the cargoes." She turned and walked back down the gangway.

Kharl frowned, wondering what he had done wrong—or if he had.

"Carpenter? What did you say to her?" Furwyl crossed the deck.

"I asked if she were the one we had cargo for, and . . . she didn't say, now that I think about it. Then, she asked how long we would be here, and I said that it was up to the captain, but that we would be here until we off-loaded. She said that she would be back with those for the cargo."

At the last words, Furwyl relaxed. "If she said that, she'll be back. They never tell lies." He frowned. "I wonder why she came aboard. Haven't seen that one before."

"She had deep green eyes," Kharl said, not knowing quite why he did.

"You leave them alone," the first mate said, "if you value your life and health. Unless, of course, they ask you. Then, I hear, you're a lucky fellow."

Kharl understood. He'd felt the power in the woman, a strange sort of power, an intertwining of golden whiteness with deep blackness.

"I'll tell the captain that they know we're here."

"Yes, ser." Kharl looked down the pier, but the druid had vanished.

At least another glass passed. Kharl was looking forward to being relieved when noon came. When he scanned the pier, he saw two druids, both with silver hair, walking down the pier toward the ship, accompanied by another figure, a man in gray, with light brown hair.

Furwyl was at the gangway almost instantly, followed by the captain. Kharl stood back, behind them.

The first druid up the gangway was not the one Kharl had met. She was shorter, with amber eyes, and she turned directly to Hagen. "Captain."

"Port-mistress . . . I had heard your assistant was here . . . I hope . . . we did not offend . . ."

The druid laughed, the sound warm. "If anything . . . I am her assistant. Dayala is one of the . . . she is of the Great Forest. She told me that your watcher"—she glanced to Kharl—"was most well-mannered, and she came to tell me that you bore our cargo. Would you mind if she and her consort have a few words with him?"

"Has he . . . ?"

"No," answered the druid Kharl had first met. "He is a most honest man. But he was injured, and we would like to see if we could aid him."

"By all means." Hagen bowed his head.

"We will talk of cargoes while they talk to your man," suggested the port-mistress.

The brown-haired man, Kharl realized, was also a druid, with the same interweaving of order and chaos, and he motioned toward the bow. Kharl followed the two up the ladder and forward until the three stood beside the bowsprit.

The man smiled politely. "Dayala said that you're from Brysta."

"I am. Are you?" Kharl asked politely.

"No, and it doesn't matter, not really. I'm from Wandernaught, but you reminded her of someone I used to know." The druid shrugged.

Kharl could sense clearly the coiled power in the man, power that made the white wizard he had killed seem less than a summer mist in comparison. "I don't think we've ever met."

The other laughed. "We have not, and I doubt we'll ever meet again. But one never knows. If you don't mind, would you answer a few questions?"

"I suppose so." Kharl was wary.

"Justen . . . he still suffers from the injuries to his ribs. We should help there first," suggested Dayala.

Justen shook his head, then laughed, before speaking. "She has the right of it. She usually does. I trust you won't mind if we repair the rib that hasn't begun to heal right?"

One of his ribs wasn't healing right?

"It was broken inside, and there's . . ." The man frowned. "Let's just say that if you got hit again there, you might not live through it."

"You can do that? Without cutting into me?"

"It will not hurt," said Dayala.

"Why . . . would you . . ."

"Because it's better for us, and better for you. We'll explain afterward."

Kharl nodded.

"It's easier if we touch you. Do you mind?"

"As long as you don't jab," Kharl said dryly.

Their touch was so light that the carpenter almost did not feel either of their hands, hers on his wrist, and Justen's on the back of his neck. What he did feel was a golden warm darkness flowing into his chest, then an easing of a tightness that he had not even realized was there.

The two lifted their hands from Kharl.

"Your own order can finish the healing, and that will take time," Dayala said. "Try not to injure yourself for the next eightdays."

Kharl frowned.

"You can sense order and chaos, can you not?" the woman asked.

Kharl looked to her, then to Justen.

"It could be that you haven't recognized them that way," Justen went on. "Sometimes, when you see a person, is there a whitish fog or mist around them, one that others don't see? Or a darkness? The white means that someone is using chaos, the dark that he or she is using order . . ."

"Like you do?" asked Kharl.

"I'm somewhere between a druid and a gray mage," admitted the druid. "You seem drawn more directly to order. You work with both wood and iron, do you not?"

"I was a cooper."

The druid nodded. "You must have been very good, and I daresay that the better you got, the poorer your business became and the more unseen enemies that you gained."

"Something like that." Kharl had the feeling that the other could see inside his head, and his feelings. "What do you want with me?"

"Dayala and I don't want anything from you or with you. She feels that you are an ordered soul who could do much good wherever you go. It's obvious that you don't quite understand what has happened to you. Not totally, anyway. It's simple enough. You want order and what you'd call truth in your life, and you try to create it. Most people have trouble with that kind of directness, and because you don't understand your power, you haven't yet figured out how to be direct and ordered with yourself without unintentionally imposing that order on others."

Kharl was still wary, but he could sense none of the white chaos about the druid. What chaos the druid had was bounded in strips of golden black, or perhaps they were wound together. "Most times when I've tried to do the right thing, in recent years, it has not gone well . . ."

"It is often that way when one such as you discovers himself," Dayala said. "You must try to learn more about who you are and what you can do . . ."

"You also need to understand," Justen added, his tone sardonic, "that order, fairness, and justice, all those things you value, generally are less well regarded than gold, coins, and possessions by most people, and especially by those in power."

"How do you know so much about me?" asked Kharl.

"It is written within you," answered Dayala. "Your spirit holds the honest darkness of order, and your thoughts the power of chaos. Your back and your ribs bear witness to the cruelty of others. Your captain is a good man, and he thinks well of you."

"But the sea is not your home," added Justen, "although it can help you find where you belong."

"Where might that be?"

Justen laughed. "That's up to you. But . . . if you choose to leave where you were born, you will need to return there before you depart to make a new home. Otherwise, both will war within you."

Dayala frowned.

"Did I say something wrong? Again?" asked Justen.

Kharl looked from Justen to Dayala.

"In time," she said, "when you are sure, return home, and do what you must do. Do it with care, and with thought, and not with hatred. Hatred will destroy you."

The two druids looked at each other and nodded, then stepped away.

Kharl felt so dazed that he just watched for a moment, then started to follow them.

From the ladder she was descending, Dayala looked at Kharl. "We all must find ourselves by ourselves. Only after that can we find others."

Kharl stopped, then waited a time before descending and walking back to the quarterdeck.

Furwyl appeared. "Are you all right?"

"I'm fine. Surprised, a little dazed." Kharl shook his head. "They did something to my ribs . . . took away most of the pain."

The first smiled, wryly. "Lucky man. Most folks they leave alone. Only heard of them healing a few. All of 'em lived to a healthy old age." He paused. "Good omen for the rest of the voyage."

It might be, but was it a good omen for Kharl? The idea of having to return to Brysta—for any reason—wasn't exactly appealing. Not at all.

LVI

The next trading leg—from Diehl to Southport—was the longest yet between Candarian ports, taking seven days, partly because of the tacking required, and because Hagen used the *Seastag*'s engine sparingly to avoid burning any more coal than he had to. It was also busier for Kharl and Tarkyn, with all the rigging repairs necessitated by the Gallosian cannon, repairs that they had put off because of the rough seas between Ruzor and Diehl and had not finished in Diehl.

The *Seastag* neared the outer edge of Southport harbor in midmorning, under harbor rigging and with the paddle wheels providing a good portion of the ship's headway in the light quartering breeze. Kharl stood on the foredeck, enjoying the luxury of not having to be a part of the winch or deck crew and looking out across the blue waters of the harbor toward the dwellings scattered on the hillside above the harbor, white structures set amid the greenery. While the buildings of Southport looked far more recently constructed than any of the Candarian ports where the *Seastag* had so far docked, the port had a very different feeling—at least to Kharl. Was that because he was finally feeling healed?

Kharl couldn't help but frown as Hagen brought the *Seastag* past the outer breakwater, a long rampart of white stone stacked together, but not mortared or joined. Cut stones, he realized, but stones later broken, then piled to form the breakwater. Or had the breakwater once been a white stone wall against the Eastern Ocean, a wall broken by time—or cannon? Or the remnants of something else piled into the offshore waters?

Tarkyn stepped up beside Kharl. "Good to be in a warmer port. Not so gray and chill here. Not too hot, either, not like Swartheld."

"Is all of Hamor hot all the time?"

"Some of it's just warm. Mostly, it's hot." Tarkyn snorted. "Atla's the worst. Like standing between a pair of coal stoves. Happy we're not going there this voyage."

Kharl saw four long piers, two without ships tied at them. He didn't see a pilot boat, but the *Seastag* continued toward an empty pier. "How does he know which pier? Or does it matter?"

"In Southport? It matters. The Marshal's Arms'll make you move your vessel if you're three rods off center in your berth." Tarkyn pointed. "See the white banner with the green square? And the flag with the number one? Tells the captain he's got the first berth on that pier."

The paddle wheels slowed as the *Seastag* neared the designated pier, where two line-handlers waited.

"Forward line!" ordered Bemyr. "Aft line."

Once the lines were secured to the white bollards, the paddle wheels *thwupped* to a halt, and the deck crew walked the *Seastag* in toward the pier.

"Double up! Make it lively!" ordered Bemyr.

The *Seastag* was soon snug against the fenders that cushioned her planks from the pier, a long solid structure entirely of white stone, all of the same shade, but with stones of differing lengths and thicknesses. Kharl could also sense something odd about the way the pier felt, as though it were ancient. He looked to Tarkyn, standing beside him. "What do you know about Southport?"

"It's just another port."

Kharl looked at the sections of white stone that comprised the pier. He could sense that deep within the stone there was chaos overlaid and linked with order. "I don't think so."

"You don't think so?"

"Your second's right, Tarkyn," said Ghart from behind the two carpenters. "Some say it's the oldest port in Candar. That pier there, the Marshal of Southwind had it built some two centuries back, all out of stone dredged from the harbor bottom. Came up without moss, just like it'd been fresh-quarried. See how sharp the lines are. No one knew how long it had been there, either."

"Another of your stories." Tarkyn snorted.

"Ask the captain, if you don't believe me. Or one of the Marshal's Arms, if you dare."

Tarkyn just grunted, not looking at the second mate. Kharl repressed a smile.

"I'll be giving the in-port deck watch schedule, carpenters," Ghart added. "Tarkyn, you'll be having the afternoon watches, and Kharl, you'll be having the evening watches for the first two days. Then you two will switch. We don't have that much to off-load here, but we'll be staying a few days to give the crew a break. That's what the captain promised."

"Can I go ashore for a bit after we're secured?" Kharl asked.

"Don't see why not, so long as you're back by the fifth glass past noon."

"Thank you." Kharl nodded and slipped down to the carpenter shop, where he reclaimed his staff. Then he made his way back to the main deck, carrying the black staff. He had decided to take it, whether or not it falsely marked him as a blackstaffer. He'd seen enough to realize that Candar was a dangerous place, at least as deadly to the unprepared as . . . He struggled for a comparison . . . as Brysta had been for him?

Ghart looked at Kharl—and the staff. "Remember. Back by the fifth glass."

"I'll be here," Kharl promised.

Ghart just nodded.

Kharl walked down the gangway and along the white stone surface of the pier toward the harbor buildings and the city beyond. The stone blocks of the pier had clearly come from different structures, but from what he could see, there were no markings, no letters, and no inscriptions on the stone. Who would have gone to the trouble of cutting so much stone without so much as a single letter or carving? And why, if Ghart had been telling the truth, would the stone have been dumped into the bottom of the harbor?

At the foot of the pier stood two women, each wearing an armless blue tunic over a long-sleeved white undertunic. In one hand, each held a long truncheon. Each also wore two scabbards suspended from their leather belts, holding paired shortswords, one on each side, the kind reputed to have been used by the women of Westwind and the Legend.

The taller woman looked at the staff. "You intending to stay here?"

Kharl had to concentrate. The way the woman spoke was different. After a moment, he shook his head. "I'm the carpenter second on the *Seastag*."

"Why the staff?"

"I was given it in Nylan and told to discover who I was. So I signed on as crew. After a while, the captain decided my experience as a cooper fitted me to help the carpenter."

The patroller—or Marshal's Arm, if that was what she happened to be—nodded. "Most won't trouble you." She paused. "You looking for anything?"

"Just some time on land, maybe something to eat. Have to be back before long."

"Enjoy yourself. Best taverns are beyond Third Circle."

"Thank you." Kharl nodded politely and continued past the two and toward a squarish structure set on the other side of the stone-paved avenue fronting all the piers. Behind him, he could sense the two patrollers talking, but not what they said.

He walked past the square white stone building with the lettered sign on one side. The first line, he could read. It said: Port-Mistress. The lines below were in different languages. One, from the swirls of the letters, he thought was the old tongue, and he suspected the third line was in Hamorian. The fourth—that one he couldn't even have guessed.

There was actually a signpost on the avenue, proclaiming it as First Circle. That probably meant that all the roads around the harbor were circles. Kharl decided to follow First Circle for at least a few blocks, heading more toward what looked to be the center of Southport.

After he walked past the warehouses west of the port-mistress's building, Kharl passed a large chandlery, then a cooperage. Both were wooden-framed buildings, painted shades of blue. He continued on, walking past a cotton factor's. Looking down the avenue, he just saw more shops and warehouses, some of white stone, others of plank and timber, but all in some combination of white and blue.

A number of wagons, most drawn by two horses, passed him, some heading in his direction, others passed him in the direction of the pier holding the *Seastag*. Some of the teamsters were men, but an equal number were women. The next cross street headed to his right, up a gradual slope, and bore the name Hill Road. Kharl turned onto it, immediately passing a small spice shop and another shop that displayed vials of oils; aromatic oils, he surmised from the scents that wafted into the street.

At the next corner, opposite a café of some sort, he stopped and studied the area, taking in a cabinetmaker's establishment across from the café, and a potter's beyond that. Most of the shops and dwellings had front porches with long, overhanging eaves, and rain barrels set at the corners to catch runoff from the tiled roofs.

Looking beyond the intersection, Kharl could see, farther uphill, where Hill Road continued and turned to the northeast, rising evenly toward a gap in the forested hillside above the regularly spaced dwellings on the lower hillside. He looked at the hillside higher still, noting that despite the covering of trees there was a pattern, almost as if the entire hillside had once been smoothed, then regular sets of rounded mounds, all of differing sizes, had been placed there, with the trees being added later. There was something . . . He nodded to himself. Buildings, or dwellings, had once been spaced there, on each side of long and regular streets, and they had covered the entire hillside, and they had fallen into ruins and been covered by time and vegetation. That also suggested that few, if any, people had lived in the area, because the ruined dwellings had not been extensively quarried for building stones.

The cooper walked on uphill for more than a kay before the houses began to thin out, each having more ground, including small orchards with trees in orderly rows and stone-walled meadows. The wall stones were neatly cut and mortared, but even from the side of the road where he walked, Kharl sensed that they were old.

A young woman walked downhill toward the center of Southport, pushing a handcart and accompanied by a girl who barely came to her waist. As the two neared him, Kharl saw, in the railed space on the top of the handcart, several baskets covered with cloths.

Her eyes strayed from Kharl to the staff, and a faint smile crossed her lips as she spoke.

Kharl didn't understand a syllable of the clipped words, although he thought she was asking him to buy something. At that point, he noted the single shortsword at her belt.

She spoke again, haltingly, in what was not her native tongue. "The buns . . . the best."

Kharl was hungry. That he had to admit. "How much?"

She looked puzzled.

Kharl fished two coppers out of his wallet and held up one.

She shook her head.

He held up two.

She nodded and lifted the cloth off the top of a basket set in a rack on the cart. Then she pointed to the raisin buns and held up one finger. Kharl handed over the two coppers and waited to see her reaction. She studied the coins, then nodded.

Kharl took the largest bun, easily the size of a small loaf. "Thank you."

She smiled a last time before continuing onward.

Kharl found that it took him little time to eat the entire bun. As he finished, he licked his fingers and wished he had an ale, but all he had seen on the road nearby were dwellings.

Several thoughts crossed his mind. First, he wondered about the woman with her daughter. The patrollers in Southport had spoken a version of Brystan, or perhaps Brystan was a version of what the patrollers spoke . . . but the woman had not. Was another language spoken in Southport? Or did the patrollers at the port know two tongues? He hadn't thought about it, but he certainly should have.

The second thought was more troubling. Why was he climbing up the road? He'd started out just to look around, but he had found himself almost compelled to continue uphill. Why? He studied the road and the dwellings, their neatly tended gardens and orchards that had already fruited and been picked, with the trees' leaves graying for winter.

There was a pull of some sort. Not exactly like the white mist or the blackness of Nylan, but similar, and it seemed to be coming from somewhere slightly uphill and to the east. After a moment, Kharl shook his head and resumed walking. After another hundred cubits, he found his feet turning right onto a lane that wound away from the main road. The lane turned more to the east and, after several hundred rods, passed through two stone posts, half-buried in berry bushes and set nearly fifty cubits apart.

Ahead was a much larger mound—one that was a least three hundred cubits in length and fifty high. It had no trees upon it, just low bushes and tall grasses. Kharl stopped well short of where the foot-trod path came to a gradual end in browning grass and blotted his forehead. All the walking had left him warmer than he had anticipated.

There was a sense of sadness, of ancient sorrow, emanating from the mound, and the feeling of attraction had subsided. Kharl kept looking, but he saw nothing out of the ordinary. He could only sense a diffuse and ancient chaos emanating from the mound, and that chaos was subtly but clearly different from that which he had experienced with the white wizard.

"Well . . . have you figured it out yet?"

Kharl turned to see a thin white-haired woman, wearing a faded gray tunic trimmed with scarlet, a garment that appeared almost military, yet one that was tailored to her. A miasma of blackness surrounded her, as it had the mage in Nylan.

"I beg your pardon?" he said politely.

"What drew you here, of course." She pointed to his staff. "That's the black staff of a beginning mage. Most never make it beyond that. With your age, you're probably one of them."

"I'm not a mage. I'm just a ship's carpenter taking a walk," he replied. "What are you doing here?"

"Getting late berries from back there, and, when I feel like it, waiting for folk like you. They all come here, sooner or later." Her laugh was knowing, but full and almost soft, not the sort of cackle Kharl would have expected from a gaunt white-haired woman with eyes that had seen too much. "It's the power in the mound. What would you do with it, if you could?"

Kharl thought about denying what he'd sensed, then shrugged. "Nothing. I wouldn't know where to start. Anyway, it's the wrong kind of power for me. Could be that any kind is."

"Power will come to you," she replied. "Best you think about how you will use it, or it will end up using you." She turned.

"Is that all you have to say?" Kharl asked.

The woman stopped and half turned. "What else would you have me say?"

"I don't know . . . You have a certain power yourself . . ."

She laughed once more. "Nothing at all, a trifle. When you see true black power, you will understand that. At least, I would hope so. Good day, carpenter." She turned and walked through the grass and northward into the bushes . . . and then disappeared.

Kharl just looked for a time, then shook his head. He studied the mound once more, but could find nothing beyond the ancient sadness and strange buried combination of order and chaos. He finally walked back to Hill Road and downhill toward the harbor. When he reached Third Circle, remembering what the harbor patroller had said, he turned southwest, searching for a café or tavern that looked both inviting and not terribly costly.

In the first block he walked along after turning off Hill Road, he passed a goldsmith's, then a coppersmith's and a jeweler's, while on the south side of the street, he could make out a shop window filled with fine cabinetry of all types, and another displaying a gray cloak trimmed in a gold brocade. A tall gray-haired woman in shimmering black trousers, a white shirt, a gray jacket—and the paired shortswords at her belt—nodded as she passed him. An older man, also well dressed, but in a rich dark gray tunic and jacket and without weapons, smiled politely.

Kharl had the definite feeling that, while there might be taverns on Third Circle, his wallet would be far lighter if he stopped in any of them. He decided to walk another block or so before heading down closer to the harbor.

"Carpenter! Ser!"

Kharl turned at the call, because he couldn't imagine anyone calling him that unless it was someone from the *Seastag*. He saw a sailor standing beside a patroller outside a shop across the street. In the doorway was a tradesman in a leather vest, gesturing animatedly to the patroller.

Kharl crossed the street and stopped several cubits short of the trio, now standing in front of a narrow window displaying various items crafted from silver. It took a moment for him to recall the sailor's name. "Yes, Flasyn?"

"Ser . . . they think I took something . . . but I didn't."

"Wexalt says that your sailor made off with an object from his counter." The patroller was an older but muscular woman in the same armless blue tunic as those worn by the harbor patrollers. She held a similar truncheon, with the shortswords at her belt, and inclined her head to the tradesman.

Kharl disliked the tradesman on sight, although his face was open and guileless, and he offered an apologetic smile.

"Can't afford to lose things these days."

The words were false, genuine as they sounded, and Kharl tried not to show his dislike and skepticism.

"Ser . . . I didn't take nothing . . . I didn't."

Kharl looked at the patroller, then at the merchant, who carried the faintest hint of the unseen white chaos. "What is he supposed to have taken?"

"He lifted a silver rose. He must have dropped it when he knew he'd been seen."

Kharl looked at Flasyn. "Why were you in the silversmith's shop?"

"Ser . . . my Berye . . . she . . . well . . . I was lookin' for something special for her, but he told me to leave, and seein' as I wasn't welcome, I left straightaway . . ."

The man's words felt true, and Kharl turned to the merchant. "Do you do the silverwork?"

"What sort of . . ."

"I just wondered. You don't seem like a silversmith."

"My brother handles that. I take care of the accounts."

Kharl nodded, looking more directly at the man. "Did you see Flasyn take this rose?"

"It was missing. No one else was in the shop recently."

Kharl forced a smile. "That could well be, but that does not mean Flasyn took it, or that anyone did. That's why I asked if you had seen him take it." The carpenter fingered his beard. "Can you honestly say you saw this rose in the shop just before Flasyn came in?"

"He's the thief! You should be questioning him."

Kharl turned to Flasyn. "Did you touch anything in his shop?"

"No, ser. Couldn't have. Only things that are out are big stuff, trays."

The patroller looked at Kharl and the dark staff, then at the merchant, then back at Kharl. "Is that staff yours?"

"It is, ser."

"Where did you get it, if I might ask?"

"It was given to me in Nylan by the Brethren who—"

"Thought so." The patroller looked to the merchant. "Do you really want to make that complaint, Wexalt?"

The merchant licked his lips nervously. "I could have been mistaken, I suppose. It is missing, but I didn't see him take it . . ."

"I thought it might be something like that . . ." The patroller smiled at Kharl. "Better take your man back to your ship, ser."

"We'll be heading back." Kharl fixed his eyes on Flasyn. "Now."

"Ah . . . yes, ser."

As he turned toward the harbor and the outer pier that held the *Seastag,* Kharl did hear the patroller's words.

". . . better be more careful, Wexalt . . . real staff . . . no one can even hold one of those unless it's theirs . . . anyone who holds one doesn't lie . . . you'd look like a fool . . . and if anything happens to one of those blackstaffers . . . doesn't often . . . usually anyone who tries ends up dead . . . not too patient with games that hurt folk . . ."

Kharl had hoped to have a bite to eat, but he was going to have to forgo that. He also had more to think about, especially about the comments of the woman on the hillside.

LVII

In the growing darkness of the late-fall evening, Kharl stood on the quarterdeck by the gangway, looking blankly down at the white stones of the pier, then up to the west, above the hills beyond Southport. There, the sky was fading from a deep purple to a violet blackness, and the stars were so clear that they seemed not to twinkle at all. The air was still comfortably warm, and only a hint of a breeze blew in from off the Eastern Ocean to the south.

"Any of the crew back yet, carpenter?"

Kharl turned to face Furwyl. "Not yet, ser." Except for Flasyn, and he wasn't about to mention that to the first.

"Most of them won't be back until after Bemyr relieves you. They missed shore leave in Ruzor. Be harder for some of them here."

Since Furwyl seemed in a talking mood, Kharl asked, "Why would that be?"

"Southport's another place where the Legend is strong. Marshal of Southwind is a woman. Women run things. You saw those twin short-swords the Arms carry?"

"They're Westwind-type blades, aren't they?"

"That they are, and they can throw them as well as use one in each hand. Most women here are armed, and they won't hesitate to use them. They'll also use them on any man who seems to be getting the better of a woman. That said . . . some of them like sailors a lot, but they want to do the choosing. Some of the crew have a hard time with that."

"What happens?"

"The captain has to pay their way out of the wayfarers' gaol." Furwyl laughed. "Usually means they end up owing a good chunk of their crew share to the captain. They remember that. It's about the only thing that some of them recall. Let me know if there's any trouble. I'll be in my cabin."

While the first's cabin was little more than a pantry-sized oblong with two bunks, he didn't usually have to share it with anyone, Kharl reflected. "Yes, ser."

The deck was empty, and dim, the only lights being the stem and stern night lanterns, and the larger lantern that shed faint illumination on the quarterdeck and the top of the gangway.

It had been a strange day, as many had been in the past two seasons. *Something* had happened to him. Everyone looked at him differently. But was that just because of the staff? Or had they always and he just hadn't seen it? Or had it happened sometime in the last eightdays? He fingered his beard.

It couldn't be just the staff. He'd been having problems with some people before that. He'd angered Egen by keeping him from Sanyle. Why had he done that? Not because anyone had told him, but because he had felt that what Egen had been doing was wrong. Why had he felt that? Because he had felt it. There wasn't a better answer.

He nodded slowly.

That suggested to him that doing the right thing was attuned to order, to the blackness he had seen in Nylan, in the druids, and in the strange woman on the hillside. He had always sensed it, but never thought much about it. He had just accepted those feelings, but others had not. Charee had been more concerned with how what he did affected the family. While Charee would never have harmed anyone, she also would not have gone out of her way to help someone if it might cause trouble for her or her children. Kharl had done what he felt was right, without thinking, and the result had been disastrous.

He frowned again. He didn't want to be like Charee—he *couldn't* be that way. Yet doing as he had been doing was going to get him in trouble again, before long. What could he do differently?

He laughed softly to himself. The answer was what the woman on the hill had said—to think about how to use his enhanced senses. Not to act thoughtlessly from his feelings but to learn to think about how to act in response to others' actions. In a way, he had done that with Flasyn, without truly understanding why. He'd only known that saying that the merchant was the thief would have only made matters worse.

Kharl looked out to the white oblong that was the pier. Despite the lack of light, it seemed clear enough to him. His night sight had always been good, but lately, or since leaving Brysta, it had seemed even better. But was it his eyes?

Musing on that thought, he closed his eyes and tried to sense the pier and the gangway. Even without looking, they seemed clear to him. Was that just his imagination?

He concentrated on the nearest part of the *Seastag*'s railing, then reached out and tried to place his hand just above the varnished surface. He opened his eyes.

Even in the dimness he could tell that his fingers were but a span above the wood, and for the first time, he knowingly perceived the difference between what he was sensing and what he was seeing. He shivered as he stood there on the quarterdeck in the darkness, a darkness that was far less than that to him.

What next? He had a little more power than he once had had. He frowned. No . . . he had known that the staff had given him some power, or he had thought it had been the staff, but from what the mage in Nylan had said, the two druids in Diehl, and the woman on the hill, and what he had just discovered . . . he had always had the ability. He just had not known it. His life had been like that—always learning late what he should have known earlier.

That would have to change. How . . . he wasn't quite sure, but whether it meant reading more of *The Basis of Order* and trying to find things in the book that he could do—or try—he had to so something more than travel and watch and react.

He had to.

LVIII

Three days later, the *Seastag* steamed out of Southport and headed westward. Kharl found himself glad to be at sea, because he'd spent much of the in-port time working with a shipwright to replace the metal rigging fittings that the Gallosian cannon had damaged or blown away. He'd decided against any more expensive meals, and read several more chapters of *The Basis of Order*. After three and a half days at sea, when *Seastag* tied up at a rickety wooden pier in Dellash, Kharl was still trying to figure out how he could put some of what he read into actual practice.

No one had told Kharl much about Dellash, so that he'd finally had to ask Ghart, who had told him that Dellash was the port on the isle of Esalian. That Kharl had known, but not that it had been held by Lord Fentrel until, less than ten years before, the Duke of Delapra had enlisted a renegade wizard to bring down the hold around Fentrel, then taken the isle.

The *Seastag* was the only ocean trader in the port that afternoon, and Kharl had taken *The Basis of Order* up on deck to read, since he would be taking the evening in-port deck watch once more. He had settled himself on the foredeck, with his back against the railing, out of the brisk northerly wind, and was debating where to begin, when he heard voices.

". . . run a tight ship, Hagen . . ."

". . . don't keep a ship unless you do, honored Synadar. Would you like to go below to discuss matters?"

". . . nothing to discuss we can't say out here. You have the brimstone?"

"That we do—all hundred and fifty stone. It was a rather costly cargo."

Kharl frowned. The customs enumerator at Ruzor had claimed the brimstone was two hundred stone. Or was the other fifty stone for another buyer? That had to be the answer, but Kharl wondered who the other buyer might be.

"How so?"

"The Prefect of Gallos wished to purchase it. We had to leave Ruzor rather quickly."

"And you sold him none?"

"No," replied Hagen. "I did not know for whom you acted. Were it him, I saved you coins. Were it someone at odds with him . . . that would have been even less wise."

"Some captains would not have shown such . . . restraint . . ."

"Some captains might call it stupidity to overlook a quick and high profit," replied Hagen. "Those are the ones who will die coinless or with a knife in the back."

"Stupidity? You have such contempt for extra coins?"

"I like coin as much as the next man," Hagen said. "But you don't enjoy them by betraying committed buyers. Not for long."

"Such noble words, such honesty . . ." Synadar's laugh was mocking. "So ethical . . ."

Hagen laughed. "You have your cargo of brimstone. Would you have it were it not so?"

"No . . . but you would not have ported here."

"Nor would I have ever been able to, and what would that have cost me, year after year?"

"So much for your vaunted honesty, Hagen . . ."

"Are you ready to have it off-loaded?"

"Such haste."

"Haste indeed," Hagen agreed. "Haste to obtain your coins. You surely understand that?"

"I have them in the strongbox. Come . . . you can inspect them and begin off-loading."

Kharl did not budge as the two men moved away.

He had felt Hagen's honesty, and the chaotic dishonor of the trader. Hagen had acted fairly and honorably, but under the guise of self-interest, and the trader had accepted self-interest even while he had scorned the ideas of fairness. Was that deception on Hagen's part?

Did the book have any passages on deception and honesty? Kharl began to leaf through the pages until he found a section that looked like it might address his questions.

> The greatest danger in practicing deception is not the reaction of others, whether it be anger or cupidity. A greater danger is the cultivation of contempt for that which is. Deception is a practice of contempt, contempt for those whom one would deceive, and contempt for the world as it is. Just as understanding what is must be the first step toward using order, contempt for a true vision is the first step toward being the tool of power rather than its enlightened user . . .

Kharl nodded. That made sense, but it didn't offer him anything to *do* . . .

He kept reading. In time, he came to another section.

> . . . often those inexperienced in using order will force raw order upon an object, thinking that such an effort will strengthen the object. Such an effort will indeed strengthen the object, even as it weakens the one who attempts this, but only so long as the would-be mage lavishes his strength. When his strength is spent, the object will become once more as it was. Far better is to study the object, and to learn how it is tied together with order and chaos, and to gently change those bonds in keeping with what the object is, for if weak bonds are properly replaced by strong bonds within the object itself, those bonds will remain strengthened, just as black iron remains stronger than iron forged without ordering . . .

Kharl sat up. He had black iron on his staff, and there were iron brackets in the carpenter shop. Could he compare the two somehow? He closed the book and stood, uncoiling in the brisk afternoon wind and stretching, before heading below.

The shop was empty, and Kharl eased his staff out of the overhead bin where he had replaced it and set it on the narrow bench against the bulkhead. Then he took out an iron bracket and set it on the bench, directly beside the banded section at one end of the staff.

He looked at the two metals. The black iron was darker, indeed blackish to the sight, while the iron of the bracket was a duller gray. He couldn't compare their weights, and he already knew that the black iron was harder. So he closed his eyes and tried to sense the difference between the two. Almost instantly, he could feel the aura of darkness tied to the black iron.

He opened his eyes, and he still saw the difference. Was that because he was learning how to use some sort of order-sensing? He tried to sense the linkages or ordering within the black iron. At first, nothing happened. All he could feel was the order-darkness. But he *knew* there was more there. He tried to see if he could sense a difference in the grain of the metal. That made a difference, because the iron bracket somehow felt rough, almost jagged, in comparison to the black iron bands on the staff.

Could he make plain iron into black iron? Somehow, the bracket looked large and heavy, even though it was only slightly larger than his hand and but a fraction of a thumbspan in thickness. Kharl bent down and looked in the bins below the bench, where he found an iron nail. He straightened and set it on the bench beside the staff.

Then he concentrated on sensing just how the black iron felt, how the grain of the metal almost locked together. Could he somehow smooth the "roughness" of the nail into a pattern like that of the staff bands? He tried just imagining, visualizing that change. Nothing happened.

Could he use his order-sense more like a forge hammer, in a regular rhythm, striking, shaping?

How long he concentrated on that Kharl was not sure, except that a good quarter glass had passed, and the nail was darker—not quite with the smooth orderedness of the staff's black iron, but far more ordered and . . . solid.

As he looked at the nail, he felt light-headed and had to reach out and steady himself with a hand on the bench. He looked down at the iron nail once more, which was no longer gray iron, but a form of black iron.

"I did it . . ." he murmured.

But he felt so weak—and all for a little nail.

He sat down on Tarkyn's stool and took out the book. Doggedly, he began to skim through pages.

Black iron should only be created while being forged . . . attempting to change less-ordered cold iron into black iron is possible only with great effort, enough to exhaust even the strongest of mages . . .

Kharl didn't know whether to shake his head or laugh. Once more, he had almost gotten himself into danger because he hadn't been patient enough. He took a deep breath, then reached out and slipped the black iron nail into his wallet. Sometime, he might find a use for it, but if not, it might be a good reminder that he needed to try to learn more before he acted.

Then, that had always been his problem—except where he had not acted at all.

LIX

Once through the Straits of Esalia and past Summerdock, where the *Seastag* did not port, Hagen brought the ship onto a course to the northwest for most of the day. In late afternoon, as Kharl took a break from working on a replacement for a top gaff that had splintered, and stood near the bow, he checked the position of the sun. Then he glanced to starboard, where he could just make out the thin line of darkness that was land. From what he could tell, the ship was headed back eastward. A glass or so earlier, Kharl had felt that the ship had begun to pitch more than earlier in the day, and ahead, the swells were deeper.

He glanced up. Rhylla was standing just forward of the paddle wheels. Kharl walked toward the third mate.

"Ser?"

"Carpenter. How are you coming with that gaff?"

"Be done later this afternoon." Kharl gestured toward the distant shore. "Thought we were headed to Hamor."

"We are. The captain heard that the *Suntasan* went aground night before last, broke her back on the reefs of Cape Feer. So we're headed to

Biehl first. He didn't tell anyone, not even the officers, until we were clear of Dellash."

Kharl cocked his head. "Are we trying to get to pick up a cargo that the *Suntasan* would have taken?"

"It's cargo—fine china. Captain thinks we can take their cartage. No one else knows yet." Rhylla paused. "Some skippers know that the *Suntasan* went aground, and there might be some that know Captain Ceagir was the regular shipper for the china folk, but the ones who know that don't seem to be in this part of the Eastern Ocean. Captain thought it was worth a try."

"China's worth that much?"

"This is very special china, for the emperor's household. There are almost always special shipments in late fall, and they have to get to Swartheld before the turn of the year. That's what the captain said. We might even get a bonus if it works out."

"There any pirates around here?" Kharl's tone was dry, not quite ironic. "I'd heard of Delapran pirates."

"Most of them were killed or hanged." Rhylla laughed. "The rest . . . not in these waters, this time of year. Pirates would be east of Biehl, looking for better pickings. Besides, there wouldn't be many buyers for stolen china marked for the Emperor of Hamor. Pirates like goods that can't be traced. Most thieves do."

Kharl nodded. That was true of other malefactors, even lordly ones. Egen certainly tried to keep his deeds hidden. "Better get below and back to work."

LX

In the late afternoon of threeday, Kharl stood just aft of the bowsprit, looking out at the town of Biehl, wondering if he should go ashore and try to find a decent place to eat. After a time, anything tasted better than ship fare, although not too many eightdays earlier, he would not have felt that way. He smiled at that thought.

Age hung over Biehl, so much so that the carpenter wondered if it had *ever* been new. The stone edges of the single pier were rounded, as if every sharp corner had been worn away by time and water. Seaward from the pier was another set of gray columns and dark stones barely covered by harbor waters, the remnants of another pier. The one pier that held the *Seastag* jutted out into the River Behla, a narrow river that, from the marshy grass that choked both shores farther inland, had once been far larger.

Across the stone causeway that doubled as harbor wall and access road to the pier was a short row of structures—their lower levels plastered and painted a pale blue. Both plaster and paint were worn away in places, exposing the old yellow brick beneath. The upper levels of those buildings were of weathered planks buried beneath layers of paint.

A much-painted but faded sign bearing the crossed candles of a chandlery was set above the sagging porch of the building just across from the foot of the pier where the *Seastag* was tied. To the left of the chandlery was a cooperage, its frontage less than half that of what Kharl's had been in Brysta. A third building bore no sign at all.

Kharl turned, trying to make out the ruins that Furwyl claimed lay on the eastern side of the river, but he could see little above the marsh grass except irregular patches of trees. The mixed odors of dead fish, mud, and salt water swirled around Kharl in the late-afternoon breeze that gusted off the blue-black water north beyond the harbor. Whitecaps topped the choppy harbor waves.

To the northwest of the pier, well beyond the harbor and the dwellings, was a small bluff less than twenty cubits higher than the water of the harbor. At the top of the bluff was a long pile of stones, from which grew bushes and occasional trees. Kharl thought that the stones might have once been a fort guarding the harbor, but it was clear that it had been generations since the fort had been used—if indeed it had been a fort at all.

"Feels like it's dying, doesn't it?" asked Ghart, from behind Kharl.

"The town? It does," Kharl replied. "Did we get that china?"

"Captain says we got the china consignment, and that we've even got space for some clay."

"Clay?"

"Biehl clay is the best in Candar, maybe anywhere in the world. Has been so long as anyone can remember. We can stow it just above the bilges, replace some of the ballast, and sell it in Hamor.

Be loading tomorrow, setting out early the next morning."

"Somehow . . . hadn't thought you could make coins on clay." Kharl laughed.

"You can make coins on just about anything, if you buy it cheap enough," Ghart pointed out. "Captain's always telling us that it matters more what price you buy at than what price you sell. You buy low enough, and you can sell anywhere at a profit. Even in Swartheld, with all the world trying to undercut you."

"That's if the quality's good," Kharl said.

Ghart grinned. "He says that, too."

Someone cleared his throat, and Kharl turned.

"I'm headed ashore," Tarkyn said to Kharl. "Need some ale, and anything besides ship fare. Want to join me?"

"I'd like that." Kharl had no in-port deck watch until midday the next day, and he liked the thought of eating with Tarkyn, rather than alone. "They take our coins here?"

"Folks here will take any land's coins, with pleasure." Tarkyn gestured. "Coming?"

"If my coin's good, I'm with you."

"Have a good time, carpenters," Ghart called, as the two headed down the gangway.

Tarkyn snorted. "Never have a good time, not one that doesn't cost more than you'd want to pay, or more than that, but there's always a chance for good fare."

"Or better than ship fare," Kharl pointed out.

"Not hard to do better 'n that."

Kharl followed Tarkyn's lead as the older man turned left on the causeway, and the two walked south toward the main part of the ancient town.

"Haven't been in Biehl in years." Tarkyn glanced at the chandlery. "Looks about the same, shabbier maybe. But it'd be hard to get much shabbier. There's a better tavern down here, past the old square and across the way. Used to be, anyway."

Kharl followed the older carpenter down two long blocks, past warehouses, some boarded shut and others with doors that sagged on their hinges. Nothing they passed could have been built in Kharl's lifetime, and he wondered if some of them had even seen paint or stain in that time.

Three blocks away from the harbor, the two men reached a square of sorts, an area once paved with smooth granite, but close to half of the paving stones had been replaced with bricks or cobblestones or, in some places, with clay. In the center was an obelisk, and unlike the stones of the town, it was sharp-edged, a crisp stone monument at odds with the decay that surrounded it.

Kharl could sense that the stone had been reinforced with order, order forced into and through the very essence of the granite, an ancient order. "What's that? Do you know?"

"Locals told me it's as old as Biehl, maybe older, to some ancient emperor of Cyador. Maybe he came from here. Lots of old and strange things in Candar, especially in the west." Tarkyn shrugged. "We go down that street there."

The street to which Tarkyn pointed looked to hold structures merely old, as opposed to ancient, and most had been maintained. The Crown was a narrow building, less than twenty cubits wide, sandwiched between a felter's and an unmarked structure that might have been a boardinghouse, or something less reputable.

A rotund woman in blue met them just inside the door. "The two of you?"

It took Kharl a moment to understand her words.

Tarkyn had no such difficulty and replied immediately. "Two, for supper."

Despite the narrowness of the place—and Kharl wasn't sure what to call it, because it was neither café nor tavern—it was deep enough to hold a good ten tables in the public room. Most of the tables were taken, and the woman seated them at a smaller table along the wall.

"Hope it's as good as last time," said Tarkyn.

"When was last time?"

"Maybe ten . . . eleven years back." The older carpenter smiled. "Things don't change so much here."

A younger woman appeared. She looked to the older carpenter.

"A good dark ale," Tarkyn said.

"Lager. Pale ale if you don't have it," added Kharl.

The woman nodded, then said, "Tonight we have poached sea trout, fresh caught, with pasneti noodles. We also have boar steak with fried apples and baked golden yams. We also have net noodles with the fish stew, and chops with fried potatoes. Everything is five coppers."

"The chops, not overdone," replied Tarkyn.

"The boar steak," Kharl added, glad he had brought a silver or two with his coppers.

"Thank you." With a smile, the woman stepped away from them and turned toward the rear of the public room, presumably toward a kitchen.

"Good food costs more." Tarkyn stretched and took a deep breath. "True anywhere you go."

"You must know the good places to eat in every port."

"Some don't have any." Tarkyn glanced up.

The server returned with two tall crystal mugs, setting the dark one before the older man, and the lighter brew before Kharl. "Three coppers, each, sers."

Kharl extended four. He thought Tarkyn did as well. She smiled and slipped away.

In the momentary silence, Kharl caught some words from the nearest table.

". . . haven't seen them before . . ."

". . . sailors from that ship just ported . . ."

". . . not sailors . . . must be officers, mates . . ."

Kharl found it strange to be considered an officer, even a subofficer.

"You got a feel for wood, don't you?" Tarkyn took a long pull of the dark ale. "Ah . . . tastes good. Nothing better 'n good dark ale."

Kharl thought the dark brews chewy, much preferring pale ale or lager. "Guess I've always had a feel for woods. Liked to work with white or black oak best. Red oak . . . just didn't feel the same."

"What about spruce . . . pine?"

"Depends on the tree."

"Doesn't everything?" Tarkyn laughed. "No tree's the same as another, no animal, no person, no ship . . ."

"Is that why you've stayed on the *Seastag*?"

"Couldn't find a better captain, not anywhere. Be a good lord, too, were he minded. Top carpenter, that's as good as I'll do. So . . . the ship matters most." Tarkyn paused as the server slid a large light blue platter in front of him. Another one went before Kharl.

Kharl set out a silver, as did the older man.

In a moment, there were two stacks of five coppers, one before each man, although the coppers were of differing sizes and thicknesses.

After just a few bites, Kharl decided that the boar steak was one of the better meals he'd had, perhaps the best since the one he'd had in Lydiar, and the fried apples were perfect, just between crisp and chewy, without being heavy.

"You're enjoying the grub?"

"Very much."

"Thought you would. You should have been a ship's carpenter from the first. Might even have made it out of the fo'c's'le early on."

"Have you always been a ship's carpenter?"

"Me? No. Started out as a cabinetmaker's apprentice in Kaerloch—little place not too far from Bruel. Didn't like all the detailing, the fussiness. Finally ran away after a couple of years. Worked as a sawboy in a mill. Didn't care much for that, either . . ." Tarkyn took another pull of the dark ale.

Kharl was content to eat and listen.

LXI

The voyage from Biehl to Hamor was long—two and a half eightdays. Kharl kept busy at whatever tasks were set before him. Some of that was internal work on bulkheads and decks, anywhere that water had managed to damage wood. He even repaired one of the cover panels on the port paddle wheel. When he was not working, sleeping, or eating, he was reading or—far less often—trying to exercise his still-limited order-skills. By the time the western coast of Hamor was in sight as a low dark line off the starboard bow, Kharl had read through every page of *The Basis of Order*. He could not say that he understood everything he had read.

He hadn't attempted to turn any more cold iron into black iron. He had tried using the ideas in the book to speed the healing of several minor cuts and scrapes he had received, and they did seem to heal more quickly, but whether that was because of his efforts, he still wasn't certain. The only thing that had been certain is that the healing had not been instantaneous—and the book had said that it wasn't supposed to be.

Within the last few days of the voyage, the air had grown warmer, and damper, and the heavy long-sleeved gray carpenter's shirt had gotten uncomfortably warm. That had forced Kharl to purchase a short-sleeved gray shirt from the ship's slop chest at more than he'd wished to spend, but the shirt was well-made and far more comfortable than the heavier winter shirt.

As the *Seastag* continued southeast, the coastline of Hamor resolved itself into a line of whitish cliffs that rose to the south over calm and light blue waters. A good three kays seaward from those waters was a line of foaming water where waves broke over a reef.

Kharl stood at the bow on the starboard side. East of the *Seastag* but farther out to sea, a dark-hulled vessel without rigging steamed westward. As it drew nearer, Kharl could see the white metallic finish of gun turrets, two long guns to a turret, two turrets forward, and one aft.

"That's a Hamorian light cruiser," offered Hagen from behind Kharl. "Newer class. Three turrets. Older ones just have two, one fore and one aft."

Kharl could sense worry behind the captain's words. "Do they attack merchanters?"

"Not that I know of. But the emperor's been building up his fleet— all with bigger guns."

"Never saw a ship like that. Lord West has two ships with single turrets fore and aft." Lord West might have had more, for all Kharl knew, but he'd seen two.

"No one else has ships with that kind of power, except Recluce, and no one knows exactly what the black mages have." Hagen snorted. "No one else has the ability to mine and forge that much metal. They say the ironworks at Luba produce half the world's iron. The whole city is a forge, and you can walk anywhere, anytime, in the light of the furnaces. I don't know as I believe all that—but that's where all the engines and plates for the Hamorian fleet come from." He glanced to the south, nodding. "They do everything big in Hamor."

Kharl followed the captain's gaze. At the point of a peninsula abeam of the ship was a tall stone tower with a shimmering dome. Kharl studied the tower.

"That's the northwest light tower," offered Hagen. "At night, there's a beam of light that sweeps across the waters. More wrecks than you can count on the Heartbreak Reef there."

"Even with the light?"

"There's fog and storms . . . and sometimes at night brigands will light fires farther west and use canvas to mimic the light. Hamorian fleet patrols the waters, but they can't get inshore, not with the reefs. Sometimes they turn their guns on the ship-breakers. They've been known to kill a few. Turned a lot of rock into gravel in the process."

Kharl pondered that. Guns that could fire four kays over the reefs and hit the shore?

Hagen cleared his throat. "Wouldn't be taking that staff ashore, not in Swartheld. Folk here don't take kindly to Recluce. Never have. One place that doesn't fear the blacks. Don't think Recluce even sends black-staffers here any longer."

"Do you know why?" asked Kharl.

"Something way back . . . the mage who founded Recluce . . . they say he destroyed a Hamorian war fleet with weather magery, except for a few ships that he refitted into his own fleet . . . and that he refused to pay the emperor a single copper . . ."

"A single mage went out and attacked the Hamorian fleet?"

"Doubtful mind you've got, cooper." Hagen laughed. "Wasn't like that. They and the white mages of Fairven were trying to squash Recluce before it got started. This mage—Creslin, that was his name—destroyed the invasion fleet. Emperors don't like that."

"That must have happened a long time ago, and they're still upset?"

"No one in Hamor ever forgets anything," the captain replied dryly. "They don't learn much new, but they don't forget. That's why some captains aren't welcome here. Tread lightly onshore." Hagen laughed again and turned back toward the poop deck.

Kharl looked back toward the stone tower and the white cliffs. Were most people like that, never forgetting, and holding hard to hatred for generations, so long that most of the rest of the world had long since forgotten the cause?

LXII

Of all the ports the *Seastag* had visited while Kharl was aboard, Swartheld was the busiest. In the late afternoon, the harbor was filled with ships, some anchored in deeper waters offshore, others tied at the long and wide piers. Another set of piers ran along the far side of the bay, but all the vessels at those piers were the black-hulled warships of various sizes, all steam-powered, with iron hulls and a white superstructure and white gun turrets. Kharl had counted over thirty such vessels, and mooring space for at least triple that number, and he understood better Hagen's wariness of a land with so many warships.

He had to wonder about all that iron and all that powder. Supposedly, a white mage could fire gunpowder or cammabark. Did all the iron—and the ocean itself—protect the ships? Or were there mages on board as well?

Kharl glanced out from the quarterdeck at the pier where the *Seastag* was tied. It was not only long, but a good hundred cubits wide, with wagons lined up for loading and off-loading, and vendors with handcarts pushing them from ship to ship. The voices of the vendors filled the air.

"Silks, silks . . . the finest silks from Atla . . ."

". . . the finest wools from Recluce and Brysta . . ."

"Spices . . . brinn from Candar, brinn and astra . . ."

"Tools . . . iron tools, Hamor's finest from the works at Luba . . ."

There were so many street and cart vendors that at times the teamsters driving the wagons being loaded and unloaded had to wait, or actually drive their teams into the crowds to force them away from the ships. While Brysta had peddlers and vendors, the numbers and variety were nothing compared to those on just the one pier where the *Seastag* was tied.

For once, Kharl did not have an evening watch, but the late-morning watch the next day. So he had decided to investigate Swartheld, despite limited coins. He had not drawn any of his pay recently, preferring to leave it on account with Hagen, suspecting he'd need all of it when the *Seastag* reached Austra.

"If you're going ashore," offered Ghart, "best be real careful. Any place said to be the wellspring of chaos, Hamor is. If you were one of the younger men, I'd caution you about the girls . . . never seen such lovelies, and you go with 'em, never will again. Probably end up working in the great ironworks at Luba, or lugging stone on that Great Highway the emperor's building and rebuilding . . ."

Kharl hadn't heard of the Great Highway, but he didn't need an explanation, except perhaps why the Hamorians wanted to call everything "great." "Drugged wine or ale?"

"Or just a cosh on the back of the head." Ghart snorted. "No matter what we say, we'll lose someone. Usually one of the younger crew. Always someone who knows better."

"Anything else I should watch?"

"Watch everything," Ghart suggested, his voice wry. "The captain does."

Kharl nodded. "I'll be back before dark."

"That's what they all say." Ghart laughed good-naturedly.

Even before Kharl was halfway down the gangway, he felt a strangeness wash over him, a feeling that was both familiar and totally unfamiliar. What was the feeling? Why was it familiar? When he reached the end of the gangway and his boots rested on the wide stone wharf, he moved back, less than a body length from the hull of the *Seastag*. There, he took a deep breath and tried to recall where he had sensed that same feeling.

After a moment, he recalled. That feeling had been in Southport, when he had been at the site of the ancient ruins, with its deep-seated mixture of order and chaos. The port area of Swartheld felt similar, except there was more chaos swirling around, diffuse chaos, and that was what had felt both familiar and unfamiliar.

Carefully, Kharl began to walk down the pier, toward the buildings beyond the shoreward end of the pier. He kept his eyes moving, and his order-chaos senses alert. He passed a cart with an open grill, and the aroma of spiced roasted fowl made his mouth water.

"The best fowl in Swartheld . . ." Those words were followed by another set with the same intonation, but in a tongue unknown to Kharl. A third language followed before the vendor returned to the Candarian version of Brystan—although Kharl couldn't honestly have said he knew whether Brystan was a version of Candarian or the other way around.

"Cottons . . . cottons . . . shirts for the summer heat . . ." That vendor also pitched his wares in several languages.

"Indentured slaves . . . young men, young women . . . in the best of health . . ."

Kharl glanced across the pier, where a young man and a girlish woman were displayed, standing on a wagon bed, chained to the frame, wearing little but cloths around their loins.

". . . in the best of health and form . . ."

Turning away, Kharl stepped to his right, then stopped as a four-horse team slowly moved out toward the *Seastag*. After the wagon passed, he continued walking, keeping some distance between himself and the peddlers and others on the wharf. Ahead of him, somewhere near the end of the pier, Kharl could sense the unseen swirling whiteness that marked a chaos-wizard, although the whiteness was not as strong as that of the wizard he had confronted in Brysta.

He eased to the edge of the pier away from the chaos-wizard, closer to a three-masted clipper, an ancient vessel without steam power and with an ornate carved figure of a woman with extravagant physical charms under the bowsprit. He stopped beside a bollard and bent, as if to check his boot, his back shielded by the bulk of the bollard, as he let his own senses study the whiteness on the far side of the pier and inshore.

He could feel nothing except the whiteness. He straightened, then continued in along the pier on the side away from the white miasma of chaos.

Four darker-skinned men wearing short-sleeved shirts and trousers of a light khaki fabric marched onto the pier from the stone-paved causeway perpendicular to it. Each wore a khaki cap with a bronze starburst set in a blue oval. They also carried polished oak truncheons and wore shortswords at their belts—and pistols. Kharl had heard that the Hamorians used firearms, but he had never seen any closely. He almost could have reached out with his senses and touched the shells and the powder within, not that he could have touched off the powder, not with order, but a brush of chaos might have done so, even within the ordered metal shell casings.

Directly behind the four armsmen, clearly being escorted by them, was an older and gray-haired man who also wore a uniform, but of black and orange. The older man carried no weapons, and the only insignia he bore was a heavy silver chain from which hung a white bronze starburst medallion.

Along with the others on the pier, Kharl stopped and watched as the five halted opposite a dark red cart. Belatedly, Kharl recognized two things. First, the miasma of chaos was surrounding a thin man dressed in flowing green, and second, the man in orange and black was also a wizard, but his chaos power was contained, so that until he was within ten cubits or so, even Kharl's order-chaos senses had not sensed the power held within some sort of shields.

The four men in khaki set themselves so that two flanked the uniformed wizard on each side. Light gathered around the figure in orange and black, and the crowd moved back once more, creating a circle around the thin man in flowing green.

"You," began the uniformed wizard, addressing the man in green. "You have attempted the practice of wizardry without the permission of the emperor. You have not presented yourself for examination, and you have hidden from others that you employed the forces of chaos to deceive and to profit personally. You have preyed upon outlanders . . ."

A resigned expression fell across the face of the man in green. "I did present myself, honored mage. I presented myself, but none would see me, save that I presented golds I do not have. One cannot—"

"Silence!"

The man in green's voice continued. "I have not used wizardry. I have deceived no one. All I have done is to be too poor to provide golds—"

A whitish red fireball appeared at the fingertips of the uniformed wizard, then flared toward the man in green. *Whhhsttt!!!*

A white dome appeared around the man in green, and for a moment that dome was surrounded by the white fires of chaos, but the man in green remained behind his shield.

Kharl tried to sense what it was that the green wizard had done, but before he could truly and fully sense the chaos-shield, the gray-haired wizard flung a second firebolt, and the shield collapsed into a pillar of white fire.

Kharl had to blink, and when he could see, where the man in green had stood there was but a small pile of whitish ash in the midst of a black greasy smear on the grayish stones of the pier.

"The will of His Mightiness! Striking down evil where it occurs," intoned the gray-haired wizard. Then he turned and walked back off the end of the pier.

Even from the far side of the wharf, Kharl had noted the fine sheen of sweat on the surviving wizard's face—and the much-lowered level of chaos that remained locked around him. Clearly, using that kind of power took much energy.

At the faintest sense of someone too close to him, Kharl's hand lashed out, slamming down on the wrist of a young cutpurse. As the carpenter whirled, a thin knife clattered on the stones, and two other youths began to run.

Another man in tan appeared, his truncheon smacked the cutpurse across the temple, and the youth went to his knees. Whiteness flashed from somewhere else.

Kharl looked at the Hamorian patroller, or Watch, or whatever keepers of the peace were called in Swartheld.

"You were very quick, sailor."

"Just lucky, ser," Kharl replied, noting that the crowd had moved away from him and the patroller. He could also see the Hamorian wizard returning, something he did not like at all. With the wizard were the other four patrollers—and two dazed-looking youths with blank faces. Kharl could sense some sort of chaos laid over them.

"You are from Recluce?" The wizard looked directly at Kharl.

"No, ser. I am from Brysta, and I am the second carpenter on the *Seastag*."

The wizard looked at Kharl for a long moment, and Kharl could sense some other sort of power, grayish, brushing him lightly, like the touch of an unseen spider, but he remained still and waited.

"So it would seem. Did you see what happened here a few moments ago?"

"Yes, ser. You destroyed a wizard who had not followed the laws of Hamor."

"Those laws apply to all who walk the soil of Hamor. Do you understand that?"

"Yes, ser."

"Good." The wizard gestured to the patrollers. "Take the cutpurses to the transfer gaol." He looked at Kharl. "They will spend five years— or more—cutting and moving stone for the Great Highway. That is a light punishment. They could have gone to the furnaces at Luba."

Kharl wanted to lick his dry lips. He did not. "I understand."

"I believe you do, carpenter. Good day." Again, the wizard turned, and this time five patrollers followed him, herding the three captives before them.

As they walked away, and those in the crowd gave Kharl passing looks before moving on, he just stood by the stone column marking the end of the pier. The wizard had delivered a clear message without spelling it out. The carpenter pulled himself together, then left the pier and turned left, toward the part of the waterfront that had looked to hold shops and taverns.

Once Kharl was off the pier and onto the street that fronted the harbor, he could move more freely, without feeling so crowded. By the time he had walked past the end of the next pier, one that held but a single small sloop, there were almost no peddlers or carts, just people heading in various directions, or standing before shop windows, or coming in or out of the shops. Compared to Brysta or any other port he had visited, it was crowded.

Most of the shops seemed to carry fabrics. He counted four shops in a row—one dealing just in silks, another in woolens, a third in linens, and a fourth in cottons. In those four shops were as many bolts of cloth as in all of Brysta, from what Kharl knew.

He walked on, but then couldn't help but stop at the display window of a cooperage in the next block. The barrels were good, but not nearly so good as what he'd crafted, especially the hogshead he saw on display. Yet the cooperage was clearly profitable.

The next shop was one that handled blades. Kharl found himself wincing as he looked at the gleaming array in the display window— sabres, cutlasses, a menacing hand-and-a-half sword, an even longer and wider broadsword, and all manner of knives and dirks. He'd never cared much for blades, but he'd also never felt the revulsion that he did as he beheld the assemblage before him. Was there a difference between working blades and weapons? If so, why did he feel that way? Or had he always, and simply not recognized it? With a shake of his head, he turned and continued to the corner. Across the narrower cross street was a tavern, and one thronged from the sounds issuing forth—despite the fact that it was still afternoon.

Kharl turned left, away from the harbor, and walked along the side of the street, passing first a closed doorway without any sign or indication of what lay behind it, then a wider doorway, with a sign showing a bed, and the words beneath beginning with "Rooms for the night" in Brystan and repeating in other languages.

"Girls . . . you want one?" A veiled woman beckoned from across the street. "Come and see. Take your pleasure . . ."

Kharl kept his smile to himself and continued to walk, this time past a rope shop.

A rope shop? In any other port, rope would be in a chandlery. Was Swartheld so large that a merchant could sell just ropes of various types? He glanced through the open doorway, taking in all the coils of ropes and lines.

A sickish-sweet odor drifted down and across Kharl, a scent compounded of something burning, perhaps incense, with something stronger. He faintly recalled the smell, then nodded. Kernash—the substance smoked by those with little hope and less future.

Kharl continued toward the next major street. The grayish wooden buildings in the first block gave way to painted structures in the second, and then two- and three-story stone-walled buildings in the third, and then even taller structures, with carved cornices and wide windows above the first floors. Kharl emerged from the side street and turned right once more, glad to find himself on more of a boulevard, where several shops actually had flowers in planters beside their windows.

The second shop on the side of the street away from the harbor held hats—broad-brimmed hats for women. The third shop was a tailor's, and it displayed jackets and colorful vests, all of silk or light fine cotton, but for men.

Beyond the immaculate shops with their wide glass windows and open archways was a café under a white-and-black-striped awning. Both men and women sat at tables in the shade. Most wore shimmering white, the men in white trousers and boots, and embroidered white shirts with lace and designs in silver, and the women in loose white robes of some light fabric. The women also had filmy white scarfs across their bare shoulders, as if the scarfs would be used as cover or veils when they left the café.

Kharl strained to hear what they said, but realized that they must all have been speaking in Hamorian, because he understood not a word.

In his plain and worn carpenter's grays, Kharl felt very out of place. He kept walking.

LXIII

After returning to the *Seastag* just before sunset on the first day in Swartheld, Kharl thought, and read, then slept less than easily. He dreamed of white wizards in burgundy, in black and orange, and in flowing green—all speaking in languages he did not understand and doing all manner of wizardly tasks he could not have explained, let alone duplicated. He asked them, and they ignored him, as if he did not exist, and went on with their incomprehensible tasks.

He woke early the next morning, pooled in sweat, and not just from the heat and dampness of Swartheld. After deciding that he could not sleep longer, he eased out of his forecastle bunk, and slipped out with his clothes. He washed up as quietly as he could and then made his way topside.

In the gray light before dawn, Kharl stood at the railing near the bow. Even in the open air, there was not so much as a hint of a breeze. A light haze blurred the outlines of the buildings and the more distant piers and ships, giving them an air of unreality. For the moment, the pier was empty, without vendors and without teamsters and wagons, and Kharl relished the comparative silence. Even the city seemed hushed, and Kharl could hear the lapping of the harbor waters against the pier and against the hull of the *Seastag*.

In time, he heard footsteps, but he did not turn.

"You came back early," Rhylla said. "With all your coins, I'd wager."

"I didn't take that many," Kharl admitted. "I had an ale, and some supper. The ale was worth it."

"They like their foods hot and spicy here. I think most folks in warm places do, but for the life of me, I don't understand why you'd want to be hotter in a place that's already too hot. But they do."

"I don't, either," the carpenter replied, absently blotting a forehead he hadn't realized was so damp until Rhylla had reminded him of the heat.

"Why did you come back early? If I could ask?"

"Something about the place bothered me," Kharl paused. "And I saw a wizard, and he was wearing a uniform."

"You didn't know that?" Rhylla paused. "All wizards or mages have to work for the emperor. He pays well, they say. 'Course there's no alternative."

"I saw that, too. He destroyed a man he said was a wizard who had broken the laws of Hamor. Something about being examined."

"Huh . . . didn't know that. Just knew that all the wizards and mages worked for the emperor. Anyone who tries to get one to do something for him without the permission of the emperor—that's a death sentence."

"A death sentence?" Then Kharl nodded. In a way, it definitely made sense, at least from the emperor's point of view. "He controls the mages, and that means he controls everything."

"I wouldn't say that . . . the marshals are pretty strong, they say."

"But if the mages and wizards are all under the protection of the emperor . . .?" Kharl looked at the third mate.

"Oh . . . frig . . . see what you mean."

After Rhylla left, Kharl turned back to the railing to study the port city. Somehow, it wasn't just a coincidence that the two strongest lands in the world were the two where mages and wizards were placed to support those who governed. Recluce had some sort of council where the Brethren had a strong voice, and the emperor controlled the mages in Hamor. Candar had once been strong, but when Recluce had destroyed Fairven and the White Order, Candar had fragmented into conflicting lands. From what Kharl had seen, most of Candar, except for Southport and possibly Diehl, was in decline. Even Brysta looked shabby, but both Nylan and Swartheld looked vigorous.

Still, while all that might be true, what could a mere carpenter do about it?

LXIV

On the following afternoon, with one more day of loading to go before the *Seastag* was ready to put back to sea, Kharl decided to make another foray into Swartheld. He'd picked the late afternoon because he was off duty, because he wasn't certain he wanted to deal with the human creatures of the night who frequented port cities, and because he had the feeling that there well might be more of the emperor's mages about later in the evening.

When he left the pier, he forced himself to remain on the lower harbor way as he walked southward along the edge of the water. He hadn't thought of it before, but none of the merchanters had iron hulls, and all had sails. Some were even full-rigged and without any form of steam power. Was that because of the cost of coal? Or for some other reason he didn't know?

Yet warships were all iron-hulled, even the smaller gunboats of Brysta, and he had seen no merchanters with cannon. That made sense, in a fashion, because a white wizard could touch off gunpowder or cammabark and turn a wooden ship into an inferno. He still had no idea whether it was the combination of ordered iron vessels and the order of the sea that protected warships from mages or whether it was something else. He'd searched *The Basis of Order*, but as usual had found no definitive answers.

Ahead, there was a small crowd of men standing opposite an open window. When Kharl neared, he could see that a single woman danced slowly in the wide unglassed window of the tavern. Her body was covered with the filmy fabric Kharl had seen on the veil-scarfs of the women at the café—except the fabric was reddish and stained with the darkness of sweat. With the thinness of the fabric, little of the woman's figure was left to mystery, and her figure was good, Kharl had to admit, although not any better than Charee's had once been.

At that thought, Kharl swallowed. The sadness and emptiness still came when he least expected it.

"You want to enjoy one like this? Just a silver for a half glass . . . and she's all yours, sailor man." The big man who made the offer topped Kharl by half a head, and Kharl was not small.

"She's too costly for my wallet," Kharl said with a forced laugh, easing past the man and along the quieter space of the street immediately past the brothel. Was it just sadness? Or the sense that he and Charee had lost something over the years? Had they ever had that something? Or had their consorting just been an arrangement set up by their families and held together in the beginning by physical attraction and later by the boys? He shook his head. Why was he even asking himself such questions? He couldn't do much about what was past and gone.

Across the harbor road he caught sight of a pair of Hamorian patrollers in their khaki uniforms. He watched the pair as they walked along the street. The two never relaxed, but kept moving, and each held a truncheon at the ready.

Abruptly, after passing the patrollers, who had scarcely given Kharl a glance, the carpenter turned left, away from the harbor, and began to walk up the gently sloping street toward the better sections of Swartheld. Farther south, he discovered, he had to walk a greater distance east before he reached the more prosperous area—almost eight blocks. But he did find another boulevard with shops and flowers and cafés with awnings and wide verandas—and he felt almost as out of place as he had the first time.

Yet, why should he have felt out of place? He wondered. He was nicely dressed, if not so extravagantly as those on the boulevard. He was not poor, or without coins. He had a respectable trade, and even a position, low as a subofficer on a merchanter might be.

He kept walking as he saw another set of Hamorian patrollers. This pair walked with empty hands, their truncheons in their belts, and they smiled, although their eyes still never stopped surveying the street and the shops. A woman, her head covered by the filmy scarf that was almost transparent, nodded to the patrollers. Both returned the smile, an expression of friendliness, but continued on their way.

From a distance, he saw another of the mages in black and orange, again an older man, accompanying a single patroller in khaki. The two turned eastward, moving even farther from the harbor. Kharl thought about following the pair, but almost immediately dismissed the idea. Instead, he turned back toward the harbor, hoping to find somewhere to eat, less fancy than where he was, but quieter and better than along the harbor way.

Finding such a place was harder than Kharl had thought it would be, and he ended up walking along side streets for what seemed almost a glass before he found himself before a low, dark redbrick building with tan window trim. The still air held unfamiliar scents of food, but without the rancidness of grease, and there was little hint of chaos about the premises—except for the thin residual whiteness that seemed everywhere in Swartheld. Kharl stepped inside.

Immediately, a servingwoman in tan shorts and shirt, with a dark brown apron and sandals, greeted him. "Yes?"

"A good meal and ale or lager?"

She looked puzzled.

"Food."

She beckoned, and Kharl followed her into a long narrow room with a high ceiling. The off-white plaster gave an impression of coolness. Kharl settled into the small table against the wall.

"Drink . . . what kind?" the server asked.

"Light ale? Lager?"

She said something to another server, and got an answer back, then nodded at Kharl before slipping away. Within moments, a squarish older woman set a dark brown mug before Kharl. "Be two coppers."

Kharl extended three coins.

She studied them and nodded. "Fare's simple tonight. We've got burhka, cutlets, sea trout, and fowl in lemonweed with Luban noodles."

"How much?"

"All the same. Four coppers."

"I'll try the last."

"It's the best. Be a bit." She slipped away.

Kharl settled back into the chair and took another sip of the ale, enjoying it as it washed away the last of the dust in his throat.

Two younger men, but well dressed in white shirts and multicolored silk vests, sat at the corner table. Although their voices were not that loud, they seemed to carry to Kharl, perhaps along the smooth white plaster of the wall.

". . . don't understand the edict . . . just applies to outlanders trading here . . ."

". . . not just to outlanders like us . . . another one . . . harsher . . . for Hamorians . . ."

". . . no brimstone to Valmurl . . . but to Bruel? Why one Austran port and not the other? Not as though Lord Estloch has a huge fleet . . ."

". . . no saltpeter or cammabark, either . . ."

". . . doesn't make sense . . . Valmurlans don't use firearms . . . don't use powder except for cannon, and they've got few enough of those . . . we're supposed to give up good trade and coins . . ."

". . . careful . . ."

". . . mages don't come down here . . ."

". . . don't know where they'll turn up . . . walls sometimes report to the patrollers, too . . ."

". . . still makes no sense . . . can ship dried fruits, but not grain?"

". . . rich the only ones who can buy dried fruits . . . everyone needs bread . . ."

Their voices died away as a server brought two platters and a basket of bread to their table.

Kharl sipped his ale and considered their words. He didn't care for the implications, not at all, and he knew he'd need to mention the matter to Hagen, although he would not have been surprised if the captain already knew.

LXV

Hagen had not been aboard the *Seastag* when Kharl had returned the night before, but immediately after eating the next morning, the carpenter made his way to the master's cabin, where he knocked gingerly on the door. "Ser . . . it's Kharl. I'd just heard something . . . thought you ought to know . . ."

"Come on in, carpenter." Hagen's voice was polite.

Kharl eased through the hatch door into the captain's cabin. The space was large, but somehow not so large as Kharl would have guessed, with a double bunk built into the rear bulkhead, and a small closet, half-open, set into the left bulkhead. In the middle of the cabin was a circular white oak table, anchored to the deck, and behind that sat the captain. A stack of papers and parchment was at his left, and he still held a pen.

"What is it?"

"Captain . . . last night, I was eating at a place well away from the harbor, and there were two traders, outlanders . . ." Kharl went on to recount what the two had said, word for word.

When Kharl finished, Hagen nodded. He did not seem surprised. "I'd heard about the brimstone and saltpeter . . . but I didn't know they could sell in Bruel." A darkness dropped across his countenance, before he forced a smile. "I hadn't heard about the grain because we don't usually carry it, but it's not surprising. Hamor's been looking at invading Austra for years, and every so often they embargo goods, usually military equipment. They've had an embargo on gunpowder and camma-bark for two years, but they decided on expanding that about a season ago to include brimstone and saltpeter and a few other goods."

Kharl tried to keep his own surprise to himself. The two traders he had overheard had clearly been talking about an edict recently issued, and Hagen had known about it for nearly a season. "Is that why we're carrying brimstone back, ser?"

Hagen grinned. "You noted that, did you?"

"I noted that it wasn't all off-loaded at Dellash," Kharl replied. "Why is Hamor going after Austra? Aren't some of the lands in Candar better targets?"

"Some are weaker, but Candar lies close to Recluce. Also, it's a long voyage from Swartheld, and under steam power, a costly one, with no-where to stop for coal. Austra is much closer, and considerably smaller."

"And Lord Estloch does not have many warships?"

"He does not."

Kharl frowned. "But Austra is united under a single ruler, while Nordla has the four Lords of the Quadrant, and they agree on little, and have even fewer warships."

"Nordla is far less prosperous, is it not?" Hagen laughed ironically. "What would be the point of spending thousands of golds, hundreds of thousands of golds perhaps, if one could not plunder the land to recover it, then tariff it heavily? Why does one seek to conquer anything?" After the briefest of pauses, Hagen went on. "Some think rulers seek fame and glory in war, but both are fleeting. No . . . most wars are fought for gain, either to keep another land from gaining an advantage in power and wealth or to extend one's own power and wealth."

"That's not true if your land is attacked."

"No . . . but you can wager—with heavy odds—that the one attacking has planned on great gain. Unless the ruler is mad, and few mad rulers survive to make war, and fewer still survive their wars. Of course, such madness is the ruin of their land and their people."

"The Emperor of Hamor is not mad. He controls his own lands too well for that," suggested Kharl.

"Who would know?" questioned Hagen. "In a land as vast as Hamor, the governing is done by the emperor's minions. Good minions can conceal much about a ruler." The captain snorted. "But you are right. The emperor is most astute, and all the world may suffer for that."

Kharl could see that, and, despite the safety of the streets of Swartheld, he was less than certain that he would wish such a rule in either Nordla or Austra. He almost frowned, thinking that Lord West's son Egen would—if he had the chance—govern with the power of the emperor and even less wisdom.

"That troubles you? Well it should."

Kharl did not correct the captain. "That was all I heard, but I thought you should hear about it." He smiled. "I thought you might already know, but I was not sure."

"You see more than you let on, Kharl. That is a good trait." Hagen smiled in return. "You're welcome to remain as crew so long as you desire."

"I thank you, ser. I'm still thinking of going ashore in Austra, but I will consider your offer, and I do thank you."

"It's my gain as well." Hagen laughed, then looked down at the sheets of paper on the table before him.

Kharl stepped back and eased the hatch door closed as he left. The captain had known about the embargoes, and he remained worried about them. Despite Hagen's laughter, the worry had shown through.

As he walked back across the main deck, Kharl realized once more that there was far more to Hagen than merely a trading captain. Kharl had heard the references to other ships, but would even a merchant factor with a number of ships have known what the Emperor of Hamor was planning a season in advance? Kharl didn't think so, and that left the question of what exactly Hagen might be, honorable as he appeared to Kharl and to the other crew members on Hagen's vessels.

LXVI

When the *Seastag* had cast off from the pier at Swartheld, starting the voyage back to her home port of Valmurl, one of the crew, as Ghart had predicted, had failed to return—the fresh-faced young Wylat. Thinking of Wylat toiling on the Great Highway or the fiery furnaces of Luba, Kharl had shaken his head. He could but hope the *Fleuryl* never ported in Swartheld, because he had his doubts about Arthal's wisdom. But there was nothing he could do about either young man's fate.

The ship had traveled no more than a handful of kays northeast beyond sight of land when the seas began to turn rough, and bitter chill permeated the winds that had raised the waves and buffeted the *Seastag*. The remainder of the eightday journey was rough, although the seas had subsided somewhat as the *Seastag* neared Austra, and Kharl had found himself more and more fretful once the coastline appeared.

The winter sun hung low in the west, offering little warmth, as the *Seastag* steamed through the gray harbor waters toward the outermost pier of Valmurl harbor. Kharl was glad for his heavy jacket as he stood by the railing and looked at Valmurl. Unlike Brysta, which faced west on the Eastern Ocean, Valmurl faced east—and the Great Western Ocean. Valmurl was also an older port city, but set on a flat plain on the delta of the River Val. The bay on which the city was located was more open, and had no fortifications like the twin harbor forts of Brysta. While there were hills to the north, they looked to be low and some distance way— and were covered entirely with a whiteness that could only be snow.

Farther back from the waterfront, Kharl could see taller structures, even stone towers. Thin lines of smoke rose from hundreds of chimneys into the cold air, and a smoky haze hung over the city. The smoke and near-twilight shadows mixed together and imparted a gray cast to Valmurl, despite the late-afternoon sunlight that glinted on the gray waters between the ship and the city.

Furwyl eased up beside Kharl. "You still intending to leave us here?"

"I'd planned to," Kharl replied. "Hoped to find a place as a cooper somewhere in Austra."

"You're a fine carpenter, and a good man to have around in a tight place. Hate to see you spend the rest of your life making barrels for someone else. Hard thing to make your way in a land not your own," the first mate pointed out. "You're already a subofficer on your first voyage. Not many do that."

Kharl knew Furwyl was right, yet he hesitated. "Making my way here couldn't be that much harder than where I came from." Even as Kharl spoke, he wondered. He'd still have been a cooper, with a consort and sons, if he'd not been so unlucky to have heard Egen in the back alley. Or would he? The druids had suggested that his situation would have worsened anyway. Did that mean matters could be worse in Valmurl? Or Vizyn, if he got there? "Leastwise, I hope not."

Furwyl chuckled. "We're goin' in to refit. Be in the yards two, maybe three eightdays. You don't find what you want, get back here afore we leave—bet the captain'd take you back as carpenter second. Not the billet he'll fill except with someone he knows, and he knows all the ship's carpenters in Austra. Leastwise, he'd put you on one of his other ships."

"How many does he have?"

"Ten. At least, that was the last number I heard. All something with 'sea' in 'em . . . *Seahound, Seafox* . . ."

"And he still sails?" Rhylla had mentioned once that Hagen had other ships, but Kharl had not realized just how many.

"He's a man who likes what he does," Furwyl said. "And he likes to keep good people. Especially carpenters."

"Are good ones that hard to come by?"

"Harder than you'd think. You get youngsters barely more than apprentices . . . know a few things and think they know more, and mostly you get older men who love their ale so much that the only time they're sober is at sea."

"Where are the good ones?" asked Kharl.

"That'd be a secret." Furwyl grinned, then added, "With the

shipwrights, but they don't take many, and you got to be family . . . or close to it, or be owed more than most would owe."

That made sense. Still . . .

"Thank you," Kharl finally said. "And thank the captain. But I think I need to look and see if anyone needs a good cooper."

"You can tell him yourself in the morning when he pays off the crew. Just thought I'd put in a word with you." Furwyl nodded and turned.

Was Kharl making a mistake? Another mistake?

Kharl didn't think so, but then, he hadn't thought so before.

LXVII

The morning after the *Seastag* ported in Valmurl, and after muster, Kharl placed his few belongings into his pack, now mostly full, and, staff in hand, headed up to the main deck to see Hagen. There he waited in the chill air until after the regular deckhands and riggers had been paid. Then he stepped forward to the small table behind which the captain sat.

"You still intent on leaving us, carpenter?" Hagen's voice was cheerful, but Kharl could catch a sense of worry behind it.

"I don't know about intent, ser. It's just that . . . well . . . I wouldn't feel right if I didn't try to be what I've spent my life learning and doing."

Hagen nodded. "When you put it that way, it's hard not to see it so." The captain paused and looked down at the ledger before him, turning the pages until he was close to the end. "Your crew share, right now, is fifteen silvers, and I owe you five silvers and three for your wages."

Two golds? Kharl certainly hadn't expected that. He'd come aboard hoping to get off with what he'd had in his leather pouch. "Yes, ser. That's more than fair."

Hagen shook his head. "It's fair. No more, no less."

Kharl sensed the other's honest feelings and nodded.

"You don't have to go," Hagen said. "I'd have you as carpenter second, and carpenter first when Tarkyn decides he's had enough of the sea."

"I only asked for passage to Austra, ser."

"I know, but I'd still have you." Hagen paused. "Where are you headed?"

"I'd thought Vizyn, but anywhere that I could be a cooper."

"Coopers . . . there are more than enough here in Valmurl. You ought to stay on as a ship's carpenter." Hagen laughed. "Then, I'd be the last one to tell any man what he should be doing. That I would be." He fingered his chin. "Three good coopers here in Valmurl. None as good as you, in truth. Oldest one is Dezant. He's off the Traders' Square. Then there's Kundark, and he does mostly slack cooperage, and his place is on the south side of the city, by the Guard Barracks there. You might try Chalart. He's on the north side, back of the refit yards. He supplies barrels for merchanters, mostly. You can tell any of them that I sent you. It might help, won't hurt.

"You don't like Valmurl . . . go and see Vizyn, but you'd better take a coaster. It's a good nine hundred kays. Of the ones in port now, take the *Norther* or the *Southshield* . . . tell 'em I sent you. You don't like it, then turn around and come back. Offer's open until we leave Valmurl."

"Thank you. How long will you be here? For refitting?" Kharl added quickly.

"Half a season, I'd guess. Takes longer to refit in winter, but there's little enough trading to be done, and I'd like to have the engineers go over the engine after that problem off Worrak."

"Is there anything special I should know about Valmurl?" Kharl asked. "Things that'd be obvious to you, but not to me? If you don't mind, ser."

"Valmurl is much like Brysta, save that it is the capital of all Austra, and there is but one lord. Lord Estloch has a good heart, and, unlike many rulers, he would be as fair as possible and still hold order within the streets. Still . . . dark streets are dangerous . . . especially harborside, and there are few patrollers past midnight. The wealthy are as they are in any city."

If those words were not a warning, Kharl wasn't a cooper. "Thank you."

"You change your mind, and there'll be a place for you, if not here, then on one of the other ships."

"I appreciate that, ser, and I'll just have to see."

"That you will. Good fortune."

After hoisting his pack onto his shoulders and securing his silvers and coppers in his concealed leather pouch, Kharl walked down the gangway of the *Seastag*, perhaps for the last time, and past the wagons already lined up to receive the cargo being off-loaded. While the pier was not so crowded as those at Swartheld, more than a score of loaders and others swirled around the area opposite the *Seastag*. Among them, he saw no patrollers, although more than a few men carried blades of various styles and lengths.

As Kharl reached the foot of the pier, he saw a wagon, with a platform. On the platform stood a blond girl, one certainly younger than Sanyle or Jeka. Despite the chill of the morning, the girl wore but the filmiest shift, and in the morning light, it was most clear that she wore absolutely nothing beneath, except for the bronze cuff on her left ankle, a cuff attached to a bronze chain. The chain was bolted to a bronze circlet affixed to the side of the wagon. The girl's face was pale, and her green eyes carried sadness.

Four huge men with cudgels stood there—one at each corner of the wagon.

A man in a rich deep blue jacket stood on the stones of the street, his voice pitched to carry. "Beauties for indenture . . . young, beautiful girls . . ." His eyes took in Kharl's staff, and there was the slightest hesitation before he continued. "Girls for every taste and pleasure . . ."

Kharl glanced down the pier toward the Hamorian merchanter tied up beyond the *Seastag*. A blonde beauty—and the girl was attractive—would be welcome in Swartheld. The girl's eyes did not meet Kharl's or any other's.

"Blonde . . . redhead . . . any kind of beauty you'd like . . ."

Kharl turned abruptly, his lips tight together as he walked away from the slaver. Indenture or not, the process was slavery. He'd hoped for better in Valmurl. His eyes moved from side to side, taking in the handful of people out so early. Most seemed well-dressed, and he saw no one in rags or begging.

He thought over Hagen's words. "Lord Estloch has a good heart . . . would be as fair as possible." He understood the message beneath. Lord Estloch was either weak or having troubles in holding on to his land. Or perhaps those beneath him had too much power. Whatever Hagen had meant exactly, it was clear enough that matters were not as Hagen would have had them, and that troubled Kharl, for he knew Hagen to be a fair and more than decent captain and man.

Should he seek passage to Vizyn, and seek out Taleas, the scrivener whom Tyrbel had written? Or first check with the coopers that Hagen had mentioned? After a moment, he decided to visit the coopers in Valmurl. Why travel to a destination where the prospects were unknown until he exhausted the possibilities nearer at hand?

As he walked along the cobblestoned streets, avoiding the too-frequent potholes holding ice and mud, and the gutters that needed cleaning, he studied the shops and the narrow-faced brick dwellings squeezed tightly together. For the number of dwellings, he saw few enough men and women on the streets, although he still saw no beggars or peddlers or tinkers.

Trader's Square was six long blocks west of the harbor, but it was still early when Kharl reached the square. Despite the winter chill, the air was still, and he had unfastened his jacket to keep from getting too warm. He stood at the edge of the square for several moments. The square was a good twenty rods in length and ten in width, with the center simply an open, paved space. A handful of carts had been pulled into place in the center of the square, but some of the shops and factor's buildings were yet shuttered. The cooperage was on the far south side of the square, not exactly on it, but on the corner street leading into the square. The building was perhaps another ten cubits wider than Kharl's had been, and featured double doors in front, with a front loading dock to one side. That suggested that there was not a usable alley behind the cooperage.

Kharl shrugged and stepped through the open doors and into a workroom nearly as deep as his own had been. He noted more shavings and sawdust than he would have preferred, but the cooperage was still relatively neat and clean, and the brick walls had been swept and cleaned recently. As he glanced around the shop, Kharl could see four figures working. One was slighter and smaller, probably an apprentice.

A young man, perhaps four or five years older than Arthal, stepped from the workbench at one side to meet Kharl. "Ser?" His eyes flicked across the staff and came back to Kharl.

"I'm looking for Dezant," Kharl said.

"Yes, ser. He's at the miller's right now. Is there anything that I could help you with? Are you interested in tight or slack cooperage?"

"Are you his son? You seem to understand . . ."

The young man smiled. "I'm Elont. There are three of us working with Father."

"He's fortunate, indeed. There must be quite a demand to keep you all so busy."

"Valmurl does require many barrels," replied the young man cautiously.

"But not quite so many as you would like?" suggested Kharl.

"It's always better to sell more than less. What kind of cooperage would interest you, ser?"

"I'm afraid my interest is a shared crafting. I've been a ship's carpenter, and my father was a cooper. I wanted to see your shop." All of that was true, if not telling the entire story.

Elont smiled politely, disappointed. "It's the best in Valmurl."

"So I had heard, and I'm glad to see it."

"You'd be better off, ser, to remain as a ship's carpenter these days, than to open a cooperage here."

"I had no thought of opening a cooperage," Kharl demurred. "Certainly not now, but one must think of the future as well."

"You're certain we couldn't sell your vessel some cooperage?"

"The captain is well aware of your work, and he would be the one to order it," Kharl replied politely. "I appreciate your kindness." He inclined his head.

"Thank you, ser."

Kharl eased out the door, grateful at least for the momentary warmth in the shop. Outside, he looked around, trying to gain his bearings. According to Hagen, Kundark was on the south side of the city, by the Guard Barracks. Kharl readjusted his pack and turned southward, his breath still steaming in the chill air.

Ahead, he glimpsed two children in rags, the first ones he had seen so shabbily dressed. One—a girl—went to her knees before a man in a solid gray cloak of warmth and style. Kharl could not hear the words, but her pleading position was all too clear.

The man glanced around, twice, stiffened, then shook his head, walking away.

A shrill whistle sounded. The boy vanished into an alley or serviceway, and the girl scrambled to her feet, but too late and too slowly to avoid the patroller who grasped her roughly by the shoulder. As Kharl moved closer, he strained to hear the patroller's words.

"... begging, you were ..."

"... wasn't beggin' ... wasn't ..."

"... off to the indenturer's ... Begging's against the Lord's Law. You know that."

"... no ... not that ..."

"... pretty little thing like you ... fetch a good price in Hamor ... won't be cold there, either ..."

Kharl winced at the thought of the beggar girl ending up like the girl on the dock, but he did not try to interfere, much as he would have liked to, and he only watched as the patroller dragged the child down a side street. His guts churned, much as he imagined Charee both telling him he'd done what was wise and asking him why he hadn't done so earlier.

He kept walking, but it was a while before he felt any calmer. A good half glass later, he stood across the street from the stone walls surrounding the Guard Barracks. He had completed a circuit of the streets facing onto the Barracks, but had not seen anything resembling a cooperage to the Barracks. Two uniformed figures stood as sentries outside the gate. One was scarcely more than a boy, and the other looked to be at least as old as Kharl.

The younger sentry looked at Kharl.

Kharl looked back and, after a moment, the youthful guard dropped his eyes. Kharl turned and started down the narrow lanelike street that angled northwest from the corner of the barracks. Fifty cubits or so down the lane, in front of a seamstress's shop, a white-haired woman in a patched coat swept dust and old snow away from the doorway of the shop.

"I'm looking for—" Kharl began.

"Speak up. You looking for something, fellow?"

"A cooper named Kundark. I'd heard his cooperage was here."

"It was. Over there." The woman pointed to the burned-out shell of a building a hundred cubits farther along the narrow lane.

From what Kharl could see, the cooperage had been about half the size of Dezant's shop, and the blaze had not been all that recent. "What happened?"

The woman shrugged. "No one knows. No one's seen Kundark. Consort and son died in the fire. Terrible blaze it was."

"How did it start?"

"No one knows." The woman looked away from Kharl and resumed sweeping, muttering to herself, "Stupid question ... outland blackstaffer."

After a long look at her, and a longer one at the burned ruins, Kharl turned and retraced his steps back northward in the general direction of where he had understood the refit yard to be.

Valmurl stretched much farther to the north than Kharl had thought, and it was close to noon before Kharl reached the workshops on the ancient street opposite the refit yard and the three dry docks—all empty. The three largest structures facing the harbor and yards were shuttered and locked, large barnlike buildings whose exterior planks and timbers had weathered into faded gray. Grimy powdered snow lay drifted into the corners where the plank walls met the frozen ground or the worn and cracked cobblestones of the street.

Kharl's face and hands were numb from the chill, even though he had periodically thrust his hands up under his jacket.

Between the two shuttered and larger structures on the northern end of the block was a smaller building, one with unshuttered windows and a half barrel displayed on a bracket to the right of the front loading doors. Kharl made his way to the cooperage and, with a shrug, opened the door and stepped inside.

A single gray-haired man straightened from where he stood over a machine that looked to Kharl as though it were a combination planer and router of some sort.

Kharl stepped forward. "You're Chalart?"

"That's me." The cooper's eyes raked across Kharl. "You another cooper looking for a place?" Before Kharl could reply, the wiry man went on. "Not enough orders for me and my boy, and certainly not enough for another mouth."

"How did you know?" asked Kharl.

Chalart snorted. "You got that look and a pack on your back. Buyers don't wear packs. Seen more . . ." He shook his head. "Wager you're a good cooper, too."

"One of the best," Kharl said.

"Then . . . why are you here?"

"I'm from Nordla. The lord's son didn't care that I stopped his pleasures with my neighbor's daughter."

"Think things be different here?"

"I'd hope no one would want to kill me," Kharl replied ruefully.

"You might get that." Chalart studied Kharl. "What have you been doing?"

"Ship's carpenter."

"Keep doing it. I know a half score of coopers that'd jump for your position."

"How did things get so bad?" Kharl asked.

"Ask the Emperor of Hamor . . . or Lord Estloch. I'm just a cooper, trying to hang on till things get better. They might, someday. Never know." Chalart looked down at the wood in the planer.

Kharl took the hint. "Thank you. The best of fortune to you."

"And to you."

Once outside, where the wind had shifted and now blew, colder and icier, out of the northeast, Kharl studied the refit area, seemingly almost abandoned, from the empty dry docks to the cold gray harbor waters with an increasing chop—and not a single vessel tied to the one pier adjoining the dry docks. After several moments, Kharl turned back toward the harbor. Should he spend good silvers to get passage to Vizyn to find Taleas and see if the scrivener could help him? If he didn't go, how would he know if there might be a place for a cooper? Nine hundred kays might make a difference. And it might not.

The walk back south and east was long, but Kharl found the coaster pier by midafternoon. Standing at the foot of the pier, he studied both the *Norther* and the *Southshield*, then decided on the *Southshield*, a smaller version of the *Seastag*—twin-masted with midships paddle wheels.

He walked down the dock to the ship, and up the gangway to the sailor on watch, who could have been Tarkyn's younger brother, gray-haired rather than white-haired, but square-faced and grizzled. The sailor watched, but did not speak as Kharl neared.

"I was looking for passage to Vizyn," Kharl said.

"Let me get the second." The watchstander rang the bell twice, but said nothing more.

Kharl did not wait long for the second mate, a narrow-faced woman within a few years of his own age, with gray eyes and short hair.

"We're not hiring," she told him bluntly.

"I was looking for passage to Vizyn."

"You a blackstaffer?"

"No. I grew up in Brysta. I've been the carpenter second on the *Seastag*."

"Don't take deadheads."

"I'll pay passage, if it's not too much. Captain Hagen said to tell you that he sent me."

"Why'd he say that?"

"The *Seastag*'s going into refit. I've been his second carpenter, but I'd heard there might be a need for my skills in Vizyn . . ."

The second laughed. "Four silvers. Three more for return passage if you decide to come back on the same trip."

"Is Vizyn that bad?"

"It's cold. Snow everywhere. Everyone knows everyone else. Don't care for outsiders."

Kharl thought. He wasn't going to be a cooper in Valmurl, not when no one would take him on and when he didn't have the golds to set up his own shop. The same might be true in Vizyn, but would he always look back and wonder if he didn't go there and see? "When do you leave?"

"In about a glass."

"What sort of quarters? Food?"

"Four gets you a bunk in a space for two, and meals with the crew. We just run two meals a day at sea. You're the only passenger this run, so you get more space. If you need more gear, be back here in a glass. You can pay then."

Kharl smiled wryly. "Got all the gear I'll need. You the one who gets the silvers?"

"Me or the captain."

Kharl eased the silvers out of his wallet and tendered them.

"Welcome aboard. Name's Herana."

"Kharl," he replied.

"I'll show you your spaces and then have you meet the captain." She turned.

Kharl followed, noting that the deck was clean and that what he saw of the vessel looked shipshape. Then, Hagen had recommended the *Southshield*.

LXVIII

True to Herana's words, Captain Harluk had cast off from the coaster pier at Valmurl in late afternoon and steamed out of the harbor. Once clear of the harbor, Harluk had shut down the engine and kept the *Southshield* heading due east until well after sunset. Then, in the dimness after twilight, in seas that were not quite so heavy as those the *Seastag* had encountered on its way to Valmurl, the captain had brought the coaster onto a northerly heading.

Kharl's cabin was but big enough for two bunks, one atop the other, although he shared it with no one, and there was space enough under the lower bunk for his pack. He had been forced to angle the staff to get it to fit through the passageway and into the cabin.

Supper on the *Southshield* had been distinguished mainly by the hot bread and peppery gravy spread over slices of meat so salty Kharl hadn't been certain what it was, perhaps mutton that had been dried, before being boiled and covered with gravy. Still, with the bread, and some hard cheese, and dried apples, Kharl had found it far better than most meals he had eaten in the eightdays before signing on the *Seastag*.

In the late twilight, well after eating, Kharl had made his way on deck and stood slightly forward of the paddle wheel casing, aft enough that the spray from the bow did not mist around him, although there was more spray across the deck than on the *Seastag*, doubtless because of the *Southshield*'s narrower beam.

At times, the dark waters shimmered with a luminescence that was not light, but the darkness of order. Although Kharl could not have explained how order-darkness could create light within the very ocean, he felt and knew that somehow that was so.

Now that he was actually on his way to Vizyn, he had more questions of himself.

Why was he spending silvers, so hard gotten, to travel to Vizyn? Just because Tyrbel had written Taleas? How could there be a place for a cooper there when there were none in Valmurl, certainly much larger?

Or was he carrying out the trip because he had already decided that was what he should do? When did a wise man change plans? Why?

"You're a hardy one."

Kharl turned to see the second mate less than three cubits away, almost lost in the darkness. She stepped closer, then stopped.

"Thinking," he explained.

"You could do that in a far warmer place," she said with a laugh.

"Then . . . I probably wouldn't think. I'd just fall asleep," he admitted.

Herana stepped closer, stopping a good cubit short of Kharl. "That's a sailor's answer."

"That's what I've been for the past seasons."

"And you're leaving a good ship with a good captain without knowing where you're going or what you'll do?"

Put that way, his actions seemed foolish. "Does seem strange," he admitted.

"One way of putting it." After a moment, she asked, "How'd you get that staff? It's a real Recluce blackstaff."

"It belonged to someone else. She was murdered. I tried to return it to the Brethren when I got to Nylan, but they said it belonged to me and that I could keep it or they'd destroy it." Kharl shrugged. "Couldn't see a good staff being destroyed."

"That means you're a mage."

"No. I'm no mage. I was a cooper, then I became a carpenter."

"They don't let just anyone who shows up with one of those keep it," the second pointed out.

"They did say that I was drawn to order," Kharl admitted. "But I'm not a mage. Doubt if I ever could be one." At the uneasiness that settled over him with those words, he quickly added, "Not like any of them. Maybe I could put a bit more order in my work—things like that."

"You probably already do. Captain Hagen looks for folk like that."

"He does?"

"That and more. Some folk say he's the lord's left hand, seeing as they're cousins, seconds, though. Don't know as I'd buy that, close as folk say they are. Captain Harluk doesn't, and there's little that escapes him, either."

"I thought there was something about him, even when he first came to the cooperage . . ."

"You had your own cooperage?"

"I did. That was a while ago. Things don't always turn out the way they should."

Herana laughed once more. "Life's like that." Then she nodded to him. "Take care up here. Farther north we go and the colder it gets, deck could get icy and slippery."

"I'll be careful," Kharl promised, watching as the second slipped away aft, back into the deeper shadows not touched by the lamps from the poop deck.

After a time, he turned and headed back to his cabin. It wasn't that much warmer than the deck, but the lack of wind and chill spray made it seem so, and the day had been long.

LXIX

In his winter jacket, hands thrust inside it to keep them warm, Kharl stood midships, just forward of the paddle wheel frame, where he was partly sheltered from the wind blowing from the stern, as the *Southshield* eased its way up to the single squat pier at Vizyn. His pack and staff were at his feet. The small harbor opened to the northeast, looking out on gray waters that might have been liquid ice from the chill carried by the wind. The hempen fenders that cushioned the hull from the pier crackled as the *Southshield* came to rest against the dock, and icy fragments sprayed forth in the morning air.

Everywhere that Kharl looked, there was white, from the steep hills that encircled the port town to the snow-covered evergreens on those hills. The roofs of the dwellings and buildings in Vizyn were covered with snow, and the streets that Kharl could make out were snow-packed. Had there been any sun, the glare would have been unbearable, but thick and low gray clouds covered the sky, and in places obscured the tops of the taller hills to the west. Smoke from chimneys drifted upward in grayish lines, eventually merging with the low clouds.

"Double up, now!" came the command from aft.

Kharl waited until the ship was secured, and the gangway down to the pier before shouldering his pack and picking up his staff. He moved back around the midships paddle wheel and toward the quarterdeck area where Herana stood.

The second mate looked at Kharl. "We'll be casting off early morning tomorrow. There'll be space back to Valmurl if you need it. Don't carry many passengers in the winter, just timber and some hard coal."

"Thank you." Kharl glanced beyond the pier. "You were right. There is snow everywhere."

She laughed.

Kharl smiled in return and made his way down the gangway. The pier itself was generally clear of snow, but he saw patches of dark ice here and there. He decided to follow the wider street that was mostly clear of snow and lined with shops. The shop nearest the harbor, unsurprisingly, was a chandlery and looked to be open. Kharl stamped his boots on the planks of the porch, swept clear of snow, unlike parts of the street, before stepping inside and carefully closing the door behind him.

The man who was sweeping the floor stopped and looked up, his eyes taking in the long black staff. He appeared to be Kharl's age, although his beard was streaked with white and bushy. "Could I help you?"

"I'm looking for a scrivener named Taleas . . ."

The chandler tilted his head slightly, frowning, before he smiled and answered. "His place is about seven, eight blocks toward the center of town. Go up the street till you get to the White Deer. Turn right at the corner. Should be two–three hundred cubits farther, on the left."

"Thank you."

"Interest you in some winterbread? Fine travel food."

Kharl smiled. "After I find Taleas . . . then we'll see." He nodded and turned. Again he was careful to close the door behind him when he left and stepped back outside. His breath was a white plume in the cold air permeated by the mixed odors of both burning wood and coal.

Kharl's ears tingled after several hundred cubits, and he could understand why the few people he saw on the streets wore caps or hats, generally with earflaps. He kept walking up the street, alternating putting one hand and then the other inside his winter jacket, a jacket that was clearly too light for the cold of Vizyn.

Healthy plumes of whitish smoke poured from the chimneys of the White Deer, and Kharl was almost tempted to step inside the inn, if only to warm himself. He could feel the chill creeping into his toes, and his ears and fingers were beginning to get numb. But the chandler had said that Taleas was but a few hundred cubits from the inn. So Kharl turned right and kept walking. He walked a good three or four hundred cubits down the rapidly narrowing street. He saw a cobbler's shop, a tiny coppersmith's, and dwellings cramped together with only small side yards heaped high with snow, but saw no sign of a scrivener's shop.

He turned around and retraced his steps, this time going in the other direction from the White Deer. The street did not narrow, but widened slightly, and the dwellings seemed larger and better kept. The fifth dwelling—more like a small cottage surrounded by snow-draped conifers—had a carving of a pen and an inkpot on the flat surface below the eaves that sheltered the small front porch. The short stone walk had been cleared and swept, and Kharl walked up it and onto the porch. He rapped gently on the door, then waited.

In time, a rotund figure in gray—gray trousers, gray shirt, with a heavy gray sweater over the shirt—cracked the door and peered out without speaking.

"I'm looking for a scrivener called Taleas."

"Let's say you've found him." The rotund man looked over Kharl. "You a blackstaffer?"

"No."

"Too bad. Could use one around here. Seafarer?"

"I have been—second carpenter. I used to be a cooper. A scrivener named Tyrbel said that I should see you if I ever got to Vizyn."

The rotund man nodded. "How are his sons?"

Kharl frowned. "He has none. He never did. Unless there's another scrivener somewhere named Tyrbel. I meant the one in Brysta."

Taleas nodded again. "What do you know of Tyrbel lately?"

Kharl shook his head. "He was killed by an assassin before I left Brysta. That was one reason why I left. We'd been friends and neighbors, and I feared that I would be next."

"What happened to the assassin?"

Kharl glanced around, then, seeing no one close to the scrivener's door, replied, "I killed him with a cudgel."

Taleas laughed ruefully, once. "What's your name?"

"Kharl."

"You look like the fellow he wrote about." The door opened wider. "Come on in. I don't know as I can help you much, but I can at least offer you some hot cider, a bite to eat, and let you thaw out before a hot stove."

"Thank you." Kharl followed the scrivener into the cottage, and then into a room off the front sitting room, where a wide and plain desk was set against a stone interior wall that suggested the room had been added later. On the other outside wall was a square iron stove from which radiated heat. On the top of the stove was a kettle. Kharl leaned the staff into the nearest corner.

"Sit down. Sit down," Taleas said.

Kharl gratefully shed his pack, placing it on the frayed hooked rug covering the worn plank floor, then took the plain wooden chair, leaving the one with the cushion for the scrivener.

Taleas took a woolen pad and used it to lift the kettle, then poured the steaming cider into a mug set on the corner of the desk before easing the kettle back onto the side of the stove. "Go ahead. I've already had two mugs this morning." He reseated himself in his own chair.

"Thank you," Kharl said again, leaning forward and stretching to take the mug from the desk. He took a small sip of the hot liquid, grateful for the warmth, both from the drink and from the heat of the mug on his chilled hands.

"What was this business with Tyrbel? He wrote that you might be coming this way, and that you might need a position as a cooper. He said you'd done him a favor he couldn't repay."

Kharl almost winced. He doubted he'd done Tyrbel any favors at all, although he'd meant well. "Ah . . . he'd sent his youngest, Sanyle, to deliver something, and she was on her way back, just after twilight. Two men decided that they wanted her favors . . . she called for help, but I was the only one who heard." Kharl shrugged. "I stopped them, and she got home safely."

Taleas raised his bushy eyebrows. "You a swordsman, too?"

"No. They had blades. I had my cudgel. That was the problem." Kharl decided that the scrivener would get the entire story one way or the other and went on with a rush of words. "I didn't know one of them was Lord West's youngest son, not until later. Then he attacked and beat up a black-staffer . . ." Kharl made the story as quick as he could, including the assassin, and a shortened version of his own hiding out until he had gotten aboard the *Seastag*. "So that's how it all happened and how I got here."

Taleas rocked forward and back in his chair. "Tyrbel said you were the sort who'd do what he thought was right, without much regard for the results."

"It's been my undoing at times."

"Doing right thoughtlessly can also be the wellspring of chaos," Taleas said ironically. "You got that staff from the blackstaffer?"

"I tried to return it in Nylan, but the Brethren said it was mine. It's helped at times, but . . ." Kharl smiled ruefully. "I can't say I know much about it."

Taleas chuckled. "You'll learn."

Kharl realized he wasn't totally sure he wanted to learn how to use it.

"You'll learn, or you'll end up like poor Tyrbel." Taleas tilted his head. "The only cooper who might even think about needing help is Almard, and that would only be for a few years, until his eldest is of apprentice age. He would not pay well."

"For now, I need little except for food, some clothes, and a roof over my head."

"That is all you'd get from Almard. The others can offer nothing." Taleas smiled sadly.

"Is it just the winter?" asked Kharl.

"Life has always been harder here than in Valmurl. The winter is longer, the summer shorter, but the fishers brought in good catches, and they salted them and sold them. With the winter ice, they could keep the fish almost fresh. Vizyn's fish was prized everywhere, and that was why we once had so many coopers. Then the fish disappeared from the Winter Banks. The only sources of coins left are the timber, and some of the hard coal, but there's getting to be less and less of that." Taleas shrugged. "Were I younger . . . but I have some coins laid by, and Elmaria gets some rents from the land she got from her father. Vizyn has been our families' home for so long we cannot count the years. Where else would we go?" He offered another sad smile. "Besides, in these days, one place is much like another."

Much like another? In what way? Kharl drained the last of the warm and welcome spiced cider. "Are you saying there is little difference between Candar or Recluce or Hamor or Austra?"

"Those that have the wealth and power decide. Here, we have a little wealth. Elsewhere, it would be less than nothing. Have you not seen that?"

Kharl thought for a moment before responding. "I think that wealth and power have always decided matters." He paused before adding, "I would worry more about how they decide. Not whether they decide."

Taleas laughed abruptly. "Well said! Well said! Perhaps you should have been a scrivener, or even a justicer."

"I'm a carpenter who's been a cooper, and hopes to be one again. Nothing more."

"I fear, friend Kharl, that is your problem. Tyrbel wrote as much, and in but a few words, I can attest to what he wrote. For a cooper or a carpenter, you think too much. And you think too deeply, and you are inclined to act on what you believe. If you do not act, those actions you do not take will eat you from within. If you do act, those in power will eat you from without."

"You make my plight seem hopeless," Kharl observed.

"Difficult, certainly," Taleas agreed.

"Just how would you suggest that I escape this . . . situation?" asked Kharl, in spite of the fact that he was certain he would not like the reply.

"You must obtain wealth or power, or obtain the protection of one who has them."

"Ah . . . just obtain wealth and power, or a friend who has both . . ." Kharl shook his head. "I fear I will have trouble even finding a cooper to take me on."

"You may indeed," Taleas said agreeably. "Perhaps I have said too much. That is a failing of those of us who have grown old."

"You are doubtless right about the cure to my situation, but the cure seems as hopeless as the situation," Kharl replied. "I thank you for your hospitality, but I should be finding Almard."

Taleas rose from his chair. "That should not be difficult. He is well outside the town. Just follow this road until you come to the mill. His house and shop are on the other side of the road from the mill. I would judge it is two kays."

Kharl stood and reclaimed his pack and staff. "I wish I had brought better news."

"You brought news in good faith, and you stood by Tyrbel as best you could. That is rare in any times, but rarer still in these." Taleas paused. "Just a moment." He scurried from the room, moving more quickly than Kharl had thought he might for a man of his age and bulk, returning almost immediately, extending a pair of worn but still well-stitched and fleece-lined leather gloves. "These were once a friend's, and they were left to me." He held up a small and wiry hand. "As you can see, they are far too large for me, but they will do you good, and do me none."

"I could not take your—"

Taleas pointed to his belt and the heavy gloves stuffed there. "I have good gloves."

"Thank you. I appreciate your kindness." Kharl decided that to refuse the gloves would be but a gesture, and a foolish one. "I do. I would that I could repay you in some fashion."

"Oh . . . you will. You already have in a way. Now . . . pull up the collar of your jacket to shield your ears," Taleas added as he escorted Kharl back to the front door.

Kharl did so.

"Give Almard my best, not that he'll care, but it won't hurt." Taleas opened the door.

"Thank you." Kharl stepped outside and bowed to the scrivener.

"Do what you can, young fellow. All I ask." Taleas smiled and closed the door.

As Kharl headed out the road that led from Vizyn, he pondered the scrivener's words about one place being much like another. Was that because people were alike? Somehow, those words went with what the druids had said to him, although he would have to think over why that might be so. He also had not considered himself a young fellow, but compared to Taleas, he was.

By the time he had covered the two kays on the snow-packed and chill road and reached the mill, clearly shut down for the winter, he was especially grateful to Taleas for the gloves. Without them, his hands would have been blocks of ice.

Almard had a cottage much like that of Taleas, with a barnlike shop attached to the left side of the cottage by an enclosed walkway. The walkway was half-buried in snow piled there—presumably from clearing the space in front of the shop's loading dock, although Kharl only saw a single set of wagon tracks in the packed snow.

He walked to the workroom door and rapped, once. After a moment, he rapped again.

"Come on in, and close the door, if you would."

Kharl stamped his boots clear of snow and stepped inside. Once there, he surveyed the work space, which looked as though it had indeed once been a barn. While Kharl's breath did not steam, the cooperage was still chill, and only a handful of barrels were stacked inside, just behind the loading doors. The forge that had been added later, to the right side of the barn, was cold, and had been for a time. A single cylindrical iron stove sat in the middle of the work space. Kharl could feel the heat, but he was distracted slightly to realize that the stove was not a true cylinder, but had six vertical sides. He'd never seen a stove shaped like that.

Almard stepped toward the door. The cooper was a heavy man, just a shade shorter than Kharl, but carrying a good two stone more than the carpenter. "What can I do for you?" Although the words were hearty enough, Kharl could sense a falseness behind them.

"Taleas sends his best," Kharl began. "He said I might stop and see you."

"You be needing some cooperage?" Interest sparked in the eyes of the heavier man.

"I was wondering if you could use an assistant cooper. He said that you might."

"Not hardly. Not any more 'n he'd need another scrivener. Not with the heart of winter comin' on."

"I heard there was good fishing here, even in winter," Kharl suggested.

"Used to be. No more. Why'd you think there'd be any place here? Not enough work for those of us still left."

"I'd heard about Vizyn a while back," Kharl replied. "It took some time to get here."

"Waste a' that time, you ask me." Almard gestured toward the barrels by the loading dock. "That's what I got for the last two eightdays, and they're still waitin'."

"I'm sorry." Kharl nodded. "The best of fortune to you." He stepped back and opened the door.

Almard did not say a word as Kharl stepped back into the afternoon chill, closing the door behind him.

After taking a deep, slow breath, Kharl headed back toward the harbor. While he had not checked with any other coopers, it was clear enough from what he had seen of Vizyn that it was not the place for him. So he might as well tell Herana or whoever was on watch on the *Southshield* that he'd need the return passage to Valmurl. It was also clear that he'd spent almost a gold on nothing.

He winced within the winter jacket at that thought.

LXX

After leaving his pack and staff in the cabin on the *Southshield*, and paying a few coppers extra to be able to sleep on board that night, Kharl had turned around and walked back to the White Deer for an early supper. Behind him a crew of men used a short crane to swing lengths of planks from heavy wagons on the pier to the ship.

The clouds had not lifted, and the streets were hard, either with cold cobblestones, or clay frozen just as solid. A few stray flakes of snow fluttered down around Kharl, but they had stopped by the time he reached the inn.

A woman in a heavy gray tunic and trousers met Kharl as he entered the White Deer and stood in the archway to the public room. "Ale or food or both?"

"Both."

"Got a small table at the side. Early enough you can have it to yourself."

"Thank you." Kharl followed her.

The public room of the inn was close, but warm, with heat oozing out from the hearth on one side of the room and the large iron stove on the other. There were close to a half score of tables, most of them long and narrow, but there were three smaller tables against the outside wall, and the server led Kharl to the one closest to the hearth, for which he was grateful. His feet were cold, almost numb.

"What do you have?"

"Not much choice tonight, fellow. Got fowl pie or stew. Three coppers, either way."

"Which is better?"

"Most times, the fowl pie. I'd go for the stew tonight."

"Then I will. Light ale?"

"Berk's lager's better. Two coppers either way."

"I'll try the lager." Kharl flashed five coppers, and the server nodded and left.

Within moments, the woman had returned. "Lager. Be a bit for the stew."

"That's fine." He handed her the two coppers, and then a third. With a smile, she was gone. He took a sip of the lager—not so good as many, but passable, and despite the cold outside he was thirsty. Something hot, like cider, would have been too cloying.

A group of men in sheepskin jackets entered the public room and took the long table nearest to Kharl without a word to anyone. When the server appeared, one of them just announced, "Hard jack for us all."

Kharl took another sip of his ale, listening to the newcomers.

". . . been a cold one this winter . . . a sow's burden keeping the mill-race ice-free . . ."

The cooper frowned. The mill he'd seen had been closed. Or were the men from a sawmill?

". . . already broke one of the bars . . ."

". . . coins though . . . and they're hard enough to come by now . . ."

". . . still cold as a lord's heart . . ."

". . . say that every winter . . ."

"Well, it's cold every winter."

Laughter welled up at the long table.

The server reappeared with a large bowl, a spoon, and a small loaf of rye bread, setting them before Kharl. He handed over four coppers and received another smile, a brief one as she hurried back to the kitchen. She reappeared in moments carrying a tray on which were five steaming mugs that she set down, one after the other, before the men at the long table.

"That's a lass!"

Kharl took a small mouthful of the stew. It was thick, tasty, and only slightly overpeppered, and the vegetables actually had not been cooked to mush. The bread was still warm, if slightly dry. Still, it was the best meal he'd had in days. After several mouthfuls, he began to pick up on the conversation at the long table once more.

". . . hear about what happened to Heyol's cousin down in Gyran? The innkeeper . . . well, he was an innkeeper till they hung him . . ."

". . . for what?"

". . . for nothing . . . magistrate there strung him up for some law no one ever heard of . . . He never studied no books to be a magistrate . . . just got the job 'cause Lord Estloch liked him. Justice . . . what he thinks it is . . ."

"... better than they got in Elkyn ... magistrate there hung a fellow for puttin' lead in his wine ... said it was poison ..."

"... nothin' anywhere that says that ..."

"... just wanted wine to taste better ... who could blame him for that? ... hung him anyway."

Kharl frowned. Tyrbel had told him something about that years back, about how powdered lead made wine taste better, but how too much of it was a poison that drove men mad if they drank it too much and too often.

"... who's he to hang an innkeeper for some fool law no one ever heard of? Magistrates and justicers ... just tools for the lords and them with coins ..."

"... be good to have a justicer ... understood people, not coins ..."

Kharl had to wonder about that. From what he'd seen, most people didn't want to be understood. They wanted to do what they wanted to do, whether or not others got hurt. He took another swallow of ale from the mug.

"... save that kinda dreams for hot nights in summer ..."

"... hot nights ... not gonna happen ... not here, not there, not anywhere ..."

Another burst of laughter rose from the table beside Kharl.

Before long, he would head back to the *Southshield*. There wasn't anything else he wanted to do or anyone else to see in Vizyn. Of that he was certain.

Carpenter and Mage

LXXI

The voyage back from Vizyn to Valmurl was swifter, but colder and rougher, than the trip north to Vizyn had been, and Kharl was more than glad when the *Southshield* finally tied up at the pier in the harbor at Valmurl late on a cloudy fourday afternoon.

Herana stood by the railing as Kharl neared the gangway. "You going back to the *Seastag*?"

Kharl grinned sheepishly. "If Captain Hagen'll take me back."

"I'd wager he will." Herana offered a broad smile, one that carried a trace of laughter in her gray eyes, and took away the lines in her narrow face.

"Let's hope you're right." Kharl returned the smile and, staff in hand and pack on his back, headed down the gangway.

Valmurl didn't feel all that much warmer than Vizyn. Was winter that cold in all of Austra? Kharl glanced at the warm gloves Taleas had given him, and for which he remained most grateful. He owed Taleas something, both for his honesty and the gloves, but how, and with what, could he repay the scrivener? Taleas had said Kharl had repaid him and would again, but he'd never explained, and Kharl hadn't asked. A sense of sadness passed through him as he thought of another scrivener. He continued to make his way down the pier toward the harbor way.

"You! With the staff!"

Kharl turned.

Three men in yellow-and-black tunics—uniforms of some sort—stood on the stone causeway at the shoreward end of the pier. The shorter armsman on the right pointed at Kharl. "Best get back on whatever ship you came in on."

Kharl forced himself to look at the lead armsman directly, but openly, and not with hostility, despite the anger in the man's voice. The fellow had no hint of chaos, and Kharl did his best to project directness and honesty as he replied. "I'm a carpenter on the *Seastag*. I went to see friends while the ship was in refit."

"Who's the master?"

"Hagen's the captain, Furwyl's the first . . ."

"Get back out to the refit yard then, and, if you know what's good for you, don't carry a dark staff like that, not now."

"Yes, ser. I will, ser, but I was traveling, and a staff helps . . ." Kharl paused as he realized that there were more of the uniformed armsmen everywhere. "What's happened? When I left . . ."

"Lord Estloch was murdered, that's what."

"Oh . . . that's not good."

"Worse 'n that. Be on your way." The words were gruff, but no longer hostile. "And get that staff put aside soon as you can."

"Yes, ser," Kharl replied politely, wondering why the guard had backed down so quickly. Then, he was glad the man had.

He made his way northward toward the street he thought led to the refit yards. He'd only been in that part of the harbor once before, seeking out Chalart to see about a position as a cooper. Had it only been little more than an eightday before? It seemed longer. Once he was away from the main part of the harbor, he saw no more guards in uniform, but there were few people out and about, fewer than he would have thought just from the cold weather and the chill wind.

When he reached the refit yard, Kharl stopped short of the single pier and looked northwest. It was easy to pick out the *Seastag* in the last dry dock. The other two dry docks were empty, as they had been earlier.

He made his way past the single pier and then along the edge of the water until he stood on the stone edge of the drained dry dock. The ship was resting on keel blocks and angled supports, and was also tethered with heavy hemp cables that ran from the masts and bowsprit to bollards twice the size of those in the harbor. Kharl looked down at the mud-smeared stone base of the dry dock, then toward the gangway.

He walked to the gangway, but stopped short as Ghart appeared from a small shed set short of the gangway.

"You didn't like the country life so well, I see," observed Ghart.

"They weren't too interested in having a good cooper, just a cheap one," Kharl said, knowing he was shading the truth somewhat.

"That's the way of the world," Ghart replied. "Captain told me you'd most likely be back. Never took you off the crew list."

Kharl didn't know what to say to that.

"He's done that more 'n once. Did it for me after my first voyage. Been with him ever since. We're all in the bunkhouse there." Ghart gestured toward the low stone structure set back from the refit area, and north of the warehouses and Chalart's cooperage. "Need to take your gear there, then report back here." He grinned. "Tarkyn said you'd be back. Been saving some work for you. We're about through for today, but he'll still want to see you."

Kharl laughed. "He was hoping I'd be back."

"That he was." Ghart's eyes darted toward the southwest.

Kharl could sense the second's concern. "What's going on? I saw armsmen all over the port."

"Someone murdered Lord Estloch the day before yesterday. Crossbow quarrel from the woods while he was hunting. No one knows who. He'd disinherited his eldest years back. Said Ilteron was cruel, and that cruelty didn't serve a land well. People have been saying that he—Ilteron, that's the older one—that he was behind the killing, and that he's got an army and the support of Guillam. Guillam's the head of the factors' council, and most of the factors and crafters leastwise listen to him. Some even say that Ilteron's marching out of the Shiltons against Lord Ghrant—that's his younger brother—and the one Estloch had named as his heir."

"Where's the captain?"

"He's in the Great House. He grew up with Lord Estloch, and Lord Ghrant sort of thought of him as an uncle. Sometimes, he'd advise Lord Estloch. That's what they said." Ghart looked at the dry dock. "We're supposed to be out of here by the end of the eightday after this one. Wish it were sooner. Ship in dry dock is like a man with his legs broken."

"They've got guards in uniform—black and yellow—at the piers in the main part of the harbor," Kharl said.

"Black and yellow—those are Lord Ghrant's personal guards. The Austran regulars are black and green."

"You don't think he trusts the regulars? Lord Ghrant, I mean."

"Don't know as I'd trust anyone, were I in his boots," Ghart replied. "Better get your gear over there in the bunkhouse. Tarkyn said you'd a lot of catching up to do."

Kharl laughed again as he turned from the gangway and headed toward the bunkhouse.

LXXII

After a passable supper in the common room of the bunkhouse, a fair night's sleep, and almost no comment by others in the crew about his absence, except a few jokes about coopers, the next morning Kharl was hard at work. Tarkyn had set up a lathe and a planer in a shed on the northern side of the dry dock, a shed kept passably warm inside by an ancient woodstove and surrounded outside by seasoned oak planks stacked chest high. Kharl's task was to rough-finish the planks to the measurements Tarkyn had already made.

"I thought the shipwrights were the ones working on the *Seastag*," Kharl said.

"They do the hull. Captain's paid extra to have the whole hull checked for shipworms. Problem is . . . no one can afford to have every plank in the ship copper-treated. Just treat the hull and main timbers. Turns out that there were places where they ate into the interior planks. We get to craft the planking for the sections bein' replaced."

Kharl's eyes went toward the timbers stacked high outside the shed. "All those?"

"Probably not, but there's a whole section in the main hold . . . and another just above the bilges in the forward hold . . ."

Kharl had to smile. Fairness aside, there were reasons why Hagen had wanted him back.

"So you rough-finish the ones for the main hold to size, while I'm down getting the sizes for the forward ones . . ."

"Leaving me the hard work," Kharl joked.

"Beats being a cooper without a copper to your name," retorted Tarkyn with a mock-gruffness. "Should anyway . . ."

"That it does, most honored master carpenter." Kharl grinned and offered a deep bow.

They both laughed. Tarkyn was still chucking when he left.

Kharl had been working in the shed for well over a glass and had a goodly sized pile of planks ready for Tarkyn when the door opened. He looked up to see Hagen closing the door and moving toward the lathe. Kharl slowed the lathe and stepped back.

"Hard at work, I see," said the captain. "Glad to have you back."

"Yes, ser. I've got some catching up to do. Have to say that I'm glad to be back, ser," Kharl replied. "And I appreciate your kindness. I do."

"Even with everything Tarkyn had waiting?" Hagen's eyes twinkled for a moment.

"Even so." Kharl paused. "Might I ask what's happening in Valmurl with Lord Ghrant?"

Hagen's countenance turned sober. "It's said that his older brother Ilteron has landed an army at Bruel, and the highland barons of the west have thrown in with him."

Bruel? Where the Hamorians could still send brimstone? Kharl decided not to ask, not yet, instead saying, "I'd heard that Ilteron was a cruel sort. Why would they support him?"

"They can accept his cruelty more than the rule of his brother. They dislike the reforms that Lord Estloch forced on them and Lord Ghrant is said to favor. Especially the right of peasants to buy their way out of indenture. They claim that they'll lose all their lands because the peasants will all leave."

"How will most peasants ever raise that kid of coin?" asked Kharl.

Hagen looked sharply at Kharl, then smiled wanly. "Most won't. It doesn't matter. The highland lords are used to being absolute rulers over their lands. The merchants and factors have more power in the north and east, and most won't support Ilteron because they feel that his rule will ruin trade and factoring."

"Are the east and west of Austra that different?"

"They are indeed."

"Will the merchants and factors stand behind Lord Ghrant? I'd heard that someone on the factors' council . . ."

"Guillam has left Valmurl. The others will hold for Ghrant, but it will be a hard battle because Ilteron has more than a few companies of Hamorian-trained free armsmen."

"Free armsmen?"

"Armsmen who serve the highest bidder."

"The Emperor of Hamor is paying them, you think?" asked Kharl. "With the brimstone going there, isn't that likely?"

"How would one know? I would guess so, but that isn't something that's proof . . ." Hagen shrugged. "The highland barons love warfare, and they have waited for years to take revenge on the easterners and merchants."

"If they are so warlike, how—"

"They are fewer, and they could never long hang together, and when Lord Estloch's great-great-grandsire subdued them, he stationed arms-men all along the borders and stopped their raids. It was bloody, because the easterners lost twice as many men, but Lord Isthel kept the highlanders from getting enough food. After three years, they were starving, and he marched into the highlands and leveled all their keeps and took all their weapons. For two generations, he and his son gar-risoned the west." Hagen laughed, ruefully. "Then the garrison com-manders became the lords of the highlands . . ."

Kharl shook his head.

"Seems like what the fathers learn, the grandchildren forget," Hagen said. "Enough of that. I'm keeping you from your work, and we'll need the *Seastag* back afloat as soon as we can." He nodded. "Good to have you back." Then he was gone.

Kharl turned his attention back to the planer and the next set of mea-surements. As always, he recalled his father's maxim: Measure twice, cut once.

But he still fretted about landowners who seemed just like Egen. Did every land have them? What did it take to keep them from their evil? Was greater power or violence always the only answer? Then he shook his head, ruefully. Just what could a carpenter do?

Abruptly, he stopped.

Taleas had said that if he did not learn more about himself and the staff, he would end up as dead as Tyrbel. With turmoil everywhere he went, those words carried more impact.

LXXIII

For the next several days, Kharl and the rest of the crew worked from just before dawn to after dusk. By twoday of the following eightday, Kharl and Tarkyn had replaced all the damaged planks in the *Seastag*, including several that Tarkyn had not realized were damaged, but that Kharl's order-senses had discovered. Kharl had been careful enough to show the damage with a hammer and chisel, rather than claiming anything.

In the evenings, on a straight-backed chair pulled up under one of the few wall lamps in the common room of the bunkhouse, Kharl had taken to reading and rereading sections of *The Basis of Order*.

He was puzzling over a phrase—"the greater the concentration of order within objects, the greater the amount of free chaos in the world."

At that moment, the door to the outside opened, and a gust of wind whistled through the room for the instant that it took a short and stocky man in a brown cloak to enter and close the door behind him. The newcomer glanced around the common room before his eyes lighted upon Kharl. Nodding, as if to himself, he stepped forward.

Kharl closed the book, still holding it, and stood. Although he had never seen the man, he could sense the darkness of order surrounding him.

"I've heard about you—felt you as well." The man was well muscled, if graying, and his hair and the tunic under his heavy brown cloak were almost the same shade. He pulled up a chair and seated himself but a few cubits from Kharl.

Kharl sat down slowly. "Felt me?"

"Bit old for a blackstaffer, though."

"Blackstaffer?" Kharl shook his head. "I'm not from Recluce. I'm a cooper from Brysta. Or I was." Who was the man, and what did he want with Kharl?

"You can't stay as a ship's carpenter forever, much as Hagen would like to keep you. Sooner or later, you'll do too much, or one of Lord Ilteron's mages will discover you're here."

"An assistant to a carpenter?"

"You're a better carpenter than Tarkyn is. He knows it, and that's why he has you doing the precise work. He's been around long enough that it doesn't bother him, and it makes his life easier." The other smiled.

"Why are you here?" Kharl asked. "Who sent you?"

"No one sent me. I came to see you, to offer you some insight . . . if you're interested. You should be, if you've got any sense."

Kharl still felt uneasy and off-balance. "Why did you mention Lord Ilteron? And not Lord Ghrant?"

"Lord Ghrant doesn't have any mages."

Kharl guessed. "He has you . . . doesn't he?"

The other smiled. "Such as I am, I suppose. I couldn't do much against true chaos-wizards. My little tricks wouldn't even slow them down. That's why I stay away from the Great House. I'd just call attention to Lord Ghrant's lack of magery."

"What kind of tricks?"

"Each skill has to be learned. Most cannot be taught."

Kharl snorted. "I can't teach coopering to everyone, but I can teach it to those who have the good hands and the wish to learn. I don't see that magery is that much different."

"It's not. But the costs are so much higher if the student is ungrateful." The mage, if indeed he happened to be one, rose from the chair. "Now is not the time or place to talk. If you want to learn more, not that I can offer you more than a small portion of what you could do, you need to come find me. I'm in the Nierran Hills. That's just northwest of here."

"You walked here?"

"Why not? It's only five kays, and I had to see who was creating such an order-focus. Besides, I could use the exercise."

"Order-focus?" Kharl frowned and, when the other did not respond, asked, "Who told you to come to me, and how would I get away?"

"Just tell your captain that you're going to see Lyras." He wrapped his cloak around himself and walked to the bunkhouse door. With a brief wave, he was gone.

"Who was that?" called Reisl from the corner where he and several others were gaming.

"I don't know," Kharl said, then added, "He said his name was Lyras, but I've never seen him before."

Reisl offered a cryptic smile and went back to gaming.

Kharl looked down at the book in his hand, thinking about what Lyras had said about the costs of magery being so much higher than those of coopering. After a time, he opened the book once more and began to read. He found it hard to concentrate on the words . . . or what they meant.

LXXIV

By midmorning of fiveday, Kharl knew he needed to talk to Hagen. After three days of thinking, of evenings spent reading *The Basis of Order* and learning little new from it, the words of both Taleas and Lyras had continued to hammer at him. So . . . during a break from working with the lathe to turn shafts for a bench back in the mess, Kharl eased away from the shed and toward the other side of the dry dock, where Hagen and Furwyl were standing and surveying the *Seastag*.

Kharl stood well back, under a welcome and even slightly warm sun, with the first clear skies in almost an eightday, waiting for the captain and first mate to finish their conversation, hoping for a break before too long.

". . . tomorrow . . . the caulk's set . . . after that?"

". . . timbers not as seasoned as we'd like, ser," Furwyl replied. "We'll have to watch that for near-on half a year . . . couldn't get the best seasoned timbers, not ones that'd take copper . . ."

". . . try for the first of the eightday."

"Yes, ser." Furwyl headed toward the building that held the ship-wright's foreman.

After studying his vessel for a time, Hagen turned. "You wanted to speak to me, carpenter?"

"Yes, ser." Kharl stepped toward the captain. "The other night I had a visitor."

"Lyras. I heard."

"He said I should visit him, and that all I had to do was tell you." Kharl waited.

Hagen laughed. "That old devil! Maybe he does know something. By all means, go and see him. Work in the morning and see him in the afternoon. See what you can find out."

"About what?"

"About anything. He won't tell you unless you ask."

"He already told me that Lord Ilteron has some white wizards," Kharl ventured. "He didn't say how he knew or where they came from."

"He never does," Hagen replied. "With matters as they are, it's more important than ever that you go and see him. All I ask is that you tell me anything you learn about what may be happening here in Austra."

"Are you sure . . ."

Hagen looked hard at Kharl. "You might turn out to be a mage. You might not. If you are, we'll all be better off for it. If you're not, Lyras will tell you that as well, and you'll be a better carpenter for it. Either way, I'm better off, and so are you."

"Yes, ser." Kharl wasn't certain that magery, especially any magery he might learn, would be that helpful to others. So far, his actions hadn't exactly benefited those close to him, but he wasn't about to say that.

"Tell Tarkyn I'm having you visit Lyras. He'll understand. I'll be here mornings. If something can't wait, Furwyl knows where to find me."

"Yes, ser."

Hagen took a last look at the dry-docked *Seastag*, then walked back toward the stern, squinting as his eyes peered at the lower hull.

Kharl headed back to the shed that held the lathe and Tarkyn. He'd little more than entered it and closed the door before Tarkyn stopped the lathe.

"What did you and the captain talk about? Saw you with him," Tarkyn observed.

"I told him about Lyras, and what he told me. Captain said he wanted me to go see Lyras in the afternoon, more than once, if necessary."

Tarkyn fingered his chin. "That'd figure, the captain being thought so close to Lord Estloch and now Lord Ghrant. He can't visit Lyras, and no one'd think twice about your going." He chuckled. "Even if it's as much for your good as his."

Kharl shrugged helplessly. "What . . . the captain said. Those were his words . . ."

"I'm sure they are." Tarkyn looked at the lathe. "Best you get back to the lathe so that this old man doesn't have to do too much by himself." The gruff words were belied by the twinkle in the eyes of the white-haired carpenter.

Kharl chuckled and took over at the lathe.

Still, he felt guilty about leaving the carpentry shed at the dry dock not much after noon, but Tarkyn had almost shooed him out the door. "Captain has a reason for everything. Go!"

Kharl went. He decided against taking the staff, but he did persuade Ghart to let him take a cudgel from the weapons locker. He covered the first few kays, through the streets and out the north road from Valmurl, easily enough. Then the stones of the north road gave way to damp and sometimes slippery clay, and he wished he had a staff for balance as his steps slowed.

All in all, it was well into midafternoon by the time Kharl found Lyras, who was outside a modest cottage of red sandstone, stone smoothed and polished into an even finish, with a dark slate roof, glass windows, and green-painted shutters and front door. The dwelling was long and narrow, no more than fifteen cubits wide, but it ran back a good forty, Kharl judged.

The mage was on the south side, pruning dormant berry bushes with a pair of long-handled shears. "Wasn't certain I'd see you, Master Kharl." Lyras took a last snip with the shears.

"Kharl . . . I'm no master."

"Word is that you're a master cooper, and you might be a master of more than that someday. Let's go inside. I can have Zera heat up a kettle of something to warm us." Lyras walked to the low front stoop, two steps above the front walk. There he set down the shears, then opened the door, holding it for Kharl to enter.

"Thank you." Kharl wasn't that cold, not after a walk that had left him all too warm, but he appreciated the hospitality.

A roundish brown-haired woman appeared at the back of the front room that extended the width of the cottage.

"My consort, Zera," Lyras said, before turning to her. "This is Kharl. He's the one I told you about. If you wouldn't mind warming up the tonic . . . dear?"

"I've already put it on." Zera looked to Kharl. "I've some shortbread. Would you like some?"

"That would be most welcome . . . if it's not . . . I wouldn't want . . ."

Zera laughed heartily. "No . . . you won't be eating us out of hearth and home. We've plenty." With a smile, she slipped through the doorway leading out of the front room.

Lyras gestured to the pair of chairs set several cubits back from the iron stove located in the northwest corner of the room. "We can talk here."

Kharl sat, and, after a long silence, looked at the older mage. "I'm here."

"And you want immediate enlightenment."

"No. I'd settle for a useful hint or two. Or an exercise that would teach me something."

"You can already detect chaos at a distance, and you can tell when people do not tell the truth. That is more than many who claim to be mages. Why do you wish to know more?"

Kharl thought for a moment before replying. "I don't know. I only feel that I should."

"So you can become wealthy and powerful, perhaps?" A slightly ironic tone colored Lyras's words.

"It would be good not to be coinless," Kharl countered, "but I have enough coins."

Lyras nodded. "So you came to see me without being able to explain why, and you want my advice and help, but you can't tell me where you'd like this advice?"

Kharl nodded, and was saved from having to make an immediate response by the arrival of Zera, carrying two black mugs. She handed one first to Kharl, then one to Lyras, and slipped out of the front room, only to return with a small platter that she set on the low table between the town chairs. Without speaking, she left as quickly and as silently as she had entered.

"It's a sweetened redberry cider," Lyras explained. "Takes the chill off the bones." He took a sip. "Ahhh . . ." Then he reached for one of the oblong shortbreads.

Kharl followed the older man's example and found the hot drink neither too hot nor too sweet. He also had a shortbread. "It's good. So is the shortbread." After a moment, and another bite of shortbread, he looked at Lyras. "Why are you here? Outside of Valmurl?"

"Why not? It's a pleasant place, and far more comfortable than a few rooms in the Great House. I'm not that good a black mage. You're already stronger than I am, and you've had no training at all. There's no use for a weak mage in Recluce, and none of the lords in Austra or Nordla really want any powerful black mages in their lands. The Emperor of Hamor just uses mages up." He gestured toward the window to his left, the one over-looking the berry bushes he had been pruning. "I know enough to help them produce and make jams and jellies, and no one pays much attention. Sometimes, I'd go to see Lord Estloch, but I never knew whether I'd done more good or harm. He let me stay because a weak black mage is much less trouble than a weak white wizard, who can still be obviously dangerous."

Kharl wondered about the words—obviously dangerous. "I saw a white wizard once. He gathered young people, mostly girls, and when he was done, they died. Not a mark on them."

"Did he look younger afterward?"

"I don't know."

"He probably was younger. His body had more concentrated good chaos, the strength of youth. What happened to him?"

"He died." Kharl had said too much. "But . . . you must be from Recluce . . . you know so much . . ."

"Ah, yes. I must confess that I was born in Reflin. My father was a baker, and a poor bakery it was. I didn't learn a thing. Zera does all the baking, and a good thing it is." The mage took another sip of the redberry cider, then looked at Kharl. "My talking isn't going to help you much. Of course, not knowing what you want doesn't help much either."

"I know what I want," Kharl said. "I want to put things to right. I'd liked to have done that in Brysta. I just didn't know how."

"What was wrong in Brysta?"

"My consort was hung for a killing she had nothing to do with. I was flogged for trying to defend her and for stopping the lord's son from taking his pleasure by force with a neighbor girl. Another man was hung because he told the truth about the lord's son . . ."

"Ah, yes . . . telling the truth. That's often the recipe for disaster. Even a poor mage recognizes that. What else?"

"A weaver girl had to hide in a rendering yard because the tariff farmer seized her mother's house and shop and tried to force her into indenture at a pleasure house. That white wizard—the one I mentioned— was working with the lord's son and killed young girls for his use, and no one even seemed to notice."

"It's that way in most lands. It has been more often than not," Lyras pointed out. "Why should it be different in yours?"

"It should be better everywhere, but a man wants to see things better where he was raised."

"Not all men. Not even most men."

"I'm not most men."

"No. You're not." Lyras laughed. "Become a justicer. That way you can change some of those things."

"A cooper? As a justicer?"

"Haven't you ever heard of the Justicer's Challenge? All the world knows about it. It's a practice that's only accepted here and in Nordla."

"I've heard of it," Kharl admitted. "Didn't seem like something for a cooper."

"It's seldom used." The older man laughed again. "That's because no one dares. Failure means that the challenger suffers the fate of the accused—the punishment of each of the five accused comprising the challenge." Lyras took another sip from his mug. "Forget about that now. What you really need is some exercises that will help you understand what power you may have and the limits of that power."

Kharl managed to refrain from saying that he'd already said that.

"I have several suggestions," Lyras went on. "Some order-mages are weather mages. There is a way to tell if you have that talent. Take a kettle and put it on a hot stove. Watch the steam. Try to move the cloud of steam around. It works better in a cold room—"

"Steam . . . and weather?"

"Oh . . . clouds are made up of water, like steam. Where do you think the rain comes from? Then, others are healers. Serious wounds create an angry reddish feel within them. If you can sense and remove that kind of chaos . . . that's what a healer is."

"An exercise?" asked Kharl.

"There aren't any that I know of. Oh . . . if you can study small animals with your senses, and feel how order works in them, that might help. I've heard that there are earth mages, who can sense the flow of order and chaos in the ground beneath, and some of them are smiths. As a cooper . . . maybe you come by that naturally. In hot metal . . . right from the forge fire, the order bonds are weaker, and chaos is, well, more fluid—that's how the black engineers on Recluce make all that black iron . . . another trick, really only a trick . . . is to use your senses to let light flow around you. Light flows like water in a way, you know. Unless you're very good with order-sensing what's around you, you'll be blind, but sometimes it's useful not to be seen . . . never could do that one myself, but I've seen it done . . ."

Kharl continued to listen, feeling that, perhaps for the first time, he was getting an idea of what order-magery was all about—or rather the feeling, beyond words on the pages of *The Basis of Order*, that what the words had hinted at could actually be accomplished.

"... Now there's one last thing. About that staff. There was a reason why they wouldn't take that back, one that they didn't tell you. You need to look up a phrase in *The Basis of Order*. You have a copy, don't you?"

"Yes," Kharl admitted grudgingly.

"There's a phrase in there about staffs, blackstaffs. It's important ... and that's probably more than I should have said, and don't ask me more."

"Why not?" Kharl asked bluntly.

"Because it's something you have to find, or it won't mean anything. Tell it to someone directly ... it never works. Already, I may have told you too much."

How could anyone be told too much? But then ... he'd tried to tell his boys things, and they'd had to learn for themselves. "Thank you." Kharl paused, trying to make sure he remembered everything that Lyras had said. "Why did the Emperor of Hamor send chaos-mages, and not order mages?"

"I'm scarcely the emperor," Lyras pointed out. "But I'd guess that's because comparatively weak chaos-wizards can create much destruction, and there weren't any strong order-mages here."

Kharl didn't quite understand the connection, and it must have shown on his face.

"Oh ... you don't see. But then, how would you know?" Lyras shook his head. "Because black mages serve order, they preserve and strengthen ties and forces. So ... a strong order-mage couldn't throw free chaos at a white wizard, but he could walk through all that chaos with his order shields and strike one blow with a staff or something— not a blade—and destroy the white wizard. But ... the emperor didn't think there were any order-mages in Austra."

"So the mages he sent to support Lord Ilteron—"

"Ilteron is only a hill baron. His sire couldn't strip him of his hill lands in the Shiltons, much as he would have liked to. Ilteron's been building his own personal guards for years. Lord Estloch chose to ignore that, although I warned him."

"Why does everyone think Ilteron was behind the lord's death?"

Lyras snorted. "The timing, for one thing. Lord Ghrant reached his majority last year. If Estloch had been killed before that, there would have been a regency, and doubtless wiser heads, such as Hagen and

Lady Renyra, would have been on the regency council. Lord Ghrant's inexperienced, but he wants things his way. But he doesn't like people arguing with him; he hates personal confrontation. He's the sort that's happy to order someone else to shed the blood, but doesn't want to strike the blow himself . . ."

Kharl had his doubts about relaying that to Hagen.

"And then there's Malcor. He's been bowing and scraping all over the Great House for the last two years. Lord Estloch dies, and Malcor vanishes without taking his leave and reappears back in the hills, making a visit to Ilteron. Also, Malcor is known to be excellent with a crossbow."

"Doesn't anyone else know this?"

"Several score, I'd imagine, but none with the nerve to say such out loud. There's no gain in it. It won't bring back Lord Estloch. It raises the question of why anyone who would state that didn't tell someone before, and, should Ilteron succeed in overthrowing Ghrant, which is most likely, it subjects the speaker to the loss of lands and life. So . . . everyone is silent."

Kharl understood that. He just hadn't thought that powerful lords and landholders would behave in the same fashion as crafters, although, upon reflection, he could see there wasn't any reason why they wouldn't.

"You had thought lords might speak up?" asked Lyras.

"I had considered it, but not for long."

"They speak out for the truth less than crafters, for they have more to lose, and little to gain from the truth. That's why no one trusts them, and they trust each other even less."

"It's a wonder that anyone speaks the truth," Kharl said.

"And when they do, examine their words closely." Lyras stood. "It's getting close to sunset, and you'd best be heading back. The parts of Valmurl north of the refit yards aren't the best in full night, even with your sight."

How did Lyras know about his night sight? Or was that something that even minor mages had? Kharl stood and set the empty mug on a side table. "Thank you. Might I come back when I've had a chance to consider what you've said?"

"I'd not be stopping you." Lyras opened the cottage door for Kharl.

"Until then." Kharl nodded as he left the stoop.

He walked quickly down the path to the road, then turned southward, trying to sort out everything he had heard over the afternoon. He certainly wanted to try out some of the exercises and tests Lyras had suggested, if only to see what he might be able to do.

And he had promised Hagen to pass on what he had learned, little as it seemed.

LXXV

The next morning was sunny, but the air felt damper, and Kharl could see clouds just above the horizon to the northeast. Since he had promised to report to Hagen on what he had learned from Lyras, Kharl found the captain even before he went to the shed to work with Tarkyn.

Hagen listened as Kharl reported on what Lyras had said. When Kharl had finished, Hagen tilted his head, not quite nodding, then tugged on his earlobe. "Lord Estloch had told me about the personal guards, but I don't think he wanted to believe Ilteron had hired so many. As for Malcor, that I can believe. He comes from the old line."

Kharl didn't know anything about the old line and decided not to ask. "And no one, not one lord or factor, said a word?"

"Oh, doubtless they're all telling each other now that they knew it all along and that they each had told Lord Estloch in confidence, but that for reasons of his own, Lord Estloch chose not to act. By sunset, every one of them will believe it."

Kharl thought he understood better why Hagen preferred the sea to the Great House in Valmurl.

"You aren't that surprised, now, are you?" asked Hagen.

"No, ser. I'd have to say that I'd hoped for better, but I didn't expect it."

Hagen smiled, sadly. "That's a good precept. Hope and work for better, but don't expect it. Are you going to see Lyras again?"

"I'd thought to, ser, but not for a while. Wouldn't do any good right now." Kharl wasn't sure that another visit would help, not until he'd had a chance to try out some of what the mage had suggested, at least. He also wondered about the mysterious references to the staff.

"That's probably for the best. When you do, let me know if you find out anything else."

"Yes, ser. I'll be heading back to the shed now."

Hagen just nodded, his thoughts clearly turning elsewhere.

Kharl was the first in the shed. He'd fired up the old stove and was setting up the lathe when Tarkyn arrived, closing the door behind him.

"So . . . what'd you find out from Lyras?" asked Tarkyn. "Didn't want to ask last night, not till you talked to the captain and not with other ears around."

"Ilteron has some white mages, and it's likely that someone named Malcor killed Lord Estloch."

"Malcor . . . name's familiar. Don't know why."

"I'd never heard of him, but the captain had. Said he was out of the old line."

"Oh . . . him. His father was the out-of-consort son of Lord Estloch's uncle. The uncle had but daughters, and couldn't pass on the title. That's how Estloch got it."

Kharl thought he understood, not that it made sense to him. A son was a son; a daughter was a daughter. Both were children. For a moment, the images of Arthal and Warrl flashed to mind, and he swallowed, wishing that he could have done more for them . . . somehow. But there wasn't much else that he could do. Not at the moment.

"Anything else? That you can say?"

"There wasn't much else. Lyras talked about why the Emperor of Hamor didn't send his best white wizards to Austra."

"That's trouble."

"And Ilteron has more personal guards than anyone knew. That was about it."

"Wager that's more than most folks knew. Captain pleased?"

"He seemed to know most of it, except for Malcor. He's worried about something."

" 'Course he's worried. He's trying to advise a lord who's barely more than a boy, and that lord's going to be attacked by his brother who's being supported by the Emperor of Hamor . . . I'd worry, too."

So would Kharl. Left unspoken was the understanding that Hagen was so closely linked to Estloch and Ghrant that if Ilteron triumphed, Hagen would lose his ships or even his life if he didn't flee Austra.

"You about ready with that lathe?" asked Tarkyn.

Furwyl had added another project for the carpenters—a second weapons locker beside the ladder to the poop deck—and he'd said Hagen wanted it finished in the next few days.

"Second weapons locker, along with everything else," Kharl said, half to himself, as he made the final adjustments to the lathe settings. "That's not good . . ."

"These days, not much is," countered Tarkyn.

Kharl couldn't say much to that.

By the end of the day, when he left the carpenter shed, Kharl still had questions swirling through his head. The clouds had moved in from the northeast by midafternoon, and a fine cold rain filtered out of a dark gray sky.

He'd really been too busy to think in any depth about what Lyras had said, but the questions hadn't gone away. Although Kharl had not tried it, not having a forge that he could use while not being watched, he thought, just from his earlier efforts with iron, that he might be able to forge something like black iron. What he would use it for was another question. He clearly had no feel for what lay deep beneath the earth, although he could sense life and patterns within perhaps a cubit of the surface.

Kharl moved quickly from the shed to the bunkhouse. He was headed for the mess and common room when he recalled the kettle test suggested by Lyras. With a half smile, he made his way to the door of the kitchen area and slipped inside. As he had hoped, there was a kettle on the huge and antique iron stove.

Kharl stared at the kettle. While, with his senses, he could feel the swirl of order and chaos in the steam that poured from the spout, he could not seem to move it. He thought he could stop the steam, because when he concentrated on touching the bits of order and chaos, the steam cloud did not change shape, but he did not try that for long, since that was all he seemed able to do and since he didn't want anyone noticing. As far as moving the steam, light as it might be, he could not. While he didn't know how, even in a general way, he doubted that was the problem.

"What you looking at, carpenter?" asked Yilyt, the ship's cook. "Watching us cook isn't gonna get you fed earlier."

"I wondered what you were fixing."

"Got some kalfin—good white fish—hard to come by. Be frying that up . . ."

Kharl nodded. To him most fish tasted the same. "Thank you." He slipped out and went to the washhouse adjoining the bunkhouse. The only water was cold—ice-cold—and washing was a trial, but Kharl had always preferred being as clean as he could reasonably be.

Since he knew supper was still not ready when he headed back through the rain that was changing to a colder and heavier downpour, he stopped for just a moment and picked a leaf from the scraggly plant outside the front door to the bunkhouse. He wasn't sure whether it was a bush or a weed. Probably a weed from the broad leaf with the thornlike tips.

Carrying it gently in his left hand, he stepped into the common room. Except for several riggers that he knew only by sight and name, the tables were mostly empty. Kharl sat down at one end of a bench. He set the leaf on the table and looked at it, both with eyes and order senses.

Even though he had picked it, there was still some sense of life, although that was fading. Kharl could sense the way the order and chaos ebbed, almost like tiny threads, notched or "hooked" at the ends. Almost on a whim, he tried to link those "hooks."

The leaf looked subtly different.

When Kharl touched it, it felt as hard as iron. He undid the twists in the order and chaos that he had somehow created, and both order and chaos disintegrated into minute fragments, a touch of white mist and one of black seeping unseen into the air. The leaf itself went limp. He could tell it was also dead, totally dead.

Somehow, he could make things so hard that they were like armor, but doing so would kill anything living. He just sat there in thought for a time.

Argan and Reisl slid onto the benches across the table from Kharl, setting platters down. At the *clunk*, Kharl looked up.

"Better get some. Looks good," said Reisl.

"Oh . . . thank you." As Kharl stood, he looked at the table for the leaf, but all that was left was a whitish powder. Almost dazed, he walked to the end of the mess line and waited for his platter, then picked up a mug of a very poor ale, and returned to the table across from Reisl and Argan, sitting down, and taking a swallow of the ale. He was thirsty.

"What were you doing?" asked Argan. "We came by and you were looking at some funny leaf. Didn't even hear us."

"Coulda fired a cannon at you. Don't think you'd have moved," added Reisl.

"Guess I was tired, or hungry," Kharl replied. "We've been working on a second weapons locker. Got the frame tied to the poop frames, and we'll have most of it done tomorrow. If the rain ever lets up. Got water-proofs over it now, but we'll still need sunlight to do it right."

"Another weapons locker?" Reisl looked at Argan. "Can't say I like that. Captain hear something about more pirates?"

"Maybe it has to do with the lord out west, the one that's rebelled against Lord Ghrant," suggested Argan.

"Say the Hamorians might back him," mumbled Reisl, looking at Kharl. "What do you know about that?"

"Some folks say he's got a white wizard and more personal guards than most hill lords," Kharl admitted. "He's the brother of Lord Ghrant."

"Brother against brother, and lords, too. That'd be nasty. Be glad when we're outa dry dock," Reisl said.

Kharl just nodded. The kalfin was actually fairly good, firm under a crispy crust, and the potatoes were less lumpy than usual.

"Think we'll get back afloat by next eightday . . ."

". . . Hemmen or Brysta next port . . . captain hasn't said . . ."

Kharl didn't say too much during supper, but tried to be pleasant and not withdraw into himself.

When Reisl finished, he looked up at Kharl. "Too wet to go to the inn. You want to join the game?"

Kharl smiled. "Thanks, but I had a long day."

"Just asking."

"Better that I don't." And it was, for more than a few reasons, since Kharl suspected he would have been tempted to try to use his order-senses on the dice.

Instead, after returning his empty platter, he walked outside into the cold rain and stood under the eaves of the bunkhouse next to the wall. He studied the small puddle at his feet, just looking at it for a moment, then taking it in with his senses, trying first to see what the patterns of order and chaos might be, and then following them. He touched the water, ever so lightly, with what he thought of as his order-sense. It seemed to grow still, the way the steam had. Then, he could sense almost what were little hooks on each of the fragments. Somehow, he looked, and thought, and *twisted* the hooks so that they all locked together.

He almost staggered, because he could feel that he'd exerted some great effort. He looked down at the small puddle, and watched as water droplets falling from the edge of the eaves splattered on the smooth unmoving surface of the water. Had he turned the puddle to clear ice?

Slowly, he bent down and extended his fingers. The changed water was more like cool glass, perhaps slightly warmer than the water had been, but definitely not frozen. He straightened and then stamped his left boot heel on the glassy puddle. The puddle was as hard as stone or steel.

Kharl took out his belt knife and bent down, drawing the tip across the hard water. Even with the unchanged water falling from the eaves and coating the order-hard water, he could see that the knife made no impression, not even the faintest scratch. After a moment, he replaced the knife and looked at the hard water.

Finally, he concentrated and *untwisted* the hooks of order and chaos. The water shimmered and a faint steamy fog rose from the puddle as the colder water from the eaves struck what had been order-hardened water.

Kharl was suddenly exhausted, as though he had worked at a forge or a lathe all day, then run five or even ten kays. He'd wanted to try some of the other things Lyras had suggested, but he was tired, far too tired. Without looking back, he slowly trudged back inside the bunkhouse, past Reisl and the deckhands gaming. He nodded to Reisl, and got a smile in return.

As he continued down the hallway, past the rooms for the mates toward the bunkroom, he could hear the voices behind him.

". . . something about him . . . scary . . ."

". . . good man," Reisl answered. "You'd keep to yourself, too, if you'd lost everything he did . . . consort, children, cooperage . . ."

". . . 'sides," said another voice, "he's the one found the friggin' ship-worms . . . could be we'd all be in the deep locker . . ."

The voices faded out as Kharl slowly undressed and climbed into the bunk. The blackness of sleep was more than welcome.

LXXVI

On oneday morning, Kharl and Tarkyn were attaching the last set of hinges on the door to the second weapons locker. The sky overhead was almost clear, with a faint haze to the west, but a chill and light wind blew out of the north with a dampness that cut through Kharl's winter jacket.

Tarkyn stepped back and nodded. "An eightday or so, and no one'd know that it hadn't been there from the time the ship went down the ways."

"Better that way." Kharl checked the racks inside and closed the door. The hasp fit over the lock staple perfectly. He slipped the fitted dowel in place to keep the door shut. Once they were back afloat, Ghart would replace the dowel with an actual lock, but at the moment, no lock was needed, since there were no weapons inside the locker.

"Captain ever say why he wanted another locker?" Kharl had asked before, but Tarkyn had always deflected the question.

"Don't give up, do you?"

"You think I ought to?" countered Kharl. "Would you?"

Tarkyn chuckled, then glanced around the deck, empty except for the two carpenters at that moment. "Didn't say. Not exactly. Said something about ports not being as safe as they used to be, even Austran ports."

"He thinks someone might try to take over the ship?"

"With what he said, the thought had crossed my mind." Tarkyn frowned. "Then, could be he didn't want to give the real reason. Could be he didn't have one, except a feeling."

"Could be," Kharl agreed.

"You going back to see Lyras any time soon?"

"I hadn't planned on it." Kharl offered a laugh. "I haven't figured out half of what he told me last time." Nor had he had a chance to try several of the ideas Lyras had suggested. He hadn't found the passage in *The Basis of Order* about staffs, and he hadn't been successful, so far, in trying to become invisible. But that could have been because he was still tired. Or maybe he was missing something.

"Mages are like that." Tarkyn paused. "You're getting like that."

"Must be getting older, like you," Kharl countered.

"Reisl said he saw you looking at a leaf in the mess the other day. Just looked at it, and it got real stiff. Then, after a bit, just fell apart into white powder. Scared him stiff. He likes you, but still scared him." Tarkyn waited.

Kharl almost swallowed. He hadn't realized that Reisl had been watching that closely. After a long moment, he finally said, "I didn't mean to scare anyone. It was something Lyras suggested. Told me to study little things. I did it wrong. The leaf was almost dead anyway, but . . . I didn't help it. It's hard work. I had to go to bed early that night. I was that tired."

"For doing that to a leaf?"

"Well . . . I was outside studying the rain," Kharl added. "That was hard, too. No one ever told me that even learning little things about magery took so much strength." He was pleased that he'd managed to tell almost all the truth without revealing too much, and not much more than Tarkyn already knew.

The older carpenter nodded. "Heard that from others. Said that one of the mages that destroyed Fairven—or might have—had been a big brawny smith . . . came back a skinny old man. Others never came back at all."

"I could see that. Just the little things, just studying things, and I felt so tired, like I'd worked a forge all day. I guess that's why I keep telling people I can do a few things, but that I'm not a mage and might not ever be one."

Tarkyn laughed. "I'd believe that, except for one thing."

Kharl raised his eyebrows in question.

"You're the kind that never gives up . . . leastwise about that sort."

Kharl wondered. Hadn't he given up in a way about Charee, and about Warrl?

"Trouble coming," said Tarkyn, looking over Kharl's shoulder.

Kharl turned and watched as Furwyl crossed the gangway between the ship and the edge of the dry dock and made his way across the main deck.

"You about finished?" asked the first mate.

"Just did," Tarkyn said.

"Good. Put all your tools back in the carpenter shop below, and the ones you carried over to that shed. Then get your personal gear back aboard. We're refloating the ship. Captain wants us out of here and ready to sail morning after tomorrow. We're moving to the Lord's Pier soon as we get clear."

"Mind telling us why, ser?" asked Tarkyn.

"Captain didn't say much, except that we needed to be ready to shove off."

Kharl wondered how much of Hagen's urgency had been created by the reports of conflict between Lord Ghrant and his elder brother.

LXXVII

By threeday evening, after two frantic and hectic days, the *Seastag* was back in Valmurl harbor proper, tied to the innermost pier for oceangoing vessels, the so-called Lord's Pier. The last of the wagons that had been lined up on the pier had been unloaded in late afternoon, and the cargo stowed below. Now, the pier was empty, except for an occasional sailor. But a handful of vessels remained in the harbor, and no others at the Lord's Pier.

Because the day had been warmer, and because the light was brighter, Kharl had come topside to read and found a quiet place forward of the paddle wheels. Hunched in his winter jacket, wearing a glove on the hand that held the book, but not on the one that turned the pages, in the dusk he looked down at the open page of *The Basis of Order*. He had read the words before, but he read them again.

> Order cannot be concentrated in and of itself, not even within the staff of order, and no man can truly master the staff of order until he casts it aside.

How could anyone master something that he cast aside? And why should anyone cast aside something as useful as a staff?

The next words had not been much more help.

> For order cannot be divided in two without its power being diminished by four, and if it be divided into four parts, then its power is less by another fourth, so that the total of all portions is but one sixteenth of what it would have been undivided. Likewise, so it is with a staff imbued with order for whoever wields it . . .

Kharl closed the book. He would have to think even more about what those words meant. He almost wished he'd gone to see Lyras again, but he'd had so little time when he hadn't been busy or so tired from work and from what efforts he had made to try to do more with his order-abilities.

"You're not tired now," he murmured to himself. Not so tired as he had been, anyway.

He tried to recall what the mage had said about making himself invisible to others, something about letting light flow around him, that light flowed like water. But from where did it flow? Kharl glanced at the western sky above the roofs and towers of Valmurl. Some light flowed from the sun. Did it flow from lanterns or fires or torches? He had not found anything in the book about invisibility, or how to do it. He'd found very few references to light, and most of those referred to the chaotic nature of light, how it was not ordered.

He paused. He'd tried to let light flow around him before—a number of times—and nothing had happened. Lyras had said that becoming invisible was a trick, but one he'd never mastered. And he thought Kharl could? The carpenter laughed to himself.

Still . . . what was the harm in trying?

Could he try to order the light, use his senses to smooth it around him? As if he were really not standing there on the deck? He just leaned back against the chill wood of the paddle wheel frame and closed his eyes, trying to feel or sense the light.

Nothing—he sensed nothing. Except . . . something like a whispering white breeze. Was that light? He tried to ease it around him, as if he were not there. Nothing seemed to change, and he opened his eyes—only to find that he couldn't see. He was surrounded by blackness.

He swallowed and pushed at the light, and his sight returned.

For a time, he just sat there in the chilly dusk, breathing heavily and holding on to *The Basis of Order*.

What had he done? Did being invisible mean that he wouldn't be able to see? He tried to recall what Lyras had said. Something about needing his order-senses? Then Kharl remembered. "You'll be blind." He shivered.

He considered. He'd been blind, and now he wasn't. So . . . what was it? If the light flowed around him, and he needed light, even a little bit, to see . . . He shook his head. It was so obvious. He really hadn't been blind. He just hadn't been able to see because he'd had no light to see. But did that mean that others couldn't see him?

Slowly, he stood. Did he want to try again? If he didn't, how would he learn? But he also recalled that moment when he couldn't see. He took a slow deep breath and tried once more.

The second time the blackness was just that—blackness, no light. He tried to place where he was with his order-senses, and began to feel what was around him. Then, carefully, he eased his way aft, toward the quarterdeck where Rhylla had the deck duty.

He could sense her as he neared the railing, but he tried to make no sound. She turned, then leaned forward as if peering in his direction. Then she turned toward the gangway and pier.

Kharl slipped back forward and around the paddle wheel frame before he released his smoothing of the light. He sighed—deeply.

Again, he was tired. Not so drained as when he had hardened the water, but tired.

He paused. Could he harden something like the air he breathed? Into an invisible shield before him?

Kharl stood on the deck, letting his senses try to feel the air before him. For a moment, he just stood there, almost entranced, as he could see the tiniest fragments of order and chaos hanging in the air. Slowly, he concentrated on a square section of air a cubit before his eyes, *twisting* the hooks of order and chaos together.

Then he reached out with his hand, gingerly. The air was hard . . . hard as if it were an invisible metal plate. He tried to push it, but it did not move or give way. He yawned, and his eyes blurred.

He could feel his knees turn to water, and he sat down on the deck, harder than he wanted to. Then, blackness washed over him.

"Kharl? You all right, fellow?"

The words slowly penetrated, and Kharl looked up at the shadowy figure of Rhylla. "Tired . . . was reading. Guess I just fell asleep." He pulled himself to his feet.

"You look tired. Tarkyn must be working you hard."

"Sometimes. Times, I just work myself too hard."

The third laughed. "From anyone else but you I'd call that a load of sowshit."

"Could be from me," Kharl admitted. "But I am tired."

"Best not to sleep on the deck—not in port. Never know who might slip aboard."

"You're right. Thank you."

Rhylla turned away.

Kharl reached up, trying to see what had happened to the air shield. It was gone. Did that mean that it took his own concentration to maintain it . . . or that it would melt away in time? He wasn't sure he wanted to spend the effort to find out. Certainly not at the moment.

He slowly headed for his bunk in the forecastle. If he were going to use the air as a shield, he needed to become better at it, or the effort would likely kill him faster than whatever he was trying to protect against. More practice might help . . . he hoped.

He yawned again as he stepped through the hatchway. He *was* tired.

LXXVIII

Fourday had come, and gone, as had most of fiveday, and still the *Seastag* remained tied at the Lord's Pier. Kharl and Tarkyn had spent the majority of fiveday cleaning out and reorganizing the carpenter's shop, in an effort to undo the effects of the thrown-together stacks and lengths of wood and the hurriedly stowed tools required by the hasty reloading that had accompanied the rush of leaving the dry dock.

Kharl slipped the black staff into the longer overhead bin, still thinking about the passage in *The Basis of Order*. Why was it important to cast aside such a useful tool as the staff? He did not doubt the book, but he did question his own understanding of the words. "That should do it."

"Leastwise, gave us time to do it right 'fore we set to sea," grumbled Tarkyn. "When we set to sea. If we set to sea."

"You think we're waiting for cargo?"

"At the Lord's Pier? More likely waiting for . . ." Tarkyn broke off and turned in the stool.

Kawelt stood in the hatchway of the carpenter shop. "Kharl . . . got a visitor here."

"Visitor?" Kharl couldn't honestly think of anyone. Arthal? But his son wouldn't have even known that his father served on a ship, let alone which one, and Kharl doubted that Arthal would have cared, not given the way he'd left the cooperage.

"Second from the *Southshield* . . ."

Herana?

"You're not thinking of changing ships?" asked Tarkyn.

"No. I don't know why she'd . . ."

At the word "she" Tarkyn laughed. Even Kawelt looked amused.

"Go on . . . We're done for the day."

Kharl slipped on his winter jacket and gloves and headed topside, where he made his way to the quarterdeck. Herana and Ghart stood by the railing, talking.

". . . good man . . . carpenter and a fighter . . . a deck-stander . . . guess that's all right . . ."

". . . doesn't talk much about himself . . ."

Both turned as Kharl neared.

"Carpenter," said Herana, "we're in port till tomorrow. Thought you might like to join me for an ale. Ghart says you're not on the watch schedule until tomorrow morning."

Kharl looked to Ghart.

"Still don't have that cargo," Ghart said. "Go have an ale. Just take a look at the pier now and then."

"Yes, ser." Kharl nodded.

"See you later, Ghart," Herana said to the *Seastag*'s second mate.

Kharl followed Herana down the gangway, then drew abreast of her on the pier. He inclined his head to her. He wasn't quite sure what to call her, since he was neither passenger nor a crewman under her.

"I was glad to see you came back," she said. "Somehow, I didn't see you as the type that would have liked Vizyn."

"You were right, but I had to see."

"You don't like being a ship's carpenter?"

"I like it. I'm not certain it's what I should be doing."

"If you like it, and you're good . . . ?"

Kharl laughed. "Once I was a cooper, and I was good at it, and I liked it. But, for all that, things didn't turn out so well."

Herana turned toward the open doors of the Crimson Pitcher. Kharl followed her inside. The tavern was half-empty, and they found a table in the far corner of the main public room. As Kharl seated himself across from her, he couldn't help but overhear words from a table nearby.

". . . said the regulars being marched south. . . going to let Ilteron have Valmurl . . ."

". . . Lord Ghrant never was a fighter . . ."

A server appeared.

"Dark ale," Herana said.

"Lager. Pale ale if you don't have it," Kharl added.

"Three for each."

Kharl showed his coins, as did Herana.

"Be back in a moment."

"Ghart said you'd had to leave Brysta. Was that what you meant by things not turning out?" Herana's voice showed interest, but was not insistent as she looked at Kharl.

"Something like that." Kharl paused, then waited as the server set down two mugs before handing over his coins. Once the woman left, he said, "Board outside said two."

"Everything's getting dearer. All the taverns are asking more."

"Because of the fighting between Ghrant and Ilteron? What's Captain Harluk going to do with the *Southshield* . . . if Ghrant and Ilteron start a battle here in Valmurl?"

"Steam off to where they're not fighting," suggested Herana. "Wait until everything clears, then go back to carrying people and cargo where they want to go. What else can he do?"

"Not much," Kharl replied. He took a swallow of the pale ale. He would have preferred lager, but he wasn't about to complain about what he couldn't get.

After another silence, Herana asked, "You think things will work out better for you here?"

"I don't know. Once I thought that anywhere would be better. Now . . . seems like people are mostly the same everywhere. There's always someone . . ." Kharl shrugged and shook his head.

"You see that on ships, too. Thought I'd get away from that by going to sea," she said. "Don't have as many folk, but they're the same."

"Why did you go to sea?" Kharl asked. "Not that many women do."

"What was I going to do? Can't have children—consort near-on killed me when he found out."

Kharl winced. "I'm sorry."

"Don't be. Was a long time ago. Made it easier. My brother knew Harluk. He carries a lot of passengers, especially in the summer. Helps to have some women in the crew. Turned out I was good at it." She looked at Kharl. "You have a consort?"

"Not now. She was hung by Lord West for murder. She didn't do it . . ." Kharl gave as brief a description as he could of what had happened. ". . . and that was how I got to be a carpenter on the *Seastag*."

"Daresay you left out a lot."

Kharl nodded.

"Your sons . . . not real grateful, were they?"

"Don't think young people ever are. They know better. I did, too, back when I was their age."

"Is that what happened with your consort?"

Kharl didn't understand the question.

Herana laughed . . . softly. "My problem. Everyone got consorted. So did I. Then I discovered he didn't love me, just wanted children . . . sons."

"You couldn't have any." Kharl shook his head. "No . . . maybe I didn't want the children enough. Was always trying to do more, bring in more coins, so that we'd have enough . . ."

"Were you in love with her?" asked Herana. "Your consort?"

The question was a shock. Kharl bit off a retort. Why was she asking? He looked at her, but he didn't sense anything from Herana except concern, and certainly there was no trace of chaos around her. Finally, he said, "At times . . . I still miss her . . ."

"That's not the same."

It wasn't. Kharl knew that. He also wondered if that was why he tried not to think about Charee much. "When we were younger . . . she was good-looking, not quite a beauty, but she turned heads. I thought I was in love . . ."

"Now you aren't sure?"

"There's more than a few things I'm not sure about these days," Kharl admitted. He forced a grin. "Like why you're so interested in a carpenter second."

"Because you're honest, and when you're not, you're trying to be . . . Not that many men who are. Because I'm either the one giving orders or taking them. Because it's good to talk with someone not on the *Southshield*. Because . . . whatever happens . . . you're not the kind to be nasty . . ." She looked directly at him. "Enough said?"

Kharl couldn't help but smile. "Enough said." He doubted that Herana would ever be more than a friend, but he had none, and certainly none who had sought him out.

"Ghart says you're more than a carpenter . . ."

"Not yet. I'm not as good a ship's carpenter as I should be."

A roll of laughter from two tables away was so loud that neither could speak for a moment.

"... and if you think I'd believe that, Lord Ghrant is as well-endowed as a prize bull ..."

"... and your mother has whiskers tougher than iron nails ..."

Kharl could sense the chaos rising around the table. He touched Herana's arm "... need to get out of here ... along the wall there ..."

The two were almost to the doorway when the table went over and men piled into each other. They kept moving until they were out in the cool twilight air.

Kharl took a deep breath.

"You knew that was coming," Herana said.

"I heard the words."

"You knew."

"I had a feeling," Kharl admitted. "Took me a while to learn that it's best not to ignore those feelings." He nodded toward the harbor. "I probably ought to get back."

She nodded.

They turned toward the harbor.

LXXIX

Kharl had been back aboard the *Seastag* for almost two glasses, a good glass after sunset, and according to Rhylla, no wagons had shown up with cargo. Nor had Hagen set a day or time for leaving, except that he expected that they could sail anytime in the next few days.

Because he'd been so restless that he knew he couldn't read or sleep—especially as early in the evening as it was, he'd made his way back topside and settled out of sight against the railing near the bowsprit, warm enough in his winter jacket and gloves. He was trying to sort out too many matters—from what he felt about what had happened over the past year to where he wanted to go and what he wanted to do. He really had no answers, not ones that made much sense, and what he read in *The Basis of Order* confused him as often as it explained things.

The ale he'd had with Herana had made several things clear. First, he definitely missed feminine companionship. Second, he liked Herana's company, but that was all. And third, he'd lacked a closeness with Charee for a long time, something he'd missed without knowing it. Or perhaps, he just had come to accept matters as they had come to be.

At the sound of hoofs on the pier, unusual after sunset, Kharl turned and looked down and aft. A rider had reined up and dismounted. He started up the gangway, and his voice carried. "Captain Hagen! Captain Hagen!"

Although the single lantern from the quarterdeck cast but faint illumination, Kharl thought the man wore a uniform, but not the black and yellow of Ghrant's personal guards.

Kharl turned and moved aft, slipping around the paddle wheel frame in the darkness. He decided to try to cloak himself by using order, and concentrated on having the light flow around him. The dimness that surrounded him turned into absolute blackness, and for a moment he stopped, disoriented. He made an effort to sense his surroundings and, more slowly, continued toward the quarterdeck.

The evening deck watchstander was Ghart, and he was talking to the newcomer.

"I've called the captain, ser, and he should be here in a moment."

Sensing Hagen coming from aft, Kharl stepped back, as quietly as he could. While no one could see him, people could still hear him, and Hagen could certainly walk into him, and that would not be what Kharl wanted.

"Captain," offered the slender man.

"Majer . . . my cabin?" asked Hagen.

"I . . . think not. Perhaps aft and above."

"As you wish." Hagen turned and crossed the deck.

The majer followed, and then, quietly, so did Kharl, several paces back, cautiously, climbing the ladder up to the poop well after Hagen and the majer. Kharl stopped less than five cubits from Hagen and the other man, possibly the son of a lord, as well as an officer, Kharl judged, certainly someone of high stature from his few words and carriage.

". . . would do almost aught to support Lord Ghrant," Hagen offered.

"For now, what is of most concern to him is that you take his consort and sons to Dykaru. Tonight, if at all possible."

"That is a goodly distance," said Hagen.

"He does not want them threatened by Ilteron. Where else in Austra could they be more distant?"

"Or safer," suggested Hagen, "seeing as it serves the center of the ancestral lands of Lord Ghrant."

"If you agree, they will be arriving shortly."

"Under the cover of darkness. Are matters that precarious here in Valmurl? Or does he fear that they soon will be?"

"Lord Ghrant does not want a pitched battle over Valmurl. If he wins, it will be a meaningless victory, because it will destroy the city. That is why he is moving south, and why he is making it known to Ilteron that he is."

"And what if Ilteron takes Valmurl and does not follow Ghrant?" asked Hagen.

The other man laughed, harshly. "If Ilteron cannot dispose of Ghrant quickly, he will lose. He is known to be cruel and unforgiving. He has stated that he is strong and Ghrant is weak. If he cannot best Ghrant soon, that gives the lie to his words. And . . . he has already killed Lord Bowar in a fit of anger. The longer the fight goes on, the more it favors Ghrant, and even the highland lords know that. Ilteron will have to fight Ghrant in the south. The southern lords will never support Ilteron, and it was for that reason, as well you know, Lord Hagen, that Lord Estloch disinherited . . ."

Kharl nodded to himself. It did not totally surprise him that Hagen was called "lord."

"I did not wish to see Austra torn in two, and yet what I did not wish has still come to pass," Hagen said in a voice so low that Kharl had to strain to hear the words.

"If Ilteron does not press the fight to Lord Ghrant," the majer went on, "eightday by eightday, the lords of the east, then the north, will slowly come back to Ghrant, for he will not rule them with an iron fist and curtail their powers. Ilteron will, and many follow him but through fear."

"The *Seastag* is ready to set to sea," Hagen said. "We will do what your master wishes, and I hope that your words are what comes to pass."

In his concealment, so did Kharl.

"What will be will be, and the right will triumph," answered the majer.

"Of that, I am certain," returned Hagen, and Kharl heard the irony in his voice. "Let us hope that it is the proper right. For do not all men and lords believe that what they wish is right?"

There was silence from the majer, and Kharl could sense a swirl almost of chaos—anger, he thought.

"Come, majer," Hagen went on. "Relying primarily on one's cause as being right is an invitation to difficulty and defeat."

"I have noted, Lord Hagen," came the stiff reply, "that those who are convinced of the rightness of their cause are more likely to persevere and triumph."

"They're also more likely to show scorn and contempt for their opponents and to sow the seeds of future conflict. I have no love of this conflict, majer. No good will come of it, only less evil. I support Lord Ghrant, as I have told him to his face, not because he is a great lord, but because he has the chance to become one, while his brother can only become worse."

The cool matter-of-fact words spoken by Hagen chilled Kharl, but the majer remained agitated.

"Ser . . ."

"Enough." Hagen's single word, delivered in a tone of cold command, silenced the majer. After a moment, he went on. "We do not live in a world where all is good, majer. We must do the best we can with what we are given. We have the better cause, but it is far from perfect, and to think otherwise is vain arrogance. I await the Lady Hyrietta and her sons."

"Ser. They will be here shortly." The majer's words were clipped, but Kharl had the feeling that the man was still seething.

Still holding his shield around himself, Kharl quickly made his way back down to the main deck before the majer, hurrying forward past the paddle wheel on the starboard side. Then he released the shield. Even the dimness of night was welcome after the blackness he had endured.

Kharl had always felt that Hagen was more than a mere captain or factor, but from the majer's reactions it was clear that Hagen held far more power in Austra than Kharl—or most of the crew—had realized. It was also obvious how Hagen regarded Lord Ghrant.

Kharl had barely considered those facts before the sound of hoofbeats on the pier signaled the departure of the majer. In the comparative silence that followed, Kharl pondered whether he should head to his bunk in the forecastle—or if he could even sleep immediately—when he heard footsteps.

"Thought you might be here," said Furwyl. "Cold as it is, most nights you're up here."

"It's not that cold, ser," replied Kharl.

"I'm from Dykaru, and it's a fair sight colder here in winter than there. Anyway, captain wants to see you. He's up on the poop, forward of the wheel."

"Yes, ser." As he turned and headed aft across the foredeck, Kharl wondered if the captain had sensed his presence, or if Hagen had a task for him because of the majer. He made his way across the main deck not at all quietly, then up the ladder.

Hagen was standing at the rail, looking westward toward Valmurl.

"Ser . . . you asked for me?"

The captain did not move for a moment, then turned. "I did. I'd like to ask you to undertake a different duty for the next few days. You'd share it with Ghart and Esamat."

Kharl waited. He only knew Esamat by sight and name, a wiry top rigger, but the combination of the three was definitely strange.

"We're going to have a passenger, a lady and her two sons, and we'll be carrying them south to Dykaru. She'll have my cabin for the trip, and I'll be needing a guard in the passageway at all times. You're good with that staff or a cudgel, and I can trust you. You're also older, and that helps."

"Yes, ser." Kharl wasn't about to say no, not when Hagen had done so much for him. "If I might ask . . . is this Lord Ghrant's consort?"

Hagen looked hard at Kharl.

"Ser . . . I don't know much, but I heard that Dykaru was where Lord Ghrant's from, and if you're giving up your cabin, and want a guard all the time . . ." Kharl frowned. "But . . . maybe I'm speaking out of turn, but wouldn't she have her own guards? Maybe I'm presuming too much . . ."

"You're not presuming. I keep forgetting that you've seen more than most. It is the Lady Hyrietta, and she will have a detachment of guards. I don't have the greatest trust in those guards, and they will be stationed outside the passageway, but I want you or one of the others in that passageway at all times, even when she or the boys are on deck. No one is to enter the cabin, except her, the boys, their nurse, and me. No one."

"You're thinking treachery, ser?"

"Ilteron is famous for that, and I want to make sure nothing happens on board the *Seastag*." Hagen paused. "You and Ghart and Esamat are to be here when she comes aboard. I also want her to know that only the three of you—and Furwyl and Rhylla—are to be in that passageway, but none of the crew and officers except me are to enter the cabin."

"Yes, ser."

"Stand by somewhere on the decks. When you hear a carriage or mounts, join the others outside the hatchway on the main deck."

"Yes, ser." Kharl nodded.

"Ghart will have a cudgel for you—unless you'd prefer the staff."

"Cudgel'd be better in the passageway, ser."

"I thought as much."

Kharl climbed down the ladder. The engineers had to be firing up the boilers, because he could smell coal as he moved forward, almost all the way to the bowsprit, where he stood at the railing and looked out at the city to the west, with its mostly shadowed shapes and intermittent torches and lamps. How many people out there knew that their futures hung on what happened between two brothers? And how many truly knew the alternative represented by each? Kharl knew that he didn't. He'd heard bits and pieces, yet he suspected he'd heard more than most people. Was it always that way?

Not more than half a glass had passed before Kharl heard hoofs on the pier and the wheels of a carriage. He hurried aft to the hatchway leading to the captain's quarters. Ghart and Esamat were already there.

Esamat looked at Kharl and smiled. "Even 'fore the captain said it, figured you might be one."

Kharl shrugged. "Surprised me."

Both Ghart and Esamat laughed.

Kharl could hear Hagen's voice coming from the quarterdeck, and another's voice. Neither sounded pleased, but Kharl said nothing and neither did the two standing beside him. More time passed, and then a group of people moved across the dimness of the main deck, led by Hagen, who carried a lantern.

Behind Hagen was an undercaptain in the yellow and black of Lord Ghrant's personal guards, followed by a young woman who had to be Lady Hyrietta. The Lady Hyrietta wore a dark blue cloak and a brimmed hat. Neither could hide that she was slender, if full-figured. Her dark hair had been braided and mostly tucked under the hat. Slightly behind her came her sons. The two boys were young. The older one held his mother's hand. The younger was being carried by another woman, gray-haired, but not that much older than Kharl.

Hagen stopped short of the three sailors, inclining his head to the lady. "Lady Hyrietta, as I explained," Hagen said, "these three men will be your inside guards. The tall one at the end is Kharl. He's one of the ship's carpenters. He also cleared almost the entire deck of a pirate vessel attacking us. The light-haired one is Esamat. He used to be an assassin in Hamor. While that was several years ago, he's still quite good. Ghart is the second mate, and he served a tour as an undercaptain with Lord Estloch. He's also the one who killed Varrot."

The faintest hint of a wry smile crossed Hyrietta's heart-shaped face. "You take your duties most seriously, Lo— . . . Captain."

"I know where my duty lies, lady. Now . . . let us proceed." Hagen looked at Ghart. "You'll have the first watch, Esamat the second, Kharl the third."

"Yes, ser."

"You three wait here." Hagen turned to the undercaptain. "If you and your men would also wait here while we settle Lady Hyrietta and the heirs?"

The undercaptain nodded, politely, but with scarcely more than minimal approval.

Kharl surveyed the armsmen who stood behind the undercaptain. There were twelve, and they ranged in age from one barely a few years older than Arthal to one close to Kharl's age. The undercaptain was bearded and graying, an older officer who had made his way through the ranks, Kharl surmised.

Hagen returned shortly and immediately addressed the undercaptain. "You understand the arrangements. Your men will guard the hatchway here, on the outside. The only people to enter the passageway are me, the officers, and these three men."

"Yes, ser."

Kharl could tell that the undercaptain was not totally pleased with the arrangement.

Hagen offered a smile. "No man does two jobs well. Your men only worry about one area, and mine only worry about one."

The undercaptain nodded.

Hagen looked to Kharl and Esamat. "You two best get some sleep. You'll be roused in your turn with the rest of the duty."

"Yes, ser."

Neither Kharl nor Esamat spoke until they were back on the main deck and well back from the two personal guards in yellow and black.

"The captain worries," offered Kharl.

"Wouldn't you? With the lord's lady and his heirs in your hands?"

"That I would." Kharl paused. "Do you know if Lord Ilteron has any ships?"

"None of his own," Esamat replied. "Leastwise, not that I've heard. He's in tight with the Hamorians, though."

"We'd better hope that they've no warships near."

"Not likely, and the captain's a better seaman than any of them. With the engine and favorable winds, no ironbound ship could catch us."

"Then we'd best hope for favorable winds." Kharl hoped a great deal more than that was favorable.

LXXX

Slightly before four glasses after midnight, Kharl pulled on his clothes and readied himself to relieve Esamat. In the darkness, he took up his cudgel and made his way across the deck to where two armsmen in yellow and black guarded the hatchway to the captain's cabin. Hagen was waiting, as was the undercaptain.

"This is Kharl. He's one of our three guards." Hagen held up the small lantern he was carrying so that the light fell on Kharl's face.

The undercaptain nodded, and one of the guards stood back so that Kharl could open the hatch and step inside.

The passageway was a good twenty cubits long, but less than three wide and barely four high, so that Kharl had to duck his head to avoid hitting it on the overhead. There were doors on both sides for the mates' cabins, and then smooth bulkheads for the last ten cubits leading to the captain's cabin. Esamat rose from a stool set aft of the last doors. As the other man did, Kharl noticed that two changes had been made to the passageway. A bracket had been added to hold a small lantern, and a small watch bell had also been added where Esamat had been standing his watch.

"The bell is only if we get attacked or threatened," Esamat said. "Captain refilled the lantern maybe half a glass ago." The rigger stretched. "It's been quiet. Hope it is for you."

"So do I."

After Esamat left, Kharl took his position in the passageway outside the captain's cabin. For almost the first three glasses, except for Hagen's retiring to the first's cabin, the only sounds in the passageway were those of Kharl's breathing and his own movements.

Then, about a glass before Kharl was due to be relieved by Ghart, Hagen reappeared from the cabin that he was sharing with Furwyl.

"Quiet, Kharl?"

"Very quiet so far, ser."

"Let's hope it stays that way, but don't wager anything on it."

"No, ser."

"And don't hesitate to ring the watch bell there if anything looks wrong. Anything at all, you understand."

"Yes, ser."

With a nod, the captain left the passageway.

Kharl heard him say, "Good morning," to the armsmen outside on the deck before he closed the hatch.

In the next half glass, Furwyl appeared, as did Rhylla, then Bemyr, and they all went topside. Ghart was obviously still sleeping.

Then Kharl heard a high childish voice from behind him, loud enough to penetrate the closed cabin door.

"Mommy . . . want to go home . . . don't want to be here . . ."

". . . be going to the summer place . . ."

". . . don't want summer . . . want home . . ."

". . . we'll go home later. Your father will be coming to meet us . . ."

". . . want home . . ."

About that point, had the boy been his, Kharl would have gotten somewhat more forceful.

Lady Hyrietta merely murmured something else that Kharl could not hear.

". . . no . . . home . . ."

"No! That's enough, Kyran!"

Kharl smiled. The Lady Hyrietta wasn't all that much more patient than he was.

The voices subsided to murmurs, and Kharl studied the passageway, hoping that nothing did happen on the voyage southward, and especially not on his watches.

LXXXI

On the second day of the voyage, and less than a glass after sunset, Kharl was standing his second passageway watch of the voyage south to Dykaru. The seas were almost calm, and Hagen was on deck. In fact, all the mates were somewhere topside.

The Lady Hyrietta and her sons were in the cabin. The nurse had left the cabin a short while before, and from the silence, Kharl gathered that she and Lady Hyrietta had put the boys to bed and that the lady was reading or resting herself, while the nurse was on deck for a breath of night air.

After three glasses in the passageway, Kharl was due to be relieved in about a glass, and he was ready for that. Standing duty in the narrow passageway left him feeling restless and confined. Inadvertently, his thoughts skittered back to his imprisonment in the Hall of Justice in Brysta. *Hall of injustice,* he thought, wondering if better justicers would have helped, or if they would have been run out or dismissed by Egen or Lord West.

His lips curled into an ironic smile. People didn't really want justice, not unless they were desperate. Even he hadn't wanted justice so much as freedom. His thoughts were interrupted by a dull thump outside, from the main deck.

Kharl stiffened, easing off the stool and grabbing the cudgel, then turning as the hatch opened. He could sense someone outside—lifting something—a crossbow. That left Kharl as a target more vulnerable than a grounded goose, outlined by the lamp on the bulkhead. He did the only thing he could think that would help, using his Talent to bind the very air into a shield, hoping that he was in time, and that he could hold the shield long enough.

Clank! Thunk! The crossbow quarrel dropped to the deck, bent.

The armsman in black and yellow charged toward Kharl, his sabre extended and clearly expecting a wounded, if not a dead or dying, guard.

Kharl raised the cudgel slightly, but stayed behind the hardened air.

The armsman thrust, his blade striking the invisible shield. The sabre blade shattered, metal scattering across the deck and bouncing from the lower parts of the bulkheads.

At the momentary look of astonishment on the armsman's face, Kharl released the minute order-chaos hooks holding the air solid, and struck at the man, the cudgel slamming into the attacker's lower ribs.

"Oooof . . ." The armsman dropped the useless sabre hilt, trying to dance back and draw a long knife, but his steps were wobbly.

Kharl's were not, nor was his aim off. His second blow was to the man's knife arm, and something cracked. His third shattered a kneecap, and the man toppled, slowly, sprawling onto the deck. The armsman did not make a sound, but lay on the deck, writhing.

Kharl stepped forward, his cudgel ready.

The attacker's good hand went to his belt, and then to his mouth. He swallowed something.

Kharl grabbed for the man's arm, but with a second swallow, the armsman convulsed. Kharl began to ring the bell that Hagen had attached to the bulkhead.

"What—" Lady Hyrietta's head peered from the captain's door.

"Lady! Stay there and bolt the door!"

Hyrietta did not argue, and Kharl heard the bolt slam home.

Within moments, Ghart and Hagen burst through the hatchway from the main deck.

In the dim light from the small lantern, Hagen looked down at the still-convulsing armsman.

"I tried to stop him without killing him, ser," Kharl said. "But he took poison before I could get to him."

"Poison?" Hagen looked to Ghart, then back at the fallen armsman, who gave a last shudder before slumping into silence.

"He put something in his mouth."

"He did something to the outside guards," Hagen said, his eyes darting from side to side, checking the passageway. "Could have offered them something to drink—water, wine. Both are dead. Poisoned, I'd say."

"But . . . he'd been with Ghrant for years . . . that's what they said."

"Treachery . . . that has always been Ilteron's way . . ." Hagen turned to Ghart. "Go find the undercaptain and tell him what happened. Then take care of this one. Don't let anyone inside here. The undercaptain can look from the hatchway if he insists."

"Yes, ser."

Ghart made his way back onto the deck, closing the hatch behind him, leaving Hagen with Kharl in the passageway.

Hagen looked at Kharl. "He picked you."

"I suppose he did."

The captain laughed, mirthlessly. "Bad choice."

"You knew they would," Kharl said.

"I thought, if there were any treachery, that they would. I'd hoped that his personal guard would have been above subversion. I wasn't about to wager the lady and the heirs on that hope, though."

Ghart reappeared. "Undercaptain's on his way."

"I'll talk to the lady." Hagen turned and walked to the door to his cabin, where he knocked. "Lady Hyrietta? Hagen here."

After a moment, the door opened a crack, then more.

"I need to come in for a moment." The cabin door closed behind the captain, and Kharl could hear the sound of voices, but not the words.

Ghart looked at the body of the dead armsman, then at the deck near Kharl's boots. He bent down and picked up the crossbow quarrel, its tip bent back.

"He must have hit something," Kharl said. "He shot, then charged me."

Ghart studied the deck again, this time picking up the shattered sections of the sabre. "I suppose he missed with this, too?"

Kharl shrugged. "He tried to get me. I used the cudgel. Maybe he wasn't used to fighting in a narrow space."

Ghart laughed, humorlessly. "We'll leave it at that, but I think I'll just make sure all this goes overboard. It's probably better that way."

"No one would believe I was that lucky," Kharl said.

"You're right about that," Ghart replied as he turned with the bent quarrel and broken sabre fragments.

Before long, Kharl could hear voices outside the hatchway.

"Poisoned . . . bastard poisoned his own mates . . . You want me to believe that?"

"I daresay that *Lord* Hagen doesn't much care what you believe, undercaptain. He knows what happened, and he knew it was likely . . ."

The undercaptain was furious. Kharl could feel the anger.

"You see why the captain wanted two sets of guards?" asked Ghart, his voice calm.

". . . and your man killed him so we can't find out . . ."

"No . . . Kharl disabled him, but he wasn't quick enough to stop him from taking poison."

"You want me to believe that . . ."

"One moment."

Ghart reappeared in the passageway. He shook his head as he bent and grasped the dead armsman's tunic and dragged the limp form out of the passageway, mostly closing the hatch behind him.

". . . face is blue . . ."

". . . poison does that . . . better believe it."

Kharl waited, wondering if there would be another attempt to get to the lady and her sons. Yes, he decided. The question was merely whether the attempt would occur on the *Seastag* or elsewhere.

While he could hope that the attempts occurred where Hagen might prevent them, he had his doubts. Whenever there might be another attempt, it would be with greater stealth or greater force—or both. He didn't doubt his own courage . . . but he did worry about knowing enough to deal with something that was less obvious.

LXXXII

Although Kharl and two others assigned to the passageway duty remained especially alert for the last two days of the voyage, there were no more attempts to attack either the armsmen or those standing duty in the passageway. Nor did the ship encounter any other vessels, not any that Kharl knew about, in any case. The seas had been calm, and there had not been much need for carpentry during the short voyage, for which Kharl had been grateful.

On a bright and much warmer eightday, one that was calm and windless, the *Seastag* steamed into the small harbor at Dykaru and tied up at the single narrow pier that served oceangoing vessels. At least a company of armsmen in yellow and black held the pier, as well as two squads of lancers in the same colors. Waiting opposite the spot where the *Seastag* tied up was a coach of golden oak, trimmed in black.

Wearing only a heavy gray shirt, Kharl looked beyond the pier, at Dykaru itself, not quite a city, rather a town composed of clusters of buildings, most of them with white plastered walls and orangish brown roof tiles. The trees were all broad-leafed, rather than the evergreens predominant in the north, and had remained green, rather than graying the way leafed trees did in the colder climes. On a low hillside to the west was a keep with light gray stone walls. The walls of the interior buildings were white and roofed in the same tile as the dwellings and structures in the town proper.

The harbor itself was empty of larger vessels, except for the *Seastag*, and a handful of fishing vessels at the smaller wharf to the west of deepwater pier.

From the foredeck, Kharl watched as the Lady Hyrietta and her sons crossed the main deck to the gangway and made their way down to the carriage. Hagen walked beside her the entire way to the coach, and the nurse followed. The armsmen in black and yellow surrounded them. After escorting the lady, her sons, and the nurse to the coach and closing the door, the captain bowed and stepped back. The lancers and the coach began to move, and then the armsmen on foot fell in behind.

Once the pier was clear, Hagen made his way back up the gangway.

Kharl watched as the captain stopped on the quarterdeck and surveyed the ship, then turned forward and made his way toward Kharl. The carpenter waited.

Hagen stopped several cubits away. "I wanted to thank you. I wasn't totally fair, but I knew I could count on you, and there aren't many in the world so trustworthy."

"I don't know that I am," Kharl replied.

"In the things that matter you are. You've proved that time after time, but then, you probably did in Brysta as well."

Kharl had his doubts about that. Instead, he asked, "What do you think will happen?"

"Ilteron will bring his forces south and attempt to crush Ghrant before most of the lords, landowners, and factors come to understand how evil Ilteron truly is." For a moment, Hagen's lips tightened. "Doubtless the Emperor of Hamor has suggested that he can spare wizards, ships, and armsmen for but a limited time, in order to force Ilteron to act quickly."

"So that there will be a war that weakens both sides and leaves Austra divided and in chaos?" suggested Kharl.

"For a former cooper, you have come to understand matters quickly, far more quickly than most of the lords of Austra, I fear."

"Several times, you have been addressed as 'Lord,'" Kharl said.

"And you would like to know why?"

"If it would not trouble you."

Hagen laughed once. "I am a lord, of sorts. My father was the arms-commander for Lord Estbach. Lord Estbach was Lord Estloch's father and the one who became Lord of Austra when his own brother died without proper heirs. My father was gifted with the lands of South Shilton. They are most rocky, fit for goats and sheep, if that, and without meadows, trees worthy of the name, or even a sizable stream. For that reason, and because my father was much respected, no one much cared about the gifting. After my father's death, I borrowed against them to purchase my first vessel. I was lucky in my trading, and was able to repay the loan. I have not borrowed since, and consider myself most fortunate in that respect."

"I don't think that's the entire tale," replied Kharl, "but I'd not ask for more."

"I was also the head of Lord Ghrant's personal guard for a brief time, a few years back. It was not a happy experience for either of us."

From what he had seen of Hagen and heard of Ghrant, Kharl could not say that he was surprised.

"It was not a position I desired," Hagen said, "but Lord Estloch prevailed upon me, and because of what I felt I owed, I did what was necessary and as quickly as possible, and Lord Ghrant and I remained on speaking terms. And there you have it, carpenter and mage."

"I'm not a mage," Kharl replied. "I can do a few things that use order, but I'm far from a mage."

Hagen smiled. "You're hard on yourself."

"Not any harder than you are on yourself, ser."

Hagen shook his head ruefully. "I think not, but the passing years will tell."

"When will we put back to sea?"

"Not for a time yet. None of the cargo is that urgent."

Kharl nodded politely. It was clear that Hagen intended to see what happened, perhaps even have the *Seastag* standing by as a way for Ghrant and his family to leave Dykaru—and Austra—if necessary. "You think things could get bad here?"

"If there's a fleet from Hamor that appears offshore . . . that will tell you how bad it is."

"I hope not."

"Nor I, but my luck hasn't run that deep in recent years." Hagen inclined his head. "Thank you again." Then he turned and was gone.

Kharl glanced out to the west at the peaceful view of the white-walled buildings of Dykaru, set against the greenery. After a time, he turned away and headed down to the carpenter shop. With little carpentry to do, he would try to glean more from *The Basis of Order*.

LXXXIII

For the next day and a half, Kharl and Tarkyn worked on minor repairs to the exterior of the paddle wheel frames. The repairs were not immediately necessary, but there was little point in postponing them, since the damage would only increase over time, especially in winter. They also put another coat of finish on the new weapons locker, taking advantage of the warmer weather in Dykaru.

After completing the locker's finish work in the late afternoon, Kharl had taken a break and stood on the aft part of the poop, looking to the northwest, out across the harbor and the white walls and tile roofs of the town. Well beyond the keep of Lord Ghrant, he could sense something in the distance. He guessed that if he could have seen farther, he would have seen or sensed a white mist, the kind that surrounded a chaos-wizard—or wizards.

"You feel something?"

Kharl turned to see Hagen standing by the wheel platform.

The carpenter shrugged. "I'm not certain, but I think there's a white wizard coming toward Dykaru from the northwest. There'll be more than one, but I don't know how many."

"If so, I can't say I'm surprised," Hagen replied. "Ghrant's arms-commander—and most of the regular officers—thought that Ilteron would take Valmurl first. That never made sense to me."

"Why not?" asked Kharl, in spite of himself. "He'd gain control of the capital and the largest port in Austra."

"Ilteron's strength is in the west, and he's not that well loved in the east. Why fight over a city that Ghrant's abandoned? All he would do would be to damage what he hopes to gain. If he defeats Ghrant, Valmurl will be that much easier to take. In fact, most would accept his rule as necessary, if not exactly welcome."

"Even if they don't care for him?"

"The alternative would be worse. If Ilteron defeats Ghrant, he will either kill him and his family or drive them from Austra. He will try for the first. It makes matters much easier." Hagen's tone turned dryly ironic. "Once that happens, what can the landholders do? Support someone else and prolong the war and destruction? Even if someone managed to kill Ilteron, and if one of Ghrant's sons survived, or Ilteron's, at best, Austra would be looking at a long regency, at worst another ambitious lord trying to seize power from underage and untried heirs. And that would make it far easier for the Emperor of Hamor."

"If I happened to be Ilteron," Kharl suggested, "I'd be looking behind me as well as before. That'd be more true if I won."

"You're even more suspicious than I am, mage."

"As suspicious, perhaps. Not more. You must have considered that long ago."

Hagen laughed.

"How long will we stay in Dykaru? Until the outcome is certain—one way or the other?"

"Unhappily."

Kharl understood that. "Is there any way you can help Lord Ghrant?"

"At the moment, I know of nothing else to be done. I have no arms-men, only a handful of unarmed vessels. We'll have to see what opportunities arise."

If any do, thought Kharl bleakly.

LXXXIV

Two more days passed, and Hagen remained onshore somewhere, leaving Furwyl in charge of the *Seastag*. After finishing the paddle wheel frame repairs, and giving the first weapons locker another coat of finish, because it looked too worn compared to the new locker, Kharl and Tarkyn retreated to the carpenter shop, where Tarkyn continued to work on his scrimshaw, and Kharl read and reread *The Basis of Order*.

Kharl searched the book for something that might explain what he had done by hardening the air and the water, but he could find nothing that mentioned what he had done, not in so many words. One passage offered a general thought:

> Order is like glue, in that it links all together, while chaos is but the opposite. Its power lies in separating . . . and when even the smallest bits of that which surround us are separated, basic fire and the heat of flame are released. A chaos-wizard channels that fire and flame, and yet he must use order to do so, lest he be separated from himself by the powers of separation . . .

So he had been using order like glue? Kharl frowned. It made sense in a fashion, and yet, it did not, because no glue could turn air into a shield against a crossbow bolt.

He let the book drop, considering. Nowhere in the entire book, he realized, was there actually a description of how to use order or chaos to accomplish anything. There were only insights, observations, and explanations about the world or how matters worked. Had it been written that way on purpose? Or because it had been written by someone who was making discoveries as he wrote?

"Won't learn how to be a mage from reading," suggested Tarkyn, looking up from the scrimshaw.

"I know. But I look for hints and ideas, and then I try to see what I might be able to do."

"Any luck?"

"I found the weak hull planks," Kharl pointed out.

"I'm glad of that. Wouldn't have wanted to swim my way to shore. Too much work."

"You can swim?" asked Kharl.

"Used to be able to. Was a sawboy, and fell into the millstream. Owner's son pulled me out, then taught me something about swimming. Claimed it was easier than training a new sawboy every few eightdays. Really not all that hard. Just keep your arms in the water and move 'em slow."

"That's all?"

Tarkyn laid down the scrimshaw. "Look. You're floating in the water. You lift your arms out of the water and thrash, and two things happen. There's more weight up over you, and that pushes you down. And . . . your arms aren't doing anything to keep you afloat." The older carpenter snorted. "Everything's like that. Do it slow and easy, and you get in less trouble. Flap and thrash . . . doesn't work. You see an eagle flying— wings move slow-like."

Kharl nodded. "You're right. Just hadn't thought of it in that way." He could swim, but no one had taught him that way.

"Most times, you discover something," replied Tarkyn, "you haven't found anything new at all, just looked at the same thing differently. It's like you see it for the first time all over again." He picked up the scrimshaw and studied it. "Then . . . life's like that, if you really live it."

Life's like that . . . if you really live it—the words seemed to echo, to resonate through Kharl. Had that been his problem all along, that he'd never really looked at life? But did anyone? Really? Unless something happened and he was forced to reconsider everything that he thought he had held dear?

He looked down, blankly, at the open book.

LXXXV

On sixday, after he and Tarkyn had completed another round of minor repairs, and when the duty day in port was done, Kharl decided to take shore leave. Hagen had still not returned to the ship, and Ghart had merely admonished Kharl not to stay too long.

Kharl left the *Seastag* about a glass before sunset and walked in the empty pier toward the avenue along the stone wall that marked the edge of the harbor. Unlike Valmurl or Swartheld, there were no guards or patrollers on the pier or the avenue that fronted the harbor. He walked alone, and that was how he often felt, for as a carpenter and a subofficer, he was neither an officer on the *Seastag*, nor exactly a crewman.

The second street to the right off the harbor avenue was wider, almost a boulevard, and Kharl turned onto it, walking to the northwest, past a cobbler's, then a cloth factor's, where all manner of colored linen and cotton fabrics were displayed. The pavement itself was of oblong limestone blocks, and with raised sidewalks on each side of the street proper, but the boulevard was nearly deserted. At the first cross street, he looked to his left, and saw a group of men in the black and green of the Austran lancers. Two men in gray cloaks looked at the lancers from the small porch of a silversmith's.

"... do more good if they were out north ..."

"... don't seem to care what's good for Austra ..."

"... who does, these days?"

One glanced at Kharl, then the other, and they stepped back inside the shop.

Halfway up the next block, Kharl stopped under a green awning, turning and peering through the open, arched doorway. With the high-arched ceilings and the tables, it looked like a tavern or a café, but out of the close to twenty tables, only two were taken—one by four officers in green and black, and one by two white-haired men.

An older woman appeared, wearing a brown apron over a tan shirt and trousers. "Yes?"

"I wondered if you were open?"

"We are."

"Everything is so deserted. I wasn't sure."

"We're open." The gray-haired woman turned with a sigh and, walking with a limp to one side of the public area, seated Kharl at a table under a wall arch.

"What will you have? Lager and dark ale, and some redberry—that's all we have."

"Lager. What about food?"

"Fowl with groundnuts and sauce or zatana."

"I'll have the fowl."

After she limped away, Kharl studied the table, a wood he'd not seen, light like white oak but with irregulars swirls in the grain, dark lines intertwined with brilliant gold ones.

"Lager." The server set the tall green mug on the table. "Three coppers."

Kharl handed her four.

"Thank you." She paused. "You off the ship?"

"Yes."

"They say your captain is waiting, in case he needs to take the lady and the heirs to Nordla or Candar."

"He's waiting, but I don't think that's the reason. He hasn't said." Kharl offered a smile he hoped didn't look too forced.

"Those in charge never do." With a sound halfway between a sniff and a snort, she turned, then stopped. "Be a bit for the fowl."

"That's fine."

After the woman retreated, Kharl took a swallow of the lager—cool, but not cold, and more welcome than he had thought it would be. He glanced around the public room, taking in the arches on each side and the paintings hung on the flat wall surface between the arches. The one directly across from him showed an old-style, full-rigged ship under full sail, with a spit of land on the right side—presumably leaving Dykaru. The one farther away, across the room and to his left, showed a black-haired man lifting a large mug and smiling. The background was that of the same public room where Kharl sat, subtly different, looking perhaps newer.

Kharl took another swallow of the lager, thinking.

"Here you are, ser. That'll be three."

Kharl looked up, blankly, for a moment, his thoughts interrupted by the arrival of the fowl, accompanied by some type of yams and a basket of bread. Then, he handed over four coppers.

"Thanks be to you, ser."

Kharl ate slowly, enjoying the combination of the mildly hot but creamy sauce, the piquant taste of the fowl, and the crunchiness of the toasted groundnuts. He wasn't that fond of yams, but dipping them in the sauce helped that problem. As he ate, he listened to the four officers, using his order-senses to boost his hearing.

". . . don't understand why we're getting pushed back . . . bastard lord's only got forty companies of lancers . . ."

". . . doesn't count the wizards . . . can't fight fireballs, and can't use rifles or cannon."

". . . retreating too much . . ."

". . . not for long. No place left to retreat . . ."

A laugh—bitter—followed. "Can't get any farther south."

"Ilteron'll go for the keep."

"Better hope so . . ."

One of the officers stood. "Time to get back."

". . . before we can't . . ."

Kharl watched as the four left. With an attack taking place, he had to wonder what they were doing where they were. Or was that just another of Ghrant's problems? He was beginning to understand—he thought—why Hagen had not stayed long as Ghrant's arms-commander. But since the four were regulars, that did not say much for the Austran lancers and foot and their support of Ghrant.

He finished eating, more thoughts than he could have counted swirling through his mind, then rose and left.

Kharl had not taken ten steps away from the café or tavern before he heard a dull *thump*. He looked back and saw that the lamp by the door had been extinguished and the double doors closed—probably barred as well.

He picked up his pace on the empty boulevard although he heard no sounds. He'd walked almost two blocks when the low rumble of iron-rimmed wheels on the stone pavement echoed down the boulevard from behind him. The rumbling rapidly grew louder, and was accompanied by a low moaning. He slipped into the darker shadows of an alleyway, watching as the long and narrow wagon rolled toward him. Through the darkness, he could sense the chaos of wounds, and imminent death, and the wounded armsmen lying or sitting in the wagon.

"... gone too far ..."

"... said to take this road ..."

"... didn't say to drive into the center of town ... way past the keep ..."

"... what you expect ... couldn't find his way to battle without two guides ..."

"Better where we are ... highlanders less than ten kays from the harbor ..."

"... closer by now ..."

"Captain said to stay out of town."

"... what does he know? Except about women ..."

"... girls ... too young to know real women ..."

Kharl just waited, standing against the alleyway wall, as the wagon rumbled past, down toward the harbor. Then, he stepped out and continued, following it at a distance.

The wagon with the wounded had disappeared by the time Kharl reached the edge of the harbor, and the harbor avenue was totally deserted as he walked back toward the pier, so quiet that his boots echoed. The only other sounds were the low buzzing of insects and the lapping of wavelets on the harbor wall.

Rhylla was on the quarterdeck when Kharl made his way up the gangway.

"Good to see you back. Captain called in everyone. Only missing a few."

"Are we going to leave?" Kharl glanced around, but the decks were empty. "Where is he?"

"He didn't say. He's off again. Left orders with the first." Rhylla looked more directly at Kharl. "You know something?"

"The fighting's getting close to Dykaru. Wagonload of wounded passed me on the way back to the ship."

"Doesn't look good," she observed.

Kharl could only agree with that, and he wished he knew what orders Hagen had left with Furwyl, but he wasn't about to ask. Furwyl wouldn't have told him, anyway.

LXXXVI

Kharl was aware of a murmuring around the forecastle, even before he slowly swung out of his bunk on sevenday morning. He didn't pay much attention until he was on his feet and dressing.

"... first says there's warships off the harbor ... black-hulled ships ..."

"... lots of 'em ..."

"... black ... isn't that Recluce?" asked Kawelt.

"Hamor," said Kharl. "Recluce doesn't send its ships in fleets, and they're usually invisible."

"Frig ..." muttered Reisl. "Means we're stuck here, maybe even get shelled or boarded."

"Or worse," added Hodal.

"Unless we get a storm. Then they'd have to stand off," Reisl said. "There are some clouds to the east."

"You're dreaming," Hodal said.

"Hoping ... fellow can hope ..."

"Good luck with that ..."

Kharl agreed with Hodal. Hope was a frail reed against sheer power. The carpenter did not say so, but washed up as well as he could, dressed, and made his way out onto the main deck.

He looked south from there, but didn't see anything. After several moments, he crossed the main deck and climbed the ladder to the poop, where he stood on the port side, looking south and out across the Great Western Ocean. Just on the horizon, he could make out black dots, hard to distinguish against the gray-blue of the water and the grayish sky, although there were no distinct clouds, just enough of a haze to blur the sun and the horizon. There was a light wind from the southeast, slightly more than a breeze.

"Looking to see them?" asked Furwyl, as he reached the top of the ladder and walked toward Kharl. "It's there—full Hamorian squadron. Ten ships. Not a fleet, but enough that we'll be staying here, leastwise in the light of day. They were closer in, earlier, but the sea's getting rougher. Wouldn't be surprised if we got a bit of a blow."

"That would make it easier for us to get around them, wouldn't it?"

"It would. That'd be if the captain were thinking of leaving."

"Is he taking over command of Lord Ghrant's forces?"

Furwyl laughed. "Too late for that. Lord Ghrant should have let him reorganize 'em when he suggested that years ago. Ghrant doesn't like to upset people. Weighs things, I hear, by who's upset. Sometimes, to do things right, you have to upset a lot of folk at first. Less people upset over time, but . . ." The first shrugged. "Like a ship. Lay down the law fair and firm-like to begin with, and hold to it, and you get a happy ship. You tack to every little change in the wind, never get anywhere."

Kharl had to wonder. Hadn't he tried that in life? And where had it gotten him? Run out of his homeland, his consort killed, his sons hating him, and his neighbor and friend assassinated. "That's if you have the power to lay down the law. The captain didn't, and Lord Ghrant did, but Lord Ghrant didn't do anything."

"Goes without saying, carpenter. Can't do much without both ability and power. Ability can sometimes get you power, but without power, ability's wasted, and that can lead to ruin. Power and no skill leads you to ruin. Just takes longer. That's all."

"You don't think Lord Ghrant has much ability?"

"Couldn't be saying that, now, could I?" Furwyl laughed, but there was little humor in the sound. "He could learn, if he would but listen."

"And Ilteron?"

"He seems to listen to all, and offers pleasant words. He heeds none, and uses and discards all." The contempt in Furwyl's voice was in stark contrast to the more muted words about Lord Ghrant.

Kharl walked to the stern, by the port rudder post, thinking, considering what little he knew. Ilteron had to have ridden south to attack Dykaru before Ghrant had decided to retreat there. Likewise, the Hamorian ships had to have set out from Hamor even before Ghrant had left Valmurl. How did they know? Lands and lords didn't stake ships and battles and moving lancers and troops just on guesses about where the enemy would be. They had known. But how? Spying? Wizardry? What sort of wizardry allowed them to see across vast distances and know what would happen?

He looked up and forward. Furwyl had left the poop.

Kharl made his way down to the mess. Most of the crew had eaten,

but Kharl managed to scrounge enough bread, and some cheese, and a
soft pearapple, as well as a mug of redberry. He sat down across from
Hodal and Kawelt, who were finishing up what looked like fried and
salted pork. Kharl didn't miss not having the pork.

"You see the ships?" asked Hodal.

"They've moved farther offshore, the first said," replied Kharl after
swallowing a mouthful of bread and cheese. "He thinks a storm's in the
offing."

"Told you so."

"Captain'll wait till it's just right, and then we'll be off . . ."

". . . knows what he's doing. That's why no shore leave."

Kharl had no doubts that Hagen knew what he was doing, but he
was far less sure that those actions included leaving Dykaru while the
future of Austra was yet in doubt.

". . . should have gotten here earlier. Cook had fresh eggs . . ."

". . . should have . . ." Kharl mumbled, his mouth full.

After eating, and the morning in-port muster on the main deck,
Kharl made his way down to the carpenter shop. His eyes lifted to the
overhead bin, and the staff, and the words of *The Basis of Order* came back
to him . . . the idea that a mage could not fully master his abilities until he
cast aside the staff . . . and the passage after that . . . where the words
talked about how dividing power weakened it more than just in half . . .

"Carpenter?"

Kharl looked at the hatchway, where Dasket, a rigger he hardly
knew, stood. "Yes?"

"Captain needs you, ser. Right this moment. He's in his cabin."

"Thank you. I'm on my way." Kharl had thought that Hagen was
ashore, but perhaps the captain had already returned.

Dasket hesitated, then turned.

Kharl followed him out and up the ladder to the main deck. From
there, Kharl crossed the deck and entered the passageway he had once
guarded, noting that the lamp bracket remained but the watch bell had
been removed. He knocked on the door to the captain's cabin. "Kharl, ser."

"Come in. Close the hatch."

"Yes, ser." Kharl opened the door, entered, and closed it behind him.

Hagen stood beside the circular table. His eyes were reddened, and
deep black circled them. "How do you feel?"

"Fine, ser."

"I'm going to ask you something. It's not an order, but a request, and I want you to understand that."

Kharl nodded, waiting.

"The highlanders are about to attack the keep. They broke through the regulars early this morning. Before long, it's likely they'll surround the town. Lord Ghrant will make an attack shortly, I believe, in hopes of breaking them and driving them back. He has charged me with the safety of his lady and heirs. I think you could help me."

"I'll go," Kharl said immediately.

"You don't have to."

"You didn't have to take me aboard, ser. What's right is right. I think I ought to bring my staff."

"That wouldn't hurt. We need to hurry."

"I'll get the staff." Kharl understood that Hagen had spent extra time, just to meet Kharl in private, so that Kharl would not feel influenced by others watching, and it was another measure of the man that Kharl appreciated.

The carpenter hurried down to the shop, where he reclaimed both the staff and his winter jacket and gloves, before hurrying back topside. Hagen met him at the quarterdeck. For the first time, the captain wore weapons, a sabre and a long belt knife.

Kharl followed Hagen onto the pier, a pier that grew wetter with each wave that broke against it, as higher waters surged into the small harbor from off the Great Western Ocean.

At the end of the pier waited a small detachment of armsmen in black and yellow, only eight in all. There were two mounts without riders.

Kharl had never ridden a horse. He'd seen riders mount, and he managed to do so. He struggled to get the base of the staff into what looked like a lance holder. Then he glanced at Hagen. "I'm not a lancer, ser."

"We're not riding into battle. We're only riding to get there. Just hang on to the saddle and the reins."

Kharl hoped he could.

The undercaptain and another lancer led the way, two abreast, with Kharl and Hagen riding behind them. Kharl felt that he bounced more than rode as the column moved at a quick trot through the stone-paved streets of Dykaru, eerily empty under the hazy morning sky, with the horses' hoofs being the loudest sound, echoing off the streets and white-plastered stone walls.

"We're supposed to meet the rest of the company on the orchard lane leading to the causeway," Hagen said to Kharl.

Kharl nodded, as if the words meant something, not that they did. He had no idea even what the keep looked like, except from a distance. He would have liked to try to see if he could sense the white wizards, but merely staying on the mount took most of his concentration. Still, it was faster than walking.

Before long, they reached the northern edge of the town, where the dwellings thinned, and a parklike expanse of grass and trees extended toward the ridgetop keep a kay away. Kharl could smell smoke, if faintly. The park seemed empty of armsmen, except in the distance off to the right, where a squad of riders had reined up, facing toward the white walls of the keep. The lancers wore dark blue and gray.

"We'll circle to the west some to reach the lane," Hagen ordered, turning his mount left onto a graveled road that fronted the park.

From the keep a series of horn blasts rang out, and there was the muted thunder of hoofs, but Kharl could see no riders. He took a moment to let his order-chaos senses feel the area before him. Almost immediately, he could feel an upwelling of white chaos more to the right, beyond the riders in blue and gray, who had already ridden northward, and out of sight. There had to be fighting in that direction, Kharl felt, although he could not say exactly how he knew, only that he did.

None of the armsmen spoke. The loudest sound was the clicking of hoofs on the pure white gravel of the lane. Kharl tried to shift his weight and came close to falling but grabbed the saddle and caught himself. He was not an instinctive rider; that was certain. In less than a tenth of a glass, the short column turned right onto a paved road that arrowed through an orchard toward the southwestern corner of the keep.

"From the right!"

Kharl turned in the saddle to see a good score of riders in the dark blue and gray riding toward them along a gravel service path in the orchard. Somehow he managed to turn the horse to face the attack, but he wasn't about to try to charge the attackers and try to use the staff at the same time. He fumbled the staff out of the lance holder, hoping that he could stay mounted while using both hands on the staff.

Because the others rode toward the rebels, Kharl was at the rear when the enemy lancers reached them.

Several of Ilteron's men went down, as did two of those in black and yellow, and then a lancer in blue and gray was bearing down on Kharl, his sabre coming toward Kharl in a vicious cut.

Kharl underhanded the staff, bringing it up from below the man's guard. The heavy iron-banded end slammed into the lancer's forearm, then into the side of his face. Kharl reeled in the saddle, but struggled back upright. The attacker lay on the ground unmoving.

Bringing the staff back into position, Kharl could only deflect the slash of the next attacker before the lancer was past him.

Another rider—Hagen—had wheeled his mount back and rode past Kharl, cutting down one of the attackers from the blind side.

The third lancer to charge Kharl saw the staff and tried to swing closer to the carpenter to block the staff short of its most effective length, but Kharl dropped the tip and angled it more from below, catching the attacker's sabre arm while he was still a good three cubits from Kharl. There was a cracking sound, and the sabre went flying.

Then, just as suddenly as the attackers had appeared, they vanished, except for the six or so bodies that lay on the gravel of the service path.

Kharl found he was breathing heavily.

"You wield a mean staff, even mounted," called out Hagen.

"Not . . . a . . . mounted weapon," gasped Kharl.

"We need to get to the end of the lane."

The six remaining lancers had regrouped. After putting the staff back in the lance holder, Kharl urged his mount up beside Hagen's as they rode along the remaining quarter kay of the lane toward the two short stone columns where the orchard ended and a grassy expanse separated the orchard from the keep.

As they neared the stone posts, a column of riders in black and yellow rode toward them down a causeway from the keep. Kharl could see blood splashed across the tunics of those leading the oncoming column.

"Captain Hagen! Captain Hagen!" An undercaptain spurred his mount toward Kharl and the others.

"We're here," Hagen said quietly once the other had reined up. "The lady?"

"She and the boys—they're waiting at the keep gates. The guards there have the causeway clear, and they've pushed them back. Don't know how long they can hold."

"Lord Ghrant?" asked Hagen.

The undercaptain shook his head. "He's trapped on the ridge to the north of the keep. Holding them at bay. He's trying to keep the wizards from getting close enough to fire the keep. They'd be lofting fireballs over the walls." Kharl could sense the truth of that. He also hadn't thought about wizards being able to destroy a stone keep.

Hagen looked to Kharl.

Kharl nodded. "He's speaking the truth."

"Get the lady and the boys down here as quick as you can, and with as many lancers as you can spare. We've already been attacked once."

"Yes, ser." The undercaptain turned his mount. Two riders galloped back up the causeway toward the gates, less than half a kay away.

To the right of the causeway, a squad of lancers had formed up, facing northeast, toward the chaos of battle that Kharl could sense all too clearly.

As they waited, Kharl looked down at his jacket and gray trousers, both streaked with blood, then at Hagen. "A word, Lord Hagen?"

Hagen eased his mount closer to Kharl, and the carpenter wondered how he could explain what he needed to do. Finally, he cleared his throat. "I would not see Austra become as Nordla, nor as Hamor. I would like your leave to depart for a time."

Hagen's eyes widened. "You don't owe me that. You don't owe—"

"No. This is another kind of debt. I will go, one way or another. I would like your leave."

"You may have it. You know that if Lord Ilteron's forces come to the harbor, we will depart?"

"I know." Even as he said the words, Kharl had to wonder if he were being a fool, searching for an act of meaning because no matter how hard he had tried, he had been unable to find one, not one that turned out well, at least.

"There is one thing that may help you," Hagen said quickly. "None have fought well or recently in Austra. Ilteron's armsmen and lancers will not act quickly. If you act decisively, events will favor you."

Kharl nodded. He had already seen that, and he was not even an armsman.

Hagen gestured, and one of the lancers, perhaps a serjeant, rode over and reined up. "The mage needs to get as close to the ridge as you can take him."

The serjeant looked at Kharl skeptically.

Kharl ignored the skepticism. "The closer I can get, the more I may be able to do to help Lord Ghrant."

"We'll get you closer than you'd like," came the grim reply. "You want to ride all the way?"

"The last part, if it's not too far . . . on foot, I think."

"You could use bushes for cover going up the ridge. You all right with that?"

"That would be better. So long as it's not too far."

"Thought as much. Ilteron's lancers can't ride you down in the bushes." There was a pause. "What are you going to do?"

"What I can." That was the only truthful answer Kharl had.

"Best we go." The serjeant motioned, and another rider joined them, grim-faced, and without saying a word.

The two lancers flanked Kharl as the three rode eastward past the front of the keep and turned northward down a narrow gravel path that slowly curved back eastward around the base of the ridge. Less than half a kay onward, still near the base of a long slope, the serjeant reined up. To Kharl's right was a mass of bushes, yet with an edge as clean as if laid out with a rule.

"This part of the ridge is mostly berry bushes. Been there since before there was a town, my grandsire said. Can't ride a horse through it, but it'd be slow going unless you stay on the edges."

"I'll stay beside them." Kharl dismounted and handed the reins to the serjeant. "I won't be needing the horse."

"Good luck, ser."

From the lancer's tone, Kharl could tell that the man thought him a dead man—or mad, or perhaps both.

"Thank you." Kharl took the staff and started uphill. He did not look back as the two lancers rode off.

From the feeling of lessened chaos emanating from the top of the ridge, Kharl could sense that the battle was winding down. He could only hope that he was not too late, that something could be salvaged. And from what he had observed of white wizards, he had to see if he couldn't at least stop them, and Ilteron, even if they had already slain the less-than-wise Lord Ghrant.

Kharl moved uphill more swiftly, staying beside the bushes, but not using his light shield, not yet, and not wanting to until he had to.

Within moments, he could see figures ahead—lancers in green and black and in yellow and black riding downhill, avoiding the berry bushes. Behind them came armsmen on foot. Some were pursued by lancers in blue and gray, and others stumbled, as if they had trouble walking or seeing. Some were splattered with blood, but most were not.

The carpenter tried to sense the chaos ahead, but there were two pillars of unseen white, one not all that far away, but uphill and to his right, out among the more open grassy stretches where there were but few trees. The other—and stronger focus—was close to the top of the ridge, if not at the very top.

Kharl drew back into the bushes as mounts thundered down in his direction.

"Someone's in the bushes! Could be an archer!"

Kharl dropped to his knees and willed the light to flow around him as the rebel lancers neared.

"Gone now . . . swore he was right there . . ."

A laugh followed. "They're all running, like scared coneys."

". . . won't matter . . . not in the end . . ."

". . . make sure we get to the end . . ."

Kharl barely waited until the lancers were past before he dropped the light shield and scrambled uphill. The rush of men fleeing and those pursuing seemed to dissipate, and he began to hurry across the hill.

Less than ten rods away, he could see a band of armsmen in yellow and black, using a stone pavilion as a makeshift redoubt and shield against a white wizard and a company of rebel lancers. There were bodies in blue and gray strewn before the amber stone structure, as well as many in yellow and black; but this group of armsmen loyal to Lord Ghrant had neither broken nor run, and the attackers had pulled back.

Kharl could see that no one was even looking in his direction as he crossed the slope.

Hsssstt! A reddish white firebolt arced from the wizard and flew between two stone pillars. Flame flared, and one of the defenders staggered forward, screaming, his entire body a mass of fire.

Kharl gathered the light shield around himself, forcing himself to keep moving, not to think, but to get closer to the wizard. Even from within the darkness of his light shield, he could easily sense the white energy of the wizard as yet one more firebolt flared into the stone pavilion. Another set of screams echoed across the morning.

Kharl winced but kept walking, until he was less than a rod behind the rear of the rebels.

". . . turn 'em to torches!"

". . . southern weaklings . . ."

Kharl was still a good fifty cubits from the swirling of chaos and whiteness. He could only hope that his idea would work. It should . . . but one never knew.

He took a slow and deep breath, then visualized the air around the wizard, then reached out and *twisted* all the order-and-chaos hooks, so that the air touching the wizard's body turned solid.

There was not even a sound, except the wizard pitched forward, frozen as though he had been turned into stone.

"What happened!"

"Must be another mage!"

"Where?"

Despite the other's immobility, Kharl could sense the gathering bolt of chaos, and he forced himself to wait until the last moment—even as the reddish white fireball was flaring toward him—before hardening a shield of air between him and the chaos-bolt.

Still, heat and fire flamed past him, so close and so hot he could feel the ends of his hair and beard crisp and smell the burning hair.

The second fireball was weaker. That was good, because Kharl doubted he could hold the shields for too long.

He could sense the chaos folding in upon itself, and he let go of the shield before him, but not the one imprisoning the white wizard.

The entrapped wizard continued to struggle, but the last firebolt was but a tiny eruption of flame. Then, there was a reddish emptiness, and Kharl could feel the absoluteness of death, releasing the confinement that had destroyed the wizard.

The carpenter turned back uphill and moved back across the hillside, still light-shielded.

Once he was a good ten rods away from the forces battling over the pavilion and again moving uphill beside the bushes, he released the light shield, blinking as light flooded his sight. For several moments, he had trouble seeing and was glad that the grassy slope offered relatively even footing.

Behind him, he could hear the clash of metal and the grunting of armsmen as the rebels and the loyalists renewed the conflict over the pavilion. He would have to leave that battle to the armsmen, at least for the moment, because he needed to find the second chaos-wizard.

The bushes ended, suddenly. Before Kharl the grassy slope leveled out. Ahead, a low white marble wall, less than two cubits high, and less than five rods away, encircled another larger stone pavilion. Behind or within the wall was the pillar of white chaos—and a far larger gathering of armed men, many of whom were looking downhill.

"Someone's coming!"

Kharl quickly donned his light shield.

"He's gone!"

". . . vanished . . ."

". . . just turned and ran, that's all . . ."

". . . don't know . . . might have wizards, too . . ."

". . . woulda seen 'em earlier . . ."

Kharl began to angle to his right, to where he could sense that there were fewer armed men, and slightly away from the chaos-focus. But he kept moving uphill and toward the remaining white wizard—and, he hoped, Ilteron and perhaps even Lord Ghrant.

"There's an order-mage coming . . . look for where things seem blurry!" called out a voice.

Kharl tried not to hurry, to keep his steps and pace even, as he used his senses to make his sightless way toward the stone structure that rose in the center of the paved area enclosed by the wall and crowned the southern end of the ridge.

"Go find him! The mage! He's got to be close."

"You find him . . ."

"How?"

For their confusion, Kharl was most grateful. He tried to keep his breathing even and as quiet as possible as he neared the stone wall and the men who stood behind it. He could sense an opening farther to his left, and he eased in that direction.

The white wizard who stood less than ten rods away was the stronger of the two with Ilteron. That Kharl could feel. But . . . did he need to attack the other wizard? What he really needed was to destroy Ilteron. His only problem was that he didn't know which of the armed men happened to be the rebel lord, and there were close to a hundred figures on the ridgetop.

Then . . . if Ghrant were dead, and Kharl killed Ilteron, and not the white wizard, the rebel lords would be able to continue the war. So Kharl had to deal with the white wizard—if he could.

"I know you are here, cowardly black." The voice boomed across the ridge, and Kharl could sense the chaos that amplified it. "Lyras, skulking in the back hills once more will get you nothing."

Kharl said nothing, moving along the stone wall, until he sensed a gap in the armsmen, one a good three cubits wide. He stepped up on the stone wall—and felt the reason for the gap—a fountain or pool behind it.

While he disliked using his tricks even to get to the white wizard, he hardened the water and carefully made his way to the far side of the pool, where he released the order-ties. Then he stood in his darkness, trying to gather himself together.

The stone pavilion was but another fifteen cubits before him, and he could sense both the white wizard and two other figures within the stone-roofed and columned structure before him.

"You have learned, Lyras . . . but you have not learned enough."

Kharl thought. The white wizard could sense his presence in general terms, but not with any great accuracy, or fireballs likely would have been sent his way. Kharl eased forward, trying to figure out which man was which of those under the dome. There were three, and one lay on the stone floor, still alive, but dazed. That had to be Ghrant. But which of the other two was which?

"You said . . . there were no black mages in Austra."

The surprisingly high voice came from the taller figure—Ilteron.

"It matters not. Black cannot stand against white, not in war."

Could Kharl just harden the air around Ilteron's face and head? If he made it tight enough, it ought to suffocate the lord, and it wouldn't take as much strength.

Remembering Hagen's words about speed, he *twisted* the order-and-chaos hooks together.

Ilteron staggered, his hands clawing at his face.

Kharl needed more strength. He could feel that the staff he held had strength, order, within it. Abruptly, the words of *The Basis of Order* made sense, and he wondered why he had not understood before. He . . . he had been the one to put that order there, as a tool. Perhaps Jenevra had as well, but the order in the staff was limited to what a staff could do.

He concentrated . . . not so much on breaking the staff, or even casting it aside, as reuniting the order that was his in the staff with that within himself.

A flow of darkness surged through him.

Crack . . . Without even his willing it, the staff had broken, and the iron bands that had bound it were no longer black iron, but gray.

The lower fragment hit the stones by his feet with a dull *thunk*, and without thinking Kharl dropped the useless other half.

"There!" *Hssst!*

A massive firebolt flared toward Kharl before he could try to harden the air around the wizard. Still trying to hold the hardened air tight around the dying Ilteron, Kharl flung up weaker, barely hardened air shields.

The firebolt flared around and past him, again burning his skin. But the worst of the fire flared into the rebel armsmen, and more than a half score flamed like torches. Kharl smiled coldly and stepped to the side, releasing the air shields.

"You missed!" he exclaimed.

Hsstt! Another firebolt slammed toward Kharl, and again he raised the deflecting shields.

More rebel armsmen flamed and died.

Kharl darted farther to his right. "You don't aim very well!"

With the third splash of flame, there was a cry, "Back! They'll flame us all!"

Kharl moved again. "Over here!"

Hssst! While the firebolt followed his voice, none of the armsmen were about to get close enough to attack, not when the odds were that they'd get burned to cinders.

Kharl could feel his breathing getting labored and his knees becoming weak.

Hssst!

Behind and around him, the armsmen backed away and began to run, slowly at first, then more quickly.

Kharl eased sideways and forward. Weak as he felt, he had to harden the air around the white wizard—and quickly.

"Your invisibility won't save you. You can't hide forever."

The carpenter reached out and hardened the air around the wizard, but just around his head and neck.

Hssst! The firebolt flared directly at Kharl, perhaps because the wizard could follow the order-link.

Kharl threw up his hardened air shields, then sat down. His legs were rubbery.

Hssst! Another firebolt flared around him, the heat even greater.

Then a third and a fourth bolt followed, and Kharl huddled behind his shields.

The fifth bolt was weaker, and the sixth died before reaching Kharl.

The carpenter released his own air shields, and just sat on the stone, shivering and holding the shields around Ilteron and the white wizard until both were dead. His face burned, and his entire body throbbed by the time he let go of the force holding the hardened air around the two.

But the job was far from done.

After releasing the sight shield, Kharl glanced around warily. There was no one alive within the circular stone wall, but charred bodies lay everywhere, and the stench of burned flesh roiled his guts.

He was surprised that more enemy armsmen were not returning to attack, and yet it made sense. He doubted if any of the armsmen had ever seen a battle between mages, and after a few score of the rebels had been incinerated, the rest hadn't wanted to remain close. Slowly, he crawled the last twenty cubits to the stone pavilion, partly because he didn't want armsmen beyond the wall to see him, and partly because he wasn't sure his legs had yet regained enough strength to hold him.

When he reached the pavilion, he looked around. The white wizard was a slight figure, smaller even than Ghrant. Ilteron had been even taller and broader than Kharl. The slightly built Ghrant was alive. How alive was another question.

The carpenter-mage reached out and grabbed the lord's leather harness, then began to drag the smaller man across the stones and around the fallen bodies toward the gap in the stone wall—and not the one where the pond was—nearest the side of the hill with the berry bushes. At the edge of the wall, keeping himself low, Kharl glanced around.

Armsmen and lancers were beginning to edge back up the hillside.

". . . real quiet up there . . ."

". . . you want to go, you go . . ."

". . . anything take out a white wizard . . . don't want to be the one to get in its way . . ."

Kharl just hoped that would keep them away for a moment.

He girded himself and cast the light shield. He needed to get at least a few hundred cubits downhill before releasing it. He made over a hundred cubits before he did. Thankfully, there was no one nearby when he could see again.

Then he continued, once more, to drag the unconscious lord down the hill. He had to stop every few cubits, and then rest, before dragging Ghrant farther.

Halfway down the hill, Kharl found a mount tied to a tree. Whose it was didn't matter.

He barely had the strength to lever the unconscious lord over the narrow space in front of the saddle, then untie and mount the horse himself. With the horse's first steps, Kharl struggled to hang on to the lord with one hand and the saddle and the reins with the other as he tried not to lurch from side to side.

The ride back to the port, with his selective use of the sight shield, felt as though it must have taken glasses. At times, he knew armsmen were near, and he somehow shielded the two of them and the horse, then rode on, slowly. At other times, even without the sight shield, he could not see, but he kept riding.

The sun was low in the western sky even before he reached the harbor avenue. To Kharl, it had all been a blur after leaving the stone pavilion.

Then he was on the pier and riding toward the *Seastag*. The lines were singled up, and smoke was pouring from the stacks, but . . . the gangway was down—if with four armsman at its foot.

They had sabres at the ready.

"It's Kharl! He's got Lord Ghrant!"

The armsmen still did not move.

Kharl staggered off the mount, and before he could say anything, blackness rushed over him.

LXXXVII

When Kharl tried to wake up, he could not, and white chaos swirled around him, then blackness, followed by fiery redness, shot with ugly whiteness. Arrows of pain pierced his body, one after the other, endlessly. He felt as though he walked through fire, then through the coldest of winters, and yet, somewhere in the darkness that clouded his thoughts, he knew he had walked not a step.

"Drink this . . . you must drink this . . ." Even the words burned through his ears, like flame-tipped arrows, and whatever he drank tasted like liquid fire.

Worst of all, he could not see, as if he were locked behind his own sight and light shields.

At other times, the words spoken to him, as gently phrased as they were, meant nothing. Every word was strange, as if spoken in the language of Hamor or of ancient Westwind, or even of antique and vanished Cyador.

At some point, a cooling blackness descended upon him, and his sleep was deeper, and dreamless.

Days later, he thought, he woke, without the fire, but he still could not see.

He could sense he was in a large room, with a light and cool breeze blowing across his face, a face that felt cracked and dry, and someone sat on a chair beside the wide bed. There was a darkness to that presence. A black mage?

"Lyras?"

"Yes. I could feel the battle from the north, but it took an eightday to get here. Few coasters were willing to chance the voyage with all the reports of Hamorian warships off the shores."

"Lord Ghrant?"

"He will recover, although he is yet weak."

"The rebels . . . the highlanders?" Even a few words seemed to exhaust Kharl.

"All is well . . . you need to know that, but you also need to rest."

"You . . . should . . . have . . . been . . . here."

A light laugh answered Kharl's halting words. "Me? I would have been burned at the first firebolt. I don't know how you did it. There were close to a hundred armsmen that you flamed. Yet you radiate darkness like the strongest of order-mages."

"Did what . . . had to . . ." Kharl was too tired to explain. He could do that later.

"I said you were stronger than I," offered Lyras.

"Don't feel . . . strong."

"Don't complain. Most people who took on two white wizards and companies of armsmen and lancers would be three cubits down—if anyone could find enough to bury. That includes mages."

". . . not a real mage . . ."

"If you're not a mage, then water isn't wet, and ice isn't cold." Lyras snorted. "Maybe no kind of mage I've heard about, but that doesn't matter. A mage is a mage, and you're a mage. No question about that."

"Mages . . . not that . . . stupid. . . . Ghrant still lord?"

"Oh, yes, and matters will be much better now."

"The Hamorians . . . their fleet?"

"Oh . . . that. When they discovered Ilteron was dead, they sailed off. They weren't interested in shedding their own blood. Just ours. Enough of the questions. You need to rest."

Kharl wanted to protest, but the cool darkness flowed from Lyras over him, and he could not say a word as he dropped into another deep and dreamless sleep.

LXXXVIII

When Kharl woke again, he could see. He was quartered in a corner room in the keep, with white plaster walls and a wide window, its shutters open to the south. The high bed was of triple width, and had sheets of fine cotton, the kind Charee had dreamed of and Kharl could never have afforded. For a moment, sadness washed over him, and tears streamed from the corners of his eyes. Were all luxuries that costly? He blotted the tears awkwardly, wishing he were not crying, trying to ignore the figure hovering over him.

"Are you all right?"

Lyras had vanished. In his place was a young woman wearing a dark tunic and trousers, with her black hair tied back, and very intent brown eyes.

"Just . . . I'm better." How could he explain? "Better," he repeated.

When he could speak, he asked, "Who are you?" Then he tried to look at her more closely, and, abruptly, the blackness dropped across his vision as though he had raised the light shield.

"I'm Alidya. I'm a healer in learning. Lyras summoned me."

Kharl forced himself to relax, not to think about seeing. "What happened?"

"What do you mean, Master Kharl?"

"I don't remember much after I got Lord Ghrant to the ship."

"No one could believe that you rescued him and killed the white wizards. I'm sure you know, but there wasn't a mark on them. Not on Ilteron, either. Master Lyras, he said that the ways of the black mages are mysterious . . . Is it true . . . oh, I'm not supposed to be talking, not so much. Would you like some lager or some ale?"

"Lager . . . that would be good."

"Just a moment, ser . . . I'll be right back." Her voice died away, as did the sound of sandals on stone.

Kharl sat in his darkness. Why had he been able to see, then not see? He'd tried to concentrate on seeing the young healer . . . and it was as if the concentration had brought on the blindness.

Within moments, it seemed, he heard Alidya's steps returning.

"Here, ser. I've got your lager."

Kharl managed to locate the tankard—a real tankard and not a clay mug—with his order-senses and take it from Alidya's hands. He took a slow swallow, then another, enjoying the taste of perhaps the best lager he'd ever had. Sometime after the third or fourth swallow, his sight returned, but he did not look directly at Alidya, just enjoyed the indirect light flooding around him and the distant hills to the south through the window.

"You didn't tell me what happened afterward, after . . ."

Alidya smiled. "Oh, it was glorious. Lord Hagen rallied the lancers and drove back the attackers and raised Lord Ghrant's banner. Then he sent a message to the highland lords, and, when they learned that Ilteron and the white wizards were dead, they agreed to return to their lands and recognize Lord Ghrant as supreme ruler of Austra."

"Ah . . ." Kharl couldn't believe it had been so simple. It could not have been that easy, could it?

"Well . . . he did have to send some captive officers back who saw Lord Ghrant so that they could say that he was alive, and he had to promise that he wouldn't execute any of the rebel lords. They say that Lord Ghrant wasn't happy about that."

"That was all?"

"There was one other thing," Alidya said. "The rebels wouldn't agree unless Lord Ghrant named Lord Hagen as both his chancellor and arms-commander."

Kharl couldn't help chuckling. He would have rolled with laughter if he hadn't known it would have hurt too much. Even the chuckling sent spasms through his ribs and muscles.

"I don't think that's at all funny." Alidya's voice turned prim.

Kharl managed to stop chuckling.

"Why did you laugh, ser?"

"I can't explain . . . except . . ." Kharl shook his head. "Someday . . . someday, you'll understand."

A pained look crossed the young woman's face, but she did not ask again.

"If I could have some more lager . . .?" Kharl asked after finishing the tankard.

"Yes, ser."

Kharl could only drink a third of what she brought before he had to put it down. He was far more tired than he had thought, and who knew how many days he'd been abed?

Later that afternoon, a half glass after Kharl woke from dozing off, Hagen appeared.

"Lord Hagen!" Alidya bolted upright from the chair beside Kharl's bed.

"You can go, Alidya, and close the door on the way out."

"Ser . . ."

"Kharl will be fine, and if he needs you, I'll call you."

"Ah . . . yes, ser."

Hagen waited until the door closed. "I owe you again." His mouth twisted into a wry smile. "And you owe me, after a fashion."

"Alidya told me about your having to be the lord-chancellor."

"And arms-commander."

"Lord Ghrant must not be terribly pleased," offered Kharl.

"He's relieved that he's still Lord of Austra, and Lady Hyrietta has prevailed upon him to keep whatever anger he may have to himself."

"What will you do with the *Seastag*?"

"Furwyl will become captain, and the others will move up, except for Bemyr. He'll always be a bosun." Hagen looked at Kharl. "Lord Ghrant will be honoring you."

"I didn't do it for honor."

"You'll pardon me if I didn't tell him that. I did say that you had seen injustice in your past and that you could not allow it to triumph in Austra if you could help it." Hagen grinned crookedly.

For a moment, Kharl did not understand the grin. Then he smiled broadly. "That was almost evil, Lord Hagen."

"What? To remind him that a lord's task is to seek justice? To suggest that he owes his entire rule to a man who sought justice?" Hagen's grin faded. "We are at least fortunate that he is one on whom that makes an impact. Though he will need frequent reminders."

Thinking of Ilteron—and Egen—Kharl nodded.

"You will be honored. I would guess a purse, a small continuing stipend and estate, and the support of Lord Ghrant, which is not to be dismissed, even here."

"I had not thought . . ." Kharl had indeed not thought of rewards . . . or of the possibility of remaining in Austra, and Hagen's words said that his entire future might well be different—if he desired that future.

"You had not. I know that." Hagen straightened. "But I thought you should know."

After Hagen had left, Kharl looked out through the window into the brilliant gold of sunset. What did he want? Really? Could it be that his actions might bring a reward? Could that really be so after all that had happened? Or would he need to remain on the *Seastag*? Thinking of Furwyl, Rhylla, Ghart, and Tarkyn, he reflected that a man could have a fate far worse—far, far worse.

A faint smile crossed his lips, and he closed his eyes.

LXXXIX

Once Kharl was finally alert and eating, he recovered quickly, although he was left with a scar on his left temple, a jagged red mark no longer than the width of his thumb that resembled a miniature lightning bolt. His hair had been cut far shorter, probably to trim off all that had been singed and crisped. Dead skin had also flaked off over most of his face, leaving new and pinkish skin beneath.

By the end of the eightday, he was up and walking through the keep, which was not so much a keep as a large country house, around which walls had been erected at some time, certainly not a structure designed to withstand a lengthy attack or a siege.

His own garments, doubtless too rent and bloodstained to save, had been replaced before he had even recovered with far finer garb, two dark gray shirts that were almost silvery, black trousers, and a black jacket. Even his boots had been replaced with black leather boots fitted to his feet. The garments signified changes, more than he'd wanted to consider. First, the colors—that had been obvious. The black and gray were because he was a mage, but the quality . . . that bothered him. He could not have afforded such finery, and yet it was almost plain compared to that of those in the keep who attended Lord Ghrant, although somewhat finer than that of the servants or of Alidya.

In the late afternoon of eightday, he stood on the corner of the upper terrace, outside the walls, looking to the ridge and park to the north. The winter sky was clear, and there was no wind to dissipate the mild warmth of the sun. From close to a kay away, outside of a handful of gashes in the turf, Kharl could see no sign that a battle had been fought days before.

He still had a hard time believing that his tricks with hardening air had been so successful and that everyone seemed to think that he was a mighty mage. He had managed to learn a few things about order and chaos—but he'd be in real trouble if he ever encountered a truly accomplished white wizard. That, he understood, even if no one else seemed to.

"Ah . . . the mysterious mage . . ."

At the sound of Hagen's voice, Kharl turned. He shrugged helplessly. "I'm ready to go."

"Not yet," Hagen said with a smile. "You need to stay here for a few more days. Just until threeday."

"Why then?"

"Because that's when Lord Ghrant has set your audience," replied the new lord-chancellor. "It would be most unbecoming to depart before then." Hagen grinned.

"Do I want that audience?" Kharl asked dryly.

"I would judge so, unless you want to go back to being a ship's carpenter or a wandering mage. As for the moment, I came out here to suggest that now that you are well, you might join me and several of the lancer officers for supper."

The thought of company for a meal—rather than being served in one of the small dining halls with minor functionaries he did not know—did have a certain appeal to Kharl, but he had no doubt that Hagen had more than that in mind. "Senior officers?"

Hagen smiled. "I am certain they would appreciate any information you might provide about what you saw . . ."

"Such as the officers dining in the town the day before the final battle?" asked Kharl. "While others were fighting?"

"They might not like such, but I would be indebted to you for such candor."

"And they are not likely to doubt a mage as much?"

"They know that you have no history with the Austran lancers," Hagen pointed out. "Unlike me."

Kharl thought he understood and gestured for Hagen to lead on.

The two walked back across the terrace and through a narrow bailey gate—where two of Ghrant's personal guards stood stiffly—before reentering the north wing. Kharl followed Hagen down a wide but short side corridor, one adorned with oversized portraits of men in restrained finery. The corridor ended in two double doors, the right one open.

Hagen motioned for Kharl to precede him, and the carpenter-mage did.

Inside, five officers in the green and gray of Austra stood around one end of the large circular table already set for a meal with white linen cloth and cutlery. More portraits graced the white plaster walls above the blond wainscot paneling.

"Lord Hagen . . . mage," offered a gray-haired and mustached officer with a broad forehead, pointed chin, and perfect mustache.

Hagen returned the greeting with a nod, then spoke. "I thought that it might be useful for Kharl to dine with us. He saw a side of the last battle that none of us did." He inclined his head to the graying officer. "Kharl, this is Commander Vatoran . . . Majer Reseff, Majer Tralk, Majer Fuelt, and Majer Nyort."

Kharl nodded solemnly in response, hoping he could keep the names and faces in mind throughout the dinner.

Hagen moved to a place at the table, the one that faced the doorway. "Kharl, perhaps . . ." He gestured to the chair across the table from him.

Kharl took the suggestion, but waited to seat himself until the other officers began to do so, and they waited until Hagen actually settled into his chair.

A long silence followed, one that pleased Hagen, Kharl felt.

"Commander Vatoran is the eastern district commander," the lord-chancellor finally explained to Kharl as servers circled the table, asking each man whether he preferred wine, ale, or lager. "In effect, he commands all of the lancer forces east of the Shiltons. Each of the majers commands a subdistrict, usually with between ten and fifteen companies. The organization is the same for the foot, but we'll be meeting with them later." Hagen turned to the server waiting patiently at his shoulder. "Wine. Red. The Asolo, if you have it."

Kharl stayed with lager. To him, wine was too close to sweet vinegar.

"You have not been a lancer, or an armsman, mage, have you?" asked Vatoran, his deep voice calm and even.

"I fear not, commander."

"But you have been in battle?"

"Against pirates and a white wizard. This was my first battle where both sides were lancers and foot."

Hagen made no comment, just nodded and waited.

Kharl took advantage of the moment of silence to sample the lager, a slightly edged but refreshing brew. One of the two women servers deftly slipped slices of white meat onto the gold-rimmed, pale blue china plate before Kharl, and the second added dumplings. A third followed with strips of green cetalya, then ladled a white sauce laced with black mushrooms over both meat and dumplings. Kharl cared little for the bitter cetalya and would have preferred the sauce over the vegetable as well.

"What weapons have you used? Besides your magely skills, that is?" asked one of the majers.

"I'm not one for the blade," Kharl admitted. "Cudgel and staff."

One of the other majers sniffed, but did not speak as the first majer asked, "How many men have you killed, mage, that is, with your weapons, not magery?"

Kharl didn't care much for the majer's tone, or the unspoken condescension of the other majers, but he fingered his chin before replying, thinking about Tyrbel's assassin, about the very first white wizard and his guards, and about the pirates. "I can't say for certain. I know about five for sure, before the battle here."

"The mage is being modest," Hagen interrupted. "Against the pirates alone, he took out ten men with his staff."

Kharl reflected once more. If he counted the deaths of the men killed on the ridge by the white wizard's efforts to stop him, then the total was doubtless several score.

"Would you agree with Lord Hagen's assessment?" asked Vatoran, a slight smile without humor lifting the corners of his mouth.

"Lord Hagen may have seen more than I did. He had a better vantage, and he is more familiar with fighting and warfare," Kharl said. "I was just doing the best I could." He took a bite of the meat—boar, he thought—and a mouthful of the flavorful dark bread. Then he tried a dumpling, surprisingly delicate, with a plumlike flavor.

"The mage cleared the deck of one vessel," Hagen explained, "but he lost two toes and cracked his ribs in a number of places."

"What about—"

"I think we can dispense with more questions about the mage's familiarity with weapons and fighting," Vatoran interjected, turning back to Kharl. "Did you see much of the fighting before the day that you bested the wizards and Ilteron?"

Hagen gave the slightest of nods to Kharl.

"I had not realized that the fighting had begun," the mage replied. "I was in the town, looking for somewhere to eat, and I went into a café. There were four lancer officers there, and they were eating and drinking, and talking about the fighting . . . about how close the rebels were to Dykaru—"

". . . must be some mistake . . ."

". . . sure they wore the green and black?"

"They were in the green and black," Kharl affirmed, "and when I left, I saw a wagon filled with wounded, and the teamster was complaining that he'd lost his way and that his captain didn't seem to know much about where the battle was or how to direct the teamster . . ." Kharl took a swallow of ale before continuing. "That was what I saw and heard before we got into battle the next day."

Vatoran nodded as if to himself before continuing. "I'd be most curious, mage, as to why you risked your life for Lord Ghrant. You don't have to speak to that, if you don't want to, of course. It's enough that you acted, whatever the reason."

"I'm not sure that it is, commander," Kharl found himself saying. "I used to think that myself. I was a cooper. No secret about that. So long as I made good barrels, didn't matter to me why I made them. But it did."

He shrugged. "I found that out. Heard enough about Ilteron and had seen enough of Lord Hagen to realize there was a difference. Didn't get to make a difference in Nordla, but I had a chance in Austra. That's why."

"But you are not Austran," Vatoran pointed out.

"Lord Hagen's acts had made it clear that right is right. Wrong is wrong. Doesn't matter where. If you only protect what's yours, and everyone does that, then wrong usually wins, and right loses. In the end, you do, too."

Vatoran looked as though he wanted to reply to that, but, instead, the commander frowned, then asked, "How did you get into battle?"

"Lord Hagen thought that I might be of some use in making sure that Lady Hyrietta and the heirs were safe . . ." Kharl went on to tell about the battle, but avoided any exact details about what magery he had used, only saying, "I managed to use what I knew about order to block their firebolts and imprison them in a web of order. That killed the two wizards and Ilteron. Then I dragged Lord Ghrant off the ridge and managed to get him onto a mount. It took a long time to get him back to the harbor."

"In the middle of the battle?" Vatoran's eyebrows lifted.

"That part of the battle was pretty near over. At least, no one was fighting there right then, and no one was looking at a carpenter dragging and carrying a wounded man. They were still worried about the firebolts on the top of the ridge." While what Kharl said was true—no one had been looking at them because they couldn't have seen them—the evasion of truth bothered him, but he didn't want to reveal exactly what he had done.

"And you just rode to the harbor?"

"What he says is true," Hagen interjected in a calm voice. "We were on the *Seastag*, and we saw a rider come up the pier with a figure over the saddle before him. Until he dismounted, we didn't realize that it was the mage with Lord Ghrant."

"It took a long time," Kharl added. "I couldn't get there directly." That had been absolutely true.

"I see. What did you notice about the foot and lancers in the battle that we should know?"

"Some of them—Lord Ghrant's men who held the little stone pavilion on the south side—they were brave and well-ordered. They were holding the pavilion even against the one mage until I killed him. There were others who ran and fled from the white wizards before I got there. More of them were in green and black, but there were some in yellow and black. Lord Ilteron's forces withdrew a number of rods when I was battling the last white wizard, but I didn't see any of them breaking or running." Kharl shrugged. "That's what I saw. I wasn't looking at the lancers and foot, though. I was trying to stop the wizards and find Lord Ghrant and Ilteron."

"Did you see any standards or banners . . ."

"Did you see any other rebel livery besides the blue . . ."

"What about cannon . . ."

Kharl replied to the questions as well as he could, even if most of his answers were negative. In between questions and answers, he kept eating.

After a time, Hagen cleared his throat. Loudly.

"I think the mage has been most forthcoming. It is most clear to me, both from what I saw and from what the mage and others have reported, that we have a solid task ahead of us if we are to be successful in halting other attempts by Hamor to weaken Austra." Hagen's smile to the officers was polite, but far from warm as he stood and nodded to Kharl.

Kharl stood and inclined his head to the commander. "My best to you, ser, and I trust I have not disturbed you too greatly, but I could only report on what I saw and experienced. I know too little about lancers to say anything but what I saw."

"I am certain that is so, mage." Vatoran had risen, as had the majers, and he inclined his head in response.

Kharl followed Hagen out and down the corridor.

The lord-chancellor said nothing until they were back in a small study or library, where both walls were filled with shelves brimming with leather-bound volumes. Hagen closed the door, but made no move to seat himself at the black oak desk. "That will do."

"I don't think they were happy with my words," Kharl said.

"They weren't supposed to be. I wanted them to know that more than a few people understood that some of the lancers had not responded well. Eating in town while the fighting was going on." Hagen snorted. "Running from battle while others fought . . ."

"Was that why you did not see eye to eye with Lord Ghrant before?"

"Something like that."

"Is there anything else you'd like from me?" asked Kharl.

Hagen laughed. "Just be polite and mysterious for the next few days, until you meet with Lord Ghrant, and then we'll talk about what you'd like to do next."

Kharl understood that, too. He wasn't going to get a direct answer until something else happened, probably between Hagen and Lord Ghrant.

XC

About midmorning on threeday, a youngster in a yellow tunic with black cuffs appeared at Kharl's door, with a neatly folded set of garments in his arms.

"Master Kharl, ser?"

"Yes?"

"These are for you, ser. For the audience with Lord Ghrant, ser. At the first glass of the afternoon, ser."

"Thank you." Kharl took the garments.

"I'll be here to escort you, ser." Then, after those words, the young man was gone.

Kharl closed the door and looked down at the garments—a silksheen silver shirt, black trousers, and a black jacket of fine and soft wool. They had clearly been tailored to his measurements and presumably were his to keep.

He shook his head. Never had he owned such finery—nor needed it.

What would happen at the audience? What did Kharl have to say to Lord Ghrant? What he could have said—such as the fact that he didn't think much of the discipline of the Austran forces or of Ghrant's personal guard—were not things that would have been wise to voice, and he'd already said them to the lancer officers.

He also wasn't pleased with the idea of bowing and scraping to Ghrant, who'd have been far better off to listen to Hagen from the beginning rather than having been forced to do so by events. Then, Kharl could always hope that Ghrant would be generous, although he had his doubts about that characteristic in rulers—or their offspring.

Kharl looked at the garments once more, then shrugged and laid them on the bed. After a moment, he began to disrobe. He might as well try on the new clothes. Not surprisingly, they fit well, and he looked almost impressive when he studied his reflection in the mirror above the chest set against the inner wall of the spacious chamber that had remained his.

Neither his pondering nor his pacing yielded more answers, and after several long glasses, the youth in yellow reappeared at his door. Wordlessly, Kharl followed him along the main corridor of the southern wing, up the main staircase in the middle of the sprawling structure, then along another white-walled corridor that ended in a single golden oak door. While the door was modest, there were two burly guards in the yellow and black.

"Master Kharl, the mage, here to see Lord Ghrant," offered the youth.

"We know, Bethem," said the shorter guard, smiling paternally before he turned and knocked. "The mage, ser."

After a moment, the words came back. "Show him in."

The guard who had not spoken opened the door, and Kharl stepped inside, into a study with wide windows opening to the north and west, with but a single case filled with books. The door closed behind him, almost silently, with just the faintest *click*.

The blond lord sat behind a wide desk of golden oak, unadorned, without a single carving.

"Lord Ghrant." Kharl inclined his head, politely, but not too deeply.

"Can't have too much formality here, not with a man who destroyed my enemies, then dragged and carried me to safety." Ghrant gestured to the straight-backed chairs before the desk.

Kharl took the one in the shade, so that he could see Ghrant more clearly, without the afternoon sun that poured into the room getting in his eyes.

"You present a problem, Master Kharl. A happy one, but one requiring a solution. I cannot offer you what I owe you, and that is Austra. Nor even a fraction of that." A rueful smile followed the words.

Kharl waited. He wasn't about to offer Ghrant an easy way out. Self-denying graciousness did not count for much with those in power. That he *had* learned.

"Lord Hagen has suggested that your service is worth a small estate, a stipend, and a minor lordship. It was worth more than that, but we have conferred and feel that, with your talents, those are more appropriate, with certain . . . adjustments I think you will find useful. Lord Hagen will tell you of those details at your convenience. But from this point on, you hold the lands of Cantyl, and shall formally be addressed as 'Ser Kharl.'" Ghrant smiled broadly. "You will also receive your first purse from him later this afternoon."

"You are most kind, ser." Kharl, although wary, could sense neither malice nor deception.

"Most grateful, Ser Kharl." Ghrant cleared his throat. "Lord Hagen will brief you on the details, but I did want to express my gratitude to you personally. My lady also conveys her thanks, as do my sons." Ghrant smiled, an expression both warm, polished, and somehow tired, then stood.

Kharl rose as well. "I am glad I was able to be of service, and I am very glad that you remain Lord of Austra."

"Let us hope that all my subjects come to that happy conclusion as well, ser Kharl."

When Kharl stepped out of the study, Hagen was waiting.

"Ser Kharl."

"Lord-chancellor." Kharl inclined his head.

"We need to discuss a few more details. Lord Ghrant is often brief to the point of being cryptic." Hagen's smile was rueful. "Filling in those details seems to be a large part of being lord-chancellor."

Kharl followed Hagen a good fifty cubits down the corridor to another unmarked door, which opened into a very small chamber holding but a circular table and four chairs, and a narrow, east-facing window.

Hagen did not sit down after he closed the door. "Lord Ghrant and I came to an agreement. Cantyl is set on and adjoining a headland southeast of Valmurl. The lands succeeded to Lord Estloch several years ago, but they are near none of his holdings. They consist of a small but good vineyard, some excellent timberlands, one small and fertile valley, and some most rocky hills, which provide a certain isolation. I thought you might appreciate the timberlands and possibly the isolation. There is just one rough road that eventually winds to Valmurl, but a very good, if small, natural harbor. The lands are well managed, and those who do so would like to stay. And there will be a considerable stipend for five years, and a modest one thereafter."

Kharl nodded. He was not quite sure what to say.

Hagen produced a plain leather purse. "Your stipend is one hundred golds a year for the first five years, and fifty thereafter for the following ten. This holds an additional fifty, not counted against the stipend, for your expenses and travel to Cantyl."

Kharl managed not to swallow. He'd never seen twenty-five golds at one time, let alone fifty, and probably never held more than ten at once ever—and the purse was only incidental.

"Lord Ghrant does not anticipate this, but would wish to reserve the right to call upon your services occasionally."

That did make sense, unfortunately.

"You're still not sure whether you'd want to go back to Brysta, if you could, are you?" asked Hagen. "Master and Ser Kharl."

"No . . ." Kharl paused. "I'd thought about it, but I'm certainly not welcome there." He smiled wryly. "I had thought about staying in Austra—but as a cooper. I'd never thought . . ."

"I hadn't either, when you asked me for passage," Hagen replied.

"Strange . . ." mused Kharl.

Hagen laughed. "You should have been a lord in Brysta, but Lord Ghrant's powers do not extend that far."

"Why did you press my case so far with Lord Ghrant?" Kharl asked.

"There are several reasons. First, Lord Ghrant must understand that loyalty is rewarded. I can say such, but if I do not press for it, then my words mean little. Also, you're a powerful mage, Kharl. But you need to know more to use that power effectively. Whether you choose to stay here—and if you do, and you learn what you must—I'd not be surprised if Lord Ghrant would call on you for aid and advice, and you will serve yourself and those around you far better for having a standing well gained in battle . . ."

Kharl could sense the caution in Hagen, and he almost laughed. Even Hagen was worried about his power. The laughter died within him as he considered what that meant. Would he have to worry about everyone now? Whether they would use him and his powers, or try to manipulate him from afar, through others?

"I can see you understand," Hagen said.

"I almost did not," Kharl confessed.

"The *Seastag* is leaving tomorrow for Valmurl. I've arranged for Furwyl to make a stop at Cantyl. They'll be expecting you."

"Who will?"

"The estate steward. That's Speltar. Lord Ghrant sent a messenger informing him an eightday ago."

"Lord Ghrant . . . or you?" asked Kharl wryly.

"I did have something to do with it, but he had to accept my recommendation."

"I hope it didn't cost you too much."

"Nothing at all. He'd much rather be indebted to you than, say, Lord Deroh."

The name meant nothing to Kharl.

"Oh . . . and you'll be traveling as a passenger. As an honored passenger in my quarters."

"I couldn't take . . ." Kharl paused. "You won't be on board?"

"No. I'll be with Lord Ghrant and his family . . . riding in triumph back across Austra."

Kharl realized something else. By not accompanying Lord Ghrant, his role in saving the lord would be diminished. There were advantages and disadvantages to that for him, but clearly only advantages for Ghrant.

"So that he can show his banner and reassure everyone?"

"That is most necessary," Hagen affirmed. "Long and tiring as the journey will be by road."

"The crew won't mind me as a passenger?"

"Not at all. They know you saved us all from having to leave Austra, and they're more than ready to leave Dykaru and to get back to Valmurl." Hagen smiled. "I'm famished. Are you ready to join me in a quiet meal? With no discussion about rulers and their duties?"

Kharl was.

XCI

As Kharl walked down the last few rods of the pier toward the waiting *Seastag*, the light breeze swirled the odor of burning coal around him, confirming that the ship was indeed making ready to cast off. He stopped just short of the gangway and looked westward, out over the white walls of Dykaru, and the orangish brown tile roofs, brilliant in the direct morning sunlight, then turned back toward the ship.

Ghart was grinning as Kharl walked up the gangway, carrying the new leather bag—black, of course—that contained equally new garments.

"Do anything to get out of the fo'c's'le, wouldn't you?" offered the new first mate.

"I tried." Kharl couldn't help grinning in return. "Even to keeping you from a bigger cabin."

"Only for a few days. Then you'll go off as lord of leisure."

"Not a lord. Just a minor landholder, with some rocky hills and a vineyard, I'm told. And a few trees. Maybe enough to set up a cooperage."

Ghart shook his head. "Cooper, carpenter, warrior, mage . . . and now you're going to be a lord."

"No . . . just a minor landholder," Kharl protested.

Ghart began to laugh. Finally, he stopped and looked at Kharl. "Being a landholder's worse than magery. Mages understand magery. No one understands what landholders do." There was the hint of a twinkle in the first mate's eyes.

Kharl could understand Ghart's amusement—and appreciated the fact that Ghart was amused, rather than resentful or jealous. "Maybe I'll learn enough to know why no one does . . ."

"You might at that." Ghart's head turned.

Kharl glanced to his left, his eyes taking in the figure crossing the main deck to the quarterdeck—Furwyl, now wearing a blue master's jacket. "Master Kharl . . ."

"Captain."

"Aye, and we've all gone up a little in the world, you more than us, I'd wager." Furwyl's smile was also warm and welcoming. "Though I'd not be saying that Lord Hagen is enjoying his fortune so much as us."

Kharl chuckled at Furwyl's observation. "The highland lords respect his abilities, perhaps more than do others."

"Lord Ghrant will have to listen to him now," Furwyl replied. "He'll soon be wishing that he had earlier, if he's not already."

"Lord Ghrant is already listening," Kharl replied.

Ghart smiled knowingly.

"Now that you're aboard, Master Kharl . . ." suggested Furwyl.

"I'm more than ready, captain."

Furwyl stepped back. "Single up!"

The bosun's whistle shrilled, and Bemyr's voice boomed out. "Single up. Make it lively!"

"Best I stow my gear," Kharl said. "What I have."

"Ah . . . Master Kharl," Ghart said. "You'll not be minding that we took the liberty of putting your other things in the captain's cabin as well."

"Hardly. Thank you." The carpenter-mage shook his head. "Seems strange to go from the fo'c's'le aft."

"Happens to us all, ser. You'll get used to it." Ghart smiled. "Remember when I had the smallest cubby on the *Seasprite.*"

Left unsaid was the knowledge that very few seamen made the transition out of the forecastle.

Kharl nodded and made his way past the deck crew. Seeing Reisl and Hodal there, he smiled at the two. "It's good to see you."

"Good to see you, Master Kharl," replied Reisl. "Wasn't sure we would when you fell off that horse." The deckhand grinned.

"I wasn't either," Kharl admitted. "I don't do well with horses. You could tell that." Belatedly realizing that he'd distracted the deck crew, he added, "Best let you get back to listening to Bemyr."

"Aye . . ."

As Kharl stepped away, toward the hatchway leading to the captain's quarters, he could hear the voices behind him.

". . . always said . . . something strange . . ."

"Strange or not, saved our asses more 'n once . . ." replied Reisl.

". . . never shirked any duty . . ." added Hodal.

Kharl wished he could thank the two for their words, but that would just have embarrassed them.

After stowing his bag in the captain's cabin—and he somehow felt guilty, no matter what Hagen and Furwyl said—Kharl made his way out and up to the poop deck. There he stationed himself at the port railing, watching quietly as Furwyl guided the *Seastag* away from the pier and into the narrow channel leading to the Great Western Ocean.

Astern of the ship, the white walls and tiled roofs of Dykaru dwindled slowly under the cool and clear greenish blue sky. Ahead, there were but the slightest of whitecaps on the low and rolling swells of the endless gray-blue waters.

Only when the *Seastag* was well clear of the harbor did Kharl approach the captain, standing beside the steering platform and slightly forward of the helm. The engineman stood to starboard and aft of the wheel.

"How long a trip, this time?"

"We're low on coal, but we've got favoring winds," Furwyl replied. "I'd guess four, maybe five days to Cantyl."

Five days . . . five days before he set foot on lands that were his. That . . . that still seemed more like a dream. But he would see. He certainly would. In the meantime, he watched the sea and the shrinking outline of the coast.

Once the *Seastag* was well clear of the coast, Kharl climbed down the ladder and crossed the main deck, making his way to the carpenter shop.

Tarkyn looked up from his stool and the scrimshaw he had been carving. "Wondered if you'd get down to see an old carpenter." Tarkyn's voice was gruff as usual. "Or if you'd forgot where you started."

"Don't think I'll ever forget that," Kharl replied.

"What happened to the staff? You still have it somewhere?"

"No. Got broken in the fight with the wizards."

"Must have been a real fight. Didn't think anything could break it."

"Wizardry and magery did." After a moment, Kharl added, "Fighting wizardry did."

"Wasn't sure you'd make it. You more like fell off that horse when you brought Lord Ghrant back."

"I wasn't either. Felt like I'd been run over by a herd of lancers' mounts. That was when I woke up days later. Wouldn't let me do much for more than an eightday."

"You get more than parchment from Lord Ghrant?"

"They tell me I've got some land—rocks, trees, and a vineyard—and some coins. Took what they offered. Probably stupid not to have asked for more."

"Probably," Tarkyn agreed amiably. "Coin's never been something that meant the most to you, though." He studied Kharl, a twinkle in his eyes. "Still . . . pretty fancy cloth you're wearing."

Kharl laughed. "It's plain compared to what the lords and their servants wear. Feels good though. They gave it to me when they found out I had an audience with Lord Ghrant."

"Wagered something like that. What are you going to do now? Don't think you're going to come back to carpentering now that you're a landed lord."

"Not a lord, but I did get some land." Kharl shook his head. "Still trying to figure out what to do next, whether I ought to try to get back to Brysta."

"You don't forget, do you?"

For a moment, Kharl was taken aback by the question. "No . . . I'd guess not." But he wasn't sure what he wasn't forgetting, not exactly. Or rather, he didn't want to say that he wasn't forgetting the injustice he'd experienced and seen in too many forms. Charee hadn't cared for his feelings that way. Sanyle had understood, but most surprisingly to Kharl, Jeka had. He wondered how she was doing, but he could only hope that Gharan had managed to keep her on in his shop. He still felt guilty about leaving her, but at the time, he hadn't been sure what else he could have done.

"Don't like to forgive those folks who do evil, either."

Kharl couldn't deny that, either.

"Understand that," Tarkyn went on. "Don't let revenge get in the way of doing what needs to be done."

"Try not to." Kharl paused, then added, "Thank you. For teaching me when I didn't know enough. For making sure I did learn."

"Be a piss-poor carpenter if I didn't."

"You've always been a good one."

"What I wanted. Nothing more." Tarkyn laughed. "Mostly, anyway."

"Isn't it that way always?"

They both laughed.

In time, when Kharl made his way back topside, Tarkyn's words echoed through his thoughts—*Don't let revenge get in the way of doing what needs to be done.* Don't let revenge get in the way . . . deep inside, was he after revenge—targeted against Egen and Justicer Reynol? Or against all those in power in Brysta?

Could he not just accept his good fortune in Austra, where he had become recognized and been rewarded?

He looked to port, out at the long coastline lying on the horizon. He *had* wanted to have his own place in Austra.

XCII

The trip northward along the eastern coast of Austra was both uneventful and slow. While there were following winds, as Furwyl had hoped, they were light. Kharl used some of the time, as he could, talking to Furwyl and the mates, and especially to Tarkyn, whom he felt he had come to know later than the others.

On the afternoon of the sixth day after leaving Dykaru, Furwyl fired up the engines to bring the *Seastag* into Cantyl. Kharl stood at the poop railing, watching as the rounded headland to port grew ever larger. In the black leather bag waiting below, with his garments, was the parchment patent conveying Cantyl to him from Lord Ghrant, a patent that also conveyed the lands to his heirs in perpetuity.

As Hagen had told him, the harbor at Cantyl was small, with the headland he had been watching to the south of the harbor—a fjiordlike bay—and a low line of cliffs to the north. The entrance to the bay was less than a kay in width, with steep cliffs more than a hundred cubits in height to the south and lower cliffs, perhaps twenty cubits above the gray water—to the north. The sails had been furled a half glass earlier, and with but the faintest of breezes, the *Seastag*'s paddle wheels carried the ship through the mouth of the harbor and into the bay, an irregular shape that might have fit in a square two kays on a side.

"Be hard to get in here in a blow," Furwyl observed from behind Kharl.

"Looks hard enough in calm waters," Kharl replied, thinking that the harbor would be comparatively easy to defend with a chain system such as the one employed in Brysta.

"Old salts say it was once a pirate haven, back when Austra was but lands warring with each other . . . could be just a tale."

As the *Seastag* eased closer to Cantyl, Kharl turned back to study the entrance to the harbor for a moment. It easily could have been a pirate refuge. He turned to say that, but Furwyl had retreated to the pilot platform. So the former cooper and carpenter, who was now both mage and landholder, just watched as the ship turned southward toward the pier a kay away.

Before that long, he was studying the five men who stood waiting on the narrow pier, a structure whose timbers had been bleached near-white by salt and sun and time. Two were clearly line-handlers. The other three watched the ship, and Kharl had the feeling that they were waiting for him. In the stone-walled harbor yard off the foot of the pier were two heavy wagons. One held beams, the other planks, both loads waiting to be loaded onto the *Seastag*.

Furwyl backed down the *Seastag* expertly, and the ship came to a halt within cubits of the pier.

"Lines out!" came the call from Ghart.

Kharl waited until the *Seastag* was tied at the pier before turning to Furwyl. "Thank you, both for this voyage—and for all the ones that made this one possible."

"Our pleasure, Master Kharl." The captain gestured toward the pier. "It would appear that you are expected—and that we might have a cargo."

"If you do, it would be the least I could do to repay you and everyone on board. I can't tell you how much." Kharl grinned.

Then he headed toward the ladder down to the main deck. Once there, he slipped back into the captain's cabin and reclaimed his new bag, and his old pack, before hurrying back out to the quarterdeck.

Furwyl, all the mates, and Tarkyn stood there. Behind them were a number of the crew. In the front Kharl spied Reisl, Hodal, and Kawelt.

For a moment, Kharl just looked at them. He swallowed. Finally, he spoke. "Don't know that I'm that good with words, but . . . any of you are welcome here, any time. Wouldn't be here, and have this without you."

He looked at each of the officers in turn, then at Reisl and Hodal.

Reisl grinned.

Kharl swallowed again, before he spoke. "Thank you. Thank you all."

Furwyl cleared his throat. "Master Kharl . . . were it not for you, it's likely none of us would be standing here. We'd be thanking you for our lives and our health, and, likewise, you're always welcome here."

Bemyr lifted his whistle and gave a long ululating signal.

With a smile, Kharl walked down the gangway. Once on the pier, he turned back to the ship and raised his arm in a salute of sorts to the *Seastag*. He watched for a moment, then turned to those who had been waiting for him.

A short and slight figure, balding with some wisps of reddish hair, stood forward of the two taller men. The top of his head barely reached Kharl's shoulder, but he bowed first. "Lord Kharl?"

"I'm Kharl . . ." Kharl eased the patent from the top of the leather bag. "Here's Lord Ghrant's patent to me . . ."

"Speltar, ser . . . I'm the steward of Cantyl." He took the patent almost apologetically, reading it carefully before bowing and handing it back.

Kharl slipped the parchment carefully back into his bag.

"This is Dorwan, the forester, and Glyan, the vintner," Speltar said, nodding first to a burly black-haired man close to Kharl's age, then to a gray-bearded and angular man with deep brown eyes.

Kharl studied each man in turn. "I'm happy to meet you all. I'll be needing your advice and skills very much. The only thing I know anything at all about is woods."

"Aye, ser," offered Dorwan. "That was what the message from Lord Hagen said."

"Are the timbers there cargo for the *Seastag*?"

"That they are," said Speltar. "When Dorwan heard that the *Seastag* was putting in here, a real heavy cargo vessel, we got together some timbers we could send to Nussar in Valmurl on consignment. That way, you'd have some more golds. We figured . . . well . . . they'd come in useful-like."

"Since mages aren't known for having full wallets?" asked Kharl, laughingly.

"That'd be true, ser." Dorwan grinned at Kharl.

Kharl could not sense either calculation or chaos in any of the three, only a certain wariness in the vintner. He turned and gestured to Furwyl, asking the master to join them on the pier.

After a moment, Furwyl walked down the gangway.

"Captain Furwyl is now master of the *Seastag*," Kharl said, "since Lord Hagen is occupied as lord-chancellor." He turned to Furwyl. "It appears that you were correct, captain, and that the timbers are a consignment cargo for you to take to Valmurl."

Furwyl nodded to Kharl, then to Speltar. "We would be pleased."

"Got the invoices, and the golds right here, captain," offered Speltar, who looked to Kharl, "if that would be fine by you, ser?"

Kharl nodded, stepping back slightly.

Once Furwyl had the invoices and the shipping fees, and had returned to the *Seastag*, Speltar turned to Dorwan.

Dorwan inclined his head slightly. "If you'd not mind, ser Kharl, I'll be supervising the loading."

"Go ahead. If you'd join us when you can . . ."

"Yes, ser. Be a while."

Kharl hitched the old pack into place on his shoulder.

Speltar led the way off the pier to the graveled lane that led from the pier westward and up a gentle slope covered with winter-brown grass to a series of buildings on a low hill overlooking the harbor. The path looked to be only about half a kay long.

The three had walked less than ten rods, when Speltar spoke again.

"Ser . . . begging your pardon . . . but . . . would you be bringing a consort?"

"No." After a moment, Kharl added, "My consort died about a year ago, and my sons have left the house. For the moment, I'm the only one." Kharl wondered if, with his newfound wealth, he might be able to track the boys down, perhaps even send for Arthal, or send someone to bring him back.

"I'm sorry, ser . . . we didn't know . . ."

"There was no reason that you would," Kharl replied politely. "And I appreciate your concern."

As they neared the hilltop, Kharl studied the structures. The main house was modest, at least for a landholder's dwelling, a two-story red sandstone structure only slightly larger than Kharl's cooperage had been, if one excluded the wide, roofed porch that wrapped around the entire house. The roof was of gray tiles, a patchwork of older and newer darker gray that showed replacements over the years. The shutters were dark gray, standing out against the red stone of the walls.

To the south, slightly downhill, were two buildings that looked like barns. Much farther to the north was a stream and a mill of some sort. Kharl glanced to Speltar. "Is that a sawmill?"

"Yes, ser. Lord Estloch had it built years back. That way, we can offer planks and timbers and charge more than we could just selling felled timber."

"The timberlands, the vineyards . . . how far do they go?"

"Not that far, ser Kharl . . . no more than four kays to the northwest and five to the southwest, four if you could ride due south, but you can't, not over those crags."

Kharl turned to the vintner, Glyan. "I know less about vineyards and wine than possibly anything in my life. You'll have to teach me everything you think I should know."

"You'd be wanting to know?" Glyan's tone was somewhere between ironic and amused.

"I do. I was wondering . . . Do we have a cooperage here?"

"No, ser. Oak doesn't grow well on the lands round about."

Kharl nodded slowly. "And about the grapes?"

"What would you want to know?"

"As much as you can tell me. I'll never know what you do," Kharl admitted, "but it seems to me that I ought to know as much as I can."

Glyan laughed. "That'd be taking some time."

"I have time." Kharl grinned. "And if you tell me a bit at a time, I might remember it more easily."

Glyan cleared his throat. "Well . . . ser . . . the vineyards are over the second hill there, on the south-facing slope. We only grow two grapes here, the full red and the golden green. Green's better, makes a Rhynn like no one else . . ."

Kharl listened intently until they neared the house on the hillcrest and Glyan broke off his words.

". . . and that's why we check the stones in the watering runs with a bubble level. They've got to be just so. Too little water or too much, and you've got a juice that's good for vinegar and not much more."

Kharl stopped and looked at the house. A flagstone walk led from the lane, which ran up the hill, then beside the dwelling, to the front porch, the one overlooking the harbor. After a moment, he followed Speltar to the porch.

There he set down the leather bag, before turning and looking out over the harbor, slowly scanning the water and the surrounding lands. He found it hard to believe that he owned the lands . . . lands that seemed too vast for someone considered a small landholder.

He stood and looked for some time, until he heard a cough.

"Ser," offered Speltar, "might I show you the house?"

Kharl smiled broadly. "You certainly can, then the barns and the sawmill." He turned to Glyan. "And the vineyard and the cellars as well."

As he turned toward the door, he paused. There really wasn't any reason he couldn't have a cooperage now, was there?

With a nod to himself, he followed Speltar through the door.

CANDAR

GREAT
WESTERN
OCEAN

REC

L. Kadirski